A JOB —FROM HELL

Ancient Legends

JAYDE SCOTT

D1303273

Other titles in the Ancient Legends series

Doomed
Voodoo Kiss

ISBN: 1461131332
ISBN-13: 978-1461131335

For Foxy, Silver and Tabby

You taught me the true meaning of love …

Acknowledgments

My gratitude goes to my partner for the inspiration.
You're my rock.
A huge thank you to my editor who drove me bonkers
with all the crazy talk about body language.
Thank you to my critique partners, and in particular
Christine who came up with plenty of witty lines.
And, last but not least, a huge thanks to all my
wonderful readers.

Prologue

It's said people can sense their imminent death. Maybe they hear death's song in the wind. Or the earth stops turning for a second, mourning those who are yet to pass. I spotted none of the signs when I dragged my tired body through the Otherworld, waiting for the winged demon guardians to pick me up and drop me back on the threshold to the world of the living.

It was a shiny object, beckoning to me from under a bush, that lured me into the killer's trap. As I bent down and pushed my arm into the thicket, a sharp pain pierced my skin and teeth cut into my bone. I choked on my breath, my scream barely finding its way out of my throat. Panic rose inside me, followed by a sense of dread. I was trapped. Even if the immortals heard me, they couldn't help me.

Blinded by fear, I pulled and kicked at the snarling creature peering out of the ground, all skin and bones and red, tangled hair. She was female, no doubt, but the way she tore through skin and muscles, slurping my blood, resembled no human being.

Somewhere behind me, wings fluttered.

"Get the fire demons, Octavius. Turn that thing into burned toast," someone yelled. In spite of my panic, I smiled as I recognized Cass's voice inside my head.

Fire engulfed us, bathing the semi-darkness in a fiery glow. The creature screeched, but didn't let go of my aching arm. If not even Cass's angels and demons could scare it, nothing would.

My vision blurred, my strength waning. I could feel my blood pouring out of me in a long, constant flow until I thought I was floating. From the edge of my consciousness, I realized a black, winged demon had appeared by my side. A thick flame scorched my skin. I cried out in pain, the scream hurting my ears. My eyes rolled back in their sockets. The creature hissed, the slurping continued.

Something caressed my cheeks, its touch light as a feather. My breath came shallow, and my heart slowed down in my chest. I hung onto consciousness until I realized the stabbing pain was subsiding, so I let myself fall into oblivion, eager to escape.

But I gather I'm not making much sense, so I shall start from the beginning. This is how I entered Aidan's deadly, paranormal world.

Chapter 1

The cab came to a screeching halt. I lurched forward in the backseat and dropped the phone I'd been fumbling with in the hope to get through to my brother.

"I thought only London had a reputation for bad drivers," I muttered.

"Ye'll have to get out now," the driver said.

"I'm sorry, what?" I glanced out the window at the dense trees to both sides of the forsaken road, then back at the driver. Surely, this wasn't where I had asked him to take me?

"I said, ye need to get out now, lassie."

I stuffed my cell phone back into my over-spilling handbag and glared at the man's hooded eyes in the rear-view mirror. "I'm paying you to take me all the way up there." I pointed up the winding country lane.

The driver shrugged. "I'm 'fraid I can't, lass. 'Tis too dark now and I don't want to be here at this time of day."

I cringed at his Scottish accent. I didn't understand half of what he said. "It's only seven."

He shrugged. "'Tis all dark."

"What's the deal? Do cab drivers turn into pumpkins once it's dusk? You should've told me at the airport."

The driver averted his gaze. "Ye're paying me for driving, not answering questions."

Grabbing my handbag I opened the door. No point in arguing with him because it seemed like a lost cause already. A chilly wind ruffled my hair and turned my skin into goose bumps. This was freezing Scotland. Why hadn't I thought of wearing a coat instead of locking it up with all the other stuff? "Oh, for crying out loud." I knocked on the driver's window and waited for him to roll it down. "Are you helping with the luggage or what?" He just stared back at me and shrugged. "What is it then, yes or no?" He turned away, his eyes scanning the forest around us as if he expected someone with an axe to jump out any minute.

"I don't believe this," I mumbled, opening the car boot and pulling out my suitcase, a big, ugly thing my brother Dallas gave me as a graduation gift. The thick plastic carcass was already heavy as hell. With my clothes and books in there, I could barely lift it. I hurled it up and let it fall to the ground with a loud thud, almost hitting my booted feet. This wasn't my day.

Slamming the door shut, I grabbed the suitcase when the driver rolled down his window. "Ye paying now?"

10

"I don't know what kind of taxi rip off you're pulling, but your company sucks." I opened my handbag and pulled out my wallet.

"That'd be thirty," he said, unfazed.

"You said it'd cost me twenty."

He shook his head. "It's thirty."

Frowning, I retrieved three banknotes. No point in arguing. The sooner I got going, the better. I was already late, and what sort of first impression is that? "You won't be getting any tip from me," I said, handing him the money.

"Good luck, lass. Ye'll need it."

"How far from here is it?"

"Ten minutes tops," he said with a sympathetic smile. Unfortunately, his concern didn't stretch out as far as not dumping me in the middle of nowhere with no map, GPS system, compass, or working phone.

I watched the cab turn and speed off in the direction we came from. Dragging my heavy suitcase behind me, I trudged up the narrow street. It was getting dark now. To both sides, tall trees filtered the light cast by the rising moon. No houses as far as I could see. No street lamp. Why the hell did I agree to arrive in the evening? What person in their right mind arranged for a summer temp to find this place at night anyway?

Sighing, I quickened my pace; the sound of the suitcase rollers echoing through the eerie silence of the night. Several times I stumbled over stones and almost fell, but I kept walking up the hill. The wind grew colder by the minute. I switched arms. No way would I return to the airport. This job was my only chance to save up enough money for college. Without it, I'd swap marketing classes for lessons in how to prepare the perfect cheeseburger at the local McDonald's.

Ten minutes later, I nearly bumped into what looked like a gate. I peered through the iron bars into the stretching darkness, and frowned. Could this be the McAllister mansion? I hoped so because my toes felt numb from the cold and my arms were on fire. How much longer could I carry this heavy thing Dallas called a suitcase?

Blindly, I moved from one iron bar to the next, pushing to find an entrance. On the third try I heard a click and the gate opened. I grabbed my suitcase and pushed my way through quickly. Like on cue, the gate closed behind me. Someone was probably watching behind a security system screen, laughing their pants off at the way I had to drag my luggage like a dead elephant. I raised my chin a notch, straightened my shoulders and trekked up the jagged path, my heels clicking noisily on the cobblestones.

The trees grew sparser, the path wider. Sensing someone's presence, I stopped, frozen to the spot. My heart skipped a beat. I turned, ready to scream as loud as my lungs would allow.

"You must be Amber," a girl said.

I exhaled. "You scared the hell out of me. I didn't hear you. Where did you come from?"

The girl moved a step closer and lifted my suitcase in one go, as though it weighed nothing. "The woods," she said. "Let's hurry. He's expecting you."

I gaped after her in awe. The way she ambled away, my suitcase tucked under her arm, she should be on the front cover of Weightlifter Magazine. If hiking in the woods gave one that kind of strength, then I was all for it. I'd hike until I dropped...starting tomorrow. Or maybe the next day, or the one after that. Truth be told, I wasn't into hiking in the woods at all. Or hiking anywhere, as a matter of fact. Who was I fooling? I was doomed with chubby arms and stumpy legs.

We walked up the cobbled path until we reached a huge, gloomy mansion stretching against the black canvas of the night.

"How did you get here?" the girl asked, opening a door.

"Your splendid taxi service. I've no complaints at all." I shook my head. "The cabbie wouldn't come anywhere near the house."

"Yeah, the locals are scared of their own shadows. You should've called. Someone would've picked you up."

"I did, but no one answered." I followed her in, my hands patting the walls to find my way in the darkness. My foot caught in something thick and soft—maybe a rug—and I toppled forward, biting my tongue to keep back a startled yelp. Why wouldn't someone just switch on the lights?

"Mind your steps," the girl said.

"It's okay. I'll just use my bat radar," I mumbled.

The girl made a noise that sounded like a chuckle. Eventually the lights flickered on and I squinted against the sudden brightness. I blinked several times before I peered in her direction: she was about the same age, tall, blonde and strikingly beautiful with flawless pale skin and ocean-blue eyes that shone a tad too bright. Skinny jeans emphasized her shapely legs and narrow waist. A thin top revealed strong arms and shoulders. Dressed in that skimpy outfit I would've frozen to death in the woods.

I turned away from her, focusing my attention on the interior design. We were standing in a wide hall with a tiled floor, a thick scarlet rug and sparse furniture. It looked like any doctor's reception area minus the desk, sitting opportunities and white-clad nurses.

"I'm Clare. You must be Amber," the girl said, smiling. Her voice was as smooth as silk, young but not too high-pitched. The tone was posh. The usual rich kid, I mused, the kind of girl everyone admired and envied.

"Nice to meet you, Clare," I said, curling my lips into a smile.

Clare turned toward a closed mahogany door and craned her neck. "Aidan might take a little longer. I'll show you to your room."

I frowned. "Aidan?"

Clare cocked a brow. "As in Aidan McAllister. He's dying to meet you."

"Ah. My new boss. Of course. Is he your father?"

Clare shot me an incredulous look. What was she waiting for? Was I supposed to say something? I wasn't making a good first impression here, was I? I should've researched my new boss on the internet, or follow him on Twitter to find out how he liked his bed sheets ironed and what he usually ate for breakfast. After all, this would be my job for the next two months. But I had been too busy missing my ex while letting Dallas fill out my application form.

"Aidan's a friend," Clare said, eventually. "Come on."

A friend could mean anything, but I didn't press the issue. There'd be enough time for that later. We climbed up the broad stairs to the first floor. Clare opened a door and let me in. She switched on the light and took a step aside. "Welcome to your new home."

I stopped, scanning my new bedroom. It was spacious, the exact opposite of my former matchbox boarding school room in London. Thick plum-colored curtains covered half of the opposite wall. To my right was a huge, four-poster bed with numerous cushions in the same color as the curtains. The bed was so large it'd never fit into my former bedroom. If this was the Scottish standard I had a feeling I'd get used to it in a heartbeat.

"I gather you like it?" Clare said, her voice betraying amusement.

I cleared my throat. Like it? Was she kidding? It was breath taking. "It's beautiful. Thank you."

Clare beamed as though I'd just complimented her on her fashion sense. "I'll let you unpack then and shall bring up your dinner in half an hour. Of course you can eat in the dining room, but I assume you're tired and may want some privacy before your first day of work."

"Yes, that'd be great. Thanks."

"Excellent. The TV remote control is on the night table. The bathroom's through there." Clare pointed at a door on the other side of the room. "If you need anything, I'm in the library, which is on the ground floor, the second door to the right. You can look around the house if you like, but the second floor is off-limits."

Once Clare closed the door behind her, I walked to the bed and pulled the heavy bedspread aside. The sheet beneath was of a perfect white. I opened my suitcase and threw my clothes haphazardly into the closet near the window, leaving my books and various memorabilia in my suitcase. Neatness wasn't my strongest point, but what my new boss didn't know couldn't hurt him. From all the competition, funny that I should be the lucky one to land such a well-paid job. Whatever Dallas wrote on that application form, I could only hope he hadn't pretended I was a domestic goddess. That might just mean the end of my placement, and I really needed the money.

I walked into the bathroom and reached for the light switch. The bulb flickered to life, revealing walls covered in white tiles with tiny, dark blue flowers. I peeked into the mirror above the washbasin and grimaced at my mousy brown hair that lacked a good cut, my chubby cheeks and big hazel eyes. Many called me pretty, but I knew I would never have that extra something that would make a guy fall in love with me. Cameron hadn't, or so he said before making it clear he wanted a break.

Enough dark thoughts already. Pushing my mental baggage to the back of my mind, I sighed and opened a cabinet. A toothbrush, shower gel, lavender soap and moisturizing lotion occupied the upper shelf. In another cabinet I found white towels and a bathrobe. I stripped off my jeans, red jumper and underwear, and jumped under the shower. The hot water relaxed my aching muscles and washed away the invisible signs of a long day. Wrapped in a towel, I walked back to the bedroom, and sank into the clean scent of recently washed sheets, falling asleep as soon as my head hit the pillow.

A thud woke me up in the middle of the night. Disoriented, I looked around in the soft light cast by the lamp I had forgotten to switch off. My head felt groggy as I threw a glance at my phone on the bedside table. It was shortly before three a.m. Everything seemed quiet, and yet

I couldn't shake off the feeling that something or someone was in the room, watching me. For a moment I thought I glimpsed pale blue eyes staring at me from the door. I spun around, heart jumping in my throat. No one there. No picture frames on the wall to hide a spy hole either. Shivering, I walked to the window and peeked through the curtains. The moon hid behind thick rain clouds. The room had noticeably cooled down.

I returned to my bed, pulling the sheets tighter around my shivering body, when I heard a thud outside my bedroom door. It was an old house and the rain and wind would make the wood creak, the living shapes of furniture simulating the threat of approaching danger, so nothing to worry there. Holding my breath, I listened for more sounds. The house was silent again. My bones felt stiff and tired, but any signs of sleepiness were gone. I slipped into my bathrobe, hesitating in front of the door. Should I really leave the comforting safety of my room and risk waking up my new employer? He might fire me for disturbing his beauty sleep.

Oh, sod it.

If I didn't check, I'd morph into an obsessive lunatic for the rest of the night. I crept to the door and opened it in one go, cringing at the squeaking sound of old hinges. The light from the lamp threw dark shadows on the thick rug covering the wooden floor. Mentally preparing myself to face whatever loomed in the shadows, I stepped into the cool corridor.

The hall was empty.

Chapter 2

It had been a long night of tossing and turning. In the morning, I stretched under the sheets, enjoying the pleasant heat of the room, when I realized it was already after nine. I was supposed to start my first day of work, not sleep in. Darn it. Trust me to lose a job because of some lavender-scented pillows.

I threw the sheets aside and rummaged through the closet to find a pair of black jeans and a white shirt. I pulled one out, all crumpled. Smelling the armpits, I grimaced. Why did it reek like I just finished a double shift at *McDonald's?* With one arm I retrieved another shirt while brushing my teeth with the other hand, then stopped to take another sniff and scowled again. This one didn't smell much better, but I had no more time to waste. I put it on and dashed down the stairs to the large kitchen.

The sun spilled bright rays through the double glazed windows. I peeked left and right and inhaled, relieved that no one was about. Perfect. If no one waited, then no one would know I was late. Whoever lived here was either still asleep, or they had left already. I snorted to myself. As if. The mansion was situated in the middle of the Highlands—where would they go? The forest extended for miles behind the back of the house. There were only two options: either McAllister worked from home, which wasn't likely. What with those high trees and probably no Internet connection. Or he drove to the nearest city, Inverness, which was two hours away. I chuckled, feeling enlightened because everything suddenly made sense. The name rang familiar, as though I somehow knew him without ever meeting him. I figured McAllister had to be a semi-famous writer—old, afraid of company, preferring solitude—because no one else would choose to live in this forsaken area.

I opened a few kitchen cabinets. The steel pots and pants gleamed in the morning light. The cooking utensils in our family never looked this polished. I peeked inside the drawers, marveling at the pristineness of this place. Why did I take this job? As much as it pained me to acknowledge, I knew nothing about housekeeping. Dallas said it'd be easy money so I could save enough to pay my bills, the yearly travel card and purchase books in my first year of college. The student loan covered my college fees already, but I gathered a part-time job would be unavoidable if I also wanted to eat. The money made from this summer job was supposed to help me survive until I found one that wouldn't collide with my classes.

Prepare breakfast, cook dinner, keep the house tidy, and wash some clothes. How hard could it be? But peering around, I realized this didn't look like any house I had ever entered. It was too tidy and clean, as though someone had already finished their work for the day. Used to this standard, McAllister probably expected me to scrub like five housekeepers. With most of the summer temping positions gone, it was too late to change my mind now, but I made a mental note not to believe my brother ever again.

No boss around, no work. I shrugged and went about making myself a cup of tea, then took a seat near the window. For a while I just sat there, watching the woods behind the house, admiring the dark green of the dense thickets stretching out as far as I could see. I felt the call of the woods, urging me to take a nice, long walk to stretch my legs and inhale the clean air I would never smell in London. I sighed with pleasure. What a beautiful, big house. Okay, given my experience from last night it was a bit spooky, but this was Scotland after all. You simply don't buy a house without one or two resident ghosts. Besides, I gathered I had been imagining things because last night when I finally plucked up the courage to open the door, the floor was empty. The point was, with no one around I could almost pretend I wasn't just an employee. I took another sip of my herbal tea when I heard a voice behind me. "It's beautiful, isn't it?"

Startled, I jumped, spilling some of the mug's content onto the floor. Slowly, I turned to stare at a woman's dowdy face. She was short, almost as short as me, with wiry grey hair tied at the back of her nape, blue eyes and a welcoming smile. I liked her instantly. "I was just taking a minute to admire the view," I said, pressing a clammy palm against my racing heart.

The woman's eyes creased as her smile widened. "No worries, dear. Take your time. I remember my first day here. I did the same thing. Couldn't resist the view." She put her large basket on the kitchen counter and took a seat at the nearby dining table. "I'm telling you, it's getting harder by the day to carry those things. You must be Amber. Thank goodness, Aidan's employed a housekeeper. I'm Greta."

I nodded. "Nice to meet you."

Greta jumped to her stubby feet and started rummaging in her basket. "I've brought some eggs and bacon to make you a nice breakfast. There's hardly anything to eat in this house. Aidan's always away, never eating in. Most of the time, I have to throw away what I cook." She opened one of the cupboards and pulled out a large saucepan, then placed it on the stove and retrieved a bowl to blend the eggs.

"Do you need help?" I asked, standing.

"No, you sit, dear. You must be tired from the long journey." Greta tossed several stripes of ham into the hot pan and turned to me. "Where did you say you came from?"

"London."

"Ah." Greta nodded knowingly. "Such a big place and so far away. Been there a few times." She shook her head. "Didn't like it one bit."

"I can see why."

"Aidan said you'd be staying for the summer?" Greta shot me an inquiring look. When I nodded, she laughed heartily. "I thought I'd be staying for a few months, but ended taking care of this house for the past five years now." She placed a plate in front of me and went about scrubbing the saucepan.

"Thank you," I said, a little shy. The aroma of eggs and bacon made my stomach rumble. I dug in. The bacon was crisp, but not dry. The eggs were still moist. My usual *McDonald's* breakfast never tasted this good. How the hell was I going to prepare something this delicious for McAllister? I almost choked on my food at the thought. Damn! Dallas said McAllister would be easily pleased with a bit of toast, butter and jam. Trust my brother to mess up my future job prospects because of a bad reference.

"How's the bacon, dear?" Greta inquired from the kitchen sink.

I forced my mouth into a smile. "All's great, thank you. I just realized I need to give my brother a call." And kill him.

Greta patted the saucepan dry and put it away. The kitchen looked as sparkly clean as before. I made a mental note to remember to wash the dishes rather than let them soak in soapy water overnight, which was my usual procedure.

"So you have family nearby? How lovely," Greta said.

"Just a brother. Dallas. He moved to Inverness a few weeks ago." I finished my breakfast, dropped the plate into the sink and looked around for washing up liquid.

"Leave it, dear. We have a dishwasher." Greta opened a cupboard door to reveal a large dishwasher smelling of lemons.

I placed my plate on an empty tray. "If you'll excuse me. I should get started on the housework."

22

"Of course. I'd better dash too." Greta picked up her basked and made a beeline for the hall. "One last thing. Just a word of advice, stay away from Aidan's friends." The old woman inched closer whispering, "Most of the time, it's only him, Aidan's brother and the blonde girl. But I've seen the others hovering outside the gates, glaring at me when I pass." She made a disparaging gesture with her hand. "I keep telling him they're strange."

I stared at her, utterly terrified. The job advertisement didn't mention visitors. For how many people was I supposed to cook? "How many people are we talking about?"

"Ah, the housework," Greta said, ignoring my question. "You should start with the washing. God knows what Aidan does with his shirts. They're always so dirty from the woods. If you need anything, you know where to find me." With a wave of her hand, she walked down the narrow, paved path behind the house.

I stared after her for a while. What was that all about? I hadn't seen anybody the evening before, but now I remembered the noises that woke me up. Could there have been other people in the house and Clare hadn't told me? Come to think of it, I was just an employee. No one had to tell me anything. Shrugging, I went in search of the laundry room.

Ten minutes later, I found it in the basement next to a locked door marked DO NOT ENTER. The laundry pile on the floor next to the washing machine stood almost as high as the ceiling. I kicked the pile and lowered to pick up a white shirt, my lips curling in disgust at the large brownish stains on the front. Either McAllister was into rolling in the mud, or he just enjoyed making my life a living hell because I sure had no idea how to get the dirt out of his clothes.

My phone vibrated in my pocket, startling me. Strange to have reception in the basement, but not in a bedroom. A smile stretched across my lips as I peered at the caller ID. Dallas dressed in diapers—he called it his Cupid outfit—at the last Halloween party after a glass too many.

"Hey, sis. How's life?"

"I should be barking mad at you for sending me to this forsaken part of the world. Do you have any idea what you got me into? I can't cook, or clean, or do anything around a house, and you know it."

"You'll be all right. You weren't that bad at home." Dallas paused. "Come to think of it, you were. But that's not the point. Don't worry about it, just listen."

I sighed. Of course he wouldn't show any sympathy. My brother couldn't care less about my job because he didn't like any kind of work. Part-time job or placement, he had never been one to stay in the same job for more than three weeks. "What do you want, Dallas?"

"I can't talk over the phone. Let's just meet and I'll tell you everything."

"It's my first day. I can't take off already."

Dallas snorted. "I wasn't expecting you to. I'll be there in half an hour."

"But—" I couldn't have guests over already. Was I even allowed to have visitors?

Dallas cut me off. "And keep me some of your boss's glorious lunch, won't you? I'm starving."

"No, you can't pop over just like that," I said, but my brother had already hung up on me.

24

No need to worry. McAllister was away, so he'd never know. My thoughts returning to Dallas's strange phone call, I started to sort through the pile, throwing all the whites into the washing automat.

What did Dallas want? He never visited unless he needed a favor. Getting me a job was the biggest surprise ever, like he really cared to help me after my family realized my chances of affording college were slim. He even helped me lie to Mum and Dad about my job duties. But my brother never did anything for anyone unless he had something to gain. I switched on the washing automat and returned to the kitchen to prepare lunch in case McAllister turned up.

The sudden noise of heavy footsteps jerked me out of my thoughts. I turned in time to see my brother's grinning face in the doorway.

"You said half an hour," I scolded.

He plopped into a chair and heaved his booted feet on the kitchen table, dried mud raining down on the polished surface. "I was in the vicinity."

"Of course you were," I muttered under my breath. In spite of my annoyance, I was glad to see him. Being all alone made me a little sentimental.

"Not bad." He pointed at the white kitchen furniture with its black marble counter.

"What do you want, Dallas?"

He peered at me from under thick, dark lashes, his golden skin flushing. "What makes you think I want something? Maybe I'm just here to check on my little sister, you know, make sure she's okay and all."

"Don't call me that. You're only a few months older." I shook my head. "Just spit it out."

"Okay." He breathed in and put down his legs. "There's something you need to do for me." I rolled my eyes. There it was. "No, listen. It's not just for me," Dallas continued. "It's the answer to all of our problems. You could go to college without worrying about money, and we could help Mum and Dad pay off their mortgage, and Dad wouldn't have to work in that horrid supermarket because he's too old and can't find a job in marketing."

"I'm not robbing a bank."

"Neither am I." Dallas inched nearer, his eyes darting left and right as he started to whisper, "In my new job as an environmentalist officer—"

"You're a what?" I burst into a fit of laughter. He couldn't be serious. Until a year ago, Dallas thought recycling meant giving away plastic bottles to people who couldn't afford their own.

"You're so unbelievably rude. I beat a lot of competition to get that job." He glared at me. "Now, are you going to let me finish, or not?"

I motioned with my hand, suppressing the laughter in my throat. "Go on then."

He shot me an irritated look before continuing, "I was walking around the forest, checking for damage to the trees, when I came across a hut. It was locked so I peered through the window and then saw something reflecting the light."

Pausing, he stared at me, wide-eyed, as if I just needed to switch on the light bulb over my head to understand what he was talking about.

"And? Get on with it," I said, impatiently.

"The floor was covered in soil, but—" he took a deep breath "—the stones were large enough to see. Diamonds, rubies and the likes, hundreds of them, as big as the palm of your hand. I'm telling you, we'll be rich soon.

Chapter 3

I crossed my arms over my chest, my mind unwilling to believe my brother's sordid proposition. "So you're telling me you want us to break into a house and rob it."

"No! You're not getting it." Dallas shook his head vehemently. "I didn't say it was a house. It's a hut, hidden in the woods. Whoever's keeping their stuff there is probably a little shady. After all, any normal person with nothing to hide would just lock it all in a safe, wouldn't they?"

"Great. You want me to steal from the local thug. What a delightful way to die." I turned to face him with a smile. He couldn't be serious. "Tell me you're joking."

"No one's going to die, because no one will know it was us." His hazel eyes sparkled as he regarded me. I could feel the layers of doubt peeling away slowly. He squeezed my hand. "Come on, sis."

"What you're asking of me is just crazy. I never figured I'd be a jewel thief when I grew up." I sighed. "All right. I'll think about it. So what happens if this heist turns into a disaster? I swear I'm not going to be caught dead in one of those hideous orange jumpers for twenty years."

"I thought orange was your color."

"Dallas!" I punched his shoulder.

"Come on. Do you think I'd let that happen to my baby sister? You know I got your back." Laughing, he grabbed me in a hug. "We could talk about this all day, but there's not much time, Amber. Who knows how long they'll keep the stash hidden." He threw me that dimpled smile that always made me give in.

"What's the plan then? I'm sure you have some ridiculous scheme cooked up already." I regarded him intently. If the jewels existed, Dallas wouldn't do something as stupid as stealing, even though pilfering from some thugs wasn't like taking away someone's life savings. Mum would be so proud of him. *Not.*

"You bet." Dallas moved away a few inches, draping his arm around my shoulders as he whispered, "Friday night. You wait until everyone's asleep, then squeeze out and meet me down the road. Make sure you wear black and I'll dig up the rest."

"You don't even know how to pick a lock." I felt laughter bubbling up again. Probably just hysteria at the outlook of burglary. Cameron had broken up with me because I wasn't as posh as his private school friends. It mortified him to be seen with me, particularly after I gained a few pounds when most of my friends were losing their baby fat. Soon I could add dishonesty to the long list of character traits that kept him from taking our dating to the next level.

"I'll look it up on Wikipedia. Now do we have a deal?" Dallas held out his hand. I grabbed it, shaking my head. Like usual, he was all talk, or so I hoped.

"Wikipedia? How reassuring. Why are you even waiting until Friday?" I asked. "Aren't you worried the stones will be gone by then?"

"Think about it. Everyone's out, partying, on a Friday."

His reasoning made no sense, but I wasn't going to argue. Anything could happen in five days. I knew he'd change his mind. "Just do me a favor and don't get the stuff on eBay," I said.

He winked. "You know I can't resist a bargain."

***

After Dallas left, I gave up on preparing lunch and went about finishing the household chores, fluffing up the cushions on the sofa and watering the flowers, then looked around. What do housekeepers do in a sparkling house? Would my boss notice if I didn't polish the already gleaming floors? Most likely not, which was good because scrubbing wasn't my favorite pastime. I grabbed the feather duster and waved it over the furniture, then hung the clothes on the line to dry. Bored, I glanced at my watch. Dinner wouldn't be served before six, so I had a few hours to inspect the back garden.

As I strolled around the bushes and trees, I inhaled the sweet smell of honeysuckle that stretched up the brown brick wall to the windowsills on the second floor. The drapes were drawn, the glass shimmered almost black in the bright sun. I wrapped my thick cardigan around my shoulders to fend off the cold wind, and turned my attention to the narrow path leading into the forest. The pale cobblestones, scrubbed from years of heavy rain, looked clean and polished. In the distance was a tall mesh fence obscured by trimmed rosebushes, already wilted. What was the fence for? McAllister obviously wasn't keen on trespassers. I snorted. As if anyone would find their way to this part of the country without the latest in satnavs and a good hound dog.

It was late afternoon when I returned to the kitchen to cook dinner. The freezer was filled to the brim. I prepared a vegetable stir-fry with pasta—one of the few things I knew how to cook—and made a mental note to look up a few recipes on the Internet. That is, if McAllister had an Internet connection.

By six the sky had turned a dark shade of grey, but my new boss had yet to arrive. I sat at the kitchen table, my hands fidgeting with the hem of my shirt, unsure what to do. I took a large gulp of water to soothe the dry cave of my mouth. I hadn't been so nervous since my first date with Cameron. It wasn't like me at all.

Eventually I heard the soft click of the entrance door. I jumped from my seat, holding my breath. Should I meet him in the hall, or wait? I had no idea. What did people do in movies? I dried my clammy hands on my jeans and opened the kitchen door, bumping into a tall, dark-haired guy. He reached out his hands to steady me. "You okay?"

I peered up into pale blue eyes framed by black lashes. He was stunning, tall and broad with high cheekbones, clad in ripped jeans and a white shirt similar to the ones

31

piled high in the basement, a leather jacket draped over his arm. Wearing my flat shoes, I barely reached his chin. The thought of laundry brought me back to reality. I'd been employed to wash the clothes, not stare at some guy, no matter how hot he was.

Clearing my throat, I pulled away and smiled. "You must be Mr. McAllister's son." My statement sounded more like a question.

The guy cocked a brow, amused. "Actually, I'm Aidan, your employer. You must be Amber."

"Right." I nodded, wide-eyed. How could he be my employer when he wasn't much older than me?

"I inherited the place," Aidan clarified as though reading my thoughts.

Another rich kid like Cameron. I would never be good enough for him. The pang hit me somewhere in the pit of my stomach. I ignored it because I needed this job. "So sorry to hear."

He frowned. "Huh?"

"Your parents. I mean—" I stopped, realizing I wasn't making much sense. His intense, blue gaze made me nervous, but I was a professional housekeeper and wouldn't develop a crush on my new employer. Not least because Clare and he couldn't be related, so there was only one option left. They were dating.

"Is that dinner?" Inching forward, he peered inside the huge saucepan, then took a sniff. The corners of his mouth curled downward. If he didn't like what he saw he didn't comment on it. "I usually eat in my study. Unless I have guests over, in which case it's the library."

I nodded, remembering the huge oak table I forgot to polish. "I'll bring it up. Do you go to school? Or college?" The words snaked their way out of my mouth before I could stop them. Was there even a college in Inverness? Even so, it wasn't my business. Apparently, Aidan thought the same because he didn't bother to answer my question.

He focused on me for a long second, staring through those eyes that seemed to look right through me. "I don't know if Clare told you no employee's allowed on the second floor."

I nodded and retrieved a plate from the cupboard. With shaking fingers I filled it with stir-fry, dropping some on the tiled floor, and held it out to him. On the sparkling china the noodles looked like giant worms swimming in brown, gooey mud.

"Thanks." He took the plate and sniffed, then turned to the door, his pale face flushed.

I hurried to open the door for him. "Can I get you a drink?"

"I'll get one later, thank you," he said over his shoulder.

"Well, then, I hope you'll like it," I called after him when something dawned on me. In movies servants always bring plates on trays. Why didn't I think of that? I sunk into my chair and covered my burning face with my palms whispering, "Stupid, stupid, stupid." Aidan probably already regretted employing me. I had never felt so mortified in my entire life. There I was, meeting the hottest guy ever and I cooked him my soggy stir-fry. It wasn't even Chinese; just one of those twenty-minute women's magazine miracle recipes supposed to save time and impress any date, including the prospective mother-in-law. Well, it didn't seem to impress Aidan. I could only hope he wasn't bowed over the toilet seat now, emptying the last remnants of a glorious yet light lunch, which he bought in some fancy restaurant.

"Are you all right?"

I lifted my head to peer at Clare standing in the doorway. She was wearing a short, black dress, tight in all the right places, her hair tied back in a strict bun. Her pale skin combined with a scarlet red lipstick made her seem fragile and alluring at the same time. Her eyes shifted from the stir-fry on the floor to me and then back to the stir-fry, her face betraying no emotion.

"I'm all right," I whispered, straightening in my seat.

Clare inched closer and stopped near the door to the back garden, her eyes focused on the darkness beyond. "It must've been a long first day. How did you find it?"

"It's very quiet here," I said.

"You'll get used to it." She turned and sniffed the air. Her gaze glazed over as though she was in deep thought. "This reminds me, you're not expected to work past five and certainly not to cook dinner. Aidan eats out most nights."

"Sure." The job ad specified cooking. Aidan must've said something. I blushed, mortified. It was his problem if he didn't like my food. No more cooking for me then.

"Great. I need to get going."

After Clare left, I forced down some food, cleaned the kitchen and returned to my room, thankful for a bit of privacy. I soaked in the large tub, enjoying the hot water, but as much as my body relaxed, my mind wouldn't stop leaping from Cameron to Aidan and back to Cameron, the image of my ex quickly fading from memory.

I got out of the tub, wrapped a large towel around me and placed Cameron's photo on the bedside table. With my evening routine finished, I climbed between the sheets and switched off the lights. I had been asleep for barely an hour when something woke me up.

Sitting up in the darkness, I strained to listen. Something moved outside my door. Then I heard the faintest giggle and a loud thud, and feet shuffling away. Maybe Aidan had guests over, or he and Clare were fooling around. They made a stunning couple, I had to admit that. Wrapping my covers around me, I closed my eyes, but I lay awake for most of the night, not quite able to shake off the image of Aidan McAllister's muscular arms wrapped around a giggling Clare. I was still in love with Cameron, so the sudden jealousy made absolutely no sense.

Chapter 4

For the next two days I saw and heard no one. The house was so quiet, it felt as though I lived alone. My new boss—I cringed at the prospect of calling someone my own age that—clearly liked to keep his distance and I appreciated it. No need to speak to him at all if he didn't want to. But I wanted to. I wanted him to notice me so much that I even applied makeup and put more effort into the household chores. I hadn't thought about Cameron in a day, setting a new record. To claim it had nothing to do with Aidan would be a lie.

"I'm being silly," I muttered to myself as I inspected myself in the mirror for the umpteenth time. The blue skinny jeans looked really good on me, making my legs seem so much longer. Shame Aidan wouldn't be in the woods to watch me break into the hut dressed in my best outfit.

On Friday, the house was deserted as usual. No voices, no slamming doors, no sign of anyone living here whatsoever. I left through the back, leaving the kitchen door unlocked. No one bothered to lock it anyway. As much as McAllister liked his privacy, he didn't seem too concerned about the possibility of burglary.

Dallas's car was parked down the street. I hoped his loud muffler wouldn't draw anyone's attention, but then again who would hear it in the middle of nowhere? I jumped onto the passenger seat, pushing a black backpack aside.

"You're late," Dallas said.

I glared at him. "You said to wait until everyone's asleep. That's exactly what I did." Irritated, I peered inside the backpack. "What's with the compass?"

Dallas started the car and sped off. "I couldn't get my hands on a pair of night vision goggles, so I figured a compass was the next best thing."

"You don't know where we're going?" I turned to face him, flabbergasted.

"Of course I do." He hesitated for a moment before adding, "Sort of."

"Great. What better way to spend a Friday night than with my half-wit brother, trekking through the freezing Highlands, looking for a shed to break into? You've really topped yourself this time."

He shot me a glare. "You only get thirty per cent since you keep insulting me. I know the way."

I held up the compass. "Sure you do."

"Hey, that's for peace of mind. Do you have any idea how dark it's going to be in those woods?"

"What did I get myself into?" I sighed. Expecting him to change his mind and give up on his grand plan made me the bigger idiot out of the two of us.

"Twenty per cent," Dallas said.

"Gee, why am I not doing it for free? I don't mind scrubbing toilets for the rest of my life."

We drove in silence for half an hour before Dallas cleared his throat and resumed a conversation, still scowling. "How's the job?"

I shrugged. "Okay. I've done worse."

Dallas smiled and steered the car onto a narrow path, then killed the engine. "You definitely have. I remember when you glued tattoos all over yourself in the hope to get the receptionist job at a tattoo parlor."

"I looked ridiculous." I returned the smile. "Shame they realized my body art was fake."

He gave my hand a quick squeeze. "This is our chance, Amber. We'll make it."

With a groan, I buttoned up my coat and exited the warmth of the car. The inclining track was narrow, surrounded by tall trees. The moon hung low in the sky, casting a soft glow on my brother's face. A cold wind whipped my hair against my skin. Dallas pulled out the compass, threw the backpack over his shoulder, switched on the flashlight and locked the car. I looked at him with raised eyebrows.

"Come on." He motioned me to follow and set off up the winding trail.

"Are you sure this is safe? You're not going to get us lost, are you?" I poked him in the back, but he didn't reply. I could only hope his lack of reassurance originated from deep concentration rather than from an inability to dispel my fears.

The air grew colder with every wearying pace I made. Dallas marched in silence, but I didn't fail to notice the hesitation in his steps every now and then. The trail wound upward, climbing into complete darkness. The stars in the sky looked like pale, gleaming dots too far away to cast any light through the thick canopy above our head. Although the ground was frozen and bare of twigs, I stumbled more than once.

By the time Dallas stopped to consult his compass yet again, my thighs ached and I felt blisters forming on my feet. I could hear my own panting and decided it was time to join the gym. Plopping down on the chilly ground, I remembered I wore my favorite jeans and jumped up. "So, how's that compass thing working for you? How long until we get there?" I asked.

"What are you, five? It's not far from here." Dallas resumed his walk. I took a deep breath and followed.

There was something in the air. I could feel an eerie vibe as though the air trembled. Twigs snapped, a soft humming carried over from the trees. I stopped dead in my tracks whispering, "Dallas? Do you hear that?"

My brother threw an irritated glance over his shoulder. "What now? No break."

A soft whistle echoed in the distance. "I think someone's following us." I peered behind me, noticing a blue streak of light flashing through the black night.

"You've always been paranoid." He quickened his pace.

I scanned the forest behind us, but nothing moved. Apart from the usual rustling of leaves, everything seemed deserted. Maybe I was just tired and sick from constantly tripping over my own feet. My overactive mind had to be playing tricks on me. After all, we hadn't passed any car on our way here, so no one could've followed us.

We trudged forward until we reached a clearing. The moon peered from behind dark clouds that looked like a huge, gaping mouth mocking me.

"It's got to be somewhere here," Dallas said.

I rolled my eyes. "Are you sure? We've only been marching for a few hours. I don't need to be home before morning."

"Stop acting like a baby, Amber." He tossed the backpack on the ground. "You wait here. I've got to take a leak."

I shook my head, trying to keep a straight face. "Nope. You said no breaks."

"But nature's calling. I'm taking the flashlight."

"No way." I shook my head and snatched the flashlight out of his hand. "Just make sure no one's biting anything off. Not sure we'd find it in the dark."

He smirked and slapped the back of my head like he used to do when we were children. Shining the flashlight on him, I watched him disappear into the thicket. I sat down on the damp ground, the wet grass soaking my jeans instantly. It had cost me a fortune. I considered getting up again, then thought, *Screw it.* We had plenty of stain remover stacked up in the utility closet to clean a whole shop. Besides, my feet were killing me. I peered into the darkness around me, counting the seconds.

On the horizon to my right, a blue light flashed between the trees again. What the heck? A shudder ran through me. There had to be a logical explanation. Maybe it was swamp gas, but that wouldn't make sense. We were in the woods, in the middle of nowhere. No swamps as far as I could see.

I sat up and called out, "Hey, are you finished? Hurry up." When my brother didn't answer, I jumped to my feet and walked in the direction in which he disappeared a few minutes ago. "Dallas? It's getting really freaky out here. I just saw this weird light flash. Someone might be following us."

Holding my breath, I strained to hear any approaching footsteps. There were none. The blue light flashed again in the distance. "Dallas?" My voice cut through the silence of the night, almost as loud as my pounding heart. "Come on. This isn't funny. If you're playing a prank on me I swear I'm going to kill you."

Crap! Where was he? What took him so long? My heart hammered like a drum. Rubbing my clammy hands on my jeans, I peered around me, unsure what to do. Should I start searching, or just wait? Leaning against the thick trunk of a tree I waited a few more minutes, calling my brother's name. I received no answer. My mind started to race, eager to come up with possible explanations.

Maybe he got lost. It was more likely than him playing a prank on me. He had done many stupid things in the past, but walking away and leaving me alone in the middle of the night wasn't one of them. I should never have let him drag me out here with him. I considered my options. Either walk back to the car and wait there for him, or hike through the woods and find him. A whimper escaped my throat as I pictured my brother crying out my name, thick blood pouring out of grisly wounds. What if he wasn't lost? Maybe whoever was following us found and hurt him. Going back to the car wasn't an option. I wouldn't leave my only brother dying.

Setting my jaw, I threw the backpack over my shoulder and hurried up the path, calling his name over and over again. Another flash of blue threw a soft glow on a black shack hidden behind the trees less than fifty feet away. Could this be the hut? Maybe Dallas had found it and was inside, finishing what we came for. I changed course away from the path, heading through the trees, grazing my hands as I pushed branches aside. And then I found myself staring at the dilapidated hut. I rummaged through my backpack and pulled out a flashlight, switching it on.

From outside, the wooden hut didn't seem bigger than a garden shed. A door hung from old hinges that looked as though a single kick would suffice to send the whole wall plummeting to the ground. There was no handle, just a metal rod to pull with a missing padlock. Dallas had said the hut was locked; maybe someone had been here already, raiding it before us?

"Dallas? Are you here?" I whispered even though I knew he wasn't nearby.

Before I could change my mind, I yanked the door open, cringing at the squeaking sound of rusty hinges, then shone the flashlight inside. The room seemed quite big; the wooden floor was surprisingly clean for a hut. Beneath the single dirty window—the one through which Dallas must've seen the gemstones—stretched a wide pit filled with what looked like thick mud. On the far left side was a high podium. I inched closer to lift a scroll.

The dim glow of the flashlight illuminated the golden letters as I read:

Two plus one but less than seven chosen in scarlet for Travel.

A tiger's eye for Sight, increased by ten for those reaching Beyond.

Green as the summer's morning leaf crushed in the velvet-blue sky for Abundance.

White smoke for those who may not come back from their eternal journey.

The list went on and on with one point stranger than the other. It was all gibberish to me, so I put the scroll back on the podium and returned to the pit. The mud shimmered black. If Dallas got lost, he'd never forgive me for finding the shed and not taking the gemstones. In spite of my better judgment, I kneeled down, pulled my sleeves back and dived my arms into the mud. I was up to my elbows when I reached the bottom. It didn't feel much different from the mud facials I usually spread on my face, just a little warmer and smoother to the touch. Still, who knew what was lurking down there, waiting to bite me? So, the sooner I finished the faster I could get away from this place. Taking a deep breath, I patted the ground, ready to pull back should something not feel right.

The strong gust of wind rattled the door, startling me. I flinched, stopping for a brief moment. When nothing moved, I continued my search. Eventually my fingers brushed against something hard and I pulled out a milky white gemstone the size of a walnut. My heartbeat quickened as I dropped it inside the bag and went about fishing out more gemstones.

The wind outside blew stronger, shaking the glass in the window. I sat up, my arms aching from the effort of delving through the thick mud and pulling out one stone after another. I didn't know how many I had, probably a dozen or more, all of them as large as the first one. Larger than any stone I'd ever seen, and worth millions if they weren't fake. Dallas would be so proud of me.

A twig snapped, making me jump. Maybe my brother had found his way to the shed, or it was an animal searching for food. I zipped up my backpack and slung it over my shoulder, then hurried out the door. Something rattled in the distance. *Chains?* But that made no sense. Why would there be chains in the woods?

"Dallas?" I whispered.

Feet shuffled behind the trees to my right. I snapped my head in that direction. Something or someone was out there, and judging from the lack of answer it wasn't my brother.

The smell of damp earth and oncoming storm lingered in the air. Fear grabbed hold of me as realization kicked in. Maybe whoever followed us killed Dallas and was back to get me. I was alone in the middle of nowhere. No one would ever hear my screams. My heart hammered like a drum in my ears, stifling the usual sounds of the woods. My breathing came shallow and labored as I leaned against the wall of the shed, unsteady on my legs, my eyes scanning my surroundings. I feared my irregular panting would betray my presence. When seconds passed and nothing moved, I breathed out, feeling silly. The woods sheltered all sorts of creatures, mice, foxes and the likes. They probably found me just as scary as I found them. My imagination was running wild again. It used to do that a lot lately.

Just to be on the safe side, I counted to three and dashed down the path. When I reached the clearing I stopped, panting, my sides burning from the effort. I leaned against a tree trunk and bent forward, palms pressed against my thighs, to gather my breath. Something shuffled through the thicket. My gaze darted toward the thick wall of bushes as I straightened, ready to sprint again.

A shadow stepped out of the darkness, his long, black coat swaying in the cold breeze. "Drop your backpack," a male voice demanded. It was barely more than a whisper, but there was something in his tone that left no doubt he usually got his way. I hesitated, frozen to the spot. My mind screamed to run, but my legs wouldn't budge. The man took a step closer and lifted a gloved hand. Something thin like a long string swished past me, leaving a trail of burning flames in the high grass. The air smelled of burnt wood. "I said drop it. Or you won't live to see tomorrow."

I stared at him, wide-eyed. Should I give up the bag? What was the point since he'd kill me anyway? Whatever happened, I wouldn't give up without putting up a fight. Even though my hands trembled, my mind remained surprisingly cool. I took a steadying breath. The flashlight dropped to the ground as I tore down the path, twigs snapping beneath my feet. I didn't think, didn't slow down to see whether the man gave chase, just ran until I reached the car and dropped to my knees a few feet away, shaking, my heart pounding hard.

The door opened and Dallas stepped out. "Where've you been? I've been waiting for ages."

"Get in the car. Go, go, go!" I could barely speak. My lungs sucked the cold air in, making a whistling sound.

"We're not leaving until we have the stones," Dallas said.

I grabbed his shoulders and shook. "Listen, idiot! Someone armed is following me. Either you move now, or I'll drive without you." For a moment he just stared at me, then opened his mouth to speak. I cut him off, "Get in, Dallas. Don't tick me off. From all the stupid ideas you've ever had this was by far the worst."

He mumbled something that sounded like, "I don't believe it," then held the passenger door open for me, got in and started the engine. I peered out the window into the darkness stretching behind me, only then realizing the full impact of what just happened. My heart started to race again. I could only hope my pursuer didn't see my face inside the shed.

Dallas switched on the overhead light. I spun toward him. Why wasn't he driving?

"You're sweaty and look like you've seen a ghost. Tell me what happened," he said. "I'm not going anywhere until you do." I could see the stubborn line between his brows.

"You and your stupid ideas," I shouted. "Only you could get lost going to the bathroom."

He glared. "You had the flashlight. I didn't see the way back from all the trees. When I returned you were gone."

"I called your name. You didn't reply." I took a deep breath and dropped my voice a notch.

"I didn't hear you. What happened?" Dallas prompted.

I pushed my trembling hands underneath my thighs to stop them from shaking. "I found the hut."

He shot me a disbelieving look. "You did? Did you get the gemstones?"

"Yes."

"Woo hoo!" Dallas laughed, then stopped when he registered the expression on my face. "What?"

"I told you someone followed me. We might end up dead any minute if you don't drive soon."

"What? Did they see you?"

Moistening my lips, I shook my head. "Don't think so. It was too dark, but I had the flashlight switched on inside the hut. He could've peered through the window. He followed me to the clearing where you disappeared—" I glared at him "—and asked me to drop the backpack."

"How did you get away?" Dallas asked.

"I took off like the wind." I let out a long breath.

The lines around Dallas's mouth smoothed a little. "He didn't follow you to the car, so we've nothing to worry about. At least he didn't carry a gun. No one could ever outrun a bullet, not even a cheetah like you." I shot him an irritated look. How could he be joking when I just escaped sure death? Dallas squeezed my hand reassuringly as he continued, "Listen, I'm sorry. I won't ask you to do anything like this ever again." He grinned. "Come to think of it, I won't have to because we're rich. We'll be sipping tropical drinks on a white sand beach in Mexico soon. I'll get a giant Margarita with one of those fancy umbrellas."

I rolled my eyes. I had just added jewel thief to my résumé and almost got killed by some thug, and all my brother could think of was fancy umbrellas and tropical drinks on a beach. I wasn't convinced the thug wouldn't be able to identify me, but Dallas's confidence didn't fail to rub off on me. It felt good to have someone else in charge now. "What're you going to do with the stones?"

"I'll have them inspected and then put them up for sale. I may be gone for a while until everything's sorted out. Will you be all right?"

I nodded.

"Good," he said. "Just keep cool. No one knows you."

We drove in silence. The way back to the mansion seemed much shorter. Before I knew it, Dallas stopped the car and turned to face me, smiling. "We'll be living the sweet life soon. You just wait and see."

"If you say so." I opened the car door and jumped out, my skin instantly turning into goose bumps in the freezing air. "You'll call?"

Dallas snorted. "You think I'll cut you out? Fat chance. Next time, Milady, I'll have you picked up in a limousine driving you to your mansion."

"Just be careful," I mouthed as the car sped off down the street. With a sigh, I turned and headed for the gate, hurrying down the path to the back of the house.

The lights were turned off. The windows on the second floor gleamed black in the dim moonlight. It all felt so surreal, my old life in London, my new summer job, the chase through the woods. Were the last hours real or nothing but a figment of my imagination? Didn't matter, because I was safe now. With a flick of my hand, I opened the door to the kitchen and entered when the lights flickered on and someone said, "Been out?"

Chapter 5

I leapt back at the sound of Aidan's voice, almost bolting out the door again. My heart skipped a beat as I peered at him. His cheeks were flushed, his hair was in disarray. Something burned in his gaze, a nerve twitched just below his right eye.

"You scared me to death. I'm sorry I'm getting in so late. Did I wake you?" I tried to keep my voice nonchalant, but I failed.

"No need to apologize. There's no curfew here." He wiped a smudge of mud off my face. "What happened? Got into a fight?" Regarding me through pale blue eyes that seemed to smolder, he pointed at my hands.

"Huh? Yeah, you should see the other guy." He had avoided me for five days. Why in the world was he up now, talking to me when I was all sweaty and looked like crap? I smiled and shrugged as if the bloody scratches were nothing to worry about.

"Really?" He cocked a brow. "How did you get home? Did he drive you after you beat him up?"

I could feel the guy wasn't going to let up, and a mistrusting boss's never a good boss. Sighing, I closed the door behind me as I set my brain in motion, imploring it to come up with a good excuse. "Okay, if you must know, I was stargazing." I cringed inwardly. Was that the best I could come up with?

"At three in the morning?" Aidan's lips curled into a sarcastic smile.

"Why, that's the best time to see the stars. Unfortunately, it was a bit dark and I tripped." I laughed a little too loud, hoping it didn't sound as forced to him as it sounded in my ears. "I'm such a klutz, always falling on my nose." I winced at my choice of words. Now he'd think I was the worst housekeeper in the world *and* too stupid to walk on two legs.

"I'm a sucker for staring at a sky full of shining stars." His gaze narrowed. "I love to watch them twinkle like diamonds."

Diamonds. It brought back all the guilt of helping Dallas steal the gemstones. I gulped, heat rushing to my face.

"It's not too late," Aidan said, softly.

I peered at him. It wasn't too late for what?

"I guess it's a no then." Aidan's jaw set as he turned away, calling over his shoulder, "You should clean those scratches before you catch an infection. There's a first aid kit in the top cabinet of your bathroom."

I waited until he was gone before walking up to my room. The wounds would have to heal without Band-Aid because I couldn't be bothered to rummage through the bathroom at this ungodly hour. I considered taking a shower, but I couldn't drag my aching feet beyond the bed. So I just dropped on it, exhausted but too agitated to fall asleep. By the time the sun rose through the clouds, I was still tossing and turning. With a sigh, I threw the covers aside and rose, giving up any hope on finding sleep, even though my eyes felt swollen and dry from the lack of sleep.

It was Saturday, my first day off. After a quick shower, I searched through my still unpacked suitcase for something wearable, maybe a shirt that didn't smell of *McDonald's*. In all the week's frenzy, I had forgotten to wash my clothes. After slipping into a black, long-sleeved top that emphasized my narrow waist and a pair of blue skinny jeans, I strolled to the kitchen for a cup of tea and a bowl of cornflakes.

The fruit basket was filled with fresh apples and bananas. Three small bowls of ripe blueberries occupied the upper shelf of the fridge. The other shelves were jammed with vegetables and dairy products. Whoever went shopping didn't penny-pinch. Particularly since no one but me seemed to ever consume anything.

I rinsed some blueberries under the cold-water tap and sprinkled them on top of my cornflakes, then sat down for breakfast, my thoughts returning to last night's events. Someone had given chase. Someone had been sneaking around the hut while I was inside. Hopefully, Dallas was right and we had nothing to worry about, because I sure couldn't deal with one of my mother's lectures if I landed in jail.

I finished eating, drained the bowl and cup, and headed out the backdoor in the hope to meet someone. A cold October wind rustled the leaves; the ground was still damp with last night's dew. I scanned the garden. Apart from two squirrels, I saw no one, but the loud clanking of metal carried over from the garage on the other side of the house.

As I inched nearer, I saw the large shape of a man bowed over a lawnmower, hammer in hand. I knocked on a piece of metal to announce my presence. "Hello. I'm Amber."

The old man turned, exposing a pair of remarkably red cheeks and a friendly smile. "Well, hello. I'm Harry, the gardener. You met my wife Greta the other day." He held out a dirty hand and shook mine with enthusiasm.

"Yes, I did. She made me breakfast."

"That's my Greta, always cooking. That's why I look like this." He patted his round belly. "Before marrying her I actually had a waist."

I smiled.

"Greta said you were from London."

"That's right." I changed the subject, uncomfortable talking about me. "You don't sound Scottish."

Harry wiped his greasy hand on a stained cloth. "I'm from the south. Cornwall."

"Beautiful place," I said.

"Not as beautiful as Scotland. Aidan left a note you might want to do some shopping today." He raised his eyebrows as if to question the sanity of the idea of driving to town. I could understand why. It was two hours away. "He asked me to accompany you."

"He did? That's very kind of him." I couldn't remember asking him, but I felt grateful for the opportunity, particularly since I hadn't made any plans for the weekend. Money was tight, but what the heck? I still had my student loan. Besides, I wasn't planning on spending a fortune, and Aidan would pay me soon.

"I can drive you now. The shops are open until six, but I'm tired of fiddling with this old thing." He pointed at the lawnmower.

"I'd love that." I ran back to the house to get my handbag and coat. When I returned, Harry was gone. I waited until he appeared a few minutes later with a jacket around his broad shoulders and a pair of dangling keys in one hand.

"That's the car." He pointed at a white van, the only vehicle in the driveway. He puffed all the way to the van and opened the passenger door to let me in. I jumped on the wide passenger seat and fastened the seatbelt. Harry squeezed his large body behind the steering wheel and started the engine. The car spluttered to life. Harry pulled out of the driveway before he resumed our conversation. "Greta always says a bit of exercise will do me good. But I say all this walking's of no help if I don't cut back on the beef."

I didn't want to point out that we weren't walking but driving. "You couldn't pay me to give up beef. I just try and watch my portions."

Harry laughed, gaze fixed on the road. "It's a short drive to Inverness. The streets are usually empty after ten o'clock but before ten it's hell."

"Do you drive to town often?" I inquired.

Harry snorted. "Often enough. I'm taking care of two houses since Aidan's hardly ever home, always busy with his work. Every day, there's something for me to mend. Old houses aren't so different from old people, they constantly need a doctor." He laughed. When I joined in, he continued, "Last week it was my rheumatism, this week it's my spine and next week it might be the grave."

I peered at him, horrified. "Don't say that."

"I'm telling you, my dear mother was as healthy as a horse. One day, she felt poorly and wouldn't get out of bed. A stroke, said the doctor. She spent a week in the hospital before she closed her eyes and never woke up again."

"I'm so sorry." I leaned in to squeeze his hand resting on the steering wheel.

"Well, that's life. Enjoy it while you're young. You never know what you might miss if you lock yourself up like Aidan."

So Aidan liked to stay indoors. Funny, I hadn't seen him all week. "What does—" I hesitated saying his name "—Aidan do?"

Harry shook his head. "Something with buying and selling, I think."

We drove for nearly two hours with Harry talking most of the time. Eventually, he pulled the car into a parking lot in the middle of Inverness and killed the engine.

"See the corner over there? That's High Street with all the trendy shops. I'll be at the pub." He pointed at a green building with a sign outside advertising a pint for a pound and Karaoke night.

54

"Thanks." I felt embarrassed for wasting the old man's time, particularly since I didn't really need anything from the stores. "Are you sure you don't mind?"

"You're doing me a favor, dear." Harry winked and slapped my shoulder lightly. "Greta would never let me waste a perfect Saturday morning sitting in the pub, unless I came up with a good excuse for having a pint of beer at this time of the day."

"I'll be back in an hour, then."

"No need to hurry. Take your time," Harry said.

"Thanks." I stepped onto the grey asphalt, overwhelmed by something I couldn't pinpoint. I swallowed hard, trying to calm down my racing heart at the outlook of adding my rising paranoia to my money worries. "I'll be back in two hours," I called after Harry as he crossed the street, heading for the pub on the other side of the road.

***

When I returned, laden with countless shopping bags, Harry waved from across the street through a crowd of people. I waited until he reached me and unlocked the car.

"Did you find everything you came for?" He grabbed my bags and tossed them on the backseat.

"I wish I didn't." I held up a clutch, ignoring the guilty feeling in the pit of my stomach. "I got this for half the price. The sales here are great."

"Pretty." Harry nodded appreciatively and locked the car. "You girls always find something. You must be famished. What do you say to lunch? My treat."

55

My stomach rumbled in response. "Sounds great. Thank you."

From outside, the pub looked deserted. Inside, most seats were occupied. A high shelf with various wine and beer bottles lined the wall behind the bar. The walls were covered in mirrors and posters advertising various drinks. Harry guided me to an empty table near the kitchen and handed me the menu. "This place has the finest beef and mash in town. Almost as good as my Greta's."

Someone yelled, "Ye already back, Harry? Or dinna ye find the way out?" The man's Scottish accent was so strong, I barely understood a word, but I smiled. Harry waved to a table across the room, then turned back to me.

A redhead in her forties approached, hands pressed against her broad hips as she regarded me curiously. "Who's the pretty lass, Harry? What are you keeping from your dearie?"

"She's just a child." Harry turned bright red. "Just get us a pint and water for the girl, and the best of your beef and mash."

He shot me a questioning look. When I nodded in agreement, the woman scribbled on a thick notepad and turned to leave calling over her shoulder, "I'll be right back."

"It's nice here," I said, watching the redhead as she took a couple's order a few tables away.

"Don't mind her. Most of the time, she doesn't mean what she's babbling." Harry pointed at a stage obscured by a group of visitors. "On a Saturday night, you'll find plenty of young and talented local musicians performing here. I don't know much about music, but Greta says they're good." He continued chatting until the food arrived, served by a freckled girl. The girl dropped off the plates and left just as quickly, her eyes fixed on her hands, a shy smile playing on her lips.

Harry tucked in and I followed suit. The slice of beef was so large I could barely eat half of it, but it was the best I'd ever had. Finishing my water I pushed my plate aside when my gaze fell on a pale woman leaning against the bar. She had long, brown hair tied at the back of her nape. The skin, shimmering pale like alabaster, stood in contrast to her long, black dress. I reckoned, with all the makeup giving her that white-as-the-dead look she could only be an actress or a musical performer. The frills on her long sleeves ruffled as she turned and lifted a manicured hand to her flat chest, her neck craned to the side in an unnatural angle.

"Who's that?" I interrupted Harry's monologue.

He raised his gaze from his plate and looked in the direction in which I pointed. "That's the pastor. A fine man."

I shook my head. "No, the woman beside him. The one in the black dress."

Harry squinted. "I don't see a woman in a black dress."

"Over there." I pointed impatiently to the woman standing next to the pastor. "Near the corner."

"That's the pastor, dear." He motioned the redhead to approach with the bill.

Frowning, I grabbed my coat and squeezed into it. When I looked back at the bar, the woman in black was gone.

"Ready to head home? It's going to rain soon," Harry said as soon as we were outside. A strong gust of wind blew my hair in my face. Several girls clad in short skirts and revealing tops walked past, clutching at each other's arms to keep warm.

"Sure." I pushed the eccentric woman out of my mind as I inhaled, remembering I hadn't thanked Harry for his hospitality. "Thanks for lunch," I said. "You were right about the beef. It was fantastic, the best I had in ages."

Nodding, Harry unlocked the car and held the passenger door open. He started the car and resumed his chat, but I couldn't focus. I nodded a few times in what I thought were all the right places as my stomach began to rebel. A tiny pang, like an electric shock, shot through me. Maybe the beef hadn't been so great after all, or my stomach wasn't used to so much food.

We drove out of the city center. Harry stopped at traffic lights. Through the windshield, I watched an old woman clad in an old-fashioned, buttoned up dress push a buggy across the street. The long, grey material barely swayed in the wind as she trudged forward, stopping right before us. The lights changed to green. Harry accelerated. He was going to kill them. Gasping, I grabbed hold of his arm, tugging as hard as I could. "No! Stop!"

Harry didn't even flinch as he drove right through them. He signaled and stopped on the bus lane. "What's wrong? Did you forget something?"

For a moment I just stared at him, open-mouthed, then turned in my seat to peer at the crossing. The woman with the buggy wasn't there. "Where did she disappear?"

"Who?"

I turned to face him again. "You didn't see them?" It couldn't be. She'd been standing right in front of the car.

The left side of my head started to throb like someone was hammering on my brain.

Harry regarded me intently. "See who?"

Throwing a last glance over my shoulder, I shook my head muttering, "No one."

"Are you okay?" Harry asked. The furrows on his forehead deepened. I nodded, wishing I could get home as fast as possible.

Less than two hours later, the car pulled in front of the manor, and I exited, grabbing my bags as I thanked Harry.

"If you need anything, just ring. It can get lonely here," he called before putting the van in gear and speeding off.

"I will." I walked around the back to the kitchen. It was almost three p.m. but the house was quiet. I grabbed a bottle of water and an empty glass, and returned to my room, sinking into my soft sheets as soon as I shrugged out of my boots and coat.

The woman with the buggy had been there, I knew it. There could be many explanations why Harry didn't see her. Maybe his sight failed him. Maybe something obstructed his view and the woman jumped to the side on time, unhurt. But how did she disappear so quickly?

I sat up and poured myself a glass of water, emptying it in one big gulp, then pressed the cool glass against my feverish temple, hoping I hadn't caught a cold on my first day out. I closed my eyes and fell asleep, the image of the woman in black still lingering at the back of my mind. When I woke up, darkness had descended, bathing the room in darkness. My joints felt stiff as though I'd slept in the same position for too long, but my upset stomach felt a little better already. Grunting, I stirred and pushed the covers aside. Dizziness washed over me, making me want

59

to stay in bed. I held on to the bedside table until it passed, then stood on shaky feet.

Somewhere a clock struck seven times. I had slept for four hours. The lack of sleep from last night must've caught up with me. I changed into a black V-neck shirt and headed for the kitchen when I heard laughter coming from the library. Stopping mid-stride, I held my breath to listen.

A woman laughed. Was it Clare? "Looks like you can try again to win the prize in five hundred years. I can't believe you let that pretty little thing beat you."

"She didn't," Aidan said. I could hear the irritation in his voice. "I was just too busy to notice her slip in and snatch it from under everyone's nose."

Chapter 6

A door opened, startling me. I turned to bolt back up the stairs. Halfway up, I stopped, reconsidering. I might make it before someone saw me, but the stairs would creak, betraying my presence. Besides, I didn't mind a bit of company, particularly since I barely knew anyone and really needed another human's presence before I turned completely bonkers.

Heaving a sigh I spun, staring straight into pale blue eyes. For a moment I thought it was Aidan McAllister standing before me, until I realized the guy was about the same age but a bit bulkier. He smiled and held out a hand with pale, long fingers, scanning me up and down, his eyes lingering on my throat a tad too long. "I'm Kieran." Even his voice sounded like Aidan's.

I shook his hand, a freezing sensation charging through me. "I'm Amber."

"Aidan didn't say you were this—" he gestured with his hand and laughed "—tasty."

One word flashed through my mind—Clare. Why would Aidan brag about a hamburger when he had filet mignon on his plate? I curled my lips into a forced smile. "Thank you." What did it matter if Aidan found me attractive anyway? Cameron and I were only taking a break.

"Would you care to join us in the library?" Standing a little too close for comfort, Kieran grabbed my hand and guided me toward the other voices without waiting for my answer. He didn't drop my hand when we stepped through the large oak door. All eyes turned on me as Kieran said, "I found this delightful creature sneaking off to bed without so much as a single goodnight. My dear brother's been keeping her all to himself. Remember what Mother always said, it's nice to share."

Sibling rivalry? I had no idea what to make of it, but being the center of attention made me feel awkward. I decided to ignore Kieran's comment as I peered around. I had been inside the library to clean, but I hadn't inspected the room too closely because my thoughts had been preoccupied with Dallas's plan. Taking it in for the first time, I realized the room was spacious with scarce but heavy furniture. Heavy brocade drapes in the color of rusty leaves covered the large bay window. Three leather sofas were set in the middle; mahogany bookcases covered the walls up to the ceiling. Aidan sat on the armchair to the right, dressed in black from head to toe, his pale blue eyes staring at me as though I was some sort of freak. Behind him, a soft fire burned in the fireplace, the crackling of wood carrying through the unnerving silence.

Clare jumped up from the floor in front of the fireplace, her skin flushed from the heat, and pointed at a sofa opposite from Aidan, inviting me to sit. "Amber, how fabulous that you should join us. I see you've met Aidan's brother, Kieran." Her silver dress enveloped her athletic body like a sheath. Her glossy hair smelled of roses and something else I had never smelled before—mysterious and different. Clare was always so dressed up. Wearing my usual jeans and top, I felt like the pauper standing next to the beautiful princess.

I dropped on the sofa. Kieran sat down next to me, his thigh brushing mine, and draped his arm around my shoulders. Aidan frowned but didn't comment. He probably didn't like his brother hitting on the employees. Even though he had a point and I vowed to keep all my relationships strictly professional because I needed a good reference letter, I couldn't help but feel flattered. It wasn't the norm that a good-looking guy pay me attention.

Smiling, Clare walked over to a cabinet and retrieved a bottle of something red. It looked like wine, smelled like it. Surely, she knew I wasn't eighteen just yet. She shot me an inquiring look. When I nodded, Clare poured the liquid into four crystal glasses, then handed me one.

"Thank you," I murmured. There were no snacks or drinks on the table, no empty plates or bowls. The rich kids in this house behaved nothing like the teens I knew. The atmosphere reminded me of going to a party that had been raging for hours and as soon as I walked in, someone suddenly decided to break the keg. I realized I shouldn't be here at all, drinking whatever was in my glass with my employer in a house I cleaned for a living. What was I thinking?

With trembling fingers, I lifted the glass to my mouth when Kieran inched closer sniffing the air. "This is good stuff."

"Shut up," Aidan said. It was barely a whisper, but the tiniest hint of a threat echoed in his tone.

Kieran laughed. "Please, someone teach him how to appreciate the good things in life."

The door flew open and another guy entered. He was tall and dark, long hair framing strong cheekbones and spilling onto his collar, his golden skin seemed free of any blemish. He looked like a statue: cold, smooth, and untouchable. His brown gaze fixed on me and stayed there. I curled my lips into a smile at the prospect of meeting yet another rich kid, remembering that I was nothing but the housekeeper. It was only a matter of time until they let me feel it.

"Blake, how fabulous that you should join us." Clare, repeating the same words she'd used before, seemed unfazed by his frown. "Meet Amber. She's—" Clare hesitated "—just arrived." I breathed out, thankful that Clare hadn't referred to me as the maid. Even though that was the job description, not being called one mattered. Clare turned to face me. "This is Blake, a good friend."

Blake looked me up and down, and I realized it wasn't with animosity; just cold curiosity like you'd watch a lab experiment. I sank deeper into the sofa, wishing I could make myself invisible. First Aidan couldn't stop staring, and now Blake. Was a mole growing on the tip of my nose and I hadn't noticed?

Blake crossed his arms over his chest and cocked an eyebrow toward Aidan who shook his head and turned away. The sudden silence seemed oppressive. I fidgeted in my seat, unsure what to do to break the ice. I felt like an intruder who'd interrupted an important conversation and everyone was too polite to ask me to leave.

Eventually Clare cleared her throat and said, "I heard you had a nasty fall last night. How are you?"

Four pairs of eyes turned on me, their faces blank. They were probably as grateful as I was for the opportunity to break the silence. Of course I would've been more grateful if the topic of conversation didn't involve me. "I'm fine, thanks for asking," I said.

Clare shook her head. "You shouldn't be outside after dark. It's not safe. Aidan should've filled you in on the dangers." She gave him a hard stare.

"It was just a walk," I said. What could possibly be dangerous in the middle of nowhere?

Aidan raised an eyebrow. "After midnight?"

Why all the interest? Surely we had more pressing issues to discuss. Like global warming, or the rise in hurricanes all over the world. Okay, so I had been dressed all in black and couldn't blame him for thinking I was out robbing the neighbors—if we had any. Or why else would he make it sound like an accusation? I raised my chin a notch. "I couldn't sleep."

"Next time you can't sleep, call me," Kieran said. I shuddered at how much he looked and sounded like Aidan.

Aidan glowered. "Please ignore my dear brother. He's slightly confused these days."

My heart fluttered in my chest. It was the longest I'd been able to stare at Aidan without looking stupid. I felt like a schoolgirl having her first crush, but it couldn't be a crush because Cameron and I weren't over. Clare's voice jerked me out of my thoughts.

"Sorry?"

"I said did you find anything interesting?" Clare asked.

Heat scorched my cheeks. What a weird question, as though she suspected something. She couldn't be. "Not really. I just needed some fresh air."

Aidan scoffed and rose from his chair, slamming a book on a nearby coffee table. "Well, then, it's all sorted, isn't it?"

"Maybe you aren't in the mood for company tonight?" Blake asked.

"We still have business to discuss," Aidan said, "and Amber will probably want to relax after a long working week."

Working week? Huh? I blinked. Right. I had been working. Sort of. I had also been enjoying the last rays of sun in the garden, but it was part of my household duties to check the exterior of the house remained in pristine condition, or so I told myself. Aidan was still staring at me. I realized this was my hint to leave. My leg brushed against Kieran's as I stood, placing my full glass next to the other untouched ones. "I should get going. Thanks for the invite."

Kieran jumped to his feet and offered his arm with an amused glint in his pale eyes. Aidan crossed the room in two long strides and placed a hand on the small of my back, barely touching the material.

"Can I talk to you for a minute?" Aidan said. I nodded.

"That's so like Aidan. Dying to sink his teeth into my dates," Kieran said. "Just kidding, bro."

I offered Kieran a tentative smile, deciding I wouldn't take him seriously, as Aidan guided me out of the library through the kitchen and out the back door into the garden.

It was so dark I could barely make out his features. The moon—a half crescent on the black sky—moved from behind the clouds, throwing glowing shadows across his skin. His eyes shimmered as he pulled me down on a bench and sat beside me. I shivered but not from the cold. My heartbeat sped up. What could he possibly have to say that he needed time in private? Maybe he was about to fire me.

He moistened his lips and stared at the lawn as he spoke, "Last night we were worried about you."

"Why?" I spun to face him, surprised. He certainly was hard to read. One moment, he seemed irritated by my presence, avoiding me at all costs. The next, he seemed concerned about my wellbeing. Why would he care anyway?

Aidan shrugged. "You're used to city life and may overlook the possibility of threat. There's danger everywhere, not just on the busy streets of London."

"I'm aware of that. Thanks for your concern." I knew I sounded tetchy, but I couldn't help it. For a moment, I had thought he cared because he liked me. He was just my boss. We barely knew each other, and he dated Clare. I wished I could be angry with his stunning girlfriend, but to my chagrin I realized she was as nice as she was beautiful.

"No problem," Aidan said. "We're one big family here, and I want you to consider yourself part of it. It must be hard to be away from everyone you know, all alone here with no one around. If there's anything I can do, just say it."

As he grinned, a dimple formed on his right cheek. My heart quivered. Men like him should come with a warning: date at your own risk. I smiled at my thoughts, then felt instantly guilty. Cameron and I weren't really over. He just needed space for a few months to sort out his plans for the future. It wasn't right to sit here with a gorgeous guy, engaging in all sorts of naughty thoughts.

"I really appreciate your concern." I moved away from him. It was only a few inches, but I noticed his smile disappear.

"Would you like to go back inside?" Aidan asked.

"Sure. I know you have important business to discuss." I forced a bit of cheerfulness into my voice, but didn't quite manage to sound nonchalant.

Without another word, Aidan led me down the path to the kitchen and held the door open. When we reached the hall, he halted. I almost bumped into him. He touched my shoulder to steady me and breathed in as if to speak, but stopped. Clare appeared from the library, holding two glasses of wine in her hands. "There you are. I've been looking for you." Her questioning gaze wandered from Aidan to me.

"We were outside," Aidan said.

"Ah. Blake's waiting." Clare raised her eyebrows and turned to me. Aidan hesitated, then walked away. "Come on, let's finish our wine," Clare said. "I'm glad for the company. Aidan's business talk always puts me to sleep."

She seemed her usual pleasant self. If she found it strange that her boyfriend had just spent alone time with me, she didn't show it. We retreated to the massive living room. She put the glasses down, switched on a lamp on the wall and lit several candles on a nearby table. Sinking into the soft cushions on the sofa, she patted the space next to her. "I assume you've heard theories about what's going on in the woods," Clare started. "People claim to have seen strange lights—"

"You mean like UFOs and aliens?" I interrupted, smiling. There it was, the woods topic again. I couldn't quite shake off the feeling they kept something from me.

"No." Clare shook her head, playing with the hem of her sleeve. "More like stories of legends and supernatural stuff. Anyway, people have been disappearing for a while. Mostly visitors, because the locals know to stay away after dark."

I'd known something was going on. The weird blue light, the strange sounds, the man following me, his threat. People went hiking all the time and nothing happened. Trust my brother to find the one forest that came with a deadly warning sign. Suppressing a shudder, I forced my attention back to the conversation. "I'll keep that in mind, thanks."

"It's not just that," Clare said. "Other things have happened, people coming back and suddenly seeing things."

She certainly had my attention now. "I don't understand. What things?"

Clare inched closer and dropped her voice to a whisper. "Ghosts, souls, or whatever you want to call them."

I nodded, a cold shiver running down my back. Like the woman with the buggy crossing the street. Harry never saw her, but I knew she was there. Everything snapped into place. Back in London I'd have laughed at such superstition, but I was in Scotland, the land of mystery. Here anything seemed possible.

"Did anything strange happen in the woods?" Clare regarded me intently, her long fingers with black-painted nails curling around my wrist. "Because we can help you. You can trust me. It's not too late."

Hadn't Aidan said something similar last night? I thought of the blue, flashing light, and then of the man, too dark to see, his deep voice too low to distinguish. Nothing had happened, but it could have. I shook my head. "Nope."

Clare peered at me, doubtful, but didn't persevere for which I was thankful. I didn't want to keep lying. "How do you like your new job?" Clare asked.

"It's different, but I like it." I said. Another lie.

Clare smiled. "I remember your application. You were Aidan's choice straight away. Will you be staying in Scotland after summer?"

My heartbeat sped up. He wanted me *straight away* when I didn't even have any experience. Whatever Dallas put on that application helped me beat the competition. Or Aidan liked me, even if only on a subconscious level. Somehow, I wanted him to like me. "I'll be going back to London, I think. My boyfriend, well, sort of has plans to move in together once I start college."

"The one in the picture on your dresser?"

"That'd be Cameron." I narrowed my gaze. Was she spying on me?

Laughing, Clare raised her hands. "It's not what you think. I smelled smoke and had to investigate. Wouldn't want to burn the house down, would we? Anyway, I called Harry and he said it was the heating system. You know these old houses."

"It's okay." I smiled, realizing I was overreacting again.

Clare brushed an imagined stray hair out of her face. "So, it's serious between Cameron and you?"

"I think so." I blushed, wondering why Clare seemed so interested in my private life. But then I remembered I was in Scotland. If I were to live in a house in the middle of the Highlands, where nothing ever happened, I'd probably be pursuing any piece of gossip I could get my hands on.

"Lucky you." Clare sighed. "That makes one of us."

"I thought you and Aidan—" I trailed off, embarrassed.

"What?" Clare laughed, eyes glinting with something I couldn't place. "Aidan's like family to me."

"You're not dating?" I felt stupid for asking and even more so for feeling relieved. With beautiful Clare no longer my competition, a sudden weight lifted off my chest. Not that I stood a chance with Aidan. Besides, I didn't want to be with anyone because I still loved Cameron.

"I don't think Aidan's ever thought of me as dating material. Not even after Rebecca—" she hesitated "—left. Kieran and I, ah, never mind. You're probably bored already."

"Who's Rebecca?"

Clare jumped to her feet, knocking over her wine. She caught the glass in mid-air before the red liquid could spill onto the carpet. "There's something I want to show you upstairs," she said. I hesitated when she pulled me to my feet. "Come on. It'll be our little secret. Aidan will never know."

She wanted me to break the off-limits rule? "I don't want to lose my job," I whispered.

Clare winked. "You won't, I promise."

Oh, what the heck. Since my arrival, I'd been dying to know what Aidan kept hidden up there. She assured me Aidan would never know, and I trusted her. Was I naïve? Maybe. But I needed a friend.

We sneaked to the second floor and walked past several rooms, then stopped in front of one. Clare pushed a massive mahogany door, and entered first.

I hesitated in the doorway. Questions about Rebecca burned on my tongue even though I didn't dare ask them. Why get involved in something that didn't concern me?

"This used to be Rebecca's room." Clare flicked on a switch and motioned me to follow.

The large room smelled of dust as though no one had aired in months. To the far left was a huge, carved four-poster. A large walk-in closet covered the entire wall to the right.

Clare walked over and yanked the door open. Her fingertips touched silky gowns and velvet dresses in countless colors. "I thought you might like to see these. Thank God, you're here. I have no one else around to talk about girl stuff. They're beautiful, aren't they?"

I nodded, my gaze moving over the tailored clothes when I noticed an expensive silk evening gown in burgundy red. A chill crept over me. "Are these Rebecca's clothes? May I?"

"Sure." Clare stepped to the side, watching me.

I leaned forward to inspect the gown closer. It was about my size but made for someone taller. There was nothing special about it, and yet it called to me. I felt compelled to touch it, to try it on, to feel the exquisite softness of the cool silk on my bare skin. I lifted my fingers, then pulled back.

"Why don't you touch it?" Clare whispered.

"No." I swallowed hard and turned away. Aidan still kept Rebecca's clothes. A memory was even worse than an actual girlfriend. Their love must've been the real deal since he still harbored the hope she'd come back one day.

Clare nudged me softly. "I felt the same way when I first saw it. Don't worry, I won't tell anyone if you try it on."

I peered at the dress again. Dizziness washed over me. Something pulled me forward, like an invisible hand, urging me to give it a go. With shaking fingers, I touched the gown. The sudden jolt of electricity took me by surprise, and I stumbled backwards, but my hand remained clenched around the material. My eyelids fluttered. I whimpered as my vision blurred. I felt Clare's cold breath on my neck, whispering in my ear, "Amber, are you okay?"

A pang of pain surged through my body. I opened my eyes wide. Clare was gone. Something icy, soft as the flutter of a butterfly, caressed my neck. I turned to scan my surroundings, noticing a girl dressed in the same red gown sleeping on the bed, her pale body sprawled across crimson sheets, her long, red hair spread around her like a halo. She seemed so serene, too quiet. Holding my breath, I walked closer, careful not to wake her, when my gaze fell on the gaping wound on the girl's neck. Half of it looked ripped out, but the gash bore no signs of blood.

My breath caught in my throat. I took a step back, whimpering. "She's dead." My voice came low, scared. I let go of the dress. The girl disappeared; the artificial light of bulbs replaced the semi-darkness.

"Yes, she is." Clare touched my shoulder, making me jump. "Are you okay? You're white as a ghost. Maybe you're not into fashion after all."

"I need to rest if you don't mind. The wine's made me a little dizzy." It wasn't the wine, I knew it. I had felt the same way after watching the woman crossing the street with her buggy. The woods made people see strange things, Clare had claimed. Was it true? Could there be a connection?

"I'll accompany you," Clare said.

"No need." I shook my head. Holding on to the cupboard door for support, I avoided touching the red gown again. "I'll find my way. Thank you though." Clare's gaze burned on my back as I hurried out. Several times I stumbled on the way to the first floor, but I managed to prevent a fall. As soon as I reached my room, I dropped on the bed and closed my eyes, nausea building up inside me. I jumped up and dashed for the bathroom, reaching the toilet just in time to throw up the contents of my stomach.

Chapter 7 - Aidan

I paced up and down the carpet, boiling inside, though I couldn't let the others see how much Amber's stroll in the woods had maddened me. If she hadn't been there, I'd have won the prize instead of her. Now I had to fathom a way to save her from the dangers her new ability brought upon the winner.

Kieran draped his legs over the sofa and grinned. "Amber's gone. To hell with the wine. Break out something a little more refreshing."

"Not with a mortal around," I said, irritated. I couldn't risk Amber knowing what we were; not before she recognized the bond we shared and fell in love with me.

"Shouldn't you take better care of your employees, Aidan?" Kieran said with a smirk. "Amber's a sweet little thing, and so very mortal. Letting her walk in the woods at night with half the Lore out there, hunting" he shook his head in mock concern "—let's just say the job benefits you offer suck."

I spun, jaw set. Why couldn't my brother just shut up for a change? "Bro, I swear one of these days I'm going to—"

Clare burst through the door, interrupting my words of promised torture and murder. "She's carrying the prize."

"Wow, you just broke the case wide open, Sherlock Holmes." I cocked a brow. "And you found out how, apart from me telling you?"

Clare rolled her eyes. "You're so bloody arrogant and annoying. Curb it down a little." She leaned in. "I'm still a little confused though. Why didn't you stop her from entering the shed?"

"Because I didn't notice her since I was busy chaining the Shadows and what else not to a bloody tree." I took a deep breath to control the annoyance rising inside me. "By the time I finished, it was too late."

"Amber's weak." Clare hesitated. "It didn't bother me before, but now that she's carrying the prize it'll be a problem. What're you going to do with her? How did she figure out the riddle anyway?"

A good question. No one ever had. I should've killed the mortal right there in the clearing. It could've saved me a lot of trouble. But looking at the soft curve of her neck, I harbored other thoughts. Fate chose her as my mate. If she died, I'd choose to die with her. Like me, she could never love another.

"I say we kill her," Blake said.

Kieran glared at him. "You and your constant need for slaughter. We're not barbarians."

Clare lowered next to him and snuggled in his arm. "I'm surprised you know such a big word."

"I know more than one." Kieran tugged her close. "And I'm more than happy to show you."

"Hey, focus," I snapped. "This is important." Three pairs of eyes met my gaze, eagerly awaiting every word that came out of my mouth. They always let me make the decisions. I tired of it a long time ago. "You forget the Interracial Race rule: once a contestant carries the prize, he can't be stripped off it. Either they give it up within twelve hours, or they carry the skill for the next five hundred years. Let's just hope Amber's compliant and does what we tell her to do, otherwise it might get ugly for all of us."

"You should've seen her upstairs." Clare shook her head. "She's not strong enough. She'd never survive the journey. She'd be drained before she even entered the otherworld."

"She should've dropped the backpack," I said. "It was *her* choice not to."

"What are you implying? You know she won't survive on her own," Clare said.

"Remind me later." I stormed out of the library, leaving the house through the kitchen so the others wouldn't pick up on the turmoil inside me. Since Rebecca's death I had barely touched a mortal, let alone kill them. Having Amber around was more than I could endure. As my mate, her blood's call was too strong. I fought a constant battle not to feed from her.

Why did she have to be in the woods that night? How did she stumble across the jewels when no mortal knew about the Interracial Race? It must've been a lucky shot or, in Amber's case, a not so lucky one. So many questions when I knew I couldn't just barge into her room and force the answers out of her. Not when she had yet to fall in love with me. My mood deteriorated at the prospect of courting her with half the paranormal world hunting us.

The air smelled of autumn leaves and imminent rain. I lowered myself onto the bench, staring at the empty space Amber had occupied less than an hour ago. Funny how Fate would always play tricks on me. I thought after Rebecca's betrayal, I'd never trust a girl again. Several hundred years later, I glimpsed Amber in a crowd in London during a work assignment, and I knew she was the one—my bonded mate given to me by Fate. With the paranormal race about to begin and my enemies watching my every step, I couldn't risk drawing their attention to her so I came up with a plan to lure her to Scotland, where she'd be safe while we got to know each other. She needed the money, and I could do with a housekeeper because I was sick of Greta roaming the mansion, pretending to clean while snooping around. So I made sure Amber's brother found out about the job. I should've delayed flying Amber over from London until after the race, but I just couldn't bare being away from her now that I knew who she was. Besides, this race was special. According to the prophecy its outcome would eventually lead to a war destroying the world. I *had* to have her by my side by then. Our bond would take care of her feelings and attraction for me for the time being, until I sorted out the mess the paranormal world was in.

Fate expected me to protect her, but how could I protect her from the most dangerous predator—myself?

With her sweet blood beckoning to me more than any other mortal, it was only a matter of time until I turned into a killer, unless I killed myself. But then someone else would go after her to get the prize. She'd turned from mere mortal into priceless commodity overnight. I groaned inwardly, only then noticing Clare standing behind me.

"I know what's going on." She sat down next to me so I couldn't pretend she didn't exist.

"What are you talking about?"

"Of course you wouldn't just admit it." The slightest hint of annoyance crossed her perfectly arched eyebrows. In my early years, I had thought—hoped—she'd be the one, but my senses never sharpened when I was around her.

"What do you want, Clare? You're annoying the hell out of me today, and that's not a good thing."

She inhaled loudly, irritated. "It's not about what I want, but rather what you want. I've noticed the look in your eyes. You see her when she's not present. It's painful to watch."

"Then don't watch."

"I want to help you," Clare said.

"Why?" I turned to face her.

She placed her cold palms on my cheeks. A single silver tear glittered in her eye as she whispered, "Because I want to see you happy. It's something that I'll never be."

"Your mate's somewhere out there," I said.

Clare shook her head. "He's not because he died a long time ago, and I did nothing to save him." She smiled, bitterly. "I assume you have a plan."

"I'm still considering my options."

"You don't have much time. Other people are interested in the book. You know, they won't hesitate to use her."

I hated when she was right. I lowered my head, inhaling the freezing air to shake off Amber's unmistakable scent. It didn't work. "I know that. I'll come up with a plan soon."

"There's someone who could help us." Something in her tone made me look up. She lifted a finger to my lips and lowered her voice. "If you lead Amber to the threshold of death, he can help her find the way back."

My anger flared up. The threshold meant certain death. No one had come back from that place. "Who said I'd ever let Amber do that?"

"You don't have a choice. Either she tries with you watching over her body, or she dies." Clare nodded, taking my silence as some sort of agreement. "I'll arrange a meeting then."

"What is he?"

"Better you don't know. You might not be so keen on a meeting." She smiled, her white teeth shimmering in the darkness. She was strikingly beautiful, and yet I felt nothing.

"Thanks," I said.

Amber's picture flashed before my eyes. Sweet Amber slipping into her dreadful flannel PJs that covered every inch of her soft skin. Clare rose to her feet and walked a few steps toward the house before she turned, her low whisper carrying through the eerie silence of the night. "There's something you should know."

The illusion of Amber disappeared. Sighing, I turned. "What?"

"She doesn't know you're her mate. Seems like you have competition. His name's Cameron. It's a beautiful name, isn't it?"

Cameron? I hated the guy's guts already.

Chapter 8

I knew I was still asleep when I opened my eyes in my dream, staring at Aidan's rigid shape up the hill. His gaze was fixed on something in the distance, his dark hair swaying in the cool Scottish breeze that turned my skin into goose bumps. He rubbed his fingers over his face and turned to face me, eyes shining as vivid as the stars on the dark horizon.

The damp air carried the faint mustiness of fallen leaves. Deep melancholy was palpable in the air. A whisper escaped Aidan's lips. I stopped breathing in the hope of grasping the meaning of his words. His voice grew louder, distorted, cutting through the silence like a knife, as he frowned, trying to explain something I still couldn't understand. His eyes, dark and shiny in the dim moonlight, bore into mine. I felt something pierce my heart. Knowledge and pain. Regret and hope. Love and something much, much deeper. Like a cord, wrapped around me, him, us. Then a thought struck me: Aidan's going to kill me.

My limbs turned to jelly as he smiled, beautiful and terrible at the same time. My eyes followed the perfect shape of his teeth to his fangs, and I slipped into oblivion.

***

When I woke up, bright light seeped through the drapes. I stirred and winced at my reeling head, nausea building up inside my stomach. Something happened to me in the woods, and I had a feeling it wasn't going to disappear all by itself. I got out of bed and walked to the bathroom. The ceiling light bathed the room in glaring brightness that hurt my eyes. Turning on the cold-water tap, I dived my hands into the jet of water and moistened my face. A trickle ran down my feverish temple, cooling my skin.

I sat there until my racing heart calmed down, contemplating the strange dream. Talk about my subconscious sending me a clear signal. Aidan wasn't danger per se, but the undeniable attraction to him threatened my relationship with Cameron. I started recollecting Cameron's good traits. Good looks. Check. Amusing. Check. Honest. I wavered. Cameron *was* honest. He might not tell me things straight away, like that his parents were visiting when I so badly wanted to meet them after a year of dating. But better a commitment phobe than a guy who kept his ex's clothes.

With a grunt, I rose from the floor and went about preparing myself a cup of tea in the kitchen, then returned to my bed, sipping the hot liquid. I snuggled under the covers and fell asleep, clutching Cameron's picture to my chest.

I slept fitfully through the Sunday afternoon, voices echoing in my ears. Fragments of dialogues and pictures flashed through my mind: Aidan saying he'd never trusted Rebecca, Cameron spread-eagled on his back, his throat displaying a gaping wound, and then the woman from the pub holding the gemstones in her hands, laughing as she pulverized them to dust.

It's too late, dear. You're as good as dead. Just like me.

The woman's voice still screeched in my head when I finally woke up. Realizing I hadn't eaten all day, I took a quick shower and dressed in jeans and a tight top, paying attention to my make-up. It wasn't like I really made an effort, was it? I just didn't want to look as crappy as I felt. Aidan wouldn't notice my efforts anyway. I headed down to the kitchen to heat up a ready-meal.

A strong wind rattled the windowpanes, the unnerving sound carrying through the silence of the house. I ate my lasagna, chewing each bite slowly, then washed up and dried the plate. The front door opened and closed. I put the plate and cutlery away, and stopped to listen. Footsteps passed the kitchen door before departing up the stairs. I figured people weren't keen on meeting me tonight.

I retreated to my room and switched on the TV when I heard the slightest knock on the door. I sat up and called, "Come in."

The door opened and Aidan peered in, hesitation visible in his eyes. His disheveled hair stuck out in places, giving the impression he just got out of bed. But his eyes shone with awareness as he looked at me. "Hey."

Aidan in my room? I switched off the TV, my heart hammering in my chest as I jumped up, then paused in mid-stride, unsure what to do. "Hey."

He moistened his lips. His fingers grabbed the doorknob, knuckles turning white, like he was holding on for dear life. "Do you have any plans for tonight?" His voice was nonchalant, unfazed. My first impression was wrong. He wasn't nervous, he probably just needed me to iron his shirt or fix him a sandwich. When the boss comes knocking, it's never a good sign.

I shrugged. "Nope. No plans."

His gaze fell on the photo frame on the bedside table, and for a second a frown crossed his perfect features. "We're going out. I thought you might want to join us."

"Ah." I wavered. Didn't see that one coming, but it was definitely much better than a request to clean the bathrooms. My heart skipped a beat when realization kicked in. An invitation to go out with *him*? "Like a date?"

Aidan stared at me. Why wasn't he answering the question? I figured he didn't want to hurt my feelings. He was just being friendly, nothing more. No date, no need to feel guilty. Besides, Cameron wouldn't want me to spend my nights trapped in the confinements of my room, watching TV and staring at the walls.

"Are you coming?" Aidan raised his eyebrow, a hesitant smile playing on his lips. My pulse started to race again, my reserve melting away.

I nodded. "I'd love to. Thanks."

A dimpled smile lit up his face. "I'll let you get ready, then. Take your time."

I watched him close the door, then turned to the cupboard, trying to slow down my racing heart. It wasn't a date, just a night out with a friend. Just friends. Nothing wrong with being friends with a hot guy. He wasn't my type anyway, too cool, too confident, too perfect. Cameron was confident too, but in a more look-at-me way, and who could blame him? His education was top-notch. Everyone knew he'd be a high-achiever one day. In contrast, Aidan seemed like he couldn't care less what others made of him. Faced with the choice, I'd take—

Don't go there. I shook my head and changed into a pair of skinny jeans and a tight, black top, then reapplied my make-up, paying attention to my best feature: my brown eyes. Eventually, I threw a last look in the mirror, then grabbed my bag, squeezed into a pair of high-heels and hurried down the stairs.

The others were waiting in the hall, Kieran whispering something to a smiling crowd. But the moment Aidan's gaze fell on me, I saw no one else.

"You look fantastic." He held my coat. As I slipped into it, a whiff of his male scent hit my nostrils.

I nodded, unable to form a clear thought, when Clare said, "Ready, everyone? Let's rock this party then."

The moment broke and Aidan pulled away from me, holding the door open for everyone. I kept my eyes on the ground as I walked past. Two silver SUVs were parked in the driveway. Aidan threw his brother a pair of keys. "You drive Blake and Clare. Amber's with me."

"You don't play fair, big brother," Kieran said. Clare pulled his arm, grinning.

Aidan lowered to whisper in my ear, "He's a lunatic. Trust me, you don't want to be in his car when he drives."

Kieran called over his shoulder, "I've seen grannies drive faster than you."

I smiled and hopped onto the passenger seat, peering around. This was one big car fitting all of us, and yet he decided to take only me. I had no idea what to make of it.

"Don't take him seriously," Aidan said as he started the engine and pulled out of the parking lot.

Kieran's car overtook and sped off. Suddenly, the narrow space seemed too small. I dropped my sweaty palms on the brown leather seat, clutching the material for comfort, then focused on the impressive back-lit board. The interior of the car looked like something out of a magazine. It even smelled new. How could he afford all of this? Was he even old enough to drive?

Aidan shot me a smile. "You okay?" When I nodded he turned back to the road and peered toward the sky.

This was it: the moment I had dreamed of, alone with Aidan, and my mind blacked out. Talk about the weather? Nah, too bland. About Scotland, the news, politics, anything. Fragments of an article popped up in my head: ask questions about him. Let him know you have things in common, but don't make him feel like he's been summoned to stand trial. I took a few breaths to put my slow brain into gear and steadied my voice. Never had making small talk seemed such a bleeding hard task. "How long have you been living here?"

"You mean in Scotland?" He didn't give me a chance to reply. "I was born on Skye and moved here a while back." Somewhere in the distance, backlights flashed twice and Aidan accelerated.

"Did your parents move here because of the solitude?"

He laughed. "It's quiet compared to London, isn't it? We lived there for a while, but it's not a pleasant place."

"How old are you?" I bit my lip and regarded him from the corner of my eye. It was a personal question. Maybe too personal?

"Older than you," Aidan said, avoiding a clear answer as usual.

Heavy drops pattered against the windscreen. Aidan switched on the wipers. I tried to read his expression. He appeared relaxed, hands clasped carelessly around the steering wheel, betraying nothing. Too cool, too confident—I wished I could be at ease like that.

"Time to talk about you," Aidan said. "Any regrets you moved here?"

I shrugged. "Not really. I think I'm getting used to the silence."

"If you were given the chance to stay here or move back, what'd you choose?"

What a strange question. I moistened my lips. His expression remained impassive, fixed on the street. "I don't know," I finally said. I didn't miss traffic-ridden London, but I felt bad for not missing Cameron either. "I guess I'd go back." It was a lie. I knew it the moment my mouth uttered the words.

Aidan snorted, the slightest hint of annoyance crossing his face, and then his smile returned. "You may change your mind by the time your placement ends."

"Maybe." My heartbeat sped up again. Did he want me to stay? *Don't get your hopes up.* It didn't mean anything, I reminded myself. "Harry said you work in Inverness?"

"Yes. I'm a freelancer."

A freelancer could do thousands of things. I waited for a narration of his job duties, but it never came. Should I ask, or would it sound like an inquisition? Ah, toss it. "What is it that you do exactly?"

"People pay me to do stuff for them," Aidan said. "I read on your application you're about to start college. Is marketing your thing?"

The sudden change in topic didn't fail to register with me. Whatever his job entailed, he obviously didn't want to share it with me. Was he self-conscious? "I think so. I was supposed to start an unpaid position in an agency to find out, but money was tight, so I had to get a job instead." We drove out of the woods, the rhythmical rattle of the car engine barely audible. I relaxed a bit as I focused on the white centerline of the road.

"What about your parents? Can't they help?" Aidan asked.

I shook my head. "They have their own worries. I wouldn't want to bother them with mine."

He shot me an amused look. "Do they know you're here?"

"Of course they do. I'm only seventeen." I smiled. "They think I'm interning in Inverness."

"In god-forsaken Inverness?" He laughed and I found myself laughing with him. "That's a good one. I bet every firm in London would be impressed."

"They're sweet souls. I feel bad for lying to them, and even more so knowing they trust me implicitly," I said.

The car took a sharp bend, gravel crunching under the tires.

"We're here." Aidan stepped out and opened the passenger door, then held out his hand. As our fingers met, a jolt of electricity ran down my spine and my breath caught in my throat. He pulled me a little too close, towering over me, his gaze lingering on my lips before he slammed the door and intertwined his fingers with mine. My heart hammered in my chest. What was he doing? I glanced up at him, but he turned to the side, unfazed by my questioning look.

The cobblestones glistened in the dim moonlight, the air smelled damp. Somewhere in the distance, I heard waves roll in and crash against a shore. Aidan cleared his throat and pointed at a house on the other side of the parking lot, past Kieran's SUV and two other cars. "I want to show you my favorite place in the world."

"Where are we?" I sounded breathless and unsteady. His presence made me dizzy, the soft caress of his hand playing havoc with my head.

He squeezed my hand. "Just wait and see."

The house was small with wilting green ivy climbing up the whitewashed walls. Dim light seeped through the opaque windows, the shadows inside appeared blurred. Aidan yanked the door open and guided me through a narrow hall into a large, open space. Floor to ceiling glass panes covered the full length of the wall, offering a stunning view of the angry sea below. On the opposite site I noticed Kieran, Clare and Blake together with a red-haired girl and two guys sitting on white sofas around a huge fireplace with large flames lapping at several wood logs. Kieran and Clare stood and walked toward us, the others remained seated.

Aidan grimaced and leaned to whisper in Clare's ear. I held my breath and inched closer, catching every word.

"What's Beelzebub doing here?"

"I heard that," the redhead said. She was dressed in a garish green top and loose jeans that looked like they'd been through the washing machine a few too many times. "One more of those and I'll kick your butt."

Kieran laughed. "What are you going to do, sweetheart? Send out some butterflies to tickle him to death?"

The girl scowled. Kieran draped his arm around my waist and guided me to a sofa. I shot Aidan a quizzical glance, but he walked out with Clare on his arm. I looked around. The large room was clean and tidy with almost no furniture and no food or drinks, not even a bar or background music. If there had ever been a party, someone had done a great job at removing any traces.

"You know Blake already. Now meet fabulous Cassandra, Devon—" Kieran pointed at a broad guy with cropped, dark hair and eerie black eyes "—and this is Connor."

I looked away from Blake's fake smile as Connor stood to shake my hand. He was at least a head taller than me with black, spiky hair dyed a dirty blond at the ends. "So, you're the lucky one." His lips stretched into a wide grin, his almost black eyes sparkled.

"He's talking about your job," Kieran said. "You beat quite a bit of competition."

"I did?" I blinked, guilt washing over me. Who'd have thought the employment situation was so bad in Scotland? I felt bad for lying on my application form when others needed the money just as much. I wasn't even into the whole cleaning routine.

"Move it, Cass," Kieran said as he squeezed between Cassandra and Devon, then pulled me on his lap, snuggling me between strong thighs. I scowled at him and tried to pull away. He wrapped his arm around me and laughed. I could already see, they might look alike but Aidan and Kieran had nothing in common. One was too reserved for his own good, the other the worst player I'd ever seen.

I sighed and tried to avert my attention from his hot breath on my neck when Aidan appeared in the door and motioned Kieran to step out. Blake took his place on the sofa, sitting as far away from me as possible. Cassandra excused herself and hurried out after them. She was about my height, her strange clothes emphasized her curves. As she walked past, I swear two tiny horns peeked from beneath her long, wavy hair.

Chapter 9 – Aidan

"What's a little misunderstanding between friends? Right, Aidan?" Kieran asked, laughing.

"What?" I peeled my gaze from the front door as I tuned in to the conversation even though I wasn't keen on tonight's drivel. Amber was safe with Blake. He might not like her, but he wouldn't dare disobey my orders.

"He chained us to a tree. He tried to trick us." Devon leaned against the wall of the house. The moon cast a silver light on his face. He looked and behaved like a mortal. Only a keen eye would notice that Connor and he had no shadow because they *were* Shadows, carcasses of humans on which their queen fed.

I snorted. The competition again. Boy, were they sore losers. "Why're you so surprised? The book's no longer yours."

"It would be if your beloved Rebecca didn't steal it from us." Connor took a menacing step forward and lifted one arm when Cass placed a hand on his chest to stop him. She barely reached the Shadow's shoulder, but he retreated nonetheless, as though her unspoken warning mattered.

I wasn't just any vampire but an established bounty hunter and a member of the Lore court. That job title didn't matter much during the Interracial Race, but at least they wouldn't dare attack me openly. Not here, not now. I could sense their weapons, daggers and the likes, no matter how much they tried to hide them from plain sight. They reeked of vampire blood. What was Clare thinking, bringing our worst enemies to the meeting? They wouldn't help; more likely, they'd try to find a way to screw us over and dispose of our dead bodies without the court's knowing. At least, Amber was safe because Shadows didn't kill humans. Or so legends said.

"Remind me again why Beelzebub's here," Kieran said to Clare. "Is she coming up for a breath of fresh air? I know how stuffy and humid hell can be."

Cass glared at him. "Call me that again and you'll see what I can do with a pitchfork."

Kieran grinned. "You look good when you're angry. Now say the pitchfork line again with more oomph."

"I thought she could help," Clare said.

"I should've left you at home." I shook my head. My brother was a loose cannon, always making things worse by opening his mouth, and sweet Clare wouldn't notice someone's ulterior motives if her life depended on it.

"And miss out on all the fun?" Kieran glanced at Connor and Devon. "It's a fact, Rebecca did steal the book from you. But how can you blame Aidan for her treachery? She wasn't his beloved; She just had the luck and good brains to turn us. She couldn't have picked a better bunch. Young, attractive, clever, and I'm only mentioning a couple of my qualities."

Clare elbowed him. "Stop antagonizing them. This is serious."

"I *am* serious. Look at—"

"Okay, enough," I interrupted my brother. If he didn't stop his endless chatter soon, we'd still be here at sunrise. From the corner of my eye, I peered at Devon and Connor who didn't even pretend not to be eavesdropping on our conversation. "Cass, what do you want?"

"I can help. In exchange for a favor, of course," Cass said.

Kieran smirked. "What could we possibly offer you that Daddy can't get you anyway?"

Cass narrowed her eyes to tiny slits, gaze blazing. "Why don't you turn into a bat and fly away?"

"She wants a position with the Lore Council," Clare said.

Kieran laughed. "All that fire has fried your brain."

"What would a princess need that for?" I asked. Kieran didn't call Cassandra Beelzebub for nothing. Her father was the Dark Prince himself. Why Cass walked on Earth, mingling with Lore folks and humans was beyond me.

"I have nowhere to go but up. The flames don't do my skin justice, not to mention they wreak havoc with my hair. You know how I hate dry split ends." Cass raised her chin defiantly. "You get me the job, and in exchange I'll volunteer a few soul hunters and demon guardians."

I scowled. What a load of crap. She had to have an ulterior motive. But what? "I don't trust demons."

"You don't need to trust them. Clare trusts me. The demon guardians will do as I order," Cass said.

Kieran snorted. "That's so reassuring."

Clare beamed up at me. "Sounds like a deal to me."

The whole bunch turned to face me, waiting for my answer. As usual. I groaned inwardly. I had brought Amber along because I thought I could keep her away from any chaos until I figured out how to teach her to control the prize. Throw in Lucifer's spawn, a bunch of demons and the insufferable Shadows and bedlam would be knocking on my door within seconds. So much for my plan to woo her while searching the Lore court for a way to save her from the fate she'd unknowingly called upon herself.

"We need the book. Without it, we can't perform a certain ritual," Devon said. "We want it back."

I shot him a sarcastic look. "You don't say. And I care why? So you can't start a fire with a flick of your hand. Big deal. Get a lighter." Usually, I wasn't one to belittle someone else's abilities, but the guy really irritated me. Playing friend one moment, and stabbing me in the back the next. I wasn't stupid.

"I understand the mortal's under your—" Devon hesitated "—protection. You need our help if she's to learn to control the prize."

"No way." I shook my head.

"You're getting her killed," Connor said. "May I remind you it's against Lore rules to kill humans?"

I shrugged, but not because I didn't care. I could never let on how much Amber meant to me. "I'm strong enough to lead her back from the otherworld."

"Only if you turn her into—" Connor spit on the ground. "That's against Lore rules too."

"Rules are meant to be broken," Kieran said.

"We have a proposition to make," Devon said. "If you work with us to find and then return the book, we'll let you and your clan enter the Cemetery of the Dead to perform the ritual."

Kieran sniffed. "Talk about the hidden power of persuasion. Didn't know a Shadow possessed that skill. You're threatening to shatter every belief I've had about your kind." He grinned. "You're lucky I'm a sucker for a challenge and a huge fan of magic. So let the games begin."

The Cemetery of the Dead—the place Rebecca would've killed to visit. I considered his words for a minute. With the help of the book I'd finally get what I wanted since my turning. If there was a place where the ritual might work, then on Shadow territory, among the trapped souls of the dead. And I wanted that ritual. It was my only chance to live without blood, to see the sun rise and set, and feel its heat on my bare skin.

"What do you think?" Devon asked. Judging from his self-satisfying smirk, it wasn't a question.

Clare bobbed her head. I didn't need to ask Kieran, because my brother was nodding enthusiastically, probably making signs behind my back. Yet I couldn't quite shake off the feeling the Shadows were keeping something from me.

Cass stepped between us as if sensing the battle inside me. "I'll make sure everyone plays fair. If you break your word, I swear I'll send half of hell after you."

"You mean Daddy will." Kieran grinned.

"Shut up, you two," I hissed, still considering my options. I wouldn't need blood any more or ever shun the sun again, meaning I could protect Amber day and night. She could learn to control her new ability while I watched over her. It was an offer too good to be true. "Okay, I'll keep my part of the deal if you keep yours. Cass, I trust you're not taking sides."

"You have my word," Cass said. Kieran snorted. She turned toward him, two tiny flames blazing in her green eyes. Her voice dropped a few notches. The smell of sulfur wafted past me. "You want to say something, moron?" She sounded as though several voices talked at once, layered in tone and connotation.

Not again. I sighed and lifted my hand to rub my forehead. "I've had it with you two. We're trying to seal a deal here." The fires in Cass's eyes disappeared, but she didn't back off. I breathed in, mentally preparing myself for what I was about to say. "As much as it pains me to work with Shadows, you have a deal."

"Wise decision," Connor said.

Kieran patted me on the back. "Congrats, bro. You've just sold your soul to the devil. Wait. You don't have a soul."

"I'll send out the soul hunters to find out the book's whereabouts," Cass said, ignoring him.

"We'll keep in touch." Devon and Connor walked away, glancing over their shoulders a few times as though they didn't dare turn their backs on us.

"You know I'll stand by you no matter what. We might have our differences, but you're my brother and I love you," Kieran said.

Cass laughed and flicked her hair back, revealing a milky-white, slender neck. "And I thought you two didn't have a heart. Well, technically you don't because you're dead. Even still, it was a gushy moment. If only I had a camera to capture the magic. But then again, you wouldn't show up on film."

"What's your desired position with the Lore council?" I asked.

Cass beamed at Clare, and I marveled at how little she looked like a half fallen angel—more like a little child in a candy shop. If I didn't know who her father was, I would've believed she was a normal teen with too much determination and no sense of fashion.

"Make me ambassador," Cass said. Kieran burst into a fit of laughter.

"I'll try my best." I grabbed her outstretched hand and shook it, the heat emitted from her palm scorching my skin.

Clare accompanied Cass to her car while Kieran and I returned to the house. My gaze fell on Amber sitting next to Blake. Our eyes connected, and she smiled that lazy smile of hers that had my stomach in knots.

"Is everything all right?" Amber asked.

"Just peachy," Kieran said. "No need to worry your pretty head. We were trying to figure out how to save a damsel in distress from evil forces that want to destroy her."

She laughed, oblivious to how much truth hid in Kieran's words. "Is there hope for her?"

Kieran winked. "I believe so. We're making it our personal mission to save her by recruiting some big, bad demons, scandalous Shadows, vampires, and even Beelzebub herself."

"You've been busy then," she said.

"Ignore him." I placed my hands on her waist, suppressing the urge to lower my lips onto hers and never let go. She didn't seem to believe a word of it, but if Kieran wasn't more careful she might start to. "All's great. We had some business to discuss." From the corner of my eye, I watched Blake leave quietly. I pulled Amber toward the large glass panes and wrapped my arms around her as I whispered in her ear, "This is what I wanted to show you. Do you like the view?" I could hear her heartbeat speed up. Whatever Clare said about a boyfriend, soon Amber wouldn't even remember the poor guy's name.

"It's beautiful," she said.

Like you. I bit my lip, drawing a drop of blood, the smell intoxicating. I hadn't fed in two days. If my plan worked, soon I would no longer need to.

We gazed at the dark water crashing against the cliffs below. Nothing I hadn't seen before, but standing here with the one, I felt excited, more so than the first time I watched the spectacular display of Mother Nature's force right under my feet. I inhaled her scent and pulled her back to the sofa, remembering she was mortal after all. "Did you have dinner tonight?"

Amber blushed. "I did. But I don't mind sitting with you if you want to grab a bite."

I smiled. A bite sounded good. I didn't mind one of those, but not to feed. "I'm not hungry."

Kieran shot me an amused look. "I am."

"You're not getting anything." Clare elbowed him in the ribs. "Come on. We'll sink our teeth into something on the way home."

"Hey, Amber. If you ever tire of him—" he pointed at me "—you know where to find me."

Amber avoided my gaze. I could sense her nervousness as the others left. She wasn't comfortable around me. Not yet. To gain her trust, I had to move slowly, taking one step at a time. "Tired?"

She nodded. "A bit."

Grabbing her hand, I pulled her to her feet. Even though the bond would draw her to me nonetheless, I wanted her to start loving me for who I was inside, not just because we were meant to spend eternity together. "We should get going then. You're working tomorrow. Nobody makes vegetable stir-fry like you do."

"Right. Of course, boss." Amber shrugged into her coat. I thought I caught the slightest hint of regret in her eyes.

I locked the door—more for show than out of need—and started the engine. She seemed fidgety now, her hands clasped in her lap, fingers intertwined.

"You're an experienced driver," Amber said.

I could sense the question in her statement. She couldn't keep her curiosity at bay. Maybe I had underestimated her inquisitive nature. Even though I had died at eighteen, my perilous existence as a vampire had helped me mature beyond that age.

"My family shared a love for cars," I said. Another lie told out of need. Before she could resume her questioning, I focused on the invisible bond between us, emptying my head of any thoughts, then let my mind invade hers, slowly lulling her into the sweet lure of slumber. It was the only power I held over her.

Amber breathed out and relaxed in her seat. I switched on the radio and watched her close her eyes, my mind wandering back to the conversation with the Shadows. Cass would ensure they kept their word. She simply had to. As a bounty hunter, half the Lore council owed me. Maybe I could call in those debts as well and buy us some time.

By the time the SUV pulled into the driveway, Amber's shallow breathing told me she was asleep. I stepped out, opened the passenger door and scooped her up in my arms, marveling at how light she seemed, then carried her upstairs, as silent as my abilities permitted. She only stirred once, opening her eyes, when I placed her on the bed.

The soft moonlight cast lazy shadows on Amber's pale skin. She stretched in my arms like a cat in front of a hearth, but I could hear her heart racing, hammering against her chest. Ever so slowly I lowered my lips and brushed hers, then pressed a little tighter. Her mouth opened under my gentle pressure and she wrapped her arms around my neck. Heat rushed through my body, the sensation new and frightening at the same time. My thumb brushed down her neck where the blood pumped the hardest, calling to me. My lips followed the trail, barely touching her skin. Her pulse thumped against my lips. Hunger stirred inside me. I needed to get out of here, and fast, before I couldn't control my need to feed.

It took me all my might to peel my lips off hers. Amber protested, but I could see panic in her eyes, the sudden realization of what just happened sinking in.

"Sleep well," I whispered. My voice sounded hoarse. In two long strides I was out the door, hurrying to get away from her before I lost all reasoning and bore my fangs into her delicate skin.

Chapter 10

I sat up with a jolt and watched Aidan close the door behind him. The last thing I remembered was sitting in his car and a sense of peace washing over me, and then Aidan leaning over me on the bed, our lips locked in the best kiss of my life.

I jumped up and rubbed my eyes to get rid of that unnerving floating. My phone vibrated in my handbag. Fishing through tissues, various makeup items and what else not, I retrieved it and pushed the green button to switch on the screen. A message popped up, and my heart skipped a beat, but not with pleasure. Guilt surged within me as I started to read.

Hey babe. Missed U so much. Whatcha say to nice dinner. Just U & I.

Groaning, I dropped back on the bed. Cameron had said he needed months to think. Why did he have to text me today of all days, less than four weeks after our break-up? It wasn't fair, not now when I had no idea what was happening between Aidan and me.

I rubbed my forehead, unsure what to do, when I remembered Rebecca's clothes were still hanging in the closet. Nothing was going on between us because Aidan still cared about his ex. To text Cameron back, I'd have to go to the laundry room. It was after four in the morning. Cameron had sent the message shortly after midnight. As much as I hated to keep him waiting, I couldn't bring myself to walk down to the basement now. I might freeze my feet off. Besides, Aidan could still be lurking around. I felt the tell tale heat rise to my cheeks, and touched my fingers to my swollen lips, his caress still vivid yet mortifying in my mind.

Should I tell Cameron? He may not be the jealous type, but I couldn't risk him changing his mind about us yet again. After taking a quick shower, I put on a fresh pair of flannel PJs and cuddled beneath the covers. Ignoring the sudden sense of being watched, I focused on my plans and the future with Cameron—a dinner that'd turn into a romantic declaration of love, Cameron realizing that what we shared was special, moving in together and finally meeting his parents. The pictures I conjured in my mind seemed hazy and forced, unrealistic, making me feel like a little girl hanging on to her favorite fairy tale because she couldn't let go of the one guy that didn't love her back enough. While Cameron was polite, educated and pretentious, Aidan made me feel alive. Who was the better choice? *Oh, darn it.* Sighing, I started counting in my head until I drifted off to sleep, wondering why I'd never noticed how scrawny Cameron seemed compared to my new boss.

It was past ten when I woke up. I'd overslept again, the second time in six working days. I jumped out of bed, dressing with one hand and brushing my teeth with the other. Downstairs, the usual silence greeted me. I breathed out, relieved that no one was about. I could only hope Aidan hadn't installed some sort of nanny cam to watch my every move. Remembering Dallas's words in the woods, I smiled. Paranoid. Yep. And silly for kissing my boss a week into the job. So much for keeping my job and private life separate.

Humming to myself, I grabbed a dusting cloth and went about cleaning, starting with the living room and shifting from one huge space to another like a robot. What a dreary job, the worst I'd ever done. Maybe not the worst, but not a glamorous one either.

By the time a car parked in the driveway an hour later, I had skipped the chandeliers—no way would I be able to reach the ceiling—and most of the paintings on the walls—really, who dusts those on a daily basis—and was ready to start on the ironing, which was even worse than cleaning.

As light footsteps approached, I polished with a little more fervor, seemingly engrossed in my work. The door opened. From the corner of my eye, I noticed red hair, floating around like an oversized halo. A faint whiff of smoke wafted in. "Hey. The door was open so I let myself in."

I turned to see the girl from last night—Cassandra—inch nearer. I peered up from the loose jeans and green cardigan to see whether she still wore the fake horns on her head, but Cass sported a turquoise bonnet that hung too low, covering her entire forehead and partly hiding her spectacular, green eyes. Didn't she wear the same things last night? Either she couldn't be bothered to change her clothes, or she liked to buy her stuff in bulk. Or she didn't go to bed yet.

"You don't mind, do you?" Cass slumped on the sofa and pushed the bonnet out of her eyes.

Happy for any diversion from my dreadful chores, I put down the dusting cloth. "Sorry I look a wreck. I wasn't expecting company." I fanned myself air. "You wouldn't believe how hot it gets in here after an hour of cleaning."

Cass smiled. "Oh, gosh. I definitely get you. Back home, it's so hot one can fry an egg on the sidewalk. And cleaning isn't my thing, either."

"Can I get you anything?" I asked.

"Nah, I'm good." Cass scanned the room, her nostrils flaring, sniffing the air. "Fancy place, isn't it? But kind of dark and dreary like an old, giant tomb. I prefer brighter colors to lift the mood. You know, yellow or red."

"You haven't been here before?"

Cass frowned, hesitating. "I have, but not in this room."

I regarded her for a moment. I wasn't a good liar myself, but I could tell when others were telling fibs. Why would Cass lie about such a triviality, unless Aidan and she were dating and they tried to keep it a secret? A pang of jealousy hit me full force, taking me by surprise. Inhaling deeply, I curled my lips into a smile. "What can I do for you?"

"There's this tiny inconvenience I'd like to discuss with you." Cass took off her bonnet and placed it beside her. "I've no idea how to start. Made myself this fabulous list—" she fished in her pocket for a crumpled paper that looked like she'd used it more than once "—but it's all useless."

"Just spit it out, whatever it is."

"Okay." Cass inhaled and exhaled a few times. "You may find it a bit hard to believe at first, which I can fully understand, but once you've slept over it, you'll see I'm offering you a perfectly fine explanation of what's going on."

Why did I have the feeling whatever Cass aimed at involved Aidan? And probably not in a good light. "Say it, Cass. I don't need any more cushioning."

"You've won a major prize and now half of the Interracial court's coming after you." Cass let out a big sigh. "There, I said it. Way to go, me!"

"The what?" No *keep away from Aidan*? No *Aidan's seeing someone else*? I laughed.

A frown crossed Cass's face. Two tiny, red dots twinkled in her eyes. "What's so funny? If I were you I'd be scared to death, girl."

I burst into a fit of laughter. "It's just, I thought you were going to—" Shaking my head, I wiped the tears from my eyes. "Sorry. Please go on."

Cass regarded me carefully. When I remained serious, Cass resumed the conversation. "A little birdie told me a few nights ago you were in the woods, doing something very naughty."

The jewels. She knew. Of course, they had to belong to someone. I groaned. Dallas had messed up big time.

Cass snapped her fingers. "Hey, focus. You entered a race, and since Aidan chained everyone else to a tree, they had no chance to stop you. No idea how you figured out the riddle, but you scooped the first prize. Congratulations. You've just won a vacation to a big, relaxing place called a grave."

"Who did what?" I shook my head to clear my mind and calm my racing heart. *Okay, play it cool.* I had nothing to fear. Cass's crazy talk proved nothing. "You're mistaken. Why would you think it was me?" If I went to jail because of Dallas's stupid plan, I'd kick him right where it hurt the most.

"I know you were near the shed. There was an eyewitness."

"You said it was night. How could this person possibly identify me?" I tried to keep my composure, but my voice shook. Dallas was as good as disowned.

Cass smiled as she peered at me, green eyes glinting. "He saw you up close when he demanded the jewels, but you ran with your backpack. You were wearing all black, covered in mud, and your hair was tied in a ponytail."

"I can explain," I whispered.

"I doubt that, mate," Cass snorted very *unlady-like.* "Now you're stuck with this ability for half a millennium."

Huh? "You're saying I've earned a skill for the next five hundred years? Are you serious? Shouldn't I be dead by then?"

"Technically yes, I guess." Cass squirmed in her seat, chewing her lip. "Actually, we're not really talking about a skill, rather a gift. I'm sure you've noticed it already and if not, Aidan will make you use it soon so you can get the book."

I laughed. "What can I do? Fly like Superman? See the future?"

Cass waved her hand. "Nah, it's not that grand. Would be great though, saving on airfares and all. What you can do is see and communicate with the dead."

"A necromancer, then?" I cocked a brow, amused.

"Yes or, in other words, the old spinster who talks to herself."

I stared at her. Cass's face betrayed no signs of lying. I had to find a way to give the jewels back without anyone dragging me to court. Hell, I hadn't even wanted to steal them in the first place, so no one could actually persecute me. Could they? Either way, Dallas would have to understand I wasn't going to take the blame for him. It had been *his* idea. He was old enough to deal with it. I could only hope he hadn't sold them to the highest bidder already.

"Okay, let's say I was in the woods and did enter a certain shed—" I took a deep breath and brushed imaginary fluff from the sofa "—I understand the things there must belong to someone, and I'm perfectly happy to return them. I'm even willing to pay a bit of compensation from my meager wage. Just give me a few days to sort everything out and maybe we could make a fresh start."

Cass leaned forward and squeezed my hand, unnatural warmth seeping into my skin. "I'm so sorry, but it's not that easy. You solved the Riddle of Sight by gathering the required jewels. No idea how you came up with the right answer, but those who enter the race must be content with whatever riddle they solve and whatever gift is bestowed upon them. There's no exchange or refund policy."

110

The Riddle of Sight? The woman from the pub flashed through my mind, and all those strange nightmares, and Rebecca's savaged body when I'd touched the red dress.

"You're starting to believe. As I always say, if you can't take the heat you should've stayed out of the kitchen." Cass laughed. "Kitchen—get it? You're a housekeeper and all." She cleared her throat, seemingly embarrassed. "So sorry, mate. I can't help it. It's like I'm possessed or something. Anyway, there's more. Ever wondered why no one's here during the day?"

I shook my head, not because I didn't wonder, but because I didn't want to know, since I was still processing the news that I was the top winner of a skill that, as per Cass, would bring me a step closer to an early grave.

"Never mind, I'll tell you anyway," Cass said as though reading my mind. "Your new boss's a vampire, and if you don't learn to handle him, you'll wake up dead. And I hope it's in Hell because it's more fun and heaven ain't all that."

"You're kidding?" Aidan couldn't be. Last night he sure didn't feel like a corpse when he kissed me. In fact, he felt all warm and gentle and—

Cass rolled her eyes. "Does he ever eat? Nope. Does he sleep during the day and only comes out at night? Yep. Is he so sexy you'd sell your soul to spend just a night with him? Double-yep. What other proof do you need?"

I sat up and walked to the window. Cass had a few points but, really, a *vampire*? Who believed in such a myth? What was Cass suggesting anyway? That I grab my rosary and head for the nearest church begging for holy water? Line my door and widows with salt? Sleep with a wooden stake under my pillow? Hang garlic bulbs from my bedroom door? Why was I even considering these options? The girl was ludicrous.

"You don't have to believe to know deep inside. Just listen to that voice and you'll find belief easier to bear," Cass said. "Or, in other words, suck it up and just look at the facts because nothing will work to keep him away."

Could she read my thoughts? My laughter died in my throat at the oppressing silence.

Cass crossed her arms over her chest, grinning. "That kiss between Aidan and you last night wasn't bad for a start, but I prefer a bit more oomph."

I gasped. "He told you? That moron—"

"The image rolls before my eyes like on a movie theatre screen because you can't stop thinking about it." She leaned in. "Honestly, you're good for Aidan. I've heard he's been such a grump over the last century. A little action might loosen the stiff up."

I didn't believe one word. How dare he kiss and tell, bragging to half the neighborhood? That is, if we had any.

"Ha, you wish. I know his kind. He's so uptight he wouldn't even tell his own brother. Now try me," Cass said.

"Try you what?" I blinked, unable to keep up with Cass's changes in topic.

"You want to know if I can read your mind. Ask me questions, then."

I hesitated. "How did you know—"

"Come on, mate. I haven't got all day."

"Let me think." Breathing in, I focused on the first string of words my mind came up with: *doo-da-di sausage with gravy and apple crumbs.*

Cass scoffed. "Doo-da-di sausage with gravy and apple crumbs. Seriously? You were more fun to tune into when you thought I was dating your guy."

"How did you know that?" There had to be some sort of explanation. Maybe some circus trick, like pulling a card out of one's sleeve.

"I could try the card trick for you, but I'm such a klutz most of the time. I'd probably end up with cards scattered all over the floor." Cass smiled.

I stared at her, enthralled. "How do you do that?"

"What? Oh, that." Cass waved her hand; her smug grin made her look as though she enjoyed entertaining her audience. "It's just something I do. Can be quite a pain in the butt when you're trying to sleep and the next-door neighbor keeps obsessing about the dripping water tap and whether the doors are indeed barricaded for the night."

"You're good," I said, impressed. I wished I could read other people's thoughts. Then I'd drive Dallas crazy by answering his questions before he asked them. Now, that would freak him out. "Can you hear anyone's thoughts?"

"There's a few exceptions."

"So, are you a vampire too?" I bit my lip to stifle the sudden onset of hysteria. Talking about the existence of vampires was one thing, facing one was another. I could only hope Cass had a hearty breakfast.

"Did my pale face give me away?" Cass laughed. "I knew I should've worn more bronzer. I guess I could pass for a vampire, but there's one giant flaw in your theory."

"What's that?"

Cass rolled her eyes as she pointed at the large windows. "Uh, daylight. How could I be sitting here without sunglasses and draping myself in blackout curtains?"

"Right. I forgot that tiny detail. You'd be in your crypt sleeping like my boss, or so you say." If she wasn't a vampire, what was she then?

Cass hesitated. "I can't go into detail right now. Let's just say I'm here to save your butt since Aidan's keeping you in the dark. I thought you should know what you're dealing with in case Aidan decides to bite a bit harder than the usual boyfriend." Cass tilted her head to the side, her eyes shimmering bright red like two Chinese lanterns. "Urgh, Dad's calling. Gotta dash." She air-kissed my cheeks and loitered out the door, waving as she called over her shoulder, "See ya, mate."

"Wait. You mentioned some court. Who's coming after me?" I bolted after Cass in time to see her jump into her huge SUV. Shooting me a smile, she sped off, a puff of smoke lingering in the air. Of course Cass had to disappear when I was finally warming up to the idea that maybe—just maybe—I lived in a house inhabited by immortals. What did they even want from me? And how dangerous were they really?

Returning to the living room, I slumped down on the sofa and stared into empty space. I shouldn't be slacking off during working hours, but no way could I focus on going about the chores now. Was Aidan really a vampire? I hadn't seen him around during the day, hadn't actually seen him *eat*, but he didn't look like the usual Dracula sidekicks on TV. For one, he didn't wear a cloak. He didn't turn into a blood-sucking maniac at midnight. And he seemed to travel by car rather than beam himself to places. Of course, there was the slightest chance that even vampires go with time and adapt to twenty-first century amenities. Who wouldn't rather sleep in a bed than in the confined space of a coffin with the migraine-inducing smell of wood polish? But how likely was that?

I sighed and jumped up, eager to find out whether Aidan bore a dark secret. I thumped up the stairs to the second floor and yanked open one door after another, skipping Rebecca's room. No point looking in there, because I knew I wouldn't find more than a closet full of old clothes.

There were five other rooms in total; four bare of any furniture and one locked. Kneeling, I peered through the padlock. Whoever was in there had locked themselves from the inside and left the key in. Pulling with all my might, I rattled the door, but it didn't budge. Well, there was my answer, then. You can't lock a door from inside unless you're in there. Had I kissed a creature of the night? A real living corpse? I should search the Internet and print out a vampire hunter's guide so I knew all the right places where to kick him. I snorted, anger creeping up on me. That morning I thought Aidan was such an improvement to egocentric, self-satisfied Cameron. Gee, had I been wrong. Why couldn't I just meet a normal guy for a change? Preferably one that didn't love his car more than me, or one that didn't need his five-a-day in the form of blood infusions. Was that too much to ask?

After returning to my room, I retrieved my phone and left the house through the backdoor in the kitchen in the hope to find reception. There was none, so I walked out the gates a few steps down the street until one bar appeared on the reception indicator. Shivering, I pressed two to speed-dial Dallas's number in the hope he was still in Inverness and could pick me up. His usual, stupid James Bond 007 voicemail greeted me, informing me he was on a secret mission with some hot chick.

I rolled my eyes and left him a message requesting that he call back, then briefly considered calling Cameron when I remembered in all the havoc I hadn't texted him back yet. He could wait just a bit longer because I had more pressing issues on my mind, like considering whether to pack my bags and get the hell out of there. Anyone in their right mind would just head for the nearest door, but that wasn't my style. I had never backed up from a good confrontation. After Aidan fooled me into kissing him, I felt I had every right to give him a piece of my mind.

The thicket to my right rustled. I ignored it until I heard the sound of approaching footsteps. Someone pressed a broad hand over my mouth. I spun sharply, staring straight into Connor's pitch-black eyes.

"Not a word," he whispered.

Panic washed over me. He seemed to miss we were in the middle of nowhere. Who'd hear my screams? And then the whole absurdity of the situation dawned on me. This person had been hiding in the bushes even though, as Aidan's friend, he could've just rung the bell and I would've opened. I groaned under his strong grip. Could this day get any weirder?

"I see Aidan's getting careless. He should've warned you not to leave the house." Connor pushed me forward but didn't loosen his grip. "You're coming with me."

My gaze scanned the area, taking in the asphalt slick with dew. Whatever his intentions were, I had a feeling Aidan was the harmless one out of the two. I made a step forward and stopped, shaking my head.

"What?" The edge in Connor's voice betrayed irritation. I made a gagging sound that barely found its way out of my throat, but it was enough for Connor to loosen his grip over my mouth. "Better now? Move it, then."

I closed my eyes, praying for help, even though I knew no one would come to my rescue. From the corner of my eye, I caught movement. A strong gust of wind scattered a pile of fallen leaves. Someone whispered in my ear, and for a moment I thought it was Connor, until I realized I didn't recognize the voice, nor did I understand the words. Without thinking I opened my mouth and bit as hard as I could while stomping on Connor's foot. He cried out, pulling his hand back, then toppled over as though someone just hit him over the head. Peering at me, he stood and took a step when he was sent flying backward, a groan escaping his throat. With a grunt, he collapsed against a tree. His body shook a few times as though something or someone kept hitting him. I stared, wide-eyed, unable to move my legs. What was happening to the guy?

Something whispered in my ear to get away from there before Connor woke up. I bolted up the street and through the gates toward the house. I didn't dare stop until I reached the front door, locking it behind me, then went about locking the backdoor too, but I knew instinctively Connor wouldn't follow. I figured he hadn't been lurking outside the gate because it was more fun than breaking in and kidnapping me from inside the house.

Aidan had called him a friend, but that's a relative term. His definition of friendship probably differed greatly from mine. I sensed there was some sort of fear that kept Connor from entering Aidan's property. Shaking, I poured myself a glass of water, spilling half of it as I returned to the safety of my room, still pondering.

I spent the day packing my belongings and checking my phone in the laundry room where I had reception, jumping at every sound. Dallas didn't call. Telling my parents or Cameron of my predicament was out of the question. Who'd believe me? Besides, I wasn't keen on risking their lives.

At the first signs of dusk, I grabbed the rosary my mother gave me and strode down to the kitchen to wait for Aidan. The cross was tiny, barely larger than my fingernail, but it boosted my confidence, instilling a false sense of safety in me. I poured a glass of water, spoke the Lord's Prayer and dipped the cross into it. It was the closest I'd get to holy water, but I figured a prayer was a prayer, with or without a vicar to say it.

The door in the hall opened and closed, and Aidan's footsteps retreated up the stairs. Fury rose inside me at his shameful pretense. He could claim he came home from work all he wanted, I knew he had been locked up in that room, sleeping in his coffin, or whatever.
I should've left. If he was a vampire, killing came with the job description, but Connor might still be out there, lurking in the shadows. For some inexplicable, utterly irrational reason, I trusted Aidan more than I trusted Connor. If he wanted to kill me, he could've done so instead of engaging in mindless smooching. I wouldn't let

a hot guy with a talent for pulling girls play havoc with my life. Taking a deep breath, I yanked the door open and stomped after him, fingers clenched around the water glass.

Chapter 11 - Aidan

I could sense Amber's bad mood as soon as I opened my eyes. Her usual nervousness was gone, replaced by maddening rage, and I didn't have the slightest clue what was wrong with her. I stretched and rose from my four-poster bed, kicking the scarlet silk sheets aside. A preference for a lavish lifestyle was the only thing Rebecca and I had in common. I just wished I'd known that before falling for her deception, but then again I wouldn't be here with my true love, ready to start a new life far away from the Lore court and the threat my world posed to a mortal.

The hearing was tonight, in the heart of London. I'd use my ability to teleport there. Even though it weakened me, I had to get there and back as soon as possible because I couldn't trust Amber's safety into Kieran and Clare's hands. They were strong vampires, but also careless: Clare was too trusting of everyone crossing her path, and Kieran always underestimated everyone else.

I took a quick shower and dressed in my usual ripped jeans and black shirt, then teleported onto the driveway, ruffled my almost dry hair and entered through the front door. It was a routine I performed on the rare occasions I had mortals around, bar the beauty part. That had started only after Amber's arrival.

Amber was in the kitchen. Hot waves of anger wafted from her as her heart thumped in her chest, pumping that delicious blood that kept calling me like no other. I walked up the stairs to my study when the door flew open and Amber appeared, cheeks flushed as though she'd hurried to catch up to me.

"Having one of those days when everything sucks but the vacuum cleaner?" I smiled and cocked a brow, suppressing the urge to grab her in my arms. Her heartbeat sped up, hammering against her ribcage. She moistened her lips. I stared at her mouth, wondering whether she'd slap me if I just kissed her.

"You lied to me." Amber inched closer and poked a finger in my chest, eyes widening when I didn't flinch. Fury blazed in her gaze. "I've no idea what game you're playing, but I quit. You can look for someone else to clean your house."

"Whoa, calm down." I reached for her. She lurched forward and poured the glass of water over my head, then jumped back, flabbergasted. I peered at my soaked shirt, stifling my laughter. "Don't tell me I was in dire need of a shower. You could've just advised me to buy a new deodorant."

"Stay away from me," Amber whispered.

My smile died on my lips. "What's wrong with you?"

"You know what's wrong!" she shouted.

I didn't want to point out that I wasn't exactly a mind reader so, unless she was more specific, I had no idea what she was talking about.

"Stop pretending," Amber yelled, inching forward.

I took a deep breath, suddenly noticing the smell that lingered on her skin. A snarl escaped my throat. "How did they get on my property?" I scooped her up and sat her on top of my mahogany desk, forcing her to face me. "Listen, I want you to tell me the truth. Did you invite them in?"

"Who? Your creepy, little friends? Hell, no." Amber's voice sounded sarcastic, but there wasn't just anger in her gaze. The telltale signs were there. She was starting to trust me no matter how hard she tried to pretend otherwise. But it wasn't enough yet.

"I told you to stay out of the woods," I roared. "Do you have any idea what could've happened to you? I can't take care of you when I'm—" I stopped before I said too much "—when I'm gone."

"You mean when you sleep?" Amber snorted. "Surprised I know what you are? I know *everything*, and I'm not staying in this house any longer."

I rubbed my chin, her words echoing in my mind. How did she find out? Was she afraid of me now? Damn the Shadows for trying to ruin my chances. "You know I'd never hurt you," I said softly, focusing on her mind as I tried to catch fragments of thought, but what came easily to me with other mortals didn't seem to work on her. I could influence her emotions, but I couldn't read her. I felt bad for using such a cheap trick on her, and yet I had no choice.

Clearing my mind, I met her gaze, ready to guide her on tranquil ground again so we could talk, when I noticed the barely visible bruise spreading on her left cheek near the hairline. Whoever hurt her was as good as dead. Tossing the books on the desk to the floor, I picked her up and teleported through iron-enforced walls to the only safe place I knew: my chamber. Ever so gently, I lowered myself on a sofa and pulled her onto my lap. She barely protested, her eyes wide with curiosity as she scanned the room, lingering a little too long on the disheveled bed.

"How—" Amber started.

"Tell me the truth. I'll make them pay if it's the last thing I ever do." I pointed at her cheek, trying to keep my mind from wandering to the bed and how awkward it made me feel since we barely knew each other.

Amber winced even though I didn't touch the bruise. "I left the house to call my brother when one of the guys you introduced me to the other night tried to kidnap me." Her voice sounded calm and composed, considering her words carefully. She was hiding half the truth.

"Wait a second, we'll get to the kidnapping part later." I raised my brows. "Why didn't you call your brother from the landline in the hall? Surely Clare told you to use it any time you want since there's no reception elsewhere."

She averted her gaze, blushing. "I forgot."

In spite of the seriousness of the situation I smiled. She was such a bad liar, but cute. "Okay, let's pretend you forgot, which I don't believe by the way, did you also forget I told you not to leave the house?"

"You said I couldn't walk into the woods, not to stay inside." Her eyes narrowed, challenging me.

I inhaled slowly. No point in arguing with her. I'd just make sure she'd never leave the house without me again. "From now on you stay inside, unless I'm with you."

"You can't tell me what to do. Who do you think you are?"

She looked so feeble in her annoyance, it made me feel frail too. I snuggled her head into my shoulder and whispered, "You're not going anywhere. If I need to put you in chains to keep you by my side, then so be it."

"Why would you do that? Because of the prize? I know you wanted it for yourself."

So the Shadows told her about the prize as well. No surprise there. I squeezed a finger under her chin and lifted her lips to mine. "Don't you see it? You're the prize. Your gift's just the bonus." I touched my lips to hers gently, running my fingers through her hair as I pulled her closer for a moment before releasing her abruptly.

She peered up at me through hooded eyes fringed by long lashes, her full lips glistening in the soft light. "What's wrong?" Amber asked, her voice dripped with disappointment.

"You don't want this like I do," I whispered.

"What?" She smiled that lazy grin that made my heart skip a beat, shattering the frail shell of my control. "I can assure you I do."

I shook my head. "One day you'll understand what I'm talking about." I had to keep my appointment with Layla, and find a way to get rid of that curse she called a prize.

Amber smiled. "You won't get another chance."

"You couldn't leave even if you wanted to."

"Dare me." I saw the determination in her eyes. She was a sorer loser than she was a bad liar. Someone had to give in before she did something reckless just to prove her point.

"Okay, you win. I believe you." I traced my finger along her jawline, brainstorming ways to make Layla grant my wish. Taking her by surprise was my best bet.

"So, when were you going to tell me you're a—" Amber hesitated, clearly uncomfortable with the word.

"A vampire?"

She flinched. I growled low in my throat.

"Yeah, that," she whispered.

"Maybe after our wedding?"

Amber laughed. "What makes you think I'd marry you?"

"What makes you think you'd have a choice?"

"I'm not into bad guys," she said.

She got that one right. I hadn't always been a bad guy; just since Rebecca decided to make me her personal toy. It was my Achilles spot, so I changed the subject. "How did you find out what I am? The Shadows?"

"The what?" Her confused look only strengthened my belief someone else must've told her. But who?

"I'll tell you later. Now, who else did you talk to?"

She raised her chin stubbornly. "I'm not telling on my sources."

"You know I'll find out sooner or later anyway." In fact, I'd make it my priority to find out upon my return from the Lore court.

"Do you have any idea how my parents will react once they notice my boyfriend's a—"

I stared at her. Had she just said the b-word? She squirmed, probably realizing the same thing. Denial and yet another fight was imminent. I had to give her space to think, so I lifted her and put her down beside me. "There's business I need to take care of first. This conversation isn't over though."

She eyed me suspiciously. "You're driving to town? Good. You can take me to the airport then." It wasn't a question; it was a demand. No one ever dared to demand anything from me. "I should've called a cab the moment I found out about all of this."

"Yeah, well, you didn't. I wouldn't have let you go anyway." I smirked. "I haven't changed my mind, Amber. You stay here. Clare will make sure you're not trying to escape."

She sneered, but didn't argue. I walked the short distance to the wardrobe and pulled out a leather belt and sheath that I tied around my ankle, hiding them underneath my jeans and a hip-length coat. The sheath held the only weapon that'd keep me safe inside the Lore court: a fire whip. Layla's succubi feared it like hell. Now, Layla was another matter and harder to control, but I counted on her soft spot for me, as long as she didn't find out how much Amber meant to me.

In two long strides I returned to the sofa and planted a kiss on Amber's lips. "Do as I say. Don't make me hunt you down, because I'm too good at it and you wouldn't stand a chance."

Her eyes glittered with that determination that kept telling me I'd found my match. "You can't keep me here."

"Dare me and I'll lock you up." I kissed her again and stood, hesitating. A sense of dread hit me. I was making a big mistake, and yet I knew I had no choice. Throwing a last glance over my shoulder, I hurried out the door, teleporting to London as soon as I was out of Amber's sight.

***

From outside, the estate looked like any other in East London: a broad building surrounded by hundreds of acres of dirty concrete and a high fence. Empty beer cans and wrappers littered the narrow pavement in front of the gate. Several girls dressed in tight skirts, tops and boots stood in immediate proximity, their greasy hair ruffled by the cold wind. One approached me as soon as I appeared in the shadows of a concrete wall. If she found it strange that I materialized out of nowhere, she didn't show her surprise.

"Have a fag?" the girl asked. She was in her early twenties, maybe younger. Her voice sounded low and impassive. I recoiled from the pungent smell of sweat lingering on her skin and clothes, and turned away when she brushed her long hair out of her eyes. On her wrist shimmered a tattoo: a black snake, its mouth agape, twisting and coiling like a living creature living beneath her skin.

"Beat it, succubus," I growled low enough for her to hear, but not loud enough to raise the others' suspicion.

She shrugged and turned her back on me, walking to the far end of the wall with short strides and exaggerated swaying of her bony hips. I kneeled, grinding one fist into the ground, and jumped over the high fence with no effort. Just like the succubi outside, the fence's purpose was to stop mortals from trespassing. Immortals knew better than to barge in unannounced.

I sprinted across the dark ground to the tall, grey building with shattered glass and barricaded windows, hesitating in the doorway as I gathered my thoughts. Once inside, there was no way back. But even if I wanted to, I couldn't change my mind now. Layla was expecting me. Backing off would only enrage the demi-goddess. Like a doctor's receptionist, she kept a tight schedule and expected her visitors to keep their appointments.

The brass doors opened and I stepped in, jaw set, every muscle tensed in case I needed to fight. The hall smelled of dust and years of decay. Torches gave the impression of hundreds of shadows moving across the walls—and souls they were, just invisible to the eyes of anyone apart from those boasting demon blood. I pulled out my fire whip and climbed down the stairs that seemed to stretch on forever, following the naked walls sub terrain into Layla's realm.

Chapter 12 - Aidan

Even after centuries of working for the Lore court, I still wasn't used to the overpowering smell of the cursed souls Layla kept around her, torturing them as she saw fit, never showing kindness. Layla believed the immortals around her were watching her every move, waiting for a sign of weakness they could use to their advantage. I figured she just liked being feared. It was also her way to show the immortal world her mother's reign, defined by goodwill and kindness, was over.

The scent of burned flesh and reeking wounds intensified the farther I moved. Finally, the steep staircase leveled and I opened the door to a different world. The vast space looked like a huge cave with high columns reaching up to a shifting ceiling of tortured souls. Immortals gathered in groups to watch the gruesome display of dismembered limbs, bloodcurdling cries and gaping mouths, hollow from centuries of being trapped in between life and death, deprived of nourishment. To many members of the Lore court, the pictures before their eyes were nothing but routine and probably less memorable than a horror movie with good special effects.

Quickening my pace, I couldn't help but look up at a crying mother holding her stillborn in her bleeding arms while a black, shapeless entity pierced nails into her battered body. I flogged my whip at the entity, a burning gash forming where I hit the flesh. It yelped and scurried away. I tightened my grip around the whip and turned to the right into a smaller space, then through another cavern until I reached the throne room.

The ceiling and walls here were bare of trapped souls, but the atmosphere freaked me out just the same. Smooth candle wax dripped from heavy chandeliers; the heavy scent of incense hung heavy in the air, choking me. And then there were the snakes—cobras, pythons, copperheads and what else not—resting on various divans. Ever since meeting Layla I hated snakes, almost as much as I hated the demi-goddess.

I lowered my gaze and dropped to my knees, face pressed against the cold ivory floor. Layla's breathing tickled my neck long before her succubi surrounded me, caressing my skin with long, soft fingers. They were beautiful and ready to do everything the immortals wanted, but while some visitors thought themselves in pleasure heaven, I knew to fend off their advances for my own safety. With satisfaction they brought plague into the heart of those they touched, drawing them into a world in-between dream and reality, until their victims turned into mere carcasses of their previous selves. And the most spectacular results were displayed on Layla's ceilings. Most of those who knew what happened to a succubus's lover thought they could escape that fate. Just one last touch and it'd be the last. It usually wasn't until realization came too late.

Clutching the whip until my knuckles cracked, I bit my lip and forced myself to endure their touch. Under other circumstances they'd feel the sting of my whip, but not today, not until I swayed Layla in my favor. Tongues licked my skin as a succubus whispered in my ear promises of pleasure. Listening to the sighs and groans of the low demons made me feel soiled and unworthy of Amber, but I controlled the rising anger inside me. When would Layla tire of this humiliating show? It could take minutes, hours, even days. I could only hope she was in dire need of conversation, because I didn't have days to spare.

"You may rise and approach," Layla said eventually.

With the slightest groan of irritation, I jumped to my feet and walked over to her golden throne. She had her back turned on me, long black hair thrown over one shoulder to reveal her glorious tattoo of living snakes. The snakes under her alabaster skin slithered, tongues pointing out, mouths opening and closing. Layla ran a manicured hand over her lean thigh and pulled her sheer flowing dress up a few inches until it rode just below the hips, revealing flesh I didn't want to see. And then she turned.

Green, cat-like eyes met me, cunning wafting from her. A thin black sheet of fabric barely covered her breasts, but I wasn't tempted. I knew too well what she was: a succubus deity of the higher kind with a strong need for blood and torture.

131

I bowed, more to hide my annoyance than to pay my respect, and lowered myself to her naked feet and painted toenails. The snakes slithered down her leg toward me. I inched away, watching her face carefully, taking in any sudden changes in mood.

"What? No gifts today, dearest?" Her voice betrayed a sharp edge. The snakes hissed.

Damn. In all the chaos from the last days, I'd forgotten how much she liked a gift. I peered at an approaching cobra, ready to kick the thing if it came closer. "Sorry about that. I'm here to see you with an urgent matter."

A frown formed between her thin brows as she caressed the snake's head. "This better be an emergency. I've killed others for much less."

I hesitated, considering my words. I figured she might be easier to sway in my favor if she thought her rules were broken. "It concerns you."

Layla bore her green gaze into me, irritated. "I've had my share of bad news for the day, but proceed."

Still clutching the whip, I stood to pour wine from the carafe at her feet into a dainty goblet and handed her the glass, a gesture that always pleased her. As usual, she smiled at me. I kneeled to her feet again, aware that I had to start my pledge soon before she lost interest. "I failed to win the prize in your race," I said.

She shrugged. "You know I cannot grant you Sight unless you've earned it. Wait another five hundred years and then try again. Maybe your brother can teach you how to loosen up a bit in the meantime."

I gritted my teeth at her insinuation. "My brother's reckless. And you know I can't wait five hundred years."

"Centuries of feeding on animal blood has made you cranky. Kill a few virgins and treat yourself to a real drink. Trust me, time will fly by." Her smug grin irritated me. I needed to get a grip before I lost it.

"I'm not complaining about your rules." I forced myself to grab her hand, my fingers closing around hers, before I released them quickly as temptation washed over me. Amber was the one. There'd never be anyone else. A snake slithered up my arm, onto my shoulder. I clenched my teeth, focusing my thoughts back to my plan as I said, "I'm worried about what'll happen when the others find out you let a mortal win the race."

She flicked her hair back, impatiently. "I don't care what anyone thinks. This is *my* race and I'll run it the way I see fit, just like my mother before me. You see, I'm not in the least biased, dearest. So long the rules are followed, the prize is well earned."

I knew breaking that wall of century-old indifference might prove a hard if not impossible task, but I wasn't ready to give up just yet. "But don't the rules say no mortal may ever be harmed, Your Highness?"

"The mortal's alive and well, isn't she?" Layla snapped. "If they were truly my rules, she could as well be bludgeoned to death for all I care."

I breathed out, relieved that Layla couldn't change her mother's legacy no matter how hard she tried to match her in strength. "Once everyone finds out a mortal's carrying the prize, she'll be hunted down and forced to use it to their advantage. Shadows have already tried to kidnap her. I urge you to strip her of her powers before something happens to her. You know it's just a matter of time."

Layla's eyes blazed with sudden interest. "Why do you care so much?"

"I don't." I tried to keep my cool, barely batting an eyelash. Layla was jealous of true love. If I admitted I had feelings for Amber, Layla would break the rules and execute us. "I worry about you, about the fate that might befall you if the rules were broken. Please reconsider." I grabbed her hand again. "You've been a kind ruler. Ever since you took over, the court's been thriving. We don't want to lose you." It was a big, fat lie. Few would actually care if she disappeared and never came back.

Layla's face softened. She believed me, sucking in every deceitful word. Appealing to her ego might just change her mind.

I continued, "Strip the mortal of her powers and hold another race, Your Highness. To demonstrate my honesty and loyalty, I promise I won't participate. The mortal doesn't know how to use the gift yet. She won't even notice it's gone, so there's no danger of exposure."

A succubus floated past, feet barely reaching the ground under flowing, transparent layers of chiffon as she whispered in Layla's ear. The goddess raised her eyebrows. With a flick of her hand, she sent the succubus tumbling against the wall, then smiled at me, sweetly. "The mortal's keeping the prize. This meeting's over." She turned her back on me as if I just ceased to exist. To her, I was a mere inconvenience sitting at her feet like an adoring slave.

"There's something else I need to discuss with you, Your Highness. Please, " I said before she forgot about me. Layla spun, brows furrowed.

"There you go again, killing the mood." She sighed. "Make it quick, then."

"Last time you employed my services, I brought you Pharaoh Tutankhamen's ring which you so desired. On top of my wages, you promised one favor. I'm taking you up on the offer. Here's what I want: take the mortal's prize back." I regarded her through imploring eyes. Layla couldn't go back on her word. She still needed my services.

"Did I say that?" She shrugged. "I can't remember, but the answer's no."

Fury throbbed between my eyes. "I risked everything to find you that lost ring. I wasted loads of cash and time, and barely escaped death in the hot Egyptian sun." I blinked to suppress my rage. "How can you say you don't remember?"

"And I paid you quite handsomely. I don't deny that you're my best bounty hunter." She winked. "Because that you are."

"I might not be for long."

She looked away for a moment, getting the hint, probably considering what she'd be losing in the future. Eventually she said, "My entire kingdom's at your disposal, but I can't grant you this particular wish."

I knew instinctively it was the best I'd get from her today, the best anyone might ever get. "Thank you for your consideration. I'll move on to my next wish then. A seat in court for Cassandra, daughter of the Dark Lord."

"What do you get if the chaos angel enters the court?" Layla seemed amused but not aversive to the idea. All wasn't lost yet.

"She's a friend. I'm doing her a favor, not the other way around. I suspect she wants to learn from a real master like you," I said.

"Very well. She may have a seat." Layla turned, heading for the door.

I trailed after her, staying a few feet behind. "Not just any seat. Promise me you'll make her the new ambassador." Not that her word was worth a darn.

"You give the word 'dead' a whole new meaning. You're lucky I'm a sucker for hotties. Ambassador, then. She won't last a fortnight." Layla burst out the door, ready to torture the next soul or whatever it was that took her fancy these days.

I pulled out my fire whip before the succubi came nearer and made my way out. Now I'd need a good scrubbing before I could return to Amber. Visiting Layla hadn't been worth the effort, but at least tried. Time to move on to plan B.

Chains wrapped around my ankles and wrists as soon as I left the throne room. The fire whip dropped to the floor as I struggled to break free from the invisible bonds that kept me glued to the spot. Summoning my strength, I tore through the chains and grabbed hold of the whip, but the bonds snapped back in place, impairing my movement.

Damn her and her little games. I had no time for this. "Any particular reason why you're not letting me go?" I yelled, tugging harder at the chains. "Having a bit of separation anxiety, are we?"

Layla appeared beside me, a malicious smile spreading across her lips. "Did you really believe I wouldn't smell her on you? Oh, the stupidity of men never fails to amaze me."

Groaning, I tugged at the chains, even though I knew I stood no chance unless Layla decided to release me. "I'm a member of the Lore council. You're breaking the rules," I hissed, anger choking me.

"And aren't you breaking the rules by dating a mortal? Come on, don't be cross. You surely knew you wouldn't get away with it." Layla laughed and summoned a nearby group of succubi to take me away. Countless hands lifted me up like I weighed nothing and carried me into complete darkness where they dropped me onto the naked ground. I landed on my back, pain rippling through my immortal body as the chains tightened, cutting into my skin like hundreds of razorblades. I opened my mouth, then closed it again because I wouldn't give Layla the satisfaction of hearing me cry for help. I didn't care what happened to me. But if anything happened to Amber I'd kill them all, Layla, the Shadows, the Lore court members. One by one, I'd rip their throats and leave them bleeding to death.

Chapter 13

I peered out the door just in time to see Aidan disappear into thin air. Now I knew for sure he wasn't quite like any of my former crushes. My cheeks burned. I had let him kiss me once again. Seduced by the rich kid, only to be pushed away when he had enough of me. Apparently taking care of business in the middle of the night was more important than finding out whether the attraction between us was real. Getting closer to him was a big mistake, especially after what Cass told me. How did I think this'd turn out? That Dracula and I would live in his big, old mansion happily ever after? I had been fooling myself all along.

Aidan said he'd never hurt me. Maybe he wouldn't do it on purpose, but vampires drink blood. Sooner or later, he'd want a midnight snack. Well, no one would mess with my red blood cells. Even if he could restrain his hunger, others were looking for me because I solved the riddle and scooped that stupid prize. I needed to snap out of this fantasy world and get my old life back by leaving Scotland that instant.

Wherever Dallas went, trouble followed, and now it started to rub off on me. Only I could get tangled in a mess like this with a real vampire. I rubbed my neck, my head throbbing like it was going to explode any minute. It was time to get the heck out of here, and fast, before Aidan came back and stopped me. Just because I felt madly attracted to his dark curls and pale blue eyes didn't make him trustworthy material. I should be hiding far away from here where no one would ever find me—not even Aidan with his fancy tracking skills he bragged about.

I sighed and quickened my steps down the stairs, ready to call a taxi and make a dash for the airport when Kieran stopped me in midstride, his hand squeezing my elbow.

"Go away." I struggled to free my arm when Kieran let go with a shrug.

"Late for a hot date?"

For a moment I just stared at him as realization kicked in. Goose bumps covered my arms. Was he a vampire too? My gaze studying his chalky pale complexion, I remembered his cold touch the day we met and Cass's words came back to haunt me. A vampire's sexy as hell. I must've been blind not to realize anyone looking so perfect couldn't be human. Maybe I should've strung a necklace of garlic before walking among them. Okay, that was a stupid myth, but I was grasping at straws.

Did Aidan's brother really think he could stop me? Eyeing the door, I set my jaw. If need be, I'd kick him where it counted. Vampire or not, he'd go down like everyone else.

Kieran traced his fingertips up my arm, his lips curled into a smug grin. "You're shivering. Would you like a sweater, or maybe I could turn up the heat?"

"The temperature in the house's just fine, thank you." What would Aidan think? I smacked his hand away. "I just need some fresh air to sort things out. My heart's beating a million miles a minute."

Kieran laughed. "I tend to have that effect on girls."

"You wish," Clare called from the library.

I needed to hear the voice of someone normal before I went crazy. Maybe Cameron would know how to get me out of this ridiculous situation. I pointed at the landline. "Can I use the phone?"

Kieran's eyes narrowed. "So you can call the police and tell them you're being held prisoner? Sorry, that's not going to happen."

"You're really something."

"Well, the ladies keep telling me. I should warn you, I have hundreds of years of experience."

Was he for real? I turned to face him, shaking my head in disbelief. "How could you have lived that long? You must be bored out of your mind."

"I'm pretty good at dodging angry mobs with pitchforks. And the boredom is bearable. It was worse before television was invented."

"I'm so out of here," I said, yanking my arm out of his iron grip.

"No, you're not. I'll tie you up, or handcuff you to your bed."

I sneered. As if. "Sounds tempting, but I'd rather make my phone call."

"Nope." He shook his head, still amused, irritating the hell out of me.

I smiled at him, hoping he'd fall for my bluff. "The police would laugh their heads off if I told them I was being held hostage by a group of vampires. Just let me answer a friend's call, otherwise *he* might involve the authorities."

Kieran stood his ground. "No, and don't you dare walk out that door because I'll know it. If it's a chase you want, a chase you'll get." He winked. "I'm not in hunting mood tonight, but Clare is. You wouldn't want her on your heel because she's a beast."

I backed up a few steps. He wasn't going to intimidate me. Maybe I could just sprint past him. "I don't think Aidan would appreciate you talking to me like this."

He caressed my cheek ever so gently. "He doesn't need to know."

Now he was completely losing his marbles. Or why else would he keep flirting? Why couldn't Cameron pay me this much attention? If only he knew, surely he'd come to his senses. He'd know what a huge mistake he made by dumping me, and he'd spend the rest of his life making it up to me because we belonged together, two normal people living a normal life with no demons, vampires or Shadows.

In two long strides I reached the door when Kieran wrapped his arm around my waist, pulling me back. "He's my brother and I'll do whatever it takes to keep you safe."

"Keep me safe? Ha! Don't you want to rip out my throat and drink my freaking blood? Yeah, I know all about you guys!"

Kieran rolled his eyes. "Oh, please. If that were the case, you'd be dead already."

A cold hand touched my shoulder, making me jump. "We don't feed from the source," Clare said. "You're safe with us. I promise."

Was a promise from a dead person even binding? I had trusted Clare more than any of them. I should never have bonded over wine and girl talk. I balled my fists as I glared at her. "Clare, how could you not tell me what you were?"

Clare exchanged a glance with Kieran, then met my gaze. "Would you have believed me?" She had a point there. "Vampire or not, we're friends."

I snorted. "Sure, as long as you don't come too close to my aorta."

"What was she supposed to do?" Kieran asked. "Invite you to talk over dinner? You should see the way she sinks her fangs into her meal. She may look sweet, but her table manners are horrendous. Frankly, I'm embarrassed to dine with her, especially with guests around."

"You're such a moron." Clare nudged him in the ribs. "Don't believe a word he says."

I couldn't get past the fact that Clare hadn't given me the benefit of the doubt. I still wanted to get out of here, but arguing wasn't aiding my plan. Time to change my approach. "Why are you holding me against my will? If you want me to trust you, you'll have to trust me first."

"I don't trust you because I know you're trying to run away." Clare handed me the phone. "No police, or any

142

hints to anyone. Break your word and I'll lock you in your room."

"I'm not calling the police, I swear," I said. "I just need to talk to Cameron." And sneak in a few hidden messages. Cameron was a clever guy. He'd read between the lines.

"Your ex?" Kieran raised his eyebrows.

Clare shrugged. "Sure. Just remember we're not the bad guys here."

I waited until Clare and Kieran disappeared into the library, then dialed Cameron's number. Tapping my fingers on the side table, I waited for someone to pick up. He never went to bed before midnight, always hanging out with his friends, drinking and debating into the night. I'd thought him terribly clever at that time. Looking back now, he was a boring, pretentious show-off. But I loved Cameron, didn't I? It wasn't his fault he knew so much. He surely didn't mean to come across as a snob.

It rang for a long time before the sleepy voice of a girl answered. My heart fell in my chest. It didn't mean anything. She could be just a friend. The girl said something, her voice dripping with impatience as though she couldn't wait to get back to whatever she'd been doing before my call interrupted her. What *had* she been doing? I opened my mouth to speak, but my tongue stuck to the back of my throat. I pressed the earpiece against my ear, listening for any background noise. Naked feet slapped against the tiled floor, then Cameron's low voice whispered on the other end of the line, "Who is it?" A giggle followed and the line went dead.

I stood frozen to the spot, the phone still clutched to my ear, surprised to discover Cameron's betrayal didn't really hurt. My heart was fine, my pulse still normal. It was my ego that couldn't deal with the blow. Even though a giggle didn't have to mean anything, I felt relieved for things to end this way.

Someone draped an arm over my shoulders and pulled me toward the library. I peered at beautiful Clare, at her deep-blue eyes and glossy hair. No one would ever cheat on Clare. They'd be stupid to do so.

Clare snorted. "You've no idea." She opened the heavy door and stepped to the side to let me walk past. "Sorry, I couldn't help but overhear. Better you find out sooner rather than later. Something better might be lurking around the corner already."

I nodded. Stepping into the library, I met Blake's hard stare. Why didn't I notice the signs before? His dark eyes with a golden gleam screamed vampire. His skin was pulled too tight over prominent cheekbones. My gaze scanned the furniture. I wished I had the privilege of disbelief—like the first time I joined them. The thought of one of them lunging for my throat and sucking me dry terrified me.

"What? No crossbows? No stakes to pierce through my heart? No sword to decapitate me?" Kieran shook his head, grinning. "I thought you'd come prepared."

I returned the smile. "What do you take me for? A vampire hunter? I'm just an average girl who won a prize and got stuck in your freaky world. Lucky me, huh?"

"Hold on to that prize," Blake said, gawking at me. "If things don't work out the way we hope, you can talk to Aidan from the other side. It might be the only way to reach him once he's dead."

"Don't even say such a thing," Clare said, slapping his arm. What was he talking about? I opened my mouth to ask when Clare whispered, "Ignore him. We trusted you with the phone call. Now it's your turn to trust us. You look tired. Why don't you rest until Aidan's back?"

Clare was right. It they wanted to kill me, they'd have done so already. They had never given me any reason to doubt them. I felt my fear slowly subsiding as I lay back and closed my eyes, ready to forget the world, even if just for a few minutes. When I pried my eyes open, the others sat gathered together, whispering with their backs turned on me. I sat up, dizziness washing over me. "What's going on?"

"Aidan should've been here by now." The tension in Clare's voice was palpable as she pushed a plate with a ham and cheese sandwich across the coffee table.

I eyed the sandwich, but didn't touch it. The sudden sense of dread sat in the pit of my stomach like a rock. "Maybe he's late." Blake shot me a grim look.

Kieran shook his head. "The day Aidan's late is the day hell freezes over. Usually, he's more punctual than a watch." The seriousness in his face made me wonder what Aidan hadn't told me.

"Where did he go?"

They hesitated, peering at one another, probably wondering whether to tell me or not. Eventually Clare spoke. "He's at the Lore court to see whether he can find a way to strip you of the prize. He's trying to save your life."

"Now we might need to save his life," Blake mumbled.

Whatever that Lore court was, it didn't sound like a nice place. Aidan was a big guy, he could take care of himself, or so I thought. The others didn't seem

145

convinced. My heartbeat accelerated until I could barely breathe. It was my first panic attack in years.

Clare held a glass of water to my lips, smiling, but it didn't reach her eyes. "Drink this. Aidan will kill us if we let you have a heart attack."

Listening to their conversation, I sipped the cold liquid until bile rose in my throat.

"I'm going after him," Kieran said. "You know Layla's capable of anything. If she finds out about Amber—"

Clare interrupted him, shaking her head vehemently. "She won't because she's not as strong as her mother."

Who was Layla? I peered from one to the other, waiting for someone to include me in the conversation. When they kept ignoring me, I sank into the cushions, figuring I might as well hide in the corner, playing furniture accessory.

"You got proof?" Kieran asked. "Aidan always says everyone underestimates her."

"I'm going," Clare said. Kieran shook his head. She continued, "No! It's my fault he's trapped in the Lore court. I should've stayed back to watch Amber and the house instead of going hunting during the race."

That fateful night again. I groaned, wondering when I'd be hearing from Dallas. If he just called I could persuade him to return the gemstones. Maybe that'd change things.

"Turning up at Layla's could make things worse," Kieran said. "Maybe she'll let him go. If he's not back by tomorrow we'll take action."

"You're willing to wait and risk your brother's life? Why?" Blake shouted, startling me.

"Layla's powers don't include the ability to kill instantly," Kieran said.

"Maybe it wasn't Layla. The Shadows want Amber badly." Clare went about closing the thick, blackout drapes against the breaking dawn. "I'll wait for Cass. Maybe she can help."

Kieran snorted but remained silent.

"Is there anything I can do?" I asked. "I'll do whatever it takes to find Aidan." I barely knew him, but somehow I felt a connection. It was almost as though I could hear the confusion in his thoughts and feel the pain that kept rippling through him like—*chains cutting into his flesh?* I tensed, gaze focused on the naked wall. There was something at the edge of my awareness, but I couldn't grasp it. With a sigh, I forced it to the back of my mind. Paranoid. Aidan was fine and would be back soon.

"Go to bed and get some rest. You've gone through a lot in one day," Kieran said.

Blake nodded, grimly. "Kieran's right. Tomorrow, we'll find a way to fix this giant mess you caused."

There was something else in the air, some sort of hesitation and anticipation. And then it dawned on me. The vampires wanted me out so they could discuss whatever they hid from me. I smiled and bid them goodnight, then headed out the door. Holding my breath, I pressed my back against the wall, eavesdropping.

"Layla will kill him out of spite," Kieran said.

"She won't," Clare said.

"She's killed others for less." Kieran again. "You know she doesn't like competition. Why would she want to keep him alive now he's found his mate? And don't tell me I'm

147

imagining things, because I've seen the way he looks at her."

Clare made a noise that sounded like an exaggerated sigh. "I'll talk to Queen Deidre. Maybe she'll know a way to get him out of there."

"No freaking way," Kieran said. "That Shadow kid's a vile liar and manipulator. She'll definitely want something in exchange."

"Cass will know what to do," Clare said.

"It's waiting game now," Blake said. "The sun's rising soon."

I peeled my back from the wall and tip-toed up to my room, avoiding the creaking floorboards, then locked the door behind me. Still dressed, I dropped on my bed and forced my mind into thinking mode while watching the moon disappear outside.

I flinched as a cry pierced my mind. Was I going crazy, developing schizophrenia? Someone whispered my name. Turning, I scanned the room. No one there. Kieran said Aidan had found his mate. Could he have meant me? It sounded so animalistic, and yet so right. Fact was, if I didn't give in to Dallas's stupid plan and steal the gemstones, Aidan wouldn't be trapped somewhere in a dungeon, fighting the chains that couldn't kill a vampire but destroy his will to battle a fate worse than death.

Wait, how did I know that? I sat up with a jolt as pictures flooded my mind: Aidan chained to a wall, blood oozing from deep cuts across his torso and legs as cowered shapes clad in flowing dresses prodded his wounds. The room smelled of something pungent that made my stomach churn. The moment he raised his head with a

148

glint of recognition in his eyes, I knew he could sense my presence.

I stretched my arm to help him, but no matter how far I stretched I couldn't reach him. The illusion disappeared. Sudden weariness gripped me, and I let go in the knowledge that I'd find a way to save him from those things, even if it meant sacrificing my own life. It was all my fault, and I wouldn't let him die.

The sun stood high on the horizon when I jumped out of bed exhausted, my head reeling. I'd survived the night with a bunch of vampires in the house. Another night or two, and I might put them on my friends' list.

After taking a shower and changing my clothes, I shrugged into my coat and left the house through the backdoor. Clare had said something about waiting up for Cass. Could a vampire do that? I had no idea and no intention to find out. I sprinted for the gate and stopped right in front of it, peering beyond the empty street and into the surrounding thickets and trees. Were the Shadows still hiding here? I hoped so because I knew no other way to contact them.

"Hey, guys. I'm here to talk." I kept my voice steady, hiding my trembling hands behind my back. With the tall trees around me, I felt as insignificant as greenery, but I knew I wasn't. I was carrying the prize that everyone wanted, and now I'd trade.

The street remained quiet. If the Shadows were around, they were probably waiting for me to leave Aidan's property. Or they gave up after the kidnapping failed. "Come on, you can't blame me for making a run for it. You could at least listen to my proposition. It might just blow you away." Smirking, I peered down the winding

149

street. Nothing stirred. "Fine, then. I'll give it to someone else."

I sat down on the cold ground, the freezing midday wind creeping into my bones. A cold wouldn't benefit my rescue plan. With the Shadows not showing up, there'd be no plan, I reminded myself.

Standing again, I jumped up and down to soothe the freezing sensation in my numb toes. "Come on, guys," I muttered. One last look at the closed gate and I returned to the house, hesitant to give up on my quest. I entered the hall and flicked open a leather-bound address book. Even though Aidan didn't like the Shadows, he might've jotted down their phone numbers. It was something people did, or so I figured. I didn't like my mother's aunt, yet I still sent a Christmas card every year. Not that the old lady ever bothered with a reply.

Apart from Greta and Harry's number, there were the usual emergency hotlines, which came printed on the diary. Nothing else. I frowned and flicked the book across the table. How did these people communicate with one another? Via carrier pigeons? I strained to listen for any cawing sounds, feeling stupid for even considering that option.

A car pulled up on the gravel in the driveway. Before I had time to peer out, the door burst open and Cass walked in, dressed in her trademark oversized jeans, what looked like an orange dress reaching down to her knees on top of the jeans, and a military style jacket that wouldn't be too bad were it not scorched in several places. I gaped in awe. Cass's outfit was so ghastly it could easily pass as art.

150

Cass grinned. "You think? Thanks, mate." For a minute I didn't register Cass was reading my mind. How could I forget that tiny detail? "So, what's cooking?" Cass strode to the living room and dropped on the sofa, making herself comfortable. "Rumor tells me your boyfriend's gone."

I sat in a leather chair, facing her. "He went to some sort of court and never came back. Clare should be here. She said she'd wait up."

Cass straightened and tilted her head to the side as if to listen. "Nah, she's snoozing like a stone." She slumped down again. "Are you sure he isn't just making a run for the hills? You know the usual excuse, going to buy milk, cigarettes, or whatever, and never bothering to come back."

"What?"

"Oh, goodness," Cass said. "I see I hit a soft spot. Didn't mean too. Who's Cameron?"

I grimaced. "Somebody I never want to see again."

"I was just messing with you, mate. Want me to send out a few demons to track Aidan down?"

"No need. Don't ask me how, but I think I know where he is." I ignored the demon remark. Nothing surprised me any more. Besides, no mortal I knew could read thoughts and carried two horns on the head. "At the beach house, I met two Shadows."

"Connor and Devon," Cass said. "You're playing with fire, mate."

I peered at her intently. The girl was strange, no doubt about it, but she also had something likeable about her. Could she keep her scattered mind to herself so the others wouldn't find out about my plan?

Cass clapped her hands excitedly. "Try me, try me, try me."

Oh, sod it. I had nothing to lose. "I want to meet them."

"Wow, Aidan's gone, like, five minutes, and the next guy's already peeping around the corner? Naughty." She shook her finger, laughing. The next instant, the smile disappeared and she looked embarrassed. "Sorry. It's not my style being rude and all. I just can't keep it in. It's my—" She shook her head. "There's this—never mind."

"I have a plan, but Clare & co. mustn't know," I whispered.

"You want me to keep this a secret from the others." She leaned closer, eyes gleaming, her cheeks turning a pink shade. "That's a good one. Pure chaos. Even better than chocolate. I like you."

It seemed as though I was making a pact with the devil herself. Was that good or bad?

"Definitely good." Cass winked. "I could be your go between. Aidan's hooking me up with this cool ambassador gig. Yeah, I'll be a diplomat." Her eyes lit up again. "Who would've guessed, right? I'll make you my first mission."

"Promise you won't tell anyone," I said.

Cass raised her right arm to her chest. "I promise I'll keep the secret as long as my scattered brain can keep it in. After that, it's pure chaos."

I sensed that was about all I'd get. "I'm going to strike a pact with them to help me save Aidan."

"You're really into him. Going after Layla with the Shadows' help." Cass literally glowed. "That's going to be major drama. Hope Aidan got me my ambassador position so I can watch it all live."

"Let's do this thing *now*. Do you know how to get in touch with them?" I didn't want to sound impatient, but something told me Cass could chat for hours.

Tucking her legs under her, Cass pursed her lips and straightened. She closed her eyes and started rocking back and forth, murmuring something that sounded like an incantation. I stared at her. Clearly, the rich kids had other ways to get in touch than pigeons.

"You're just too gullible, mate. You've got to meet my dad. He'd love you." She pulled a silver phone out of her oversized bag and dialed, her gaze fixed on me as she spoke, "Hey babes, it's me, listen—" she paused and tapped her chewed fingernails on her thigh "—all set? Aidan's girl wants to talk to you. Pop over now before she changes her mind. You owe me. Cheerio."

"What did they say? Are they coming?" They simply had to. Aidan's life depended on it.

Cass nodded. "They'll be here in a flash. Do you want me to negotiate? I'm quite good at it. Always get the best deal, or so Dad says."

I shook my head. "It's a tempting offer, but I have to do this myself."

Cass shrugged and jumped up. "Got it. Just a word of advice since we're now chums and all, stay within the gates. That gift of yours is quite handy. Some people would kill for it—literally. So try to stay out of the fire, okay?"

"You were right about the vampire thing," I said.

"You didn't believe me?" Cass shook her head, laughing. "Do you see angel wings on my back? I'm far from perfect—maybe beautifully flawed—but I don't lie."

"Thanks for filling me in. If it weren't for you I'd still be in the dark."

"Us girls have to stick together," Cass said.

Okay, I had to ask, now or never. "You're not one of them. What are you?"

Cass pointed at the floor. "You know the big guy downstairs who loves to steal the souls of naughty people? Well, that's my dad."

Her father was the devil himself? I blinked. Why not? I was willing to take on vampires, so why not believe in good old Lucifer too? "This is too weird. Talk about getting all wrapped up in your new guy's world."

"The shock will wear off soon."

I accompanied Cass to the door and gave her a brief hug, murmuring a thanks.

"No problem, but you owe me," Cass whispered. Waving, she jumped into her huge, black truck and sped off.

Chapter 14

Terrified, I leaned against the gate to wait. A strong gust of wind blew my hair in my face. It'd rain any minute now. I wished I had brought an umbrella because, whatever the Shadows were, I wanted to see them clearly, not half-blinded by water pouring down my front.

Cass left only minutes ago, but it already felt like hours. I wiped my damp hands on my coat and peered around, listening for any sounds. Were the Shadows nearby? How long would it take before they arrived?

Devon's tall figure, appearing out of nowhere inches away from my face, made me jump. I balled my fists. A shriek remained trapped in my throat.

"Amber." He held out his hand as if to shake mine through the thick metal rods. I regarded it, unsure whether to squeeze my hand through the rods and touch him. Then decided against it in case he had some sort of magical power up his sleeve. Devon pulled back. If he was annoyed he didn't show it. "I understand your hesitation. You've probably heard nothing but bad things about our kind."

I raised my chin, the memory of the failed kidnapping still vivid in my mind. "I haven't heard much about you. My opinion of you is based on a previous encounter."

Devon's eyes locked with mine, the black of his iris shining unnaturally bright. "Fair enough. I must apologize for my brother. He's too heated for his own good. He acted without our queen's consent. He's received his punishment already."

There was something strange about Devon that I couldn't quite pinpoint. He was too charming, too perfect, and I didn't believe a word he said. I curled my lips into a fake smile, hoping it looked genuine enough. "I've a proposition to make. You want my gift, and I'm willing to share it with you if you do something for me in return."

He didn't hesitate with an answer. "If it's in my power to grant your wish, I'll do it." No blink, no sudden movement, nothing. He was plain eerie. And probably lying.

I quivered inwardly as I forced myself to meet that liquid black gaze. "Aidan's disappeared. We suspect Layla's locked him up. I know you can help free him."

Thunder roared across the sky, making me flinch. Dark clouds gathered in the distance. Devon's face remained expressionless. "With a boss like that, he needs to consider a career change. He used to be her favorite pet. What did he do to piss her off?"

"It doesn't matter." I squeezed a hard edge into my voice. "Are you going to help or do I need to take my

156

proposition to someone else?" I crossed my fingers in my pockets, praying he'd take the bite. Truth was, I had no idea who else to contact. The Shadows were my only option.

"We'll do it." A smile crossed Devon's lips, disappearing just as quickly. "He'll be free by tonight, but you'll have to come with us."

I shook my head. "No way. I'm not going anywhere with you. I'd rather be struck by lightning. Just take the gift out of my mind. Put your hand on my forehead and just zap it out, or whatever you do." I shuddered at the thought.

Devon hesitated. "It's not that simple."

I didn't like the sound of that. Were they going to whisk me off to some laboratory and have a mad scientist cut it out of me, turning me into a modern-day Frankenstein? A chill ran down my spine. Oh, Dallas, messing up as usual. If I died, I silently vowed to come back and haunt my brother for the rest of his life. I gripped the metal bars as I inched closer. "So how does it work then?"

Devon shook his head. "It's complicated, but I can assure you that you won't be harmed. Why don't you open the gate and come out so we can talk face to face?"

How stupid did he think I was? "Trust is earned."

He raised his brows. "It goes both ways, sister."

Tiny drops of rain started to pour again, soaking my clothes. Devon winced as though the water hurt him. I pushed my wet hair out of my face and yelled over the howl of the wind, "Are you okay out here with the rain?"

He smirked. "Do you think I'm going to melt?"

"I just thought because you're a Shadow, you might need sunlight and—" I waved my hand about "—you don't look comfortable. Never mind. So you'll just take the gift and let me live?"

He nodded.

"Promise?"

"I give you my word."

What was it worth? "One more thing. Is it going to hurt? I'm not so good at dealing with pain."

"I assure you there's no pain involved." He stretched out both hands, waiting for me to grasp them. I didn't. He squinted and pulled back his arms. "So you're ready to give up your own life to save Aidan?"

"It's all my fault. I'd do anything to set it straight," I said.

"But you hardly know him." He opened his mouth to say something else, then closed it again.

"What?" I asked, irritated.

He peered at me intently. "You know he's a vampire, right?"

Did no one but me miss that tiny detail? Rain poured down on me as realization kicked in. I had fallen for a real vampire, like the ones in myths and legends. It was crazy but true. I could finally understand how a person could give up everything for someone else, even though I couldn't imagine doing this for Cameron. Then it struck me—Aidan and I shared a connection deeper than anything I ever felt with any of my exes. Hopefully he felt the same way. Too bad I might never find out.

"Your gift will help our entire civilization."

I rolled my eyes. "I get it. You're helping your race, even if it means killing me."

"Last chance to back out. Are you sure Aidan's worth never seeing your family again?"

Why wasn't he assuring me I wouldn't literally die? I faltered as the downpour intensified. Aidan meant everything to me. I'd make the ultimate sacrifice and give up my former life. Staring into Devon's eyes I said, "He is worth it."

Devon nodded. "To show our gratitude we'll see to it that your family's taken care of financially."

Well, at least my parents and Dallas would never have to worry about money again. "Deal. But you'll have to show me proof that you've kept your word before I keep mine."

Fishing in his pocket, he retrieved a tiny silver phone and placed it on the damp ground, then pushed it toward me, careful not to touch the iron bars. "Keep it switched on. The moment you hear his voice, you leave Aidan's premises and walk down this road—" he pointed at the street behind him "—otherwise he's dead."

When I nodded, Devon turned and disappeared between the trees. I picked up the phone and put it in my pocket. My old phone vibrated. I peered at the unknown caller ID, deciding I might as well answer.

"I've been trying to reach you for ages. You should switch that thing on more often," Dallas said. He didn't sound his usual easy-going self.

"I told you I've no reception." I breathed in, annoyance washing over me. "You're such an idiot. Do you have any idea what mess I'm in because of your stupid plan?"

"Listen, I have bad news and bad news. You pick."

Yet more worries. Could my life get any worse? "Just tell me."

"The diamonds are worth nothing." He paused. When I didn't reply, he said, "You still there?"

My heart fluttered in my chest. If they were worthless, maybe Dallas didn't sell them just yet. "Yeah, I am. Do you still have them?"

He hesitated. "Yeah, that's the other bad news. I couldn't sell them, not even on eBay. They're not the real deal."

"Are you telling me the diamonds are fakes like cubic zirconia?"

"Not just the diamonds, the other gemstones as well. What a waste of time, huh?" He laughed. "But there's more, sis. There's tiny symbols etched on every stone. You can only see them under ultraviolet rays. Pretty freaky, eh? So I had them inspected by a friend of mine who runs a lab."

Groaning, I kicked a nearby pile of leaves. "A lab? Oh, Dallas, please don't get us mixed up in drugs."

"Don't be silly. A science lab, obviously. Now, get this. Hold your breath and sit down." He was into show and drama big time. All eyes on Dallas.

"Just spit it out," I said, impatiently.

"Apparently, they're unknown minerals. In other words, they're not from this world. Whoa! Is that wild or what? Can you even begin to imagine?"

I blew out a breath. "Believe it or not, somehow I can."

"Now I do have some good news. I was going to ditch them when I found somebody who's interested. My buddy's coming by today to pick them up and take them to a paranormal investigator. He says maybe they've something to do with the world of vampires and

160

werewolves. He matched up the symbols with some legend he found in some old book. Says there's a race every five hundred years or something. What a load of crap, huh?"

Werewolves? Were they real as well? Nervously, I peered to the nearby bushes, wrapping my soaking wet coat tighter around me as if it could protect me. "No," I yelled. "Don't you dare give him the stones! Bring them back. Bring them back right now."

"What for?"

"I know who the owner is, and she's quite fond of her stones. Do you hear me? She's *very* sentimental. So bring them back."

"No way. What if she traces their disappearance back to us?"

I smirked. "Bit too late for that. Just do me a favor and do as I say. I might not be here when you arrive, so wrap them in something and leave them in the kitchen. And Dallas, don't you bail out on me, or I swear I'll kill you."

"What if—"

"No ifs. This is serious," I yelled, cutting him off.

"Okay." Dallas took a deep breath. "You can count on me."

Yeah. Heard that one before. "Hey, before you leave, I just want you to know that no matter how mad I get at you, I'll always love you."

"Even when you kill me?" He laughed, taking none of this seriously. "I love you too, sis."

"You mean the world to me. I wish I could give you a big hug." I tried to hide the quiver in my voice. "Take care, Dallas."

"Are you crying? Don't get all mushy on me. I'll be there as soon as I can."

After hanging up, I hurried back inside. Dallas would arrive soon with the stones. Clare said returning them wouldn't change anything, but I could at least hope. It was a waiting game now. Aidan would be safe soon, and then I'd leave the gemstones up to him. I changed my clothes and tossed the wet ones into the tumble dryer, then dropped on the sofa and stared at the walls, unable to shake off the feeling that I didn't get the best deal. In fact, I wondered whether I got a good deal at all.

Chapter 15 - Aidan

Several times, I woke up to find new succubi probing my cuts and wounds. The pain was so intense I hung on to my consciousness like a shipwrecked person onto hope that rescue was near. But I knew my rescue might not come for a while. How long did I have before the succubi's poison coursed through my body, molding my will to theirs until I longed for what they had to offer? I had no idea and no wish to find out either. Where was Kieran when I needed him? The corners of my mouth cracked as I tried to call him even though I knew words were useless. My powers were weakening and any telepathic bond between us would be lost in the depths of Layla's magic-infused dungeons anyway.

Something moved before my eyes. I focused my gaze as the chains cut deeper into my flesh. A pang of pain rippled through my body and I let out a cry, hating myself for nourishing Layla's self-satisfaction on which she thrived. The flicker of a girl appeared; a tiny shape with huge, brown eyes I would never mistake, not even in death.

Amber inched nearer, almost touching me. The succubi shifted, but didn't notice her. Was I dreaming, imagining my mate? I clenched my teeth, suppressing another cry. No need to worry her. Amber stood in front of me now, a deep frown set between her brows, the succubi's flowing dresses brushing against her jeans. I opened my mouth to speak out a warning. *Don't come nearer. Don't let them touch you.* "Amber." My voice was barely louder than a whisper, but if she could see me, she'd sense the warning.

The succubi hissed, pushing their nails into my flesh. A new wave of darkness washed over me, and with a last glance at the one I loved, I let go, eagerly falling into oblivion that'd gift me a few merciful moments of peace.

***

I lifted my head, waiting for that vengeful probing to come back with full force. When it didn't, I opened my eyes warily. Had Layla tired of me? No chance in hell. Did she come up with a new plan to force me into submission? That was a more likely explanation.

Through my hazy gaze I first noticed the succubi cowering near the opposite wall. The soft light of a torch highlighted the fear in their pale faces. What scared them? The chain around my neck cut deep as I tilted my head to the side, gnashing my teeth against the blinding pain, and peered at Devon's face.

"Hold still." Devon's eyes—two dark pools that seemed to suck in the light—glazed over. The chains loosened a bit, but not enough for me to squeeze through. Devon shook his head.

Two Shadows appeared beside him, a slender girl and a tall, blond guy. I turned my head away, not out of respect but to avoid disrupting their concentration, so they could continue their voodoo stuff, or whatever they were doing.

Meeting Shadows here was the last thing I expected. I was dying to know why my life-long enemies were helping, but I'd save my questions for later. Someone had asked them for help, and I had a strong feeling it wasn't my dear brother. I groaned at the thought of Kieran storming the Lore court this very moment, falling into Layla's trap while Amber saved my life. The chains came loose and the pain ebbed to a bearable level.

"Get him out now. I can't hold them in place," Devon hissed.

"I'm not touching a vampire," the girl screeched in a Scottish accent, like I carried some contagious disease. "Especially not a bloody one. That's disgusting."

While their banter continued, I forced my body into motion, squeezing through the maze of chains now floating mere inches away from my wounds. Several times I came too close, the sudden pain leaving me on the brink of unconsciousness. My legs gave way beneath me, and I dropped to the floor moments before Devon's concentration slackened and the chains tightened in mid-air, holding onto something that wasn't really there.

I rose to my feet and turned to face my enemies. "Thank you."

Devon scowled. "Don't thank me, thank Amber."

165

I glared after him as he turned to leave. What kind of deal had she made with them? Did she even know what she was getting herself into?

"Let's get outta here," the blond guy said.

The succubi hissed yet didn't move. I had no idea how the Shadows kept Layla's slaves complacent, but it seemed to work. With a wary glance back, I followed Devon out of the dungeon through narrow catacombs with torches on the walls, wondering how the Shadow knew the way so well. The stale air smelled of earth and decay, of burned flesh and body fluids. If the Shadows were bothered, they didn't show it. My head throbbed badly. I swallowed down the bile in my throat, and kept walking.

A fresh breeze caressed my skin. Devon quickened his pace until we reached an opening and stepped out into the night. I realized we were out of London, surrounded by trees and grass. The girl retrieved a silver phone from her pocket and held it to my ear. "Tell her we've kept our part of the bargain and that you're okay."

At the second ring, Amber's unsteady voice answered, "Aidan?"

"Yes, I'm okay. They broke me out. I'm coming home." I barely had time to inhale before the girl snatched the phone away.

"Our deed's done," Devon said, but he didn't leave. "You're lucky we're not here to kill you."

The girl tapped her booted foot on the ground as she peered at me, hate pouring from her unnaturally black eyes. The phone in her hands vibrated. A brief nod toward Devon and the Shadows sprinted into the night without another word.

I turned to inspect my surroundings. To my right, railway tracks stretched into the woods; to the left were concrete buildings surrounded by high fences. Dogs barked somewhere in the distance. I had no idea where I was, but there was no doubt I had higher chances surviving here than in Layla's dungeon.

A peek at the black sky told me it was before midnight. I had to find a way to warn Kieran of Amber's pact with the Shadows—if it wasn't too late already. Ignoring the pain in my thighs, I walked to the buildings. They looked like warehouses locked for the night, but I gathered somewhere in there had to be a phone. The dogs threw themselves against the fence, crazed by the smell of blood. I hesitated for a moment, then climbed up the fence as fast as I could and jumped to the other side, landing on my feet. Canines pierced my flesh, tearing through the muscles and tendons in my legs. Baring my fangs, I spun and growled at them, ready to fight for my life.

Chapter 16

Clare and the others were gathered in the library, plotting Aidan's rescue, going through possibilities over and over again as though they had all time in the world. I excused myself and slipped away before anyone noticed my jumpiness. One mistake, and all could be lost. Devon's warning echoed inside my mind. *He'll be dead.* I shook my head, shaking off the thought at the same time. No, Aidan wouldn't die. Not if I played by the Shadows' rules.

The first time the phone vibrated on the washing machine, I held my breath. Could they have done it already? The phone vibrated a second time and I pressed the response button. Lifting it slowly to my ear, I whispered, "Aidan?" It wasn't a question; it was hope coming from somewhere within my heart—the part that no other but he could ever fill.

"Yes, I'm okay. They broke me out. I'm coming home," Aidan said.

I wanted to ask him what happened, when he'd be back. Hundreds of thoughts raced through my mind, relief washing over me like a warm rain shower in the summer, pleasant yet leaving me yearning for more. But in those few moments, my throat felt dry, unable to form a word. And then the line went dead.

They had fulfilled their part of the bargain, and now it was time to fulfill mine. I'd spent the entire day pondering over my options. Run out of the house as fast as I could, praying the vampires wouldn't catch me, or pretend to have business outside and hope they'd be too busy to question my word?

Buttoning up my coat, I snuck up the basement stairs. The door to the library clicked shut as though they tried to prevent me from spying. I exhaled with relief and quickened my pace before anyone changed their mind and decided to pay me attention after all. I reached the telephone in the hall when the door to the library opened again and Kieran peered out. "Need something, Amber?"

Of course someone had to spot me. Trust my crappy luck. My heart skipped a beat. If he didn't go back inside soon, the Shadows might kill Aidan after all. I regarded Kieran. I'd do anything to get rid of him, even knocking a vase over his head. "No, you just keep polishing your fangs or whatever you guys do in there."

"Vampire jokes. Cute. Didn't see that one coming." He hesitated in the doorway.

Oh, come on. I didn't have time for his nonsense. "Listen, I know I'm great company, but I need to get a sandwich and then call my parents. Shouldn't you be working on a plan to rescue Aidan anyway?"

He nodded. "You know where I am if you need me."

I waited until he closed the door, and then bolted through the front entrance because it was the fastest way to the gate. As soon as I stepped out a gust of wind blew my hair in my face, whipping it against my skin. The air smelled damp. The night was pitch black, the moon hiding behind a veil of heavy clouds. My mind was on full alert, my ears strained to hear any sound that might break the deep silence. The house remained as quiet as the night.

For one moment, I considered flipping my phone open to see where I stepped, but I didn't dare in case someone saw the light. Throwing a last glance over my shoulder, I dashed for the gate. Several times I stumbled when the heels of my boots dug into the gravel. The moment I squeezed through the gate I knew the Shadows were waiting though they didn't show themselves until I walked several feet down the road.

A girl, tall with long dark hair, stepped in the way and clutched my arm as though to guide me toward the headlights in the distance. I didn't miss that fleeting look to the side that told me the girl was afraid of what might happen if her mission failed. Whatever the Shadows wanted with someone who could see ghosts, it probably went beyond a mortal's interest in the afterlife.

As soon as we reached the black SUV, someone held the door open, then shone a flashlight in my face. I squinted against the glaring brightness mumbling, "Yes, you're kidnapping the right person."

I jumped onto the backseat. The girl sat next to me, smiling as if relieved that I was cooperating. Did I have a choice? I grimaced and turned away, my heart racing in my chest as the car sped off. The driver—all curly hair and thick eyebrows overshadowing black eyes—peered at me through the rear-view mirror. Should I keep quiet and obliging for my own sake? Nah, that wasn't my style. Besides, if they wanted to kill me they'd have done so already.

"Hi there. You probably don't know me yet. I'm Amber, in the flesh. Proud winner of the coveted prize and a big bag of worthless jewels. I see I've won a free trip to Shadow World." I paused, my heart drumming in my ears. "Given my worth, I hope you're accommodating me in a five star hotel."

"Congratulations on winning the gift. You outsmarted everyone," the girl said.

I smiled. "No applause, please. But I'm glad to see you're not a sore loser."

"It's so nice of you to share," the girl said. She sounded as though she believed every word. Was she serious?

"Like I have a choice. But yeah, I'll play nice." The race was played out every five hundred years. Clearly, I was born in the wrong century. "So, what happened to the limo, caviar and wine? I like to travel in style when I win a trip. This vacation blows already."

"Shut up," the driver said. The girl shot me an apologetic look. Who did the idiot think he was? No one told *me* to shut up.

"So, guys, do you want me to try and summon up a spirit, or something?" I waved my shaking hands in the air.

171

"Who shall I conjure? Elvis? Marilyn Monroe? You just name it."

"No," the driver said.

A scaredy cat? I smiled. "If there is any spirit from the light who wishes to communicate, please make yourself known." No one answered. I touched my forehead. "Wait. I can sense a presence. Yes, it's strong. Something with P." I peered at the driver. "Anyone having an aunt going by the name of Petunia or Prudence?"

"Angel, shut her up now, or else I will," the driver hissed toward the girl.

"Do it and I'll summon Bruce Lee," I said.

"Just keep quiet for a change," the driver said.

"See what you did?" I snapped. "You broke my concentration and now the link has been severed. Now your aunty will never know that you're okay."

The girl leaned into me whispering, "I'm Angel, by the way. My mother had a very strange sense of humor."

Whoa, they sent someone called Angel to help me feel comfortable? Angel—as in a winged white being greeting one in the afterlife? Now I was scared.

"This isn't the place for this," Angel continued.

"You're right. We lack the right ambiance. Just roll down the windows so we get the wind effect. Maybe one of you has a lighter that could replace the candles. And I'll start calling our friends." I held up a hand. "Wait. The spirits are talking again. I need what?"

Angel cocked her head and whispered, "Are they talking to you *now*?"

I closed my eyes and shook my head. "Shush. They're asking very clearly for specific items." I started to rock back and forth, barely able to suppress my laughter. "Sorry spirits, go on. This ritual can't be performed without what? Ghastly jewelry? That's an easy fix. The driver's wearing the most hideous ring I've ever seen in my life. Very Asian meets gangsta rap. And what else? Talk to me, spirits." I rocked harder. "You need the medium to wear a bright scarf, big hoop earrings and gypsy clothes. Well, okay then. I'll be in touch soon. Thanks for joining us and go in peace." I opened my eyes and regarded Angel. "They want a crystal ball, too."

The driver shook his head. "Out of all people, how did *you* end up with the prize?"

I leaned back and smiled at the impressed girl, proud of my performance. It might not be worth an Oscar, but one day I'd give Whoopi a run for her money. "Talking to the dead drains a girl. Anyone got a sandwich?"

"What's it like talking to the dead as well as dating them?" the driver asked, sarcastically.

A low blow from a snarky little man. He just had to drive the point home that Aidan was dead. I shrugged and glared back at him. "Aidan's cuter in death than you'll ever be in life." He pressed his mouth tight. Angel giggled.

We drove in silence for a while, before I asked, "Where're we going?" The driver's glare hardened. Angel gave my hand a reassuring squeeze. It would've been more comforting to know where we were headed.

The moon had risen to a large crescent in the sky. I leaned my head against the window and peered out at the passing trees. We seemed to travel north along the shoreline. Every few minutes, we passed a house or two, barely larger a cottage with whitewashed walls. After a while, all I could see was vegetation stretching on forever.

The car took a sharp right onto unpaved terrain, then halted in front of high gates. The driver signaled with the headlights and the gates opened to let us through. The street wound several times before the driver stopped and killed the engine. Opening the door, Angel motioned me to follow.

The wind whirled the fallen leaves on the ground. The taillights threw a soft glow on high stonewalls that seemed to melt with the mountain behind. Angel seemed to know her way around as she brushed her hand over the weathered walls as though looking for a bolt or catch that might open a door.

I sighed, irritated. "You know when I think of prizes I imagine lying on the beach, not hiking through the woods at night. That's Clare's thing." Angel laughed, but didn't reply.

I rubbed my hands to fight the cold slowly creeping into my bones. Peering into the impenetrable shadows of the trees and thickets made me uneasy. Whatever this place was, it didn't look like anyone would ever find me. Or my body. Unwilling to go on, I peeled my eyes off the wall and focused on Angel. She was a few inches taller than me, and dressed in skinny jeans and a thin jacket. Her jet-black hair was tied in a ponytail; her features were hidden in the dark.

The sound of a rusty bolt scraping on metal echoed from somewhere inside. A moment later, an opening appeared in the stone.

"You sure took your time," Angel said as she gestured me to follow her inside the mountain. A male voice snorted from behind the door.

I peered at his obscured face, trying to make out his features. "You know I could conjure up your uncle Jack or Grandpa Henry."

The guard snorted again.

"Okay then. Your loss." I shrugged. If I could only engage them in some small talk, I might be able to persuade them to let me go. But these people had no sense of humor at all. "Anyone up for a good ghost story?"

"Come on. We need to get going," Angel whispered, tugging at my sleeve.

The narrow opening stretched into a tunnel leading deep inside the mountain. Angel guided me forward, warning me before every turn. Low whispers and chants echoed through the corridors. As soon as my eyes adjusted, I could make out details: a low ceiling, what looked like light bulbs on the walls that no one bothered to switch on, and other narrow passages that crossed ours. Realizing we were in a maze, created to make escape impossible, I shuddered. Even if I managed to get rid of Angel, I'd never find my way out.

We took a few more turns until we reached a corridor with several doors. Angel opened one and showed me into a candlelit room.

"Candles are nice. We could have a séance right here, right now," I said, my heart beating a million miles an hour. "I can summon some buddies for a big party."

"Honestly, all this talk about dead people's creeping me out," Angel said.

I glared at her. "You kidnapped me because of this ability."

"Not me. The elders." Angel regarded me curiously. I had a hunch she wanted to ask something but didn't dare.

Maybe befriending her wasn't such a bad idea because I sure could do with an ally.

"What am I doing here?" I asked.

"The elders plan on using you as a medium."

"What?" I laughed. "I'm no Whoopi Goldberg. I was just playing around in the car when actually I've no idea how this gift works. I never thought of myself as the wacky person leading a séance to communicate with spirits in a dark room, candles flickering and all." How could I explain to her that I didn't even believe in ghosts until I saw the lady with the buggy crossing the street? The idea of talking to dead people freaked me out big time. What if they possessed me and I started to do unholy things? I watched *The Exorcist* on more than one occasion. A spinning head, a creepy voice, and green vomit just weren't my thing. Aidan wouldn't find that particularly attractive.

"You can rest here before the meeting tomorrow morning," Angel said.

A meeting, or raising some zombies? An uneasy feeling settled in the pit of my stomach. I laughed, trying to hide my fear. "Oh, goodie! Muffins and coffee, I hope."

Angel threw me an apologetic look and pointed at the narrow bed near a tiny window. "These are the guest quarters. You'll probably get a nicer room once the elders find you worthy of it."

I shivered. "Don't know what good my gift's going to be when you find me turned into a big ice cube in the morning."

Angel smiled. "We have chisels."

"Any chance of getting a complementary hot cup of tea, coffee, hot chocolate?" I rolled my eyes. "Let me guess, once I'm worthy. What a rip-off."

"There's a pitcher of water on the table. I'll see you in the morning." Angel left, locking up behind her.

A musty smell hung in the air. I scanned the room. This sure wasn't the *Four Seasons*. Heck, it wasn't even a youth hostel. No mints on the pillows. No flowers to spruce up the place. No fancy wallpaper to give it a homey feeling. And worst of all—it was tiny, not to mention freezing. "Couldn't spring for heat?" I mumbled as I wrapped my coat tighter around me.

And where was the bathroom? Even jail cells have toilets. Guest quarters? More like the cell on a mental ward. The only things missing were the metal bars on the window. I hoped on the bed to inspect the window. It was too small to squeeze through, but I could see the woods stretching in the distance. We must've trekked inside the mountain. Even if I had a flashlight I doubted I'd find my way out of this place, not least because my sense of orientation sucked. Back in London I still got on the wrong train half of the time, even with a map.

In spite of the cold, I shrugged out of my coat and kicked my boots off, then jumped under the covers, ready to act against my better judgment and get some sleep. Aidan's image appeared before my eyes. He looked worried but safe. That surely made my current predicament worth it. Eager to get some sleep, I closed my eyes, but I couldn't stop fretting for a long time, tossing and turning as I kept asking myself the same question: how would Aidan be able to find me here?

***

Dim light seeped through the muddy window. The sun stood high on the horizon, but the morning rays were almost as chilly as the wind. The heavy blanket felt like cold iron, squeezing the air out of my lungs. If I didn't know any better, I'd swear I was in Antarctica, and penguins and polar bears would be peeking through the door any minute now. The memories of my giant, fancy room, lavender sheets and warm bedspread hit me full force. Talk about going from riches to rags. Okay, technically it was Aidan's riches, but still. I wished he were here to snuggle up and keep me warm. But he wasn't. Taking a deep breath, I kicked the sheets aside.

A narrow strip of light fell on my black coat, which I had draped over the back of a chair after my arrival. I squeezed into it, buttoning it up at the front, and tried the door. It was unlocked. The girl from last night—Angel—dressed in tight jeans and a thick, cream cardigan, black hair slicked back in a ponytail, leaned against the wall. As soon as she noticed me, she smiled. "Slept well?" In the glaring brightness, I realized she looked barely older than fifteen.

I nodded and examined the corridor to both sides. My spirits dropped. The air smelled stale. The passages looked all the same: grey, smooth stone everywhere with naked light bulbs hanging from the ceiling. Nothing stood out. Even if Aidan managed to find this place, he'd never find his way out once he entered.

Angel followed my gaze. "If I were you I wouldn't try running. You wouldn't get far." She sounded factual, as if it wasn't the first time she dished out this advice.

I raised my brows. "Really? Why's that?"

"The perimeter's heavily guarded." Hesitation crossed Angel's face. She clearly kept something to herself.

"It's not just Shadows guarding this place, is it?"

Angel shook her head, avoiding my gaze. "You got that part right. Come on. We'll get you breakfast before the meeting." I nodded, sensing she wouldn't tell me more, even if I insisted.

We passed several stone corridors until we reached an open space with whitewashed walls, tables and chairs, and huge flower arrangements lined up along one wall. Several Shadows stopped their chatter and peered at us, brows drawn, the plates in front of them now forgotten. My stomach churned at the aroma of toast and freshly brewed coffee.

"I've saved us the best view in the house. Why don't you take a seat?" Angel pointed at a table near a high bay window with spectacular scenery of the woods below. "I'll get us breakfast."

We were hundreds of feet above ground, but how could anyone build a place like this inside a mountain? I sat down and scanned the room. Ivy grew out of the cracked sandstone walls. Several pillars of dark marble supported the high ceiling. A fresco painting representing a sundial hung from one of the walls next to hip-high stone gargoyles covered in ancient symbols, pictures of battles and dragons. I realized I had been kidnapped by a civilization that had been kept secret for thousands of years. My fate was sealed. Where was Aidan when I needed him the most? Probably getting a good day's sleep in his comfortable vampire dungeon.

Angel returned carrying a breakfast tray with croissants, butter and cream, then disappeared again to get the coffee. "Hope it's what you usually have," she said as soon as she sat down, pushing a plate across the table.

"Is this stuff safe to eat? No poison in that jelly?" I took a tentative sip of my coffee, eyeing the croissant carefully.

"Would you like to switch trays?" Angel pushed her plate toward me.

I shook my head. "No, thanks. Sorry, my nerves are on edge."

Angel took a bite of her bagel and pointed at the mountain below. "Beautiful, isn't it? Do you like it here?"

Was she kidding? "I froze all night. My back's killing me. I want home, and I'm scared to death. But I guess the view makes it all worth it."

"You're funny," Angel said.

Smiling, I took another sip of my coffee. "I wasn't actually joking, but yeah, it's nice. It's very different from anything I've ever seen."

"Living with the same people loses its appeal after a while." Her voice quivered. "It's strange."

We fell silent as a tall, black-eyed guy approached to ignite a fire inside the marble fireplace. The flames started to leap greedily at the surrounding glass, gnawing at the logs. I resumed the conversation. "You don't seem happy."

Angel laughed. "What? What makes you say that? I had no one before coming here and am grateful for everything." She leaned forward and peeked over her shoulder, lowering her voice. "I know you're not like them. You're mortal."

"What's their deal?"

Angel shook her head, her huge, brown eyes filled with something I couldn't quite pinpoint. "I can't tell anyone. But I understand the fear you must be going through because I was in a similar situation years ago."

"You're mortal too?" I whispered, suddenly noticing the blue vein on her neck, and the freckles on her nose. She didn't have the same blemish-free skin like the others. There was no mistake: She was human.

Angel nodded. "Yes, just like you, minus the fancy abilities."

"You must've been convicted of, I don't know, robbing the local candy store. What did you get, twenty years to life?"

"I was chosen to live among them. I wasn't given an alternative because my—" Angel hesitated "—friend lives here." So, the girl hooked up with a Shadow. That was even freakier than hooking up with a vampire.

"Maybe we could break out of this joint together," I said. Even though I infused a cheerful tone into my voice, I hoped she'd take my suggestion seriously.

"You've laid eyes on a city only a handful of humans has ever seen in thousands of years. You're not going anywhere." Angel leaned forward, whispering, "I wish I could help you, but I can't let you escape." She drained the last of her cup and pointed at my untouched croissant. "You should eat up. It may take a while before anyone thinks of feeding you again."

"Even prisoners get bread and water."

"Not here. These people hardly ever eat. In a few days, they'll have forgotten you're mortal. You're stuck here with them forever."

I figured out that much, but the possibility of not seeing Dallas, my parents or Aidan again wasn't an appealing one. "I did all of this for somebody I truly care about. His name's Aidan." I felt myself blush just saying his name.

"I know all about him. Devon filled me in before I picked you up. Aidan must think you're a hero."

I smiled. "Or an idiot."

"So how long have you been into vampires?"

"What?" I snorted. "It's not like that. Not at all. I didn't go out one day looking for one, like some groupie. Aidan just kind of popped into my life. And I had to screw everything up by taking the jewels and getting this stupid prize. I messed up big time."

Angel's eyes sparkled with amusement. "Was it love at first bite?"

I had a feeling I'd get that joke a lot. "He doesn't bite. Before you ask, he doesn't sleep in a coffin either. And yes, he can be a pain in the neck. No pun intended."

Angel laughed. "You're pretty cool. I like you. I haven't been around a real mortal in years. I miss it."

"Thank you." I nodded, slightly uncomfortable. How long had the girl been living in captivity? "No one's ever said that to me before."

"Is it wicked of me to feel happy that you're here? I don't want to be alone."

I gave Angel's hand a squeeze. "No, it's not. And once rescue arrives, we'll take you with us."

Angel lowered her gaze, but she couldn't hide the scowl crossing her features. "No, you won't. I'd die if I ever left. I'd rather stay here because the Shadows aren't what everyone makes them out to be. They're kind and generous and our queen's—" She broke off. I regarded her for a moment, searching for signs that betrayed she was lying. I didn't find any.

We finished our breakfast in silence, then got up to leave for what Angel called the meeting while a tall guy started to clean our table. My heart pounded in my chest as we walked past another open space with hooded people cowered on the naked ground, murmuring the strange chants I'd heard the night before.

"Make sure you bow when you enter, and don't lift your gaze unless the elders tell you so." Angel continued her nervous chatter as she grabbed me in a hug and knocked on a door. Taking a deep breath, she opened the door and stepped to the side to let me through.

Chapter 17 - Aidan

The alpha dog bore his canines into my flesh, ripping through clothes and skin like knives. I bit down on the pain and pushed myself up from my cowering position, then kicked at the aggressive hound, knowing that if the alpha fled it'd unsettle the others. Under normal circumstances, they'd be no match for me, but the hounds were crazed by the scent of blood and my strength was weakened to the point where it'd take me weeks to recover. This was one fight I didn't want to have.

The snarls continued as I kicked the alpha again, this time in the gut, sending the whimpering hound flying against the wall. The others barked but kept their distance, unsure whether to attack or not. I snarled and made a dash for the warehouses, the muscles in my legs burning. With the dogs on my trail, I reached the first depot and snapped the lock off, then entered and pulled the door shut behind me. For a moment I felt so weak I considered feeding from the hounds, but animal blood would make me sick for days. I wasn't that desperate just yet.

Wood pallets, boxes and dusty crates lined the walls. Computer screens whirred in the office to my right. In a few strides, I reached the far side and kicked the locked door open. An old-fashioned PC screen covered half of the small desk. Buried beneath invoices and orders I found a phone and dialed the mansion's landline number. It rang a few times before Clare answered.

"Where's Amber?" I roared.

"Aidan?" Clare sounded surprised. "I thought you were—"

I cut her off. "Get Amber now!"

"Sure. She's upstairs. Wait a second." Clare put down the receiver.

The dogs outside calmed down, probably forgetting about me. I knew I had to venture out eventually to find a sleeping place for the day since I was too weak to teleport, but there were still a few hours until sunrise. First, I'd make sure my mate was safe, guarded by the two immortals I trusted the most, and then I'd start thinking about my own wellbeing.

I heard static on the line. A moment later, Clare was back on. "Aidan, are you still there?" She sounded agitated, frightened even. I knew instantly Amber was gone.

"Where is she?" I clenched my jaw, teeth gnashing.

"I've no idea. She was upstairs half an hour ago. I—" Clare's voice broke.

"I told you to watch her." Anger rose inside me. For a moment I saw Amber's injured body wandering aimlessly

185

in the semi-darkness of the otherworld, searching for what we all wanted. Once there, she'd never find her way back. My blood raced through my veins, the wish to smash something grew stronger than my self-control.

Muffled voices echoed in the background before Kieran said, "Where are you?"

My head throbbed with rage that threatened to choke me. I had to tamp it down for my mate's sake. I blinked, pushing my anger aside. The Shadows wouldn't act in haste. Amber needed preparation and training before she could fully use her new ability. I gathered I still had at least a few days. But since I was forced to sleep during daylight, time wasn't my friend right now.

Cradling the phone between my shoulder and ear, I flicked through the papers until I found an invoice with an address. I compared it with the other invoices to make sure I had the right place.

"All right, stay there," Kieran said before the line disconnected.

I put down the phone and lowered my forehead onto the desk, letting my fears take hold of me for a moment. What was the worst scenario? That the Shadows had taken Amber to their cursed place so I'd never find her. But Rebecca had found a way in, and if she could do it, then so would I.

If the Shadows hadn't broken our agreement, I'd have kept my word to lead Amber on the threshold of death, let her find the damn book and then return it to the elders. My mate was worth more than the ritual I once desperately wanted, but now I vowed to find Amber and kill one

Shadow after another. The war had been going on for too long; it was time to win it.

Less than ten minutes later, the dogs barked again. The door opened and Kieran's voice called out, "Hey, bro, you in here?"

"I can't believe the pests ripped my favorite purse to shreds," Clare said.

Forcing my aching body to move, I straightened and stood. "Was it the red one with the fancy sequins?" I asked. Clare nodded as she walked over. I grinned. "Cheers to that because I never liked the thing."

Clare slapped my back. "You look horrible."

"Sorry for the delay. This place didn't even show up on Google maps." Kieran shot me a crooked smile. "You should've told me about the poor puppies out there. I could've brought a few bones." His gaze wandered over my shredded clothes and dried blood, hesitating. He kept his thoughts to himself even though his expression betrayed his guilt.

I peered at the huge rip in my brother's jeans, caked blood covering his ankle. "Puppies, my butt."

"Okay, so he got the upper hand, but only for a few seconds," Kieran said.

"A few seconds?" Clare laughed. "You two were battling it out like sumo wrestlers. I didn't know who wanted the championship belt more, you or him."

"It wasn't wrestling, Clare. He surprised me. Just attacked my ankle out of nowhere and I lost my balance."

"Either that, or you two were making out. I swear I saw lots of tongue." She nodded at me, guilt glinting in her eyes. Their teasing was just a means to cheer me up.

"I could've easily smashed the poor pup into smithereens if I wanted to," Kieran said. "But I'm not like that. You know I have a special touch with animals."

Clare winked. "You sure do."

Kieran turned to me. "Point is, the pup bit my ankle before I made friends with him. Maybe I deserved it for screwing up big time. I'm so sorry, bro."

"We both are," Clare said, grabbing my hands.

"We'll talk about this later," I said. "Given how much you've always wanted a pet, I'm glad you enjoyed your cuddle, bro."

Kieran laughed. "You look like you had your fair share of those, too. Had fun with the succubi?"

"Save the wise cracks for home." Clare elbowed him in the ribs, regarding me. "I was worried sick about you."

Kieran placed an arm over my shoulder and squeezed. "Ready for the ride of your life?" Without a warning, he teleported. The next moment, we were in my library. Kieran let go and dropped onto the sofa, crossing his long legs, a smile playing on his lips.

"What's so funny?" My head reeled, bile rose in my throat. Teleporting wasn't my favorite means of transportation anyway, but weakened from the lack of blood I abhorred its side effects even more because they played havoc with my body.

"I've never seen you so wound up because of a girl, that's all," Kieran said. "It's hilarious to watch you make a fool of yourself."

"I'm not wound up," I roared. I wasn't, was I?

"Whoa, take it easy, bro." Kieran smirked. "How much can a mortal handle anyway? Maybe she's had enough of the whole vampire stuff. I wouldn't blame her."

Clare nodded. "Maybe she's with her family. Let's face it. We drink blood. We sleep during the day. We're dead. And worst of all—we're dysfunctional."

"Not to mention she was almost kidnapped by a Shadow," Kieran said. "I bet she's totally freaked out and headed straight for the border."

"She doesn't know she's not safe out there with that big target on her back," Clare said.

They didn't see Amber like I did. She wouldn't just disappear. I shook my head. "No, you don't understand. I'm positive the Shadows have her because they hinted at it."

Clare sat up, interested. "Start from the beginning. How did you get away from Layla?"

I recalled my escape with the Shadows' help. "Devon had a smug look on his face when he told me I had Amber to thank for the jail break. She made some kind of deal behind your back."

"You think Amber made a deal with them? That's impossible." Kieran shot me a disbelieving look.

"I'm truly sorry," Clare said. "We were working so hard on a plan to rescue you because you know I'm not keen on mourning and wearing black. It just doesn't suit me. But I swear I'll fix this. I'm calling Cass." She walked to the door, then turned. "Did you get her the ambassador position?" At my nod she left. At least some of us got what they wanted. I snorted and rubbed a hand over my face.

"Clare's right. We didn't mean to let Amber slip away," Kieran said. "We were so focused on you. If anything happened to you, I don't know what I'd do."

"I know that." My voice betrayed my irritation. It wasn't addressed toward my brother but toward myself. I should've locked Amber in her room when I had the chance.

Kieran didn't seem to hear me. "I was crazy with grief, man. I couldn't think straight. I couldn't imagine living the next millennium without you. Who'd keep me in line? Who'd tell me to stop driving like a maniac?"

I smiled as Kieran jumped up from the sofa and grabbed me in a brief, awkward hug. "You have a good heart, even if it doesn't beat," I said. "Okay, you can let go."

Kieran laughed and pushed me out the door. "Go take a shower. You look like crap, and smell even worse."

How could I indulge in the luxury of hot water when I didn't know what happened to Amber? She might be cold or hurt, my life-long enemies savoring the pain they could inflict on me by harming her.

"If your mate were hurt, you'd know it. You'd feel it," Kieran said. "Go on, take a shower, or I might end up pouring a bucket of water over your head."

Kieran was right. With a sigh, I retreated to the privacy of my bathroom and peeled off my torn clothes. In the bright light the wounds looked worse than I thought. They'd heal in a few days, but not if I didn't feed. Like on cue, a sudden pang of hunger washed over me, but I decided my immediate needs would have to wait, at least until I had scrubbed myself clean.

Under the hot stream of water, I rubbed at the dried blood until it trickled down in thin, pink rivulets, then dried myself off with a towel and pulled out a bag containing donor blood from a fridge hidden in the compartment of my closet. The blood tasted of nothing, but it soothed my physical hunger. The need to drink right from the source still persisted though.

I ripped the bag open and drank, the smell overwhelming me. I hated it because it lingered on my skin. It was almost impossible to wash off. In my early days as a vampire, I'd tried to convince myself that its constant presence was nothing but a disturbing side effect of immortality. In those days, I'd wanted to love it, gorged on it with Rebecca by my side. Blood's power, and being strong makes up for everything that's gone wrong in life. Or so I told myself—until I killed Rebecca. It was a matter of survival. If I didn't kill her, she'd have killed Blake. I couldn't let an innocent die, so I shared my blood with him, turning him into a vampire.

I finished the last drop of blood and threw the bag onto the burning logs in the fireplace. Thinking about the events that happened a long time ago, I felt a peculiar relief, wondering how little they meant to me now.

"Memories can't be laid to rest," I mumbled.

"But you can learn to forgive yourself," Kieran said from the door. "Give yourself a break, bro. I promise the demons in your head will still be there, waiting for you, tomorrow night. Cass is downstairs."

I slipped into a clean pair of jeans and a shirt, and followed my brother out. "She's as fast as a spreading bushfire. I've got to give her that."

"Yeah—" Kieran smirked "—a little too fast. It's like she's always where there's trouble." I nodded, realizing my brother was right.

***

Cass and Clare were seated on the sofa, whispering as far away from Blake as possible. As soon as Kieran and I stepped through the open door, they stopped. Cass turned to watch me, her green eyes glinting unnaturally, her open mouth sucking in the air.

"What's she doing?" Kieran whispered in my ear.

Cass puffed. "Let me guess, women are a whole new species to you, fascinating yet scary at the same time." She touched my arm. "I can't believe what Layla did to you. She's such a meanie."

I nodded. "Thanks, Cass."

"Let me get out my handy dandy make-up kit," Cass said. "You'll look good in no time. Just ask Clare. She's had one of my famous makeovers."

"Her skilled hands work like magic," Clare said. "It's amazing what she can do."

Were they kidding? Talking about cosmetics when we had no idea what happened to Amber? I took a deep breath and peered at the snacks on the table. "No, Cass."

"You sure? I can tone down that pale thing you got going. You know, give you some color. Make you look like you're—" Cass waved her hand in the air, trying to find the right word "—alive."

"No," I said. "And that's final. Now, I don't want to be a killjoy, but can we get on—"

"Your loss." Cass shrugged and applied another thick layer of bright-red lipstick.

"We don't have time for this," Blake said. I turned and shot him a thankful smile. Blake was strange, always lurking in corners, silent as a grave, but he actually seemed sane compared to my other companions.

Cass put away the lipstick and smacked her lips. "Okay, let's get down to business. You guys are wasting my precious time."

I stared at her, dumbfounded. We were wasting *her* time? Go figure.

"No idea why she's always here. She doesn't even have any powers," Kieran whispered.

"I'll get them once I turn eighteen," Cass said. "Besides, I have the power to kick your butt, and that's all I need."

I pushed the glass of water from the table into her hand, lest she jump up and challenge my brother to fight. The girl was half fallen angel; it wasn't her fault she couldn't control her temper. But my brother had absolutely no excuse. "If you don't keep quiet I'll kick you both out. I've no time for this. Amber's life depends on us and all you do is—" I shook my head in exasperation "—you should go out together because you seem to have a lot in common."

Cass snorted. "No, thanks. I'd rather join a convent."

Clare laughed. Kieran shot her an irritated look, and she quieted.

I hurried to change the subject before they started another fight. "Cass, do you know where she could be?"

"Okay, I'll bite." Cass let out a giggle. "No pun intended. Why'd you think I knew what happened to your sweetheart?"

"According to Aidan we're supposed to work together so, no more vampire jokes," Kieran said. "Got it?"

Cass narrowed her gaze. "You think you're God's gift to women. But you know what? I'm way hotter. Literally. See, I can make hell jokes too. So don't get all touchy because it's not personal. Really, take a chill pill."

I rubbed my temples, staring at them. They had to stop eventually. I'd just wait it out.

"Of course you're comfortable cracking jokes about your kind," Kieran said. "You and your demon breed are the epitome of hilarious. Just look at the way you dress."

Her eyes sparkled, her set jaw screamed murder. I raised my hand to stop further confrontation. "Cass, listen, I asked if you knew anything because you usually know what's going on, that's all."

Cass cleared her throat, her eyes moving back and forth as though she was leading an inner argument. Kieran snorted. Eventually, Cass smiled and said, "Okay, I'll tell them, but they owe me big time."

"Who's she talking to?" Kieran whispered.

"I got you the ambassador position," I said, ignoring my brother's question. "As the new ambassador you're bound to tell me anyway. If you don't play by the rules, you risk another war and you can kiss your position goodbye before you've even started your new job."

Cass tapped a finger on her chin, thinking. "That makes sense."

I breathed in, forcing myself to remain the patient, reasonable one when Cass pushed the envelope with her lack of urgency. If she continued putting off telling us what she knew, I might have to shake some sense into her.

"Cass, what do you know?" Clare said as though sensing my annoyance.

"Not much." Moistening her lips, Cass brushed a hand over her wrinkled, oversized jeans. "Yesterday morning, I came to visit Clare, and stumbled across Amber. She said she had a plan to save Aidan. She wouldn't tell me what it was, just that it involved the Shadows." Cass peered at me, all innocent green eyes, wide with fake honesty. I knew she was lying, but I let her continue. "I tried to talk her out of striking a deal with the Shadows, but she wouldn't listen. I had no idea she'd act so quickly, otherwise I would've left you a note."

"How did Amber get hold of the Shadows?" Kieran asked. "It's not like they can walk in here, what with the gold-infused bars Aidan put up around the property."

Cass shook her head. "I've no idea, mate. Maybe Amber got hold of their phone number. I've heard that Devon's throwing it around like hot cakes."

"That's very useful information, Cass." I nodded, seemingly impressed, ready to let her believe her bluff worked on me. "Can you get us inside their fortress?"

She shook her head. "That isn't part of my job duties, mate."

"May I remind you it's your responsibility to ensure no mortal entering the immortal realm, willingly or unwillingly, ever comes to harm?" I raised my brows meaningfully.

Cass groaned. "This job's kind of hard, isn't it?"

"You're not cut out for it, I knew it. Send in your notice, sweetie. No one will hold it against you," Kieran said. He was leading her on, counting on her half fallen angel nature that wouldn't let a challenge untouched. I regarded her, waiting for her reaction.

Cass lifted her chin defiantly, that dangerous glint blinking in her eyes like a siren. "I was joking, you moron. No job's too hard for me. I can't get you in because some of them are my friends and I would never betray them. Doesn't mean I don't know someone who can help."

I would've liked to point out the double standard in that. Instead, I said, "She showed you, bro."

"Didn't see that one coming from our little Cass." Kieran's lips twitched. He was barely able to conceal his amusement. If he didn't shut it, Cass would see through his pretense.

"There's this guy who works for me—Thrain. He's the best demon slash shape shifter there's ever been. He'll get you in," Cass said, proudly.

"Can we trust him?" Clare asked.

"He won't dare cross me." Cass shot Kieran a displeased look. "Unlike some other people here who don't know what's best for them."

I breathed in. *Here we go again.* She was even worse than my brother. "Cass, how fast can you get hold of him?"

"Huh?"

"The shape shifter," I said. "We need him here ASAP."

"Right. Thrain." She fell into that strange state again, like she heard something that we didn't. Her eyes twinkled a few times before her gaze cleared. "Dad's pissed with me for taking the job," she mumbled. "I told you it was a bad idea, Pinky."

"Who's Pinky? Is she okay?" Kieran whispered. "Someone forgot to take their meds this morning."

196

"I don't believe in medication," Cass said. "I'm 100% natural. No silicon, no synthetic hormones or steroids, no artificial flavors, colors or preservatives."

Kieran laughed. "Too bad, because you would benefit big time from something to make those voices go away."

Cass jumped up and pushed the table to the side. Her half-full glass shattered against the floor, water seeping into the carpet. "That's it, mate. I've had it with you! I'm going to kick your butt into next week."

"I see she's hallucinating again," Kieran yelled. "Somebody call the pharmacy!"

Before I could grab her, Cass stretched out her arm and started murmuring. Her green eyes changed to red, glinting like a lantern. The bulbs flickered; the ground beneath our feet shook. I looked in horror as Cass growled, hundreds of voices echoing at the same time. Kieran paled, frozen to the spot as he murmured, "I knew I should've let sleeping demons lie."

The paint from the walls peeled off, falling to the floor in large chunks, as something screeched outside the window. The ceiling cracked, the tiny fissures growing bigger. Cass took a step closer, sparks like thunder flying from her outstretched hands, hitting Kieran in the chest. He stumbled backward, eyes wide with surprise. Something stirred beneath his white shirt, tightening it and pulling at the material until it stretched. The buttons ripped and fell off.

The noise stopped abruptly. Cass stormed out, red-faced and angry, slamming the door shut. My brother dropped on the sofa, laughing hard with tears in his eyes. I tilted my head to get a better look.

In his lap sat a cute, white Labrador puppy, scratching at its stone-embedded, pink flea collar.

***

The demon—Thrain—arrived the next day, shortly after dark. I could smell him from a mile—incense and heat mingling with the sweet scent of blood. Although I could never quite shake off that gnawing sense of hunger that came whenever I picked up the scent of blood, my stomach turned. Taking a deep breath, I opened the door before the demon drove up the path in a shiny, black SUV with tinted windows.

Thrain stepped out, a large grin playing on his lips. "Dude, what happened to you? Someone pound on your face?" He appeared to be the dodgy male version of Cass: tall with disheveled hair, dressed in tattered jeans and a crumpled shirt.

"Yeah, I was in a giant pillow fight. Come on in." I shook his hand and stepped aside to let him walk past.

"Yo, how hard were those pillows?"

I grimaced. Not only did he dress like Cass, he also had her strange sense of humor. Must be a hell thing. As soon as we entered the library, Clare's gaze locked on Thrain, and she almost tripped over herself to greet him. "Hi there, I'm—"

"An idiot," Kieran said, rolling his eyes.

Thrain grinned and shook Clare's hand. "Well, hello, Miss Idiot."

She pointed at Kieran. "He's the idiot. I'm Clare."

"Okay, that's enough," I said. "So glad we got the introductions straightened out."

"Cass said you needed my help?" Thrain dropped on the sofa and crossed his right ankle over his left knee. Clare sat down next to him, enthralled by whatever she found so attractive about his bad boy attitude, oblivious to the reek of ritual and offerings wafting from him.

Kieran sat next to me and leaned in to whisper in my ear, "I don't get it. What does Clare see in a guy who looks like he doesn't know how to commit, is narcissistic, self-absorbed, and in dire need of shave?"

I cocked a brow. "You realize you're describing yourself, right?"

"Feel this face—not one stubble. Only cavemen don't shave. I admit, I might have one or two of those traits, but it's different."

I smirked. "You're a diamond in the rough, bro."

He shook his head. "Look at Clare. I know what she wants with a dude like him—smoldering, volcanic passion. That's an easy fix. I can erupt any time she wants."

I laughed. He didn't just say that. "Whoa, too much information. That's an image I don't need seared in my mind for the next hundred years." I turned to Thrain who didn't seem to mind Clare's gawking. "Thanks for coming. Cass probably told you we need you to get us onto Shadow territory." Kieran snorted and stared ahead, pissed that he wasn't the center of attention for a change. Blake lurked in the corner, quiet as usual.

Thrain nodded. "You've set yourself quite a goal, mate. That's almost as hard as entering hell without Lucifer noticing."

"We know that. Otherwise you wouldn't be here," Kieran said. With his ego hurt, he didn't seem to plan on turning his hostility down a notch any time soon.

I nudged him in the ribs and turned my focus back on Thrain. "Can you do it?"

Thrain laughed and winked at Clare. "Let's go."

"We should have a plan, just in case he isn't trustworthy," Kieran said.

Thrain just shrugged and leaned back. No temper flares, no fighting back—this wasn't the usual behavior of a demon. I felt temped to just jump up and go rescue Amber, but my brother had a point. We couldn't burst in there because we wouldn't stand a chance against hundreds of armed Shadows.

"You stay outside. I'm going in with him," Blake said. "I know how to deal with a demon."

I shook my head. "Not happening, Blake. Rescuing Amber's my responsibility."

"Trust your best friends," Clare said. "We've dealt with Shadows before. They wouldn't hurt me. As Blake said, you wait outside, just in case something goes wrong, but don't get too close."

Clare was naïve to believe the Shadows regarded her as some sort of friend. She always thought if she was friendly enough everyone must like her. Even after her turning, she still didn't understand that by just being called a vampire, half of the paranormal world watched her with distrust, and the other half would kill her in a heartbeat if it weren't for a few Lore rules that kept immortals from attacking each other.

"Amber's my responsibility," I repeated, quietly.

200

"Your scent's too strong. They'd spot you in a heartbeat because they're probably expecting you to come to her rescue. Look at it this way—" Clare paused until I glanced at her "—if anything happened to you, she'd stand no chance against them."

Thrain cleared his throat to get our attention. "Not trying to interrupt your touching display of concern for one another, but I'm a busy man. Either we get going *now*, or I'm off."

"We're going," Blake said. "There's no need to wait. We can discuss the details during the drive."

"Goody. Follow me." Thrain headed for the door, calling over his shoulder, "And try to keep up."

Kieran laughed. "Ever hear of NASCAR? I invented it."

I glared at him, but he just shrugged and jumped up, car keys dangling from his fingers. Throw in the word 'drive' and Kieran was ready to start the engine.

***

We drove up the Scottish coast, heading north, past one long strip of trees on both sides of the highway. The air smelled of rain and salt. The moon hid behind heavy clouds in the pitch-black sky.

"We're in the middle of nowhere. No wonder we never found them," I mumbled.

"We're slowing down," Clare said from the backseat. "This must be it."

"Where?" Kieran asked.

Clare pointed at the darkness stretching to our right. "The mountains." The brake lights in front of us came on as Thrain pulled his SUV onto a track and stopped.

"Don't say anything to piss him off. In fact, don't do anything to screw this up," I said to my brother.

"Come on." Kieran parked the SUV behind Thrain's. "Give me a little credit."

"Give you some credit? If you protected Amber the way you should've we wouldn't be here."

"Drop it, Aidan. You're not helping. Now, let's go," Clare said. I exited after her, lingering near the vehicle.

"We're close. I can smell their faint scent," Blake whispered.

Kieran snorted. "That makes one of us. All I smell is dog shit."

Leaves rustled. The long grass swayed in the wind. "You know this is the craziest thing we've ever done," Clare said, wide-eyed.

"That *you've* done," I said. My work as a bounty hunter usually involved more than trekking through the Scottish Highlands.

"Exactly," Kieran said. "Like Aidan, I live for this kind of stuff. If you want adventure, I'm the guy for you."

"I just hope Thrain doesn't screw us over and feeds us to the wolves," Blake mumbled.

I nodded. "Me too. I can't believe we're putting our lives in the hands of Cass who picked this winner."

"She says he's the best shape shifter there's ever been," Kieran said. "Yeah, right."

"We haven't seen him shift shapes, so quit judging a book by its cover." Clare's blonde hair shifted in the wind, floating around her like a halo, as she turned to stare at Thrain.

Kieran snorted. "The best? I find that rather hard to believe. The dude can't even grow a beard, he's never seen a brush, he's never heard of an iron, and—"

Clare cut in. "Classic bad boy, very sexy."

"I call it *unkempt*," Kieran said. "Don't tell me he can't afford a pair of jeans that haven't been put through a shredder. What's taking him so long anyway?"

I cocked my head to get a better view. "He's fumbling around in the glove department."

"I hope he's looking for a map and not a weapon," Blake said, leaning against a tree.

I turned to face him. Blake must be nervous. That was about as much as he talked in weeks. "You don't have to join the mission. I'm not twisting your arm."

Blake pointed at Thrain's car, ignoring my statement. "He's coming."

We watched in silence as Thrain marched over to join the waiting party, eyes glittered in the moonlight. "It's up there," he said, pointing at the dense forest on the mountain behind us. "We need to reach the trees before the clouds clear again."

"A midnight stroll—how romantic," Kieran said.

I followed the others up the path, pondering over what the demon called a plan: find a way in, save the lass, find a way out. Maybe avoid a guard or two in the process. Didn't sound like much of a plan to me, but I wasn't one to argue as long as we didn't leave without Amber.

"I should've worn my trainers," Clare muttered.

"Don't break a heel," Kieran said.

Thrain laughed. "Stilettos are hot. Just tell me and I'll carry you."

"Thank you," Clare said. "Finally, a guy with taste."

203

"Since when do tattered jeans equal taste?" Kieran nudged Thrain. "You know I'm dating her, right?"

"Kieran, I said no trouble, remember? You're not even dating her." Groaning, I shook my head. I stood a better chance rescuing Amber with the help of my iPod.

"It's best we maintain silence from here on. We're on a mission, not a dating show," Blake said.

Irritated by their endless banter, I nodded even though I was several feet behind them and they couldn't see me as we hurried up the winding path. The trees looked all the same, but I could sense we were getting closer because the air had started to reek of Shadows.

A few minutes later, we stopped. Thrain dropped to his knees and rubbed soil between his fingers. "We're not far from their main trail. The gate is to the east."

"Keep north until we reach the fence," I whispered.

Thrain shot me a curious glance over his shoulder, before he took off again. We moved at a fast speed through the trees, almost invisible to human eyes, but not undetectable to Shadows. I could already see the fence in the distance, rising high against the dark night. Rebecca had entered once without the demon's abilities, but Rebecca was an excellent manipulator. She could persuade a mortal to give away their life for her. The immortal warriors had opened the gates and let her in, unsuspecting of the bloodbath she'd leave behind. That trick wouldn't pull again, which is why we needed a shape shifter to pretend to be one of them and make sure the way was clear.

The fortress was secured by a twenty-foot, barbed-wire fence about fifty feet away. A sign warned that it was electrically charged. I focused on the gate—two guards patrolling on the other side, cloaked in black and oblivious to what was going on. Their strong, earthy smell invaded my nostrils. I knew instantly their powers were limited based on their low rank in the Shadow hierarchy. Judging from their position, size and abilities, I could easily take them down if I had to, but I wouldn't. Not before Amber was safe.

Thrain stopped and pointed at the fence, whispering to Clare and Blake, "I'll distract the guards. You jump." He nudged Kieran. "You invented basketball too? Or just NASCAR?"

"You should see my jump shot." Kieran grinned. "I know you'd feel safer with me around, but Aidan wants me back here. He claims I'm trouble."

"Shame." Thrain shrugged. "I'd have loved a race."

"He'll take you up on the offer another time," I whispered as I watched Clare and Blake disappear through the thicket. Thrain headed for the gate. Kieran and I dropped onto the ground, prepared to wait.

Chapter 18

Shooting Angel a timid smile, I stepped through the open door. To my surprise, I realized I was in a thriving terraced garden rather than a room. Bright rays shone through the glass ceiling, settling on the fallen leaves in a wealth of color. Dumbfounded, I peered around. How could there be so many plants in bloom in the middle of a bleeding mountain in freezing Scotland? I didn't even know Scotland had this many flowers.

"It's magic," the guard said, turning to face me. I recognized Devon.

"Do you mean magic in the literal sense?"

He shrugged, smiling. As usual, I was kept in the dark. My temper flared. "I thought you'd take the gift out of my head and then let me go," I snapped.

Devon cringed. "It doesn't work that way. You're part of the package."

Where did he get the impression I was keen on joining their little club? "You failed to mention I had a lifetime membership to Shadow Land."

He shrugged. "You didn't ask. Let's put it this way—" he grabbed my elbow and guided me down the cobblestone path "—I did you a favor. The company you kept was a bit shady."

I let out a huff. A Shadow calling vampires shady?

Devon continued, "Aidan's not even remotely human. You were flirting with danger. I rescued you, and barely in the nick of time."

I laughed. "So, let me get this straight. You slayed the dragon, jumped over the moat, climbed the tower of the evil king's castle, saved the princess, and rode off with her into the sunset aka Shadow Land. Why, you're my knight in shining armor."

His face remained expressionless as he nodded. "Just switch the castle for the gloomy McAllister mansion. Aidan doesn't love you because he's still in love with Rebecca. He'd do anything to raise her from the dead. Or why do you think he participated in the race?"

That certainly explained why Aidan wanted the prize so badly. But usually, there are two sides to a story. I shook my head, unwilling to let Devon twist my mind. Or maybe I couldn't handle the truth. "His plans are none of your business."

"What do you see in him anyway?"

"He doesn't leave the toilet seat up." I smiled bitterly, realizing I had no idea who Aidan really was.

"Doesn't your life mean anything to you?"

"Of course it does." I shot him a sideway glance, wondering where our conversation was heading.

"Then why on Earth would you hook up with one of the McAllister brothers? You would've been dead before Christmas."

"Now you're being melodramatic. Must be part of the Shadow charm—all dark and gloomy."

Frowning, Devon stopped in mid-stride. "Are you trying to be funny? Do you think your brother and parents would've seen the joke in bringing flowers to your grave every day?"

The thought made my heart skip a beat, dread settling in the pit of my stomach like a heavy stone. "You know my family?"

"Yes, and you bet Aidan's been watching them too. He may seem like a nice guy, sweet and charming and all that, but behind his calculated façade hides a skilled killer. He chased you in the woods. You only escaped because other immortals were around and he wouldn't risk exposure."

Avoiding his gaze, I regarded the nearby bushes with their tiny white flowers. I couldn't get the thought of my parents crying at my grave out of my mind. "I put my parents down as my emergency contacts. You know, I never even wanted this job." I took a deep breath. Was it Aidan's mission to kill me all along? It made so much sense, and yet my heart wasn't quite willing to buy it. A silly thing called hope kept clinging to me. I turned away from the tall trees with their canopies of leaves. My gaze connected with Devon's as I tried to read his expression. "Why do you care?"

Devon inhaled and scanned the area behind me, black eyes glinting. "The first night we met I knew I had to save you. I couldn't bear the thought of Aidan ripping your throat out. It took everything I had to just walk away."

"Why?" I shook my head. "I'm sorry but I don't need saving. Maybe pour all that energy into a worthy cause, like saving the whales, or the Rainforest. I hear trees are being cut down at an alarming rate."

"He's killed before and he'll do it again," Devon said. "Doesn't it make your skin crawl knowing you were bunked up with Vlad the Impaler?"

"Huh?"

"Look him up when you get the chance. The point is, Aidan and Rebecca killed hundreds in their bloodlust hunt." Devon grabbed my hand, inching closer until we stood mere inches from one another. My breath caught in my throat as I stared into his black eyes. "The Shadows fight to keep humans safe from monsters on the prowl. I know our image was tarnished when Connor tried to kidnap you. But I want you to know my brother had only the best intentions in mind. He was desperate since he didn't know how much time we had left." His tone was honest. Even though he fell quiet, I felt as though his voice was still talking to me at the back of my mind, whispering unspoken words in my ears.

"Who are you people?"

"We're the good guys," Devon murmured. His gaze turned soft as he brushed a wisp of hair out of my face. "I hope in time you come to see that. Breaking away from Aidan will be good for you. Besides, it can't be fun snuggling up to an ice cube every night." He hesitated. "Or shall I say, corpse?"

I smiled warily. "All the more reason to invest in flannel nightwear."

Smirking, Devon pulled away. "I'll end on this note. Aidan has killed his lovers in the past and I won't to let him repeat history."

"Why?"

He shrugged, avoiding my gaze. "Because I like you." For a moment, I wasn't sure I heard him right. I opened my mouth to ask in what way he liked me, but Devon took my hand and led me under the low branches of a tree on the narrow path. My hand felt strange in his as we crossed the open space. We turned right until we reached an opening in the wall and squeezed through into yet another corridor. He didn't let go of me until we halted in front of a huge door of polished metal.

Devon opened his mouth to say something when I lifted a hand to stop him. I'd heard enough. Now, I needed time to make sense of his words. "Aidan's your sworn enemy," I said, "so it's hard for me to trust you."

"You trust him more? That's disturbing." The door opened. Devon let me pass through, following a step behind. I took in the narrow stony passage with torches lit on both sides of a long aisle, marveling at how much it resembled the others we had passed. We walked in silence for a while, the dull thumps of our boots echoing from the walls.

My mind reeled. There were so many questions I wanted to ask. Did Aidan say anything? Did he know about my deal with the Shadows? But I kept quiet, praying Devon would get the hint and keep his mouth shut too because I couldn't deal with more reproach and mind control, until we reached a great hall with a marble altar set up in the middle. A strong, chilly breeze swept my hair across my face. My heart started to race, hammering against my ribcage. Judging from the distance we had put behind us, we couldn't be anywhere near the open space with its blooming trees. The scent here was different too, less flowery, more earth-like and damp, just the way a mountain would smell in the cold Scottish summer. Gazing around, I searched for the door to freedom. If I could just see it, I might be able to distract my captors and make a dash for the woods.

"You're shivering. Here." Devon took off his jacket and draped it over my shoulders. I mouthed a thank-you, careful not to give away my enthusiasm at being so close to a way out. His obliging attitude was part of his plan to sway me in the Shadows' favor. On the other hand, why would he want to deceive me when I was already cooperating? I was being paranoid again. He said he liked me. I wondered whether his words meant more than he let on. I took a deep breath and focused my attention back on our surroundings.

Devon led me past the altar to an opening in the wall, like a giant hole. Behind it stretched darkness. The dim light of the torches barely cast enough light to illuminate our way as we walked through, entering yet another corridor in this maze. A shiver ran down my spine. Even though I knew it wasn't from the cold, I wrapped Devon's jacket tighter around me.

"You okay?" Devon whispered, grabbing my hand again.

I nodded, but didn't pull away. We entered another open space. From the corner of my eye, I thought I saw motionless shapes leaning against the walls, surveying our every move, waiting in silence as if they, too, were carved of marble like the altar we passed. Had they followed, or did they keep guard? Either way, there were so many of them, even if I found a way out, how far would I get before someone spied me and raised alarm?

At the far end of the space, a dais of stairs led to an upper platform with a door. Devon pressed his palm against a carved triangle. Light flickered where his skin touched the wood, and the hinges moved with a loud groan. We entered a rock chamber, and the door shut behind us.

Holding my breath, I looked around. More torches illuminated the vast room. Oriental rugs, in the color of autumn leaves, covered the stonewalls. Thick logs burned in the huge fireplace to my right. I turned to the girl and the man seated on ebony thrones overlaid with red velvet when Devon hissed in my ear, "You're about to meet our queen, Deidre. Keep your head bowed."

Doing as he ordered, I caught a glimpse of ivory skin and silver hair that spilled onto her dress, surrounding her elfin figure.

"I want a better look at the girl," Deidre said, her thin child-like voice ringing a bell.

"Go," Devon whispered as he gently pushed me forward, bracing me when I stumbled.

Deidre held out a hand and whispered, "Come closer."

I looked up, my gaze shifting to the bearded man sitting on the throne, pale and unmoving. When he didn't even blink, I turned to the girl, taking in the hip-long, silver hair, smooth skin and dainty physique. She looked barely older than twelve, but something glittered in her black eyes; old knowledge, pride and something else I couldn't pinpoint.

Deidre drew a sharp breath, then lifted one hand, motioning me to take a step forward. "This is Amber?"

"Yes, Deidre. She was chosen by the vampire," Devon said, head bowed.

"I still can't see her face," Deidre said. I could hear impatience in her voice, so I approached, my boots making an unnerving clicking sound on the shiny marble floor, until I stood a few inches away from her.

"Chosen for what?" I asked, suspiciously, as I tried to push away the image of the girl in *The Exorcist*, a movie Dallas made me watch a few times. Eerie atmosphere. Check. Pale girl dressed in a flowing dress. Check. Weird talking. Check. I held my breath, waiting for the demonic voice to start cussing.

"I can't tell you. Revealing this particular secret shall be the vampire's pleasure, or agony, however he might see it." Deidre ran her fingers up my arm, barely touching Devon's leather jacket. "You've come to offer help in this dark hour?" Her authoritative voice stood in stark sharp contrast to her frilly dress and friendly smile.

"Yes, Deidre. Amber agreed to a pact: her skill for the vampire's life," Devon said. I shook my head. Was a verbal agreement even binding? I'd never heard of one to hold up in court. A good lawyer could surely get me out of this bad deal in a heartbeat.

Deidre's gaze never left me. She had the same coal black eyes as Devon and the other Shadows, as though they were siblings. Her lips were the color of frozen rose petals, barely moving as she whispered, "Let her speak for herself, warrior."

"Devon's right, we had an agreement." I noticed the sword sheathed along Deidre's right hip. Honestly, a sword? Could she be more psycho?

Deidre placed a hand on my shoulder, and squeezed. A freezing sensation seeped through the thick material of clothes. I imagined myself slapping her hand away, but refrained from following my instinct.

"I saw you in my dreams hundreds of years ago," Deidre whispered. "Yours is so beautiful and yet so tragic a fate. But first you'll reunite us with what is ours." Did she say *hundreds* of years? Unless my parents lied about my age, I was only seventeen. Deidre smiled coldly and continued her monologue, "You're a rarity among mortals and immortals, pure and striking. I reckon you've pledged your allegiance. Don't betray our trust or you'll die, and the vampire with you." She paused, glancing past me at Devon. A guttural hiss escaped Deidre's throat. "He thinks they share a bond."

"Only fools believe in bonds," Devon whispered. "The vampire made it up to suit his purpose."

I cast Devon an irritated look because I had enough of all the bad-mouthing. They were Aidan's enemies and I didn't trust them. They might seem more human than a vampire, but between the bloodsucker and the Exorcist kid and her black-eyed clique, I'd take the bloodsucker any time.

"Did you know he has the ability to influence your mind?" Deidre asked. "He'll feed on you night after night, sucking your blood and destroying your will to live."

"You're kidding." Aidan happened to leave that tiny detail out. At this particular moment, he didn't seem so mysterious, good-looking and eternally alluring. A chill ran down my spine. Did I trade Cameron's wisecracking, partying and womanizing for a guy with an uncontrollable hunger for human blood? My taste in men was despicable. What came next? A werewolf? A zombie?

Deidre returned to her throne, chiffon shuffling as she draped her frock around her. "That you're here shows me you're ready to beg for help, just like our Angel once did." She paused again, the sudden silence stirring a storm of different emotions in me. The Exorcist kid was lying. Aidan could neither mess with my mind, nor would he ever drink from me. And yet, he wanted something, something they all seemed to want. I couldn't trust anyone; not Aidan, not the Shadows, and certainly not bloody Dallas who brought this disaster upon me in the first place. From now on, I'd only trust myself.

"I need answers." My voice quivered. "Angel said I could never go home again."

The sudden oppressing silence hung heavy in the air. I could slice the tension with a knife. This was the moment I'd been waiting for. Maybe Angel and Devon didn't know what they were talking about. Deidre might let me go home in a few months. I should've been more specific by offering my skill for two years, three tops, and then demand to be brought home.

"You're part of our world now, Amber," Deidre said, eventually.

My heart sunk in my chest. "No."

She titled her head slowly, her voice remained soft. "It's a small price to pay for a second chance in life."

215

I shook my head. "There's been a misunderstanding. I wasn't under the impression I'd be spending the rest of my life here. I want to go home."

"To be with Aidan." Deidre sighed and brushed a hand over her dress. "You need to fight it if you don't want to be the vampire's captive for the rest of your life."

"I'm not his captive." I wasn't. Was I?

"What do you know about vampires? Nothing but a few tidbits Aidan's tossed your way. You are naïve, and he knows it. He will use that to his advantage."

Deidre was laying it thick. "How can you say that?"

"Do you enjoy being bitten, hurting until the pain makes you wish you were dead?"

"This is all too crazy for me," I said.

"You fell for his charm like many others before you. But Fate has brought you here in your time of trouble. We're the beacons of light in the darkness. Think of this world as a lighthouse, and think of yourself as a ship lost during the storm. We are your refuge providing guidance and safety. As a mortal, this might take a while to sink in, but Angel will be at your side to teach you our ways. In time, Aidan's influence on your mind will die down."

I swallowed the sudden lump in my throat. I knew I should take Aidan's side, but something in Deidre's words rang true. Ever since entering Aidan's house I felt different. Past relationships faded from my mind. I never believed in mind control, but I also never believed in immortals, magical powers and seeing the dead, and they existed. The Exorcist kid's words were starting to make sense. Aidan had kept a lot from me. "Will I ever get my old life back?"

Deidre shook her head. "I can't undo the kind of mind spell the vampire cast on you. As long as he lives, you won't find peace. The only way to protect your mind from him is to keep away. Is there anything we can get you to make you feel more comfortable?"

A bottle of Prozac would be perfect. Good old Valium would do the trick, too. Maybe a padded cell for being nuts enough to fall in love with a guy who wanted to get a little tipsy from sipping on my red blood cells every night. I smiled, bitterly. "I'm good. Thanks."

"Here's a small token of my appreciation." Deidre stood up from her throne and reached me in a few slow strides, pulling out a rectangle box wrapped in lace from the sheath of her swords. I stared at it, hesitating. The only gift I wanted was freedom. So it better be a map out of this place, a key to the dungeon door, or a pair of red heels I could click together three times saying, "There's no place like home." Anything else was just worthless stuff.

"Take it," Deidre whispered.

I opened the box and pulled out a large butterfly-shaped moonstone pendant dangling from a silver necklace.

"It's called, Butterfly of Hope. The butterfly symbolizes a new life. The stone will protect you." Deidre fastened it around my neck and took a step back to admire it.

"It's beautiful. Thank you." I wrapped my hand around the smooth metal. It felt like a warm fire against my skin, comforting me. I wondered what it really was for.

"Lead Amber back and ensure she receives a room worthy of a queen," Deidre said. "And don't veil her mind. She shall be able to find the way back to my chambers." After walking around for hours through this

217

maze, I doubted even a GPS system could help me, but I smiled in response nonetheless.

"That's unheard of. The vampire—" Devon started.

"I shan't turn away a soul in need," Deidre said, sharply.

Devon bowed and we left.

***

"It wasn't so bad, was it?" Devon asked, as soon as we were out in the open again.

"No worse than the time my appendix burst," I said.

Devon turned to face me, smiling. "You're funny. I've heard all about your ride and the wonderful séance."

"Gossip travels fast here. You should get television."

Devon's gaze remained locked with mine. For a moment, he seemed to want to say something, but decided against it.

"I bet Angel's waiting for me," I said.

He nodded, and we walked in silence to the eating quarters where lunch was served. Angel jumped up from her seat and hurried over as soon as she saw us enter. Devon said goodbye and disappeared.

"You took hours. Are you okay? What did she say? She's beautiful, isn't she?" Angel grabbed my hand and pulled me to our dining table. She started piling steaks, mashed potatoes and vegetables on two plates, then handed me one.

"You must tell me everything, but wait until it's more quiet." Angel nodded toward the curious faces staring at us.

We ate in silence near the window overlooking the woods. Angel finished first and got up to bring us coffee and dessert. She insisted I eat up. "Trust me, you'll need it. The people here don't sleep a lot. You can only keep up if you compensate with food and caffeine." I shot her a disbelieving look, but she didn't seem to be joking.

"Does she spend all her time in that dark dungeon?" I whispered so the others wouldn't hear us.

"You mean Deidre?" Angel shook her head. "She comes out every now and then to fulfill her duties."

"She seems very young, but the way she speaks—"

"It's freaky, isn't it?" Angel cut me off. "No idea how old she really is, but legend is the Fates made her queen. She took great care of me when I arrived here. She made everything easier to understand and accept."

We finished our dessert and left, passing through a narrow gate until we reached a corridor with several doors. Angel opened one and entered, motioning me to follow.

"This is where I live." She peeled off her jacket and threw it haphazardly over the back of a chair, then went about pouring two glasses of water from a bottle on her dressing table, and handed me one. "Water's good for your skin. They're all so beautiful. I'll take whatever little help I can get."

I sat on the chair and peered around. What should I say? That she was pretty and special? I thought back to that fateful night when I first met Clare. I felt the same way. With all the perfect immortals around her, no wonder Angel's self-confidence was non-existent. I decided to change the subject. "You should be an interior designer with your fantastic taste."

219

It wasn't a lie. The room was bright and spacious with white walls and a red carpet covering the marble floor. A large, glass bookshelf was mounted over a long fireplace. On the opposite wall were a four-poster bed and several blooming orange trees in flowerpots. It looked minimalist chic and expensive, straight out of a magazine.

"Thank you." Angel beamed and took a sip of her water as she pointed to a chair. I took a seat and placed my water on the glass table. "Now, tell me what Deidre said. Are they going to train you?"

"Looks like your wish was granted," I said. "I got a life sentence in Shadow Land, whatever this place is."

"Really?" Angel hugged me tight for a long moment before letting go. "I did wish on the right star."

"Guess that makes one of us."

Angel shook her head. "No, you'll love it here. I promise I'll help you adjust."

I recalled my encounter with Deidre. Angel kept asking question, forcing me to repeat the exact conversation a few times.

"I wish someone told me what to expect," I said.

"It'd have spoilt their surprise moment. If it wasn't for that vampire, your fate would be a different one."

"Really? What is my fate?" I didn't want to hear any more gossip, not before I talked to Aidan and let him tell his side of the story, but I couldn't resist.

Angel leaned closer and lowered her voice. "I heard Devon and a few others talking after you arrived. They said if the vampire finds you he'll kill you."

"So, my fate is to die?" I smiled even though fear choked me. Angel nodded, wide-eyed. I smirked. "Awesome."

She wasn't telling me anything I hadn't heard from Devon but, coming from a girl I was slowly starting to trust, the words seemed to carry more weight. Why would Aidan want to murder me when I saved his life? He could've killed me plenty of times back at the house. Then again, maybe he only kept me alive so he'd learn how to use my gift to reach his precious Rebecca, after I stole the prize from right under his nose. A thought struck me. Did he want to use me as a vessel, like when Patrick Swayze jumped into Whoopi Goldberg's body in the movie *Ghost*? No guy would turn me into a zombie while Rebecca possessed my body. I jumped at the knock on the door.

"Your new room's ready," a girl said.

"She's in shock," Angel said. "Can you come back later?"

The girl bowed and left. At the back of my mind I wondered why someone would bow in front of a mortal fifteen-year-old, but the thought evaporated just as quickly. Images of a dream flooded my memory. That fateful night when I stole the gemstones, I dreamed Aidan wanted to kill me. Could the gift have warned me? Like a premonition, or—even better—a prophecy? No, a prophecy would imply a definite, imminent death. I breathed in and out, my heart thumping. Talk about a crappy job. The pay wasn't even good enough to warrant the possibility of death.

"Hey, you're safe here," Angel said, rubbing my shoulder. "We'll take care of you."

I shook my head. No, I wasn't safe. He'd come to get me because I had what he wanted. And somehow it was all connected to his dead ex. Or why else would he still keep Rebecca's clothes and need someone with the ability to communicate with the dead, unless he planned to find and raise his zombie bride?

Chapter 19

I spent the day with Angel. Devon popped in a few times to check on us, hesitating a tad too long in the doorway, as though he wasn't keen on leaving us alone, but had more pressing issues to tend to. It was clear the Shadows were waiting for something, but no one would tell me more.

My new room was a surprise: in size very similar to Angel's, but furnished in the colors of late summer leaves, dark green and brownish-red.

Big, giant bed fit for a queen: *check*.

Over-the-top-bathroom with a Jacuzzi: *check*.

Magical skylight on the ceiling: *check*.

Wood fireplace designed in ancient rocks reflecting the love of timeless style: *check*.

The pad was like something out of the *Lifestyles of the Rich and Famous*. I spun around slowly as I took in all the details, almost expecting Robin Leach to pop up yelling, "Champagne wishes and caviar dreams."

I gave up on my escape plan because the window couldn't be opened. Besides, we were hundreds of feet above ground.

After dinner, I retreated to my room with a borrowed book, faking tiredness. As much as I enjoyed Angel's company, I felt a strong need for some solitude. Angel didn't seem too happy, but she caved in. I went to bed early with a strange feeling in the pit of my stomach.

In the middle of the night, I opened my eyes, drenched in sweat. All traces of sleep gone, I knew instantly something was wrong. A strong wind shook the trees, whistling against the double-glazed window. Somewhere outside, a door slammed. If I stayed in bed, I'd end up tossing and turning for hours, so I pushed the sheets aside and stepped onto the wooden floor.

The fire in the fireplace had died down, but the logs still gleamed orange in the dark, spreading their last heat. I walked to the chair next to the window and slipped into my jeans and shirt, the cold material turning my skin into goose bumps.

The floor groaned under my weight as I walked to the door. For a while, I just stood there with one ear pressed against the wood to listen for sounds, my heart pounding in my chest. A voice at the back of my mind told me I had to find out what was going on. Maybe it was just the guards on routine patrol or friends leaving after a late night. Should I venture out? Was satisfying my curiosity worth catching frostbites, hypothermia, or a nasty cold? I shivered. The comfortable covers beckoned to me, but something didn't feel right so, naturally, I had to investigate. My heart pounded harder. Just a tiny look, and then I'd return to the warmth of my bed.

I turned the handle quietly and paced onto the corridor. "Here goes nothing," I whispered to myself, glancing left and right.

Several torches were lit, casting flickering shadows on the walls. Low voices echoed from around the corner. Someone said my name. Were people talking about me? I wasn't into gossip, but they might be mentioning Aidan, and that I couldn't miss.

Holding my breath, I crept slowly toward the voices, when I realized there were more than two people whispering. One was female and obviously excited; the male barely said more than two words. A palm pressed against my mouth. Turning, I shrieked, but the sound remained trapped in my throat.

Blake's voice whispered, "Found her." My heartbeat sped up. Aidan was here. Somehow they had sneaked in, and now they were going to kill me. I punched and kicked, ready to scream should Blake's grip loosen, but he didn't let go. He dragged me around the corner to where Clare hung onto a guy's arm.

"That's her?" the guy asked. "I thought she wanted out. We should've brought cuffs and a gag."

Clare frowned. "What's wrong with you, Blake? This is a rescue mission, not a kidnapping."

Blake shrugged and stepped aside. For a moment, I was stunned to find myself free to move. I opened my mouth to scream, then closed it when Clare gave me a tight hug whispering in my ear, "Us girls have to stick together, right?"

Didn't look like she harbored any murderous thoughts. The other guy turned and I recognized Devon. He helped the vampires now?

My fluttering heart calmed down a little. Whatever was going on, Devon seemed to be leading the whole operation. But could I trust him? I punched him in the arm. "You have some nerve, Shadow boy. Telling me I'm crazy for dating a vampire, and here you are with a bloodsucker all over you." I let out a huff. "Guys and their double standards. How long have you been dating Clare, you hypocrite?" Devon shot Clare a questioning look.

"I'm so glad you're okay," Clare said. "Let's get out of here."

"No." I stood my ground. "Aidan wants to kill me."

Clare wrapped her arms around me, pulling me forward. "That's nonsense, silly. Now, stay quiet. If they notice us, we're all dead."

I turned to Devon. He truly cared about my welfare. Out of the bunch, he was the only one I was willing to believe. "I thought you said Aidan was the bad one and the Shadows the good ones."

Devon smiled, face flickering like bad reception on TV. "You couldn't pay me a million dollars to live here in Freak Ville. Deidre's a nutcase."

They sure liked to change their alliances. My gut feeling told me to trust them, but then again it was the same gut feeling that advised me to take the housekeeper job, and that had been a bad move.

"Ready?" Clare asked. When I nodded, she motioned the others to move. Devon shot me a lazy grin. Something moved beneath his slightly tanned skin, stretching and flickering for a few moments. It disappeared as quickly as it started, but I couldn't stop staring at him as he led us through the corridors, halting to sniff the air at every turn. Eventually, he signaled us to stop and stay put. Drawing a deep breath, he turned a corner with Blake on his tracks.

"Going out?" a male voice asked, followed by a groan and the hard thud of someone dropping to the floor.

This was getting stranger by the minute, double standards all the way. Either Devon was a traitor, or he had a mission to fulfill. He'd been preaching the peacekeeping of Shadow Land, and less than a day later he whacked someone over the head. Why agree to a deal with me when he was clearly helping the vampires to get me out?

"What're we doing?" I whispered to Clare as Devon's head appeared around the corner. Clare just shrugged and pulled me forward, glancing behind her as if to ensure no one was following.

The door stood wide open; a strong gust of wind whipped against my skin as I followed Clare out into the night. I couldn't help but picture Mel Gibson in *Braveheart*, shouting "FREEDOM" at the top of his lungs.

"We need to be fast," Blake said, elbowing Devon. "You're a big fan of races, so show us what you've got." In a fluent motion, Blake draped me over his shoulder like I weighed nothing, knocking the breath out of me.

The trees blurred to a continuous line of darkness as we sprinted past, branches hitting and scratching my arms. Hanging upside down, I held on to Blake's waist, fighting the nausea rising inside my stomach. Several times I thought I heard voices calling my name, but when I held my breath to listen, all I could hear was the howling of the wind.

A few minutes later, Blake stopped and put me down next to Clare. I peered around, dizzy from the bumpy ride, mumbling, "I hope you get a speeding ticket." The forest stretched around us as far as I could see. It didn't look different from the woods I'd visited in my childhood when camping with my parents. If it weren't for the bad weather and the scary vampires, I could've been in Cornwall.

Devon—his face flickering again like a light bulb going on and off—reached us a few seconds later. The flickering thing stopped, and I gasped. It wasn't Devon standing before me, but a tall, large guy about my age, clad in ragged clothes and gleaming red eyes. He looked like a relative of Cass's. How could I've been so stupid and fall for their trick? I screamed at the top of my lungs, hoping it'd wake up the forest and beyond. My legs turned, ready to head back up the muddy path, but Blake clamped his hand around my mouth once again, pressing me against his chest until he squeezed all air out of my lungs. Choking or not, I wouldn't surrender easily. I kicked and tried to bite, arms charging to the sides to grab hold of a branch I could use as a weapon. Clare stepped forward and restrained my legs, whispering something I didn't understand.

"Looks like the lass doesn't want to be saved," Cass's relative said.

"Give her a break. She's been in there for almost two days. Who knows what kind of stuff they filled her head with." Clare pulled a face and tightened her grip, talking slowly as though to a child. "Amber, this is Thrain. He's a

228

friend. Trust me and I'll explain later." She took a deep breath. "Bring her to the car. We'll take care of any pursuers."

I felt Blake's muscles tensing as I was pulled up again, speeding down the winding path. We took a sharp bent through the trees, and kept on running until the path disappeared in the distance. Blake stopped and peered around before he put me down. Panting, I glanced at him. Our gazes locked. Something glittered in his eyes.

The blow, too fast to see, took me by surprise and sent me flying against a thick tree trunk. Tasting blood, I scrambled up, my arms raised to protect my face, my head throbbing. *What the heck?* This wasn't quite the rescue I'd imagined. I pictured a white horse and a knight in shining armor assuring me that everything would be all right. Then it struck me—Blake wasn't the king's brave knight, but the king's hit man. To be more precise, Aidan's enforcer. He had been sent to kill me, right here, right now. The prophecy in my dream was right on. How could Clare leave me to this fate?

Blake inched closer when someone moved behind him. My breath caught in my throat as Aidan threw my assailant to the ground shouting, "I should kill you for this."

A breeze swayed the nearby bushes. Dark, faceless shapes, thin as veils, appeared out of nowhere, their mouths whispering words I couldn't hear.

Blake rose to his knees, head bowed. "I'm doing you a favor, Aidan. You're better off without her."

Aidan threw him against a tree with supernatural force, bark flying around them. "She's my mate. You're lucky I owe you for saving my life once. Don't ever come near her again, or I'll forget we were friends. Now get the hell out of here."

Blake disappeared without a look back. Aidan kneeled beside me. "Are you all right?"

The shapes inched closer. I gaped at them, trying to discern their features. "I think I see dead people," I whispered.

"Yep," Aidan said, smiling. "More vampire jokes. You're just fine, then. Once this is over, you and my brother will be BFFs." He wrapped his arms around me, pressing me against his broad chest. Against my better judgment, I leaned into him, strangely comforted. I noticed I was shaking as he carried me to the car, the dark shapes following a few paces behind. I shouldn't trust Aidan, shouldn't trust anyone, but it felt so good to be near him again.

"What happened? You just took off," Kieran asked as we reached the vehicle and Aidan squeezed onto the backseat, pulling me close.

"Just drive." His voice came low and hoarse, his warm breath tickling my cheek.

"What about the others?" Kieran leaned forward and felt for a pulse on my neck.

I slapped his hand away. "What're you doing?"

"Just checking you're living and breathing," Kieran said. "Maybe we should discuss ways to keep you that way because right now I feel like strangling you. You got me into a lot of trouble with my brother."

"I didn't mean to sneak off." He had a right to be cross.

"No, no. I get it. You had to do it." Kieran's eyes narrowed. "Believe it or not, I'm a sucker for romance.

Two star-crossed lovers who don't fit in each other's world. Kind of like Romeo and Juliet—just with fangs."

Aidan took a long breath. "I said drive. They'll find their way back."

"Yes, Father," Kieran said. He started the engine and sped down the road. I wanted to point out that I'd rather wait to see Clare was safe, but then I decided to shut up. Aidan knew what he was doing.

The tires rattled, gravel crunching under the wheels, until we reached the main road. The low humming of the engine made me drowsy. Cuddled against Aidan's chest, I fell asleep and only woke up as Kieran pulled onto the driveway and said, "Okay kiddies, we're home. Let's go grab our guns, knives, and arrows."

"He's a drama queen." Aidan helped me out and carried me the short distance to the house.

"You knocked out one of us," Kieran muttered. "You're delusional if you think it's not going to come back to bite your ass."

Aidan just shrugged and opened the door. In the bright light of the hall I spotted the deep furrows on Aidan's forehead. When he noticed me watching, he curled his lips into a smile. I didn't miss his wince as Kieran slapped his shoulder to get his attention. He couldn't fool me. I could feel he was hurt.

"I guess what happened back there wasn't very pretty," Kieran said.

"We'll talk later." Aidan's jaw set. "Lock the doors. As for Blake, he's no longer welcome here." I squeezed his hand, feeling guilty for how things turned out. If I didn't strike that pact with the Shadows, Aidan and Blake might still be friends. But it also occurred to me that Aidan might also be dead.

Kieran snorted. "I've been telling you for years Blake's a loose cannon."

"Forget Blake," I said, realizing I was still alive in spite of what the Shadows had claimed. Who could I trust? The line between friend and foe was shifting back and forth. All I wanted was my old life. I had a feeling it was time to try bargaining with Aidan. "You have more pressing problems. The Exorcist kid wants me to save the Shadow race. They're not letting me go without a fight."

"Amber's right," Kieran said. "Besides, what good is a locked door against an army of Shadows if they decide to encircle the property and wait until our blood supply dries out?"

"I know, but—" Aidan hesitated and shot me a strange glance, as if considering whether to continue "—we can teleport, they can't."

Kieran nodded and disappeared into the kitchen. Aidan led me to the library. As soon as the door clicked shut, he lowered his lips onto mine, pulling me close until I could barely breathe. Closing my eyes, I savored the soft caress of his mouth while his fingers trailed down my arm. He ended the kiss too quickly and took a step back.

"Look at me." His voice was barely more than a whisper. I opened my eyes to meet his burning gaze. He moistened his lips. "Don't play hero because this isn't a game. They could've killed you."

"I highly doubt that. You're the one with an X on your back," I said. "Actually, they loved me and even wanted me to be part of their family."

"That's one crazy family in need of psyche meds big time. Can you imagine the family portrait with all those big black eyes staring at you." He pulled me close again, cradling me against his broad chest. "Don't believe their lies, Amber. We're talking about people who've hated me for centuries. They'd promise you the world if it helped them gain your trust."

His hands clenched to fists, his face flushed. I could see how much he struggled to keep his temper under control. The Shadows had been nothing but obliging. Something stirred inside me, a deep voice echoed at the back of my mind, calling me to listen. Realization struck me with such force that I stumbled back, staring at him. "You're doing your mind games again."

"What?" Aidan's expression darkened. "What are you talking about?"

Hiding my trembling hands behind my back, I shook my head. I had to keep quiet for the sake of my safety. Aidan didn't know the Shadows had filled me in on his secret ability. I grimaced at the image of Aidan holding beautiful Rebecca in his arms, laughing at the common mortal trusting and falling in love with him. I had been such an idiot to let my guard down. If it weren't for his ability to influence my mind, I wouldn't have fallen for him so hard in such a short time. If he ever found out, my humiliation would be complete.

"Just tell me what's wrong." He touched my cheek. I slapped his hand aside, disgusted with myself. I didn't belong here and the sooner I left his world, the better.

"Don't get a hero complex." I crossed my arms over my chest and glared at him, barely able to keep my voice from shaking at his fake confusion. "I don't owe you a thing, Aidan. In fact, you owe me for saving your butt."

He frowned. "I'm most grateful, but you should've let the others handle the situation."

"Ha. If I did you'd be dead by now." I felt the first pangs of anger. Of course he'd play the good guy. He had his role mapped out in great detail: get me to trust him, and then stab me in the back—or should I say, stab me in the neck. "You're right; I shouldn't have risked my life for you, because you're not worth it."

Annoyance crossed his face. "Just listen to yourself. You let them manipulate you. Deep down you know whatever they told you was a lie." He stared at me when the door opened and Clare walked in, oblivious to the tension in the room. She slumped down on the sofa. His gaze still locked on me, Aidan said, "You took your time."

Clare let out an exaggerated sigh. "Thanks for not ditching me in the dumpster. But it's okay, Thrain gave me a lift home." She shot me a smile and winked. "I got his phone number."

"Good for you. Seems like you have more luck than the rest of us," Aidan said with a scowl.

Clare laughed. "Don't be a sore loser. I'm sure he would've given you his number—if he swung that way."

Aidan snorted, a faint smile crossing his lips. "Believe me, you have nothing to worry. Demons don't rank high on my dating list."

"Don't come running to me when he breaks your heart," Kieran said from the hall.

Clare broke into an adoring chant of how the guy called Thrain slash demon fooled the guards into thinking he was one of them. It took her several minutes before she stopped and scanned the room. "Where's Blake?"

I didn't catch Aidan's expression, but I heard his low growl. Clare's eyes popped wide open as if she understood, and I wondered whether the vampires had some sort of secret code to communicate with one another. Surely, if I figured it out, I'd be able to fathom Aidan's plan. Or I could just ask him, but I figured the chance of him telling me the truth was almost nil. Still, I could at least try.

Aidan must've seen the change in my expression because he raised his eyebrows. My gaze wandered over the cuts and bruises on his forehead and chin—now almost faded. They hadn't been there on the day of his disappearance. For some reason, he had tried to free me from the gift and risked his life. Could be a trick, but it could also mean he at least sought a way to avoid killing me. What was the whole shebang about this gift anyway? It wasn't like I could put it to any proper use. I was so useless I doubted I could do more than call the spirit of Elvis to shake his hips. How could that help an immortal? I had to know. I wouldn't let them keep me in the dark any longer.

"May I talk to you?" I jumped up from the sofa and walked to the door without waiting for his answer, assuming he'd follow. He caught up with me as I stepped into the kitchen. When I turned he stood too close, his breath brushing my lips as he gazed down at me.

I cleared my throat, unable to hold his blue stare. "Let's go elsewhere. This isn't the place to tell you what I have to say."

"Wait a second." He disappeared into the hall and returned with a blanket he draped over my shoulders. "Let's go for a walk, but not too far." He opened the door and we stepped out into the chilly night wind. "See the path over there? It winds around the house, and leads directly into the woods."

Nodding, I let him grab my hand. I didn't tell him I'd seen the path before, on my strolls during working hours. He quickened his pace, throwing glances over his shoulder every now and then as if to make sure no one was following. The moon was hidden behind impenetrable clouds; it was so dark I could barely see my hand in front of my eyes. The house disappeared in the distance, obscured by thick trees, when Aidan took a bend and stopped in front of a wide dead trunk.

"Immortals love the woods," he said as he sat on the trunk and pulled me on his lap. "They're so mystical and tragic, don't you think?"

I pressed my lips tight as I tried to fight the uneasy feeling in my stomach. Yeah, pretty tragic all right, and a great place to chase any potential victims. Who'll hear them scream when they're having their throat ripped out in the middle of nowhere? "I don't know, Aidan. I'm not immortal." Pressing my palm against his thigh, I pulled away from him, but he draped his arms around me signaling he wouldn't let me go. I sighed and peered into the darkness, mentally preparing my words.

He spoke first. "You still don't trust me, Amber. What have I done that you don't seem able to give me a chance?"

"My mother always advised me not to trust a dead person." I hesitated, considering whether it was wise to have this conversation about us, or just ask him to reveal my purpose in his game. "You have strange manners and

236

habits, and I—" my voice broke "—I don't know what you want with me."

He rubbed a hand over my tummy, gently squeezing as if to ease my nerves. There was nothing comforting about his touch though. "I know it's hard for you to believe what I am, but you figured right from the beginning there was something wrong about me. If you didn't walk into the woods that night to, uh—" he cleared his throat "—star gaze, things would be different. We could just get to know each other without—"

"There's no *us*, Aidan." I turned to face him, surprised to find I could see him clearly in spite of the darkness around us. His eyes burned with something I could not define. Anger. Frustration. My heart started to race. He seemed to buy my bluff. Maybe he cared after all. I groaned inwardly. *Drop it. Let it go. Don't even go there.* I forced myself to look away as I whispered, "What do you want with me?"

"Don't be afraid of me because I—"

Want to use your body for my beautiful zombie bride Rebecca. "Because what?" My heart hammered faster. He'd say it; I'd finally know.

He pulled something out of his pocket and squeezed it into my palm. I turned the object in my hand. In the darkness, it felt like a coin dangling from a chain. "What is it?" Whatever it was, I had no use for it. He was the enemy. All of them were.

"It's a lucky charm. I got it from my mother right before my—" he hesitated "—before I was turned into this. It saved me from sure death. I want you to have it now." I stared at him suspiciously. What was he trying to say? Why would he give me something this valuable?

"Please just accept it. It means a lot to me," Aidan said. With a soft moan, he kissed the skin on my nape, his fingers tracing slow circles on my skin. I couldn't help but close my eyes and enjoy the tingling sensation. Cameron had never been so loving, but my ex had also never needed to fool me into trusting him. "We can't return what's inside you, but we can make the best of it."

"What's that?" The feeling of warmth turned into ice. I waited for his answer, suddenly oblivious to his kissing.

He sighed and stopped, his tone turned serious. "There's something you need to retrieve for me. For us. Trust me, if I could do it myself I would. But you carry the gift now. And if we don't do this soon, others will continue to come after you. I can't protect you during the day."

"Just say what you want, Aidan." I held my breath, my heart racing again. Once I knew, maybe I could bargain with him to get my old life back.

"There's a book, a dark manuscript that once belonged to the Shadows. The one who turned me—Rebecca—stole it a long time ago. Before she disappeared she hid it, and no immortal has been able to find it." His fingers resumed tracing circles on my neck.

"So, Rebecca turned you. What happened? After a roll in the hay she bit you? Or was it all a big misunderstanding, a love bite gone wrong?" I snorted, unable to hold back my jealousy. "What's that book good for anyway?"

"Rebecca turned me, Kieran and Clare," Aidan said. "I turned Blake when she sucked him dry, ready to dispose of his dead carcass. I couldn't let her kill one of my friends.

That's why he thinks he needs to protect me. The book's one of enchantments and incantations, the most powerful in the paranormal world."

That was a touching story. Turning your friend into a vampire because the girlfriend was about to kill him. I fidgeted on his lap, unsure what to say. Eventually I decided to return onto safer terrain. "You said Rebecca stole it. I gather she didn't spend one minute in the slammer since that might be hard to do with a ripped out throat."

"How did you know about the wound? I never said that."

I shrugged. "Kind of saw her in her room, sprawled out on the bed. Trust me, she wasn't a pretty sight."

"What else did you see?" Something in Aidan's voice made me look up.

"Is there something I should've seen?"

He shook his head. "Nope. Anyway, she hid the book before she died. It's said only someone carrying your skill—Sight—can find it."

He was keeping something from me. I could sense it. The whole affair sounded suspicious to me. How convenient for Rebecca to die before anyone saw the manuscript. "But if no one can find it, how do you know for sure this book even exists?"

"Believe me, it's not just a legend. Others have longed for it. Immortals like me, but far more willing to do whatever it takes to get it." He placed a finger under my chin and lifted my head until our lips almost met. "Lore rules or not, most wouldn't hesitate to kill for it."

I held my breath, captivated by the moment, waiting for him to lower his mouth on mine. When he didn't, I said, "The books about enchantments, right?"

"I don't know much, but from what I've been told it's more than a simple spell book. It knows the answers to all kind of questions. Legend says long time ago it was written by Blye, a powerful Shadow who sought knowledge. One night a demi-goddess appeared in his dreams. She offered to share all her wisdom with him if he promised to be hers forever. Blye knew he couldn't deny her. No one denies a demi-goddess. He loved her during the night. During daytime, he worked on the book. Twenty-one days later, the manuscript was complete, but he found a horrible fate."

My interest was piqued. "What happened to him?"

Aidan buried his face in my hair, chuckling. "You don't want to know."

"That's okay. You don't have to tell me. I'll just summon him right up and ask myself." I smiled, enjoying his warm breath on my skin. "I'm sure I have a pretty good picture of what happened."

"You've no idea," Aidan said. "The book's said to be one of the most powerful manuscripts in the world. It's unique, invaluable, and of greatest benefit to the one who owns it. It's also the reason why Layla arranges a race every five hundred years. She loves to watch the bloodbath."

I considered his words for a moment. Dallas had been wrong about the gemstones. They were worthless to mortals, but worth killing in the paranormal world. As if Cameron's cheating on me wasn't bad enough. Trust

Dallas to find new ways to make my life suck even more. "What do you want the book for?"

Aidan pulled away. I could sense a certain seriousness in his voice. "There's a ritual that can take away the bloodlust and the danger of burning in the sun. Layla wouldn't take your prize away so others will continue to chase us, but with the help of that ritual I'll be able to protect you at all times."

I gazed at him as I made a decision. "I'll use the gift to find the book. In return, I want you to promise me you'll let me return to my old life. I don't want a bodyguard 24/7."

The reaction I got from him wasn't quite what I expected. Moistening his lips, he looked away and then back at me. "It's not that simple, Amber." He shook his head vehemently. "To find the book I'll have to lead you to the threshold of death. Once there, you might not be able to find your way back unless—" his expression darkened, his blue eyes glinting unnaturally bright "—you were to become one of us."

"You want to turn me into a vampire?" I snorted, flabbergasted. He couldn't be serious. None of this could be real. I was still waiting for that moment when I'd wake up from a bad dream, then laugh it all off at my parents' breakfast table.

He squirmed beneath me as though the mere thought was an uncomfortable one. "This is a choice you have to make for yourself. I'll fill you in on all the pros and cons. I promise I'll be with you every step of the way. Take some time and think it through with no pressure from me. Immortality isn't a decision to take lightly."

241

"Really? And I thought you didn't have a heart. I'm touched you're so concerned about my wellbeing." I inhaled to calm my racing heart, pictures of eternal youth flashing through my mind. And then I remembered a movie scene showing thirsty female vampires tearing a guy to pieces, blood dripping down their chin. It was just a bad B movie, but how could I know Aidan's life wasn't like that? Why else would he keep a room in the basement, locked and marked private, unless he had a stash of bodies down there? I knew all along he was a vampire, and I knew vampires drink blood, yet I hadn't really taken it seriously. I'd been stupid not to put two and two together, and admit that Aidan needed blood to survive. Maybe he dressed all contemporary, but deep inside I doubted he had also traded his blood supply for a Bloody Mary.

"Should I thank you for giving me a choice to join your legions of the undead? Hollywood would've a field day with this one." I shot him a suspicious look and pulled back just a bit, ready to dash back to the house if he so much as lifted a finger. He could say what he wanted, but I didn't trust him one bit. "Sorry, your food's not for me. Nothing beats a steak and an old fashioned cup of tea."

Annoyance crossed his brows. "Can you take this seriously for one moment?"

"Sure, as long as you promise to introduce me to all your friends. Are there any other mythological beings or legendary creatures from the supernatural world I should know of? Any zombies or werewolves I should meet? Is your childhood best friend a mummy? Was your first kiss a ghoul?"

"Quit acting like Kieran." He regarded me with raised eyebrows for a second, then said, "I'm giving you a shot at immortality here, but I want you to keep a clear head."

I scoffed. Was he really thinking I'd just jump at the opportunity of becoming a raging monster crazed by the smell of blood? "You got me all wrong here. I'm—"

He cut me off. "Don't fight it." With lightning speed he grabbed hold of my wrist and sank his fangs into the soft flesh. It wasn't painful, just a tiny sting that seemed surreal. For a moment, my body recoiled at the realization what he was doing. My mind raced, searching for ways to ward off the unexpected attack. I pushed him to free myself as a sense of peace washed over me. His grip tightened. I closed my eyes and let myself drift off, lulled in by an unspoken promise of peace and joy.

Chapter 20

"Amber? Wake up."

Moaning, I pried my eyes open and peered at Aidan's concerned face leaning over me.

The woods were still gloomy, but the moon peered through the heavy clouds, casting a soft glow on the trees to my right. My senses seemed heightened; I could see as far as the house, hear the soft rustling of leaves, and smell the sweet, faint scent of Aidan's skin. Was it the bite from the Prince of Darkness or the prize that made me perceive all those things?

I pulled my wrist away. Aidan retrieved a tissue from his back pocket and applied pressure on the two punctures.

"You freaking bit me," I said, my voice hoarse. "You're lucky I don't call animal control."

"It was the only way to let you see."

"Pull a stunt like this again, Aidan, and I'll kick you where it counts."

"I'm truly sorry."

I nudged him in the arm. "You could've turned all Dracula on me."

Aidan smiled. "Not likely. I have excellent self-control."

"Said the spider to the fly." I pushed his hand away. "Just get away from me. Why did you bite me?"

"I wanted to show you that I'm not a monster. I don't inflict pain or rip out throats."

I smirked. "Right." He failed to mention he used mind control to sedate his victims so they couldn't fight him. Pictures flooded my mind. For a while, I just sat there, trying to make sense of what I saw. *Aidan staring wide-eyed at a beautiful red-haired girl clad in a brocade gown covered in blood, sitting amidst bodies and torn limbs scattered across the floor. The same girl leaning over Aidan, licking the ghastly gash in his throat.*

Shaking my head to get rid of the disturbing images, I peered at Aidan. "You hooked up with a serial killer? Seriously, Aidan, were you drunk?"

"Never underestimate a kiss from a vampire." His eyes twinkled as he ran a thumb over my lips. "You, out of all people, should understand that."

My cheeks burned. Our knee-weakening, mind-blowing kiss still consumed my thoughts every second of the day. "You were drawn to Rebecca, I get it. She was beautiful."

Aidan shook his head. "Beauty's only skin deep. Beneath Rebecca's splendor hid a raging, psychotic, bloodthirsty monster. She enjoyed killing."

I clicked my tongue. "She was the girl your mother warned you about."

"I guess." Aidan nodded and lifted my chin to kiss my forehead. "But she couldn't hold a candle to you."

I knew he must be lying, but I couldn't help smiling. "Thank you. It's nice to know I'm your type."

"Are you B positive?"

I laughed. "You only date mortals or vampires?"

"Yeah. Zombies, werewolves and mummies kind of stink like dead meat. Not to mention, they don't clean up all that well once they start losing their hair and limbs." He started rubbing my back.

"Why was she dressed like Cinderella at the ball?"

"It was the year 1499," Aidan said. "The year my life was turned upside down."

I gawked. Was he serious? That'd make him—

"You look great for a man who's over five hundred years old and happens to be dead. I mean, you could've hitched a ride with Columbus on his epic voyage to America and helped Sherlock Holmes solve crimes. You were around to see the great plague claim millions." And my father was upset that Cameron was a few years older. He'd keel over knowing Aidan's age. What would it be like to work the graveyard shift for hundreds of years and never feel the sun on one's face?

Aidan grimaced. "Thanks for reminding me."

"Go on," I said, smiling.

"Before meeting Rebecca, I led a sheltered life with my parents and my brother. At night we'd sit around the campfire and listen to stories about people like her— vampires roaming the streets of London, feeding on the poor and homeless. I didn't believe one word."

I squeezed his hand to convey my sympathy. "Until you met Dracula's spawn."

"Yes. Rebecca was dangerous, charming, and mysterious."

A pang of jealousy hit me in the pit of my stomach. I raised my brows. "Sexy?"

Aidan rocked slowly back and forth, his gaze focused in the distance as he recalled his memories. "Yeah, that too. Something seemed odd about her though, but I couldn't place it. I never thought she was a killer, not until one fateful night when she decided I was worthy of her blood. I was never given a choice."

"I take it there's no support group for newbies. Why did she do it in the first place?"

He shrugged, his gaze lost in the woods around us, as if he was reliving the details of his former life. "Maybe she was bored and wanted a companion, or personal slave. I had just turned eighteen and was easy to manipulate. She never revealed her purpose. There's another reason why I wanted you to see the sort of vampire I am." His gaze locked with mine. "You and I—we're meant to be together."

I rolled my eyes. "The bond again. Everybody keeps mentioning it. What's that all about?" My heart pumped hard as I let my voice trail off. Something told me we *were* meant to be together, and it scared the living hell out of me.

Aidan spoke slowly. "When two people are destined for each another, they're called mates. A strong psychic connection bonds them together. That's what you and I have. Some of us will never find that rare and beautiful love of a lifetime. Blake, Kieran and Clare have been searching for hundreds of years. I've found mine and I'll never let go." He cupped my face in his hands, our gaze connecting in the darkness. "Can't you see, Amber? Losing you would be like a stake to my heart. We can make this work. I'm not a dreadful person. Being together won't be as bad as you think. Just don't give up on us."

The moonstone pendant burned against my skin. I shook my head, hesitating. His words touched my heart because they rang true. I wanted to believe him, but I couldn't.

"Falling in love with a vampire ruined your life," I whispered. "I don't want it to ruin mine." This was the stuff of nightmares, legends and horror movies, and pretty darn freaky. I knew I should get away as far as I could, but I couldn't. I felt torn inside, unsure what to do. "I care about you more than you'll ever know." I searched his eyes, trying to make him see the turmoil inside me. "I'm trying so hard to understand your world, but all of this is too much to handle." I got up from his lap and dropped down near a tree, surprised to find I could still distinguish his features in the darkness.

"There's something else you should know," Aidan whispered. "I'm torn whether to turn you because Rebecca's memory still lingers in my mind as if it all happened yesterday. Sometimes I wake up confused, unable to distinguish between the past and the present."

He was still into the bloodsucker. So much for eternal, exclusive love. "She's gone. Do you want to raise her? Is that why you still keep her clothes?" I glared at him as more pangs of jealousy washed over me. The pendant around my neck felt like hot iron, heavy and unpleasant.

Aidan opened his mouth to speak. I held up a hand to stop him. "No, don't answer that. It's none of my business. I don't want this gift you have to offer, Aidan. Killing the entire town isn't really my thing. I mean, where'd I get my nails done?"

"You wouldn't be like that." I could hear the hesitation in his voice. So, he had no idea how I might turn out.

I raised my glance to the canopy of trees filtering the soft glow coming from above. "Great, I'm sitting under the full moon with a vampire, talking about his zombie bride. I guess it could be worse. You could be shape shifting into a wolf right now."

"Werewolves aren't real."

"Yeah." I snorted. "That's a good one. After the creatures I met in the last month, I wouldn't be surprised to find myself shaking hands with a troll this very minute."

"Your sense of humor is one of the things I like the most about you. But let's get back to the nitty-gritty. As mates, we can feel each other's emotions. I know you're jealous of Rebecca even though you have absolutely no reason to be."

I jumped up from my sitting position, cheeks burning. "I'm not—"

Aidan cut me off. "We can teach you how to live a fairly normal life, but there's still a chance you won't be able to control the blood craze. I don't want you to hate me for turning you into a loathsome creature of the night. That's the reason why I can't stop thinking about Rebecca. It's not obsessive love but hate. Once we have the book in our possession, things will be different."

I ran my hand over the moonstone pendant as more pictures of blood-sucking vampires flooded my mind. As

249

much as I wanted to assure him I didn't see him as a monster, I couldn't. He had been in the wrong place at the wrong time, seduced by the gorgeous Rebecca. How could I ever blame him for that? But that didn't make him less of a monster.

"This turning thing isn't going to work for me. I'll just get your little old book and be on my way back to Normal Ville," I said.

He shook his head. "If only it worked that way."

I groaned. "Please, no more. I think I know all there is to know about vampires."

Aidan got up from the tree trunk and inched closer, halting a few inches away from me. "Really? But you haven't even asked the obvious question."

Maybe I didn't want to know the answers. Ah, yes, what the heck. I might as well go all the way. I looked up at his dark shape. "You guzzle down a pint of cold blood every night? Or do you prefer it hot like coffee? Maybe sprinkle a little anti-clotting agent in place of creamer?"

"I've no idea what you're talking about," Aidan said, dryly.

I took a deep breath, summoning up the courage to ask what I felt was a key issue here. "Do you feed on the life essence of humans?"

Aidan cringed. "Feeding straight from the source is kind of medieval, don't you think? I drink only donor's blood, although it doesn't taste the same as the real deal. It took me a long time to get used to it."

The pendant burned, scorching my skin. I could feel rage bubbling up inside me. He was a monster, no matter how he put it. How could I ever introduce him to my

250

parents? My emotions kept changing from trust to distrust, from understanding to fury, as though there were two different people inside me, fighting to take control over my feelings and actions. I tried to sound nonchalant, like it didn't matter, but it did. "So, you rob the local blood banks?"

Aidan hesitated. "Let's say I have connections."

"I can't imagine being on a warm protein liquid diet, and believe me, I've tried plenty of weight loss plans in my time."

"Morning will break soon. We need to get back to the house before the first rays of light appear." He reached me in two short strides and held out his palm. I grabbed it and let him pull me up. His stare made me feel uneasy.

"Let's go then."

"You haven't put on my mother's necklace," Aidan said, pulling it out of my pocket. His breath tickled my cheek as he touched my throat, brushing Deidre's pendant. A voice shrieked inside my head. Aidan stumbled backwards. I raised my hands to cover my ears against the ear-piercing screech.

Aidan approached slowly, his face resembled a mask of fury. "Take that off." I gawked at him, wide-eyed. He took another step forward until he stood mere inches away, towering over me. "Amber, that thing's infused with magic. Whatever it's for, it's not doing you any favors. Take it off now."

With shaking fingers I unclasped the pendant. The metal burned and twisted like a snake in my hands as I dropped it to the ground. My mind cleared as though a heavy cloud had just lifted. I inhaled to calm my racing heart.

Aidan clasped his mother's necklace around my neck and placed a kiss on my forehead. "It's just a necklace," Aidan said, as though sensing my hesitation. "I'd never influence you in order to take advantage."

I let him hold my hand on the way back. Trudging down the path to the house, something clicked into place. My rage had disappeared, and curiosity had taken its place. "Do you sleep during the day?" I asked, resuming our conversation. That much I knew already, but I needed to hear it from him. Just the usual gathering of facts.

"Unfortunately, yes. I wish it was just a myth."

I laughed. "Guess Bram Stoker got it right."

"Finding the book will give me my life back. I haven't seen the sun rise in hundreds of years." He pointed at the dark horizon. "It's the first thing I want to do with you by my side. We'll have eternal youth and—"

"Perfect skin." I giggled.

"Yes, all of it. No more blood, no more fearing sunlight."

His talk of a future together made me feel awkward, insecure, so I decided to change the subject. "If you stay outside you burn to ash?" The thought both scared and fascinated me.

He smiled. "I don't know. But I've heard the pain's unbearable, so I'd rather not find out."

The house was as silent as a tomb. We entered the kitchen through the backdoor and climbed up the stairs together. In front of my room, Aidan stopped and pressed his lips against mine whispering, "Promise you won't run away."

I nodded and wrapped my arms around his neck, hating myself for giving in so easily. I wished he'd ask if he could come in to spend more time with me. If only a few minutes. After Cameron's stunt I needed to feel loved again. Aidan pulled back.

"Sleep well." He smiled, then turned on his heel. Holding my breath in case he changed his mind, I waited until he disappeared up the stairs before returning to my room, ready to get some sleep.

***

The day seemed too long. I couldn't eat or sleep because my thoughts kept circling around my encounter with Aidan. He'd said we were meant to be together. I'd read enough magazines to know no guy would ever make such a grand statement, unless he followed a hidden agenda. Aidan lied to get my cooperation. I was willing to cooperate, but only if he promised to help me return unscathed from wherever I was supposed to travel. As much as I fancied the idea of eternal youth, I wouldn't turn into the Princess of Darkness. My parents would never get over that blow.

From behind the curtains of my window on the first floor, I watched Harry Timble examine the scrubs around the house, a black cat meowing around his ankles.

"Is this your work, kitty?" he said as he pulled out a dead squirrel from behind a bush. "Such a good girl. You get them all, don't you, dearie?"

The old man reminded me of my father who had worked so hard to give Dallas and me the best education possible. I missed my parents so much. So, I vowed to focus on damage control and get out of this situation as soon as possible. No more Aidan. No more wishing we could be together. We lived in different worlds. It would never work out.

I retreated to the kitchen to get another cup of coffee and stared out onto the back garden, my fingers playing with Aidan's pendant. The house was empty and silent. For the split of a second I was tempted to invite Harry in for a cup of tea, but then decided against it. One thing was obvious, the old man didn't know what was going on in Aidan's house. With so many questions still unanswered, I didn't trust my curiosity. I couldn't start poking around and risk arousing the old man's suspicion.

I waited until Harry headed for the garbage bins in the garage, the cat still meowing at his feet, and then left the house, following the path to the place where Aidan had shown me a part of his former life only a few hours ago. But I didn't walk as far as the tree trunk. Risking being kidnapped by the Shadows was out of the question if I was to have my old life back.

Pulling my cardigan tighter around me, I sat on the damp ground. Although the sun shone through the canopy of loose branches above my head, the freezing north wind made me shiver. In broad daylight, the woods looked divine. The dried leaves scattered across the ground gave the impression of a shaggy rug. Morning dew glittered in the grass. I sat there for a while, inhaling the clean scent of oncoming autumn and sorting through my thoughts until a plan emerged. I loved Aidan, but a relationship was out of the question. The Shadows had been right. I was a mortal and didn't belong in Aidan's world. Even if he wanted to protect me, Aidan had trouble written all over him. My parents mattered far more than a deadly romance. My death or disappearance would break their heart. To spare them the pain, I'd give up the love of my life.

Harry was nowhere to be seen as I followed the path back to the house. Would Aidan expect me to resume my job as a housekeeper? Probably not since I'd handed in my notice. I still needed the money, but my lack of funds was the last thing on my mind.

I cuddled on the sofa in the living room and waited. The grandfather clock on the wall ticked, its unnerving sound cutting like a razorblade through the silence of the empty room. I napped through the afternoon, waking several times only to fall asleep again, dreaming mostly of Aidan.

When darkness finally descended, I got up from the sofa and switched on the lights, chasing away the ominous shadows cast by the heavy furniture. In the kitchen, I found some old sandwiches. The cheese tasted sweaty, but I ate it anyway, then turned on the cold-water tap and poured myself a glass of water to rinse my mouth. After a quick shower, I changed into my favorite jeans and a shirt. The jeans smelt earthy from the woods. As usual I'd forgotten to wash my clothes, but at least the shirt was clean. I combed my wet hair, leaving it to dry naturally, brushed my teeth, applied make-up and examined myself in the bathroom mirror.

The dark shadows under my eyes were obvious. The red lipstick didn't do my flaky skin any favors, but Aidan wouldn't notice any of these because I wouldn't let him see me up-close. From now on, I'd keep my distance. No more talking about love bonds and a future together. My obsession with him had to stop because I had a job to do, which was retrieving the book so I could get the hell out of here.

I returned to the living room and sat down. Aidan hadn't told me where he usually slept, but I guessed it was somewhere in the house; maybe even in his own room or in one of the many other chambers upstairs. I thought of Harry and Greta, and for the first time it occurred to me that Aidan felt safe here and that he might find this century rather pleasant because people were less superstitious. Since nobody seemed to question his routines and habits, it made pretending to be normal easier.

Time passed slowly. Eventually, I heard the first creek of approaching footsteps. I sat up, rigid, suddenly nervous like a teen on my first date. What would Aidan look like? Would he find me pretty tonight? It didn't matter anyway because I had no interest in getting close to him.

The door opened and the dark shape of a guy entered.

I lifted my gaze. My smile froze on my lips. "What're you doing here?"

Chapter 21 - Aidan

I smelled the visitor long before I woke up, my heart beating too fast, the sweet scent of blood beckoning to me more than any other because it was so similar to my mate's. I got up with a groan and reached the food supply in a few strides, downing the content of a bag in one large gulp. Since Amber's arrival, the bloodlust was growing stronger, and biting her hadn't helped ease it one bit. In fact, it had made it stronger because I hadn't drunk fresh blood in a long time. My true powers tingled beneath my skin, ordering me to drink more of the good stuff so they would ripen to reach their full potential. But to fully embrace my real vampire nature I would risk turning into what Rebecca was. I had drunk blood from a source before and then waited it out a few weeks until the addictive need for it subsided. But this time it was different. This was the curse of having a mortal mate; her blood would always seem sweeter, more tempting than that of any other mortal.

Unfortunately the same applied to her family. Killing Amber's brother was out of the question though. How could I persuade the in-laws I was the right one for their daughter when, instead of focusing on small talk, all I could think about was how not to kill them? I could only imagine what I'd say to the prospective in-laws, "Hello, it's a pleasure to eat, I mean, meet you." I had to find the book—and fast—before I turned Amber and half of her family with or without their consent.

Kieran waited for me outside my room, leaning against the railing, an unnerving grin playing on his lips. "Fee! Fie! Foe! Fum! I smell the blood of an Englishman. Be he 'live, or be he dead, I'll grind his bones to make my bread."

Walking past, I hissed, "Shut up."

"You're right. The lyrics don't fit. I'll change the end: Be he 'live, or be he dead, I'll drain his blood from his head."

I punched his shoulder.

Kieran lifted his hands, his smile widening. "What?" He sniffed the air and moaned. "Are you having a Fangsgiving Day dinner without me again? Somebody's messy. You know, they came up with this marvelous invention in this century. It's called a paper napkin. Ever heard of it?"

Kieran wasn't going to drop it. Not until he got bored. I sighed and decided to get it over with. "Okay, say it."

"No idea what you're talking about." Kieran raised his eyebrows in mock confusion.

"That I'm a fool for putting myself through this because of a girl."

Kieran laughed, eyes glinting with self-satisfaction. "You're going about it the wrong way, bro. Girls will trip over themselves to get a bad guy. The way you're proceeding, she won't fall for you in a million years. If you bite her and she turns, the Lore court will kill you, but she'll have her bad boy. If you don't bite her, you'll end up running around in those stained shirts for the rest of your existence."

I looked down at the stains, and sighed. I had been too frantic yet again, even though I knew drinking frozen blood would never quell my thirst. "Crap. It's probably on the carpet too. Where's Clare? She's a miracle worker when it comes to removing tough stains."

"Great way to impress your future brother-in-law, by the way," Kieran continued. "You look like you took a blood bath. The only thing missing is the axe. Would Dallas really let his little sister date a crazed murderer who hacks bodies in the basement? You need to change that shirt pronto. And oh, you're welcome. I just saved you from making a complete and utter fool of yourself, but don't mention it."

I curled my lips into a fake smile. "Thanks. It's so nice to know you've got my back."

Kieran regarded me coolly. "A hobby might help ease all that hunger. Have you ever considered fixing cars, or woodworking, or maybe a DIY project around the house?"

"You're getting a big laugh out of this, aren't you?"

Kieran shrugged. "There's nothing on TV. I really hope you don't change her. If you do it's a sure death sentence, and I won't stand by and watch."

I smirked. "Just do me a favor and get Amber's brother out of the house before I have his blood stains on my shirt, too."

Kieran crossed his arms over his chest, grinning. "Yeah, killing him might not help you earn any brownie points with her. So, what's with the bad mood? Not yourself today?"

"Not really." I stared at the floor and the whirled up dust particles shimmering in the artificial light.

"I doubt you'll ever be, bro, and that's because she has you wrapped around her little finger." Kieran winked, his laughter ringing through the hall as he headed downstairs.

I returned to my room to change. I'd be the one having the last laugh when Kieran found his mate, but until then I reckoned I'd continue to be the laughing stock.

Clare wasn't in the library. I dropped on the sofa and waited for my brother to give me the all clear. Half an hour later, Kieran hadn't returned from the living room, and the scent of Amber's brother still hung heavy in the air. How could I talk to Amber, make her want me and agree to her turning if things went wrong, if Kieran didn't hurry up a bit?

A vein throbbing in my right temple, I stood and took a few tentative steps down the hall. Voices carried over; the scent seemed a hundred times stronger here. Then I heard Kieran's laughter, and I realized my stupid brother was probably having the time of his life—on my expense. Fighting the sudden pang of hunger, I clenched my hands and entered the living room.

***

Amber sat next to Kieran, laughing at something he said. My gaze was drawn to the dark blond guy to her right. Dallas, Amber's brother, looked like the tanned version of her, but his heartbeat was less frantic. The poor guy probably had no idea he was talking to a killing machine that could snap his neck in an instant.

Kieran noticed my entrance first and jumped up, putting himself between Dallas and me. For the first time in years, my brother didn't have a cracking comment up his sleeve. My back was slick from sweat as I forced air into my lungs. I pushed Kieran aside with more force than intended and held out my hand. Amber glanced up at me, startled, as though she didn't expect me to join the party. Well, as far as I remembered it was still my house. If she didn't feel comfortable introducing me to her family, she shouldn't have called them over to visit.

Amber pointed at me. "Dallas, this is my boss, Aidan McAllister. Aidan, this is my brother Dallas."

Dallas seemed oblivious to the tension in the room as he shook my hand with unnatural vigor. "You're the guy who managed to turn our Amber into a household goddess. Mum and Dad will never believe it."

I frowned. So, Dallas still thought Amber was just the housekeeper. She hadn't told her brother we were on the verge of dating? I shot her an irritated glance. "I don't know about the household goddess part. Let's face it. Amber's no Kim Woodburn or Aggie MacKenzie, that's for sure."

She scowled. "If you want a five-star menu that you're not going to eat anyway because you *eat out* most nights, why don't you just hire a cook?"

"I sense trouble in paradise." Kieran's smile was back in place as he said to Dallas, "Come on. I'll show you the house while they sort out their lovers' spat? Could take a while."

"Did you say *lovers' spat?*" Dallas raised his brows. Kieran dragged him out the door.

"What's wrong with you? Did you wake up on the wrong side of the coffin?" Amber placed her hands on her hips, her gaze throwing daggers. "Your brother couldn't keep his mouth shut to save his life. I'll tell Dallas when I'm good and ready. He had no right to spill the beans. And as for you—"

I laughed, interrupting her. "Inviting your brother over wasn't the brightest idea, especially not when you're hell-bent on keeping us a big secret." I grabbed her shoulders, ready to shake that arrogance out of her. Clare was right, Cameron wasn't forgotten yet, or why else would she not make our dating official?

Amber pushed my hands aside. "I didn't invite him. He came to visit because, with all the drama, I forgot to reply to his last message and he was worried." I knew she was lying from her racing heart. But I let her continue. "Do you really think I'd put my brother's life at risk by introducing him to a bunch of vampires looking for their next dinner?"

A bunch of vampires? Was that all I was to her? I cringed, ignoring my anger. "That's okay. It's not like I want to meet the in-laws any time soon. We all know I only hired you because you're hot."

Standing, she inched closer, barely reaching my chin as she glared up at me. "Since you keep mentioning my cooking and cleaning skills, is there something you're trying to tell me?"

Until now I had been the one to do the chasing. Kieran was right, I was going at it the wrong way. Time to play it cool. "Let's put it this way—" I took a deep breath, considering my words "—we fancy the pants off each other, but I'd rather not meet your family."

Her jaw dropped; her expression hardened. She looked like she fought hard not to slap me. I sounded like my brother, but as much as I wanted to hug her tight and admit my lie, I couldn't. Judging from her dating history, she didn't fall for good guys. "Why would I even want a guy with over five hundred years of emotional baggage?"

I snorted. "Like you have room to talk."

"I didn't spend hundreds of years with Cameron," Amber said.

"You can't move forward with your life. It's the same thing."

She glared at me. "Why don't you go out on the town and look for some fresh necks to bite? I'll be sure to have the bartender spike your Blood Light with garlic."

"My what?"

"*Bud light.* A beer?" She waved her hand in my face. "Ah, never mind. Guess at your age, keeping up with the youth is a tough task. I don't see the point in being here much longer. Let's just get the darn book so I can be on my way."

"Sure. Whatever suits you, babe." I winced at her hurt expression, which disappeared immediately behind a cold mask.

"I'm not your babe. Never will be." Keeping her head high, she dropped onto the sofa and turned away from me. "I'm so tired of playing house with you. Don't even say another word to me until you figure out how to get the book."

I regarded her profile for a moment. All the makeup in her face couldn't hide the signs of exhaustion. Her cheeks were flushed, her eyes glinting with moisture. Clearly, her ego was hurt. I could only hope Kieran's tactic wouldn't backfire. Sitting down beside her, I draped an arm over her shoulders, drawing her closer. She stiffened, but didn't pull away.

"Do you have any plans tomorrow evening?" I whispered in her ear.

Amber drew in a sharp breath, her heartbeat spiking again. "What? I'm not so sure a housekeeper should be seen with a guy of your stature."

I cocked an eyebrow. "I thought you quit."

"I did. But you wouldn't let me leave, if I remember correctly. So, technically, I'm still being paid."

Hiding my smile, I said, "We're getting the book tomorrow night—if you don't have any other plans."

She turned to face me, brows furrowed. "As a matter of fact, I do. Yeah, big ones. I'm washing my hair. But I'll make an exception because the sooner I get rid of you, the better."

I knew she didn't mean it, but the words stung nonetheless. The door swung open and Cassandra walked in. Her gaze moved between Amber and me, then to my hand on Amber's thigh. "Get a room, guys."

"I don't think so," Amber said. "You couldn't pay me to get a room with him because he's rude, pushy, selfish, disrespectful and obnoxious. Shall I go on?"

Cass shook her head. "Nope. We got the message, loud and clear. Why, I could've told you that, mate, and saved you the heartache. The last thing you want is obnoxious offspring."

"That's not even an option." Amber sighed.

Cass inched closer, as usual not able to keep her mouth shut. "Let me give you some great advice. Aidan's the finest piece of vampire meat you've ever met. But never invite a vampire into your heart, silly girl." She glanced at me, nostrils flaring, eyes sparkling like she enjoyed every bit of the chaos she created.

"Go away, Cass," I said, irritated, wishing I could just throw her butt right out the door.

"I want to get a million miles away from this moron." Amber sat up and pushed my hand aside. "But for now, the next room will have to do. I'll get Clare while I'm there."

Cass watched Amber walk out, then turned to me, eyes glinting again. "What's cracking?"

Half the time I didn't understand a word she said, and the other half she annoyed the hell out of me. "Mind your own business, Cass," I said, taking in another one of her strange attires: a colorful, baggy dress that looked like it was cut out of a tablecloth, and combat boots.

But Cass didn't seem to know when to back off. "Amber's showing you the cold shoulder, huh? Been there, done that. Nothing a little strip can't solve."

"You're suggesting I take off my clothes?" I shot her an amused look, waiting for her to start laughing. Her face remained dead serious.

"Obviously, getting naked won't do the trick." Cass rolled her eyes. "Keep it subtle, you know—" she waved a hand about "—a bare shoulder here, a naked pin there. You know the drills."

I laughed. "How do you propose I show my legs unless I run around the house naked and risk prosecution for indecent exposure in front of my employees?"

"Show a bit more fantasy, mate. I can't do all the work for you." She tapped her fingers against her painted lips. "What about a kilt? You could get away with it since we're in Scotland and all. I've heard girls are suckers for guys in skirts."

"Why're you here, Cass?" I asked, not quite able to shake off the frightening image of hundreds of hairy legs in short skirts and dresses. I shivered, focusing on how widened Cass's eyes suddenly seemed. She was about to lie. First Amber, now she. What was wrong with me that people just couldn't tell me the truth?

Cass smoothed a hand over her reddish hair to gain a few more second. "I was worried about Amber. Had to check you guys got her back okay."

I narrowed my gaze. "Since when do you care?"

"Hey, don't be like that. I really like her. We're two pals who share secrets, like sisters," Cass said.

"I'm sure Thrain filled you in."

Her voice rose a notch. "Nope. He was too busy." She regarded me, all wide-eyed innocence. "You never thanked me. Without my help you wouldn't have Amber back. Though, she doesn't seem too happy about it."

"If I thank you, will you be on your merry way?"

She held up her palms, eyes glinting. "Can't make any promises, mate."

I laughed. Getting rid of her was harder than breaking into a military base. "Thank you, Cass. I truly appreciate everything you did for us. You should trade your horns for angel wings."

She snorted. "And you thought you couldn't trust me."

The door opened again. "We'll be talking later. Don't think I'll forget," I whispered.

Cass shrugged, but I could see the relief in her face as she jumped up and grabbed Amber in a hug. Cass's gaze locked on Dallas who stood in the open door, hands in his pockets, unsure what to do. "Who's the hottie?" Cass whispered. "He's such a hunk."

"More like a chap in tacky bottoms." Amber motioned Dallas to step nearer. "This is my brother, Dallas. Dallas, this is Cass."

Dallas cleared his throat, eyes sparkling almost as bright as Cass's, but Cass spoke first. "I'm fuming you kept him from me. What a waste."

"Are you on your way to a Halloween party?" Dallas grinned and pointed at her tiny horns peeking from beneath her hair.

"Oh, this little number." Cass laughed and grabbed his arm, pulling him down on the sofa. "I'm on my way to a charity event run by the Devils in Danger Foundation. It's all about saving the Tasmanian Devil. If we don't act, they'll go extinct."

"Sounds like a worthy cause," Dallas said, seemingly impressed.

Looking away, I rubbed my neck. Whatever Cass was doing in my house, it probably wouldn't help my quest with Amber one bit. Clare walked in, and I leaned back, switching off the drivel as I went through my plan one more time. I wasn't keen on meeting the Shadows, not after the stunt they pulled on me. But to return my mate safely from her imminent trip, I had to use all the help I could get.

Nodding, I joined the laughing concoction that seemed to evolve around a glowing Cass, a staring Dallas and Kieran—the center of attention, as usual—telling a story everyone seemed to enjoy. Everyone apart from Amber, who shot me a glare. I breathed in and focused on our bond to feel her emotional undercurrents. She was mad, but not because of me. She didn't like the way Cass and Dallas looked at each other. I couldn't help but feel a wee smug. At least she wasn't having a good time either.

Without paying the others any attention, I signaled Kieran to follow me. My brother pulled a face that had the others hooting again and joined me outside.

"You're not helping your case if you come across as a cold fish," Kieran said, closing the door behind him.

"You realize we have more pressing issues than entertaining the ladies."

Kieran sighed and leaned against the wall mouthing, "Salmon."

"Whatever." I shook my head. Most of the time, I had no idea why I put up with him. "Call Devon and tell him Amber's trip is scheduled for tomorrow night. If they're still in, he should get the preparations going."

Kieran's jaw dropped. "You're kidding! Why do you think they're going to play fair this time?"

"I don't have a choice. Just do it."

Kieran regarded me for a minute, then shrugged and pulled out his phone. I returned to the living room. If everything went according to plan, the book would be found soon, and I could finally focus on earning Amber's love. If not—I clicked my tongue. Failing wasn't an option.

Amber didn't get up from her seat, but I noticed her questioning gaze, heart racing again. I sat down next to Dallas, opposite from her, ignoring the devastating call of the forbidden blood. From the corner of my eye, I noticed Amber lean forward, a frown perched between her brows, as she tried to eavesdrop on the conversation.

"Kieran filled me in on your little courtship," Dallas said. "Hey, sis, is it really such a good idea to mix business with pleasure? It's a great way to lose your job."

"Or your life," Amber muttered under her breath.

"What?" Dallas asked.

Amber smiled, sweetly. "I said it could cause strife."

"We have a fair share to work out," I said. I hated how casual that sounded.

For a moment, Dallas seemed uncomfortable. "You know about the ex in London, right?" When I nodded, he said, "You seem like a good guy. Don't break her heart like Cameron, or I'll have to kick your butt."

The mortal threatening me—if his brotherly love wasn't so touching, it'd be downright hilarious. Struggling to keep a straight face, I nodded. A minute later, Kieran appeared and gave me the thumbs-up sign. I exhaled, relieved that at least one part of the plan was proceeding according to plan. I stood and reached for Amber's hand. "Can I have a moment?" Four pairs of eyes settled on us.

She moistened her lips. "Uh, sure." I helped her up, our fingers barely touching. An electric shock ran down my spine as I tightened my grip and led her to the kitchen, then closed the door.

"What do you want?" Amber hissed.

In the darkness, I pressed her against the wall and placed my mouth on hers. She draped her arms around my neck. Something stirred inside me—the hunger I thought I had under control. I couldn't touch her, not without gulping down another gallon of donor blood. Not until she chose me and the bond we shared.

Peeling her arms from my neck, I pressed a last kiss on her lips and let go of her, then switched on the light. Amber blinked against the sudden brightness. Her lips glistened with moisture; her hair was in disarray, clothes disheveled. I probably didn't look much better.

"We need to talk about tomorrow," I murmured.

"It's done then?" She tilted her head and sighed. Her heart beat faster, her mouth tightened. She was scared. I wished I could assure her everything would turn out as planned, but I didn't want to lie. Her expression softened, and for the first time I saw something in her. As much as she fought it, she recognized our bond. I nodded. The pink tip of her tongue flicked over her upper lip. "When?"

I placed a peck on her forehead and drew her onto my lap as I sat on a chair, burying my face into the soft mane of her hair. "Before midnight."

She nodded.

"I'm scared," I whispered so low she wouldn't hear me.

"What?" Amber asked.

I shook my head. "I asked you to think about my offer. Have you made a decision yet?" I forced myself to meet her probing gaze.

For a brief moment, confusion crossed her face, then she grasped the meaning of my words and her expression darkened. "I have. The answer's no."

"I'm only trying to save your life, Amber. Think about it. With immortality, you also get an eternity of various skills."

"Like eternal youth, mind-control, and traveling at the speed of light?" She snorted.

"Among others. I can't go into detail because you're not one of us yet, but with my blood you also get my memories and knowledge. We're strong; we're not slaves to our need for blood. The Shadows have outnumbered us for centuries, and yet they can't win the battle."

"Beauty and brains. What more could a girl ask for?" She shook her head. "Don't look at me with those sad, soulful eyes. It won't change a thing. I don't need your protection. I can take care of myself without turning into what you are. The only things that should be sucking blood are leeches, fleas, mosquitoes, spiders and ticks."

"Your jokes never cease to amaze me," I said, dryly. She was clearly spending too much time with Cass and Kieran. Or where else could she have learned how to come up with one insult after another?

"You said you liked my sense of humor. All joking aside, Aidan, I'm not trying to give you a hard time, but I want to be able to lay on the beach and sip a glass of water without bursting into flames. Please understand. It's a girls' thing."

Fearing she'd make this choice was one thing, hearing her utter the words was another. I ran my fingers through my hair, wary of the calculating look Amber shot me. "Fair enough. But if things don't go smoothly and—"

271

Amber cut me off. "Then you let me die."

I regarded her, open-mouthed. The victory I could sense in her told me she saw the situation as some sort of triumph over me. Whatever sort of battle she fought against me, it was slowly starting to tick me off. "You don't mean it."

"Of course I do." She crossed her arms over her chest and raised her chin defiantly.

"Please. You know I wouldn't turn you without your consent." It was a lie. Even though the chance she'd hate me was high, keeping Amber alive was worth risking her wrath.

Shaking her head, she stood. "I'll never change my mind. So, get this book and give me my old life back. Got it?" Shooting me a last glance over her shoulder, she walked out. A few moments later, I heard the living room door open and shut.

I switched off the lights and opened the back door to let in the freezing Highland air. I wasn't surprised at Amber's reaction to my proposition. Given the same circumstances and choices, I probably would've decided the same way. She was a mortal and had no reason to trust me since I had done nothing to earn her trust. Were she any other, I wouldn't have hesitated to wait out the next race, even if it meant someone else going after the mortal. But this was different; I couldn't risk the Shadows using Amber's powers and let her die in the process.

I swore under my breath and leaned against the wall. A strong breeze ruffled the curtains. My once mortal body would've shivered, but I didn't feel the cold now. And soon Amber wouldn't either, whether she wanted it or not.

Chapter 22

How dare Aidan try to fool me into giving in to his sordid proposition? He could pay me a million bucks, but that wouldn't change a darn thing because no amount of money would make me give up my espresso.

I could picture myself at the *Coffee, Anonymous Meeting For Vampires*, talking to a bunch of sympathetic, nodding, newly turned members. "I miss my old life. I miss my coffee and tea. Sure, I love blood, but it can't replace my latte. I stare at my coffee cup and long for a sip."

The sponsor would smile and say, "These intense feelings go away after a few years. Fifty tops. Okay, newbies, let's give Amber a warm welcome."

Horrified and fuming inside, I snapped out of my thoughts and curled my lips into a smile as I tuned in to the trivial chatter. Unlike Kieran—who kept throwing me questioning glances—the others didn't seem to notice my upheaval. And that was good because I didn't want to worry Dallas. Regarding my brother, I took a sharp breath and joined in the laughter. His cheeks were flushed, eyes shining, as he hung onto Cass's every word. *Great!* As if I didn't have enough problems already. Now he had to fall for the demon and add more to the pile.

"You okay?" Kieran mouthed. With Aidan and Clare gone to take care of what they called 'important business', he seemed to have assumed the role of watching over me now.

I looked away, ignoring him. For all I knew, he could be working with Aidan on that ridiculous plan to turn me into one of them. Frankly, I had no idea why Aidan kept pressuring me into agreeing. In spite of his words, I didn't believe it'd be such a hard task to get the book—use the gift to find the place, get it, done. It wasn't exactly rocket science. No need to give up my life for it.

"You think Amber's a bad housekeeper? You should see me," Cass said, grinning.

I blinked at hearing my name. "What?"

"I was just telling Cass how surprised I was you got the job." Dallas winked. "You must've left out in your application that you even manage to burn toast."

"Luckily for her, Aidan doesn't eat toast," Kieran said.

Dallas laughed, oblivious to Kieran's double entendre. If I didn't get a chance to spend some alone time with my brother soon, I might end up forgetting my good manners. I ignored Kieran's stare as I addressed my brother in the most nonchalant voice I could muster. "I believe you came to talk about Mum and Dad?" Confusion crossed his features. I opened my eyes wide, hoping he'd take the hint. He didn't.

"Huh?"

"Their wedding anniversary, dummy," I prompted. There would be no anniversary for the next six months, but I doubted Dallas knew. As expected, his expression turned from confusion to guilt. I slapped my hand against my mouth in mock surprise, hoping I wasn't going over the top with my theatrical performance. "No! Don't tell me you forgot again."

Dallas peeked at Cass. His rosy cheeks turned bright red. "I'm not too late, am I?"

Cass's eyes shone as she sniffed the air. "Chaos coming right up."

"You'd better not be. You know how angry Mum can get." I pulled Dallas up and motioned him to follow me, lest the demon read my mind.

"Hey, do you think you could share with me?" Dallas asked as soon as we reached the hall.

"What?"

He shrugged. "You know, whatever you bought them. I'll totally pay half."

I laughed. He was so gullible, like an overexcited little boy. Who else would believe he'd scored the jackpot by stealing a bunch of fake gemstones? Would he ever grow up? "All right. Mum and Dad needn't know."

Dallas let out a big breath. "You got me scared for a second. Mum would've kicked me out. She did last year. Literally."

"Yeah, I remember." Dallas had been the only guest to turn up at the anniversary without a clue what the party was for. In an angry fit, my mother had called him an airhead, who couldn't find his brain even if it came knocking on his door. I never laughed so hard.

"Thanks, you're a lifesaver. I owe you big time." He turned on his heel to head back to the living room when I grabbed his arm.

"There's something else I need to talk to you about. Come on." Ignoring his raised brows, I pulled him up the stairs to my room. As soon as I closed the door behind us, I turned to face him. "You brought them, didn't you?"

His face lit up for a moment. "If you mean the stones, they're in my backpack in the kitchen under the table." A frown appeared on his forehead. "You told me to leave them there." I nodded. He breathed out, relieved. "What do you want with them anyway? They're worthless."

Give them back to the psychopath owner. But I couldn't tell Dallas. Not when the owner wasn't human. "I'll return them."

"You know her?"

"Sort of. Actually, no." I hurried to add, "But I have friends who do. You wouldn't believe how sentimental this particular lady is. They've been in her family for generations. Like your researcher friend, she's into legends."

"My friend deciphered some of the inscriptions. He said there's a paranormal race every five hundred years, and whoever finds the gemstones gets some kind of gift, or maybe it's a curse. We couldn't figure that out."

Definitely a curse. I puffed. "Listen, if I had any supernatural abilities I'd have used them on you already. You know, turn invisible and pull down your pants in front of Cass and everyone else."

"You wouldn't!"

"I remember a certain somebody leaving me all alone in the woods."

277

"You're never going to drop that one, are you?" Dallas said.

I grinned. "Never."

"So the owner wants to link this bag of stones to all the things that go bump in the night. Even if she finishes decoding the inscriptions, it's not like she'll ever meet a vampire, werewolf, or whatever. I mean what're the chances?"

I cleared my throat. "You'd be surprised."

"Who cares about this stuff anyway? It's a bunch of hogwash, if you ask me."

I patted his arm, eager to drop the topic. "Real or not, let's give this woman her stones back, okay?"

"What is she, some old, sweet lady?" Dallas asked. I groaned. Was he ever going to stop his interrogation?

"She's pretty old from what I hear. Not sure about the sweet part."

"Do what you want, then." Dallas seemed to be finally losing interest; his glance kept wandering to the door as though he couldn't get away fast enough. I narrowed my gaze, realizing I shouldn't have asked him to pop over.

"Are you late for a hot date?" My laughter rang fake.

"No, not at all. I'm here to catch up on my sister's life." His gaze swept over the furniture and unmade bed, then back to the door. I figured I had his undivided attention for all of twenty seconds.

I plopped down on the bed and turned to face him. "I quit my job."

"What? I thought I was the only job jumper in the family. I mean, aren't you supposed to be responsible while I get to be the reckless one?" He chuckled. "No longer, huh? What will you tell Mum and Dad when you return to London?"

"Well, thanks for asking why I quit." I pouted. Why hadn't I thought of my mother's reaction? I couldn't say I'd been fired because no one was ever fired from a work placement. Quitting wasn't an option either; I'd heard my parents lecture Dallas over and over again.

Dallas laughed. "I don't need to ask because I know. You treat cooking like it's rocket science, and doing laundry's not your strength either. It's no big deal, but with no home you'll have to live with Mum and Dad for a while. Can't wait to hear your excuse."

"I'll say the company went bust." I nodded to myself. That was definitely a good excuse.

Dallas seemed impressed too. "Not bad. Dad might buy it, but Mum—" he shook his head and sucked in a sharp breath "—she'll probably want to send the poor guys a fruit basket and a greeting card." He had a point there. Dallas's face lit up like it always did when he thought he'd come up with a cunning plan. "You could say your boss was kidnapped."

I slapped my forehead. "You've got to be kidding."

He sat down next to me and grabbed my shoulders. "No, listen! It's brilliant. Just say your boss disappeared and the police need to keep it a secret until they finish their investigation. She won't poke her nose around for months, and by then you'll have another job and she'll have forgotten all about it."

From all his stupid ideas, this wasn't even such a bad one. I might consider it. Dallas looked at me expectantly, waiting for the praise to start flowing. I nodded to please him. "It might work. I'll think about it."

Dallas walked over to my dresser and picked up Cameron's picture. "Could he have something to do with you quitting your job?"

"That's not fair," I said.

"Is it fair to display his picture when you're dating the boss?"

"Aidan and I aren't really dating. Besides, I've been meaning to take it down." It wasn't even a lie.

Dallas put the picture back. "What happened? I thought you two were going to take a break and then try and work it out."

I grimaced. "We were. Until I called him at three a.m. and a bimbo answered his phone."

Dallas blew out a breath. "What a jerk. I'll kick some sense into him the next time I see him."

"If I don't beat you to the punch," I said. He laughed, and I found myself laughing with him, forgetting my worries for a moment.

"Can we go back now? I think I'm getting a phone number tonight," Dallas said, grinning. "There's something about that redhead."

No doubt he had Cass in mind. From all the women in the world trust my brother to be attracted to a nerdy demon. It was a bad mix, like oil and water. If Dallas screwed up this relationship, her father would be on his trail, striking him with lightning bolts, sucking his soul into hell, tossing him in a fiery dungeon, and throwing away the key. Dating Cass was not going to happen in this lifetime.

"I was thinking Cass and I could watch a cool movie on Friday night at my pad. Any suggestions?" Dallas continued.

I tapped a finger against my lips, thinking. "*Drag Me To Hell, Demon Hunter, Storm The Gates Of Hell, Succubus, Blue Demon*—have your pick."

"Ah, I get it. She's into horror flicks big time. Do you think she'd wear those Halloween horns on our first date?"

I sneered. "I have a sneaking suspicion she would." I had to get him out—and fast—before bad things happened, like producing offspring. They'd give a new meaning to the expression 'demon child'. I got up and gave his shoulder a sympathetic squeeze. "I'm sorry to have to break it to you, but Cass's not available."

"She's what?" Dallas looked confused. I rolled my eyes inwardly.

"She's seeing someone," I said. "Besides, the girl has issues." Maybe it wasn't even a lie, I consoled myself. Judging from the few books I'd read on demons, Cass probably had a new guy every weekend. Granted, the books had been fiction but, apparently, basing one's work on research was all the rage in literature.

Dallas's shoulders slumped. His expression betrayed disappointment. For a moment, I considered laughing it all off as a joke, but I had to remain strong even though I hated to see his hopes crushed. No way was I letting my brother get sucked into this crazy world. It was too late for me, but not for him.

"You sure?" Hope flickered in him, then died down like a blown-out candle as soon as I nodded. It wasn't like him to fall for someone at this speed. Maybe there was something about the demon, some sort of demonic thing that drew guys to her.

I gave him a tight hug and decided to change the subject before he started asking questions. "Thanks for bringing the stones. I'll call you before I return to London."

He lifted his chin a notch and turned to the door. "Yeah, you do that." We climbed down the stairs in silence. Dallas hesitated as we reached the hall on the ground floor. "I should say goodbye."

Not if Cass kept spawning her weird magic on him. I put on my most compassionate expression. "I'll tell them for you." He didn't argue, just kissed my cheek, mumbled something about calling and took off through the backdoor, vanishing as fast as he had appeared only an hour ago. I watched him disappear into the darkness. For a while I just stood in the middle of the kitchen, rubbing my arms through the thin material of my shirt as a cold breeze blew in, ruffling the curtains. I always felt bad for lying to Dallas, but the thought that I had done the right thing consoled me. No point in dragging him into this crazy world. The sooner I got out of it myself, the better. After returning to the living room and watching Cass's face drop when I mentioned Dallas's departure, I realized maybe the demon liked him more than I imagined.

Chapter 23

Cass excused herself and left soon after Dallas, and I saw my chance to leave too. After retrieving the backpack from the kitchen, I returned to my room and locked the door, then snuggled onto my bed, still clothed. I clutched Cameron's photo to my chest, trying to conjure up happy moments we'd shared, but I couldn't remember any. The girl answering my call, Cameron's voice and the giggle still lingered in my mind. My eyes moistened. I didn't feel hurt, just a little betrayed and pitiful. Cameron couldn't remain faithful for a few weeks, and all Aidan wanted was an old book. Why did I always get the nutcases?

The soft knock on the door jolted me out of my thoughts. I knew it was Aidan before he asked to come in. For a moment, I considered pretending not to hear him, but what was the point? I'd have to face him tomorrow anyway when we retrieved the book. Straightening up in bed, I inhaled to steady my racing heart when his footsteps departed down the corridor.

Whatever he had to say, he probably changed his mind. I dropped back on the bed, unable to shake off my sudden disappointment. What had I hoped for? The guy wasn't interested in any sort of commitment, which made him dangerous to my heart and sanity. And my soft spot for him wasn't helping my case either. I should be careful, run instead of seeking his proximity, but for some reason I needed to be close to him. What did I think he'd do once he had the book? He'd send me away. The more reason not to get involved, because it'd end up in tears—and surely not his.

Wood creaked near the window, startling me. I turned my head sharply and shrieked, the sound dying in my throat.

"A little jumpy, aren't we?" The tall girl, dressed in something that looked like a sheer, black nightgown with slits on both sides of her hips and along the legs, laughed. Countless rings and bracelets adorned her fingers and wrists.

I shot to my feet, ready to bolt out the door, then stopped as my curiosity got the better of me. "Who're you?"

"Well, we know who you are, you boyfriend-stealing hussy." The girl stood with her back turned to the window, the soft light of the lamp catching in her raven hair and throwing shadows on her porcelain skin. Her cat-like eyes seemed to follow my every move, but her features betrayed no emotions. There was no need for it anyway because her eyes said it all. She had the superior air of someone who knew she might have competition, but certainly not in this room.

"Has Aidan kept my existence a big secret?" she said. "By the look in your eyes, I can tell he has. Now I'm offended." She took a step forward, long, lean legs peering between the splits in her nightgown. For a second, I thought I saw a thin snake wrapped around her ankle. But the illusion disappeared. "I'm Layla. You could call me his—" She trailed off, leaving the rest to my imagination.

Staring at the generous cleavage threatening to spill out of the thin material of her dress, I could definitely see why any guy would fall for her, but the name rang a bell somewhere at the back of my mind. *Layla*. Aidan had almost been killed by someone called Layla. Was this the same person?

I clenched my fists, my temper flaring. I knew I should be afraid—whatever Layla was, she was strong enough to imprison a vampire—but, for some reason, I felt I could deal with her. "What do you want from me?"

"I know how you feel, little mortal." Layla took another step forward. "Look at you, all lost and forlorn in this world you didn't know existed." Another step, and she reached the edge of the bed. "Give him up, and I'll let you return to your previous life." She picked up Cameron's picture and nodded. "He's pretty hot. What a shame you don't have him on your arm."

"We broke up. He needed his space," I said, dryly.

"He didn't want you." Her eyes flickered with amusement. "I can change that. How would you like it if you could have him back?"

"I don't want that cheater." I shook my head, realizing I had no idea what I had ever seen in Cameron.

"I promise he'd never ever cheat on you again," Layla said. "He'd love you with a passion he never knew existed. Surely you've had enough of this supernatural world. I can make you forget the last few days ever happened. Just go back to the one you love. He's waiting for you this very moment. Say the words and you'll never know sadness and despair in your lifetime."

I narrowed my eyes. "Why even ask me? Can't you just do it, and then all of your problems will go away?"

She sighed. "If only it were that simple. This kind of magic has to have your blessing to work."

If Cameron didn't want me for who I was, then why bother? No love potion or magic would fix that deep down it'll all be an illusion. Cameron would only love me because he had a big hex on him. But I was sold on the promise of having my old life back, which I'd wanted ever since coming here. Aidan wasn't mine to begin with. Leaving him behind shouldn't prove a hard task. So, why the hesitation?

Layla's fake smile vanished. "You should be jumping at the opportunity. I can make this boy love you. I can make the two of you rich beyond your wildest dreams. I can give you both prestigious jobs that you've been longing for your entire life. You'll never have to clean somebody's house again. Just imagine how proud your parents would be."

I stared at her calmly. Why did she hurt Aidan? The question burned on my tongue. I shouldn't care, but I couldn't help it. "What happens to Aidan if I leave?"

My words seemed to take Layla by surprise. She blinked a few times, then moistened her lips. "Well, that depends on him, of course. I'll leave the decision in his capable hands. Disloyalty usually results in harsh punishment."

He'd tried to save me from whatever I'd brought upon myself when I solved the riddle. How exactly had he been disloyal to Layla? I brushed a hand over my jeans as I gathered my thoughts, forming a plan. "I'm only a humble employee who stumbled into this mess by accident. I assure you I have no ties to anybody in this supernatural world."

"He picked you—" Layla looked me up and down "—and the reason's beyond me. I could've given him anything he wanted, but he decided to pursue this bond thing. Not the wisest choice, if you ask me."

My heart skipped a beat. It wasn't all about the book. Aidan truly believed in a bond and wanted me over this stunning girl with her gorgeous skin and sultry mouth. Somewhere inside my mind a voice screamed to run and let the vampires sort out this mess since they were better equipped to deal with whatever Layla was, but I had never been the cowardly type. I placed my hands on my hips and took a pace forward, glaring up at Layla. "You may be the prettier one, but he's not into the bitchy type."

Layla's gaze narrowed. "What did you just call me?" Several hissing snakes crawled from under her dress, slithering around her legs.

Maybe crossing her hadn't been such a good idea. Gulping, I backed off slowly toward the door. The snakes slithered across the floor like some sort of guard dogs. I never feared reptiles, but I also never stood so close to them before.

Talk about skeletons in one's closet. Aidan sure knew how to pick his girlfriends. First a crazed killer, and then psycho Medusa. This girl was as dangerous and obsessive as Glenn Close in *Fatal Attraction*—even had the crazy, bulging eyes to prove it. If she looked at me any harder I'd soon turn into stone.

"I'll think about your proposition and let you know," I said, paralyzed by fear. My heart hammered in my chest, my palms were slick with sweat. "Thanks for stopping by. Please take your stones with you on your way back. They're in that backpack over there." I pointed at Dallas's bag, then stretched out a shaking hand, secretly praying she wouldn't shake it, and curled my mouth into a smile.

Ignoring my outstretched hand, Layla scoffed. "They'll soon pulverize to dust. Now, who said my offer still stands? It was just a gesture of goodwill, and I don't usually do goodwill."

The snakes slithered closer until they stood mere inches from my feet. I pressed my mouth shut. A squeal remained trapped in my throat as I lifted my head a notch. Rivulets of sweat trickled down my spine. Would Layla's pets attack? I kicked my brain into gear, struggling to come up with a plan to bluff my way out of this situation.

"You want Aidan, I don't." I cringed at my lie. "I'll make it easy for you and leave so you can have him."

"As if I ever needed your cooperation." Layla scoffed, raising her hand. The light of the lamp caught in her rings. "Once I get rid of you, he'll be mine anyway. Guys need diversion. He had his fun, now he'll be eager to come back to me."

I quelled a nervous laugh. My bluff wasn't working. So much for my plan to play the strong girl who doesn't need a guy to protect her. Time for plan B: run, and let the immortals fight my battle. I dashed for the door, but the snakes moved faster, draping around my ankle like huge cuffs. With a hard thud, I toppled forward and banged my head against the wall, the impact knocking the air out of my lungs. I turned in time to see Layla towering over me, a wicked smile playing on her lips.

My ankle throbbed when I lifted my leg and kicked, hitting Layla somewhere below the knee. I could feel the vibration running through my body, but Layla didn't even budge.

For a moment, she looked stunned, then annoyance crossed her face and her cheeks turned an ugly reddish color. "You didn't just try that."

Pushing up on my elbows, I scrambled to my feet when I felt a sharp pain in my upper thigh. I looked down at the large head of a snake sinking its teeth into my skin, two rivulets of blood spiraling down my leg, and screamed as loudly as my lungs would allow.

Chapter 24 - Aidan

Cass had promised to ensure the Shadows would play fair. But Cass was a demon and they weren't exactly trustworthy material. I took off my shirt and threw it on the sofa in my bedroom, then dropped down beside it, absorbed in my thoughts.

I knew Amber heard me outside her door. That she decided to pretend otherwise annoyed the heck out of me. What had I done to cause her mistrust? Others met their mate, fell for one another and lived happily ever after. Why couldn't Amber and I do the same? Was that too much to ask for?

Maybe I was giving up too quickly. If the girl wanted to be pursued, then so be it. Sighing, I jumped up and retrieved a clean shirt from the wardrobe when a vision appeared before my eyes. I blinked and looked around, confused. My sight blurred again, the bond with Amber sending out a message I didn't understand. Maybe Amber was thinking of me, unconsciously sending out those vibes, drawing me to her again. It was new terrain to me. True love bonds weren't exactly a common occurrence in the paranormal world. Consequently, no one knew a great deal about them. The few who found their mates didn't share their experience so their weaknesses wouldn't be exposed.

I shrugged into the shirt, considering my next step, when Amber's scream pierced the air. In two long strides, I reached the door and sped down the stairs to her room. From the corner of my eye, I noticed my brother close behind me, asking something I didn't understand. Ignoring him, I didn't stop until I reached Amber's room and yanked the door open.

Amber lay sprawled on the floor, motionless, several snakes slithering around her body. I let out a deafening roar and dropped next to her, only then noticing the tall girl leaning against the wall. *Layla.* No need to ask what she'd done. Her self-satisfied smirk said it all. Something snapped inside me and all reason disappeared.

"I'm going to kill you." In one fluent movement I charged for Layla's throat, ready to rip it to shreds. She stepped to the side, eyes glinting as though she enjoyed a playful encounter with a lover.

"Oh, Aidan, you should see yourself. You look like a raging bull. If only I had a red cape. Andale! Andale!" Layla giggled like a child.

I prepared to pounce again, barely aware of my brother coming up behind me, grabbing me by my shoulders and pulling me back. Kicking, I let out another roar and fought against Kieran's iron grip.

"No! She'll kill you too." Kieran's voice seemed to carry over from far away, lingering somewhere at the verge of my perception, but I didn't want to control my anger. Layla had gone too far by attacking my mate.

Fate screeched in my ear to hurry up, or Amber would die. I turned and kicked Kieran in the gut, then spun to face the succubus. The snakes slithered across the floor with their mouths agape, forked tongues flicking in and out. I didn't fear her pets—it was Layla's touch that could prove fatal because it could make me lose my will. In physical strength and abilities, she wouldn't stand a chance against me—so long I didn't let her come too close.

"Nice to see you too, Harry Houdini. My, you're quite the escape artist," Layla said.

"I would've said goodbye but, you know, I was a little tied up." I ambled backward and planted myself in front of Amber. I could teleport Amber to another place, but that wouldn't keep Layla from coming after her.

"I'll let it slip by this time." Layla ran a finger down her thigh. "Nice pecks. No idea how you find the time to look this delicious with such a busy work schedule. I bet the girls at the beach go nuts when you rub baby oil all over that sculpted chest of yours." She laughed, the shrill, unnatural sound irritating my ears. "Oh wait, that couldn't happen. What with being a vampire and all. Must suck to take your dips in the ocean at night with only the boring, old moon watching you. Then again, you like boring things." She pointed at Amber. I cringed.

"Don't," Kieran whispered, sensing my fury. "She isn't worth it."

Layla continued, "How could she possibly know what you need? She's nothing but a stupid girl. I'm an immortal demi-goddess. Any man would kill himself just to catch a glimpse of me."

My temper flared up again. Blood rushed through my veins, ready to turn me into the crazed maniac Rebecca once was, if I didn't control it. "You mean until you tire of me like of all the others, and then turn me into your personal slave, captured and tortured for eternity." I snorted and kneeled down next to Amber. "Thanks, but I'll pass."

Slowly, I moved my hand to the sheath bound at my calf. My fingers clasped the fire whip when Layla said, "It doesn't matter. Given the chance, they'd do it again."

"Is that statement based on experience, or on your own narrow-minded, self-centered assessment?" I pulled out the whip and lashed. Fire burned bright where it hit Layla's skin.

For a moment, Layla's eyes widened, surprise crossing her features. When the flames scorched her chest, burning the sheer material of her dress, she cried out.

"You like rough, Aidan. I can do rough. I highly doubt your little porcelain doll could handle half of what I can take." The snakes hissed angrily, but didn't attack. Layla stifled the flames with her bare palm and took a step back. Her voice came low and menacing, barely audible. "You've just attacked a member of the Lore court. For this you'll be punished with death."

I snorted. Was she really playing the innocent card here? "You tried to kill a mortal. I only acted in my own right."

"Tried?" She laughed. "Who says your mate won't die?"

"I do." I wanted to kill her, but I didn't have time for a fight. Saving Amber's life was my priority. So, sending Layla a threat would have to do for the time being. I regarded her. "Seriously, Layla, what would your mother think? Falling for a vampire's beneath you. And stalking him day and night, sending your pets to kill the competition who just happens to be an innocent mortal who isn't even part of your court. Do you know your victim's not even eighteen? Your mother won't be pleased. Last I remember she was still the one with all the power."

Layla's face turned into an ugly mask. "Say one word and you'll suffer my wrath, and so will all of your sidekicks, like your pathetic brother and wimpy Clare."

"Whoa, did the hag just call me a sidekick?" Kieran muttered. I nudged him in the ribs, praying my brother wouldn't pursue an argument for a change.

"It's in your best interest to stay away from us," I said. Layla loved revenge. I doubted my threat would keep her away from Amber, but it'd make her spend a few days plotting. Maybe she'd give me enough time to get the book so I could protect my mate day and night, and then get rid of the demi-goddess once and for all.

"Hold on a second," Kieran said. "Did you just call me a sidekick? Like Robin to Batman? Like Donkey to Shrek, or Sam to Frodo? Isn't that precious?"

Kieran shutting his mouth was obviously too much to ask. I shot him an irritated look. "Let's get back to the topic at hand. Go away, Layla, or I swear I'll talk to your mother."

Layla puffed and moved to the window, the snakes slithering with her. "She'd never make you happy. I would because I'm a goddess." She threw me a glance over her shoulder, head tilted, revealing a slender neck and glossy, black hair, thick as a curtain.

Not tempting. Not like my Amber. I shook my head. "Find someone else. I'm not interested."

Her expression darkened. "I'll make sure to bring flowers to her grave." Shooting me another menacing grin, Layla dissipated into thin air, disappearing before my eyes. It wasn't over yet.

"Getting cocky's my thing, not yours," Kieran said, punching my shoulder. "And who do you decide to practice on—Layla of all people? Are you crazy? Now the hag will come back, you idiot."

"Next time I'll be prepared."

Kieran rubbed a hand over his abdomen. "You frigging kicked your own flesh and blood. I won't be able to eat for a week."

I snorted. "I highly doubt that."

"Okay, so maybe for a few hours," Kieran said. "Payback's a bitch."

Ignoring him, I turned my attention to Amber. A sheen layer of sweat covered her forehead. Her eyes were closed, her mouth stood slightly open, her breath came in shallow, ragged heaps. Could she hear me? I ripped open her top and jeans, examining her skin for wounds. There were several small bruises on her upper arms and two small punctures the size of a wasp sting on her left thigh where one of Layla's snakes must've bitten her. I could smell the blood where it had caked over.

"She's alive," Kieran said.

"Yes, but her heartbeat's faint."

Kieran let out a sigh before meeting my gaze. "We need to get her to a hospital. In case you haven't noticed we don't have antivenin. We're not equipped to handle her here."

I peered up at him. "And what exactly do we tell them? That we teleported over as fast as we could? That she was bitten by a pet snake of a demi-goddess who's obsessed with a vampire? They'll throw us both in the nuthouse."

"Padded cells big time," Kieran said, nodding.

"They'd never figure out what species bit her." I pushed Kieran aside and squeezed my arms beneath Amber's knees and neck, scooping her up together with her shredded clothes. She stirred, but didn't open her eyes. "Hell, I doubt they've even discovered it yet." Standing my ground, I glared, preparing for battle if need be, but Kieran didn't argue. My brother stepped to aside and let me pass. A flash of understanding mixed with something else reflected in his gaze.

"Just don't turn her," Kieran whispered.

"I'll do what I deem right."

He held up his hands. "I can't stop you alone, but I'll get Clare. Two against one." He chuckled as he continued, "And don't forget the connections Clare has. She could call an army if she wanted. They'd come in a heartbeat."

No connection Clare had was stronger than a vampire. "Interfere and I won't have a brother anymore," I muttered.

"What, no sidekick? You'll kill your own brother?"

I shook my head. "No, I'll denounce you and kick you to the curb. You've been living here without paying rent far too long anyway."

"Fine. I won't stop you," Kieran said. "You always say I make bad choices. I hope you two ride into the sunset and live happily ever after. Oh wait! That's not going to happen." He turned and walked away. How could loving Amber be a bad choice? Kieran would never understand until he found his own mate.

The corridor stood empty as I carried Amber to my bedchamber on the second floor and kicked the door shut with my leg. I lay her down on the bed and tore my shirt into wide strips that I wrapped a few inches beneath and above the punctures, then retrieved a dagger from my desk.

The bites, a nasty green color, had swollen to the size of a small egg. With the tip of the dagger I made a small incision in the middle. The venom oozed out, soaking the remaining of my shirt. Amber pried her eyes open and twisted her leg as if to pull away, her hazy gaze looking right through me. A pained moan escaped her lips, beads of sweat covered her forehead. I was naïve to visit the Lore court and trust Layla would understand why a mortal shouldn't carry the prize. Now Amber suffered because of me.

I set my jaw and increased my pressure on her leg, forcing the venom out. When the swelling deflated, I pressed my lips against her skin. The sweet flavor of her blood, intermingled with the bitter poison, spread in my mouth, making me faint for a moment. I forced myself to draw blood and spit it out until the taste of toxin dissipated, then bandaged the wound with strips of my shirt and ignited the logs in the fireplace. A strong flame lapped at the dried wood greedily, warming the room.

Amber barely stirred when I pulled the covers over her pale body and tossed the soaked shirt into the fire. The venom sizzled in the heat. I teleported to the kitchen for a glass of water and some aspirin, then peeled off my jeans and snuggled next to her, pulling her into the cave of my arm. I had done all I could to clean her blood, now I could only hope rest would get her back on her feet.

The scent of her blood lingered in the air, making me hungry. Amber moved and sighed, hands clenching and unclenching in a fitful slumber. I grinded my teeth against the temptation surging through my body. Why had I thought lying next to her, with her blood beckoning to me, would be an easy task? My fingertips grated her feverish skin, sending electric shocks through me. I groaned and turned my head to the side, trying to ignore the pain in my stomach. There she was, fighting death, and all I could think of was her blood. I draped my leg over the edge of the bed, wondering whether putting some space between us might help.

"You're a sight for sore eyes," Amber whispered, stirring next to me. I turned and found myself peering into her hazel eyes still foggy from the shock. Kissing her forehead, I gave up any hope of spending some moments away from her enticing scent. Even if I wanted to, I couldn't leave her alone when she so clearly needed me.

Amber sat up groggily and scanned the floor. "Where are my clothes? How did I get here, in your room of all places?"

"I had to find the snake bite."

She cocked a brow. "What happened to your clothes? You got bitten too?"

"You're hilarious." I handed her two aspirin and the glass of water.

Her arm moved across my chest, holding me in place. "I'm okay." She sounded breathless. In spite of the seriousness of the situation, I found myself smiling.

"You're the worst liar ever. Just take them," I said, helping her up.

"Yes, Nurse Ratched." She grimaced but swallowed the pills nonetheless.

"Why don't you get some sleep?"

She batted her eyelashes. "Doctor's orders?"

"Yep. I even wrote you a prescription. Lot's of rest, kisses, hugs, and pampering. I'll make you breakfast in bed, right before daybreak." I placed a soft kiss on her forehead.

She laughed. "I hope your cooking's better than mine."

"You like cereal, right?"

"Thanks. You saved my life," she whispered. Her hand found mine, and our fingers intertwined. A jolt of energy rippled through me. My hunger stirred stronger than before. I bit on my lip until I drew blood, but the pain did nothing to stifle the sudden craving in my veins.

"Get some sleep," I said through gritted teeth.

Amber shook her head and lifted on her elbows, placing a peck on my cheek. My heart skipped a beat. *Get a grip.* It didn't mean anything because the girl was still delirious from the venom.

She wrapped her arm around my neck. Our eyes connected. "Layla said you chose me over her. Why?"

Layla and her big mouth. I sighed, fingers twitching to press her lips to mine. Not tonight. Not when I could barely control the hunger inside me. "It wasn't a tough choice."

"But why me when you could have any other?" She moistened her lips, confused. Her question took me by surprise. Did she really not understand that we were puppets of our fate? The bond, a tiny silver thread that intertwined our lives, had chosen for us. No other than Amber would ever do.

I glanced at the dying fire, paneled walls and brocade covers, unable to come up with an answer that wouldn't scare the hell out of her and make her run a mile. *Because Fate chose you for me. Because I can't live without you. Because we belong together for all eternity.* Kieran would collapse in a fit of laughter. There were hundreds of reasons, but none I could share with her just yet. Girls like bad guys, not over-sensitive pansies who paint their girlfriend's toenails and remember to bring chocolate pralines on Valentine's Day. So, what was the right answer? What did she want to hear?

"Because I mop the floors like no other?" Amber prompted, piqued. Her brows were drawn, her gaze reflecting mistrust and disbelief. Her rapid heartbeat sounded like a drum in my ears. My body stirred, flaring up with a hunger I hadn't felt since the day I was turned.

"I love a girl who makes me laugh," I whispered.

"And did I do that a lot when I worked for you?" Her lips twitched.

I tried to hide a smile. "Only when you cooked me that dreadful vegetable pasta."

"It's called a stir-fry." She slapped her forehead. "Oh, my gosh. You don't eat food. I bet you got the biggest kick out of that one."

"Kieran couldn't stop laughing for a day."

"You haven't answered my question." She regarded me as if she could see right through me. For the first time I feared the bond might empower her to do just that. "There's something you don't want to tell me," Amber continued, pulling away from me.

"No idea what you're talking about," I muttered.

Amber stared at me, frowning. "I can sense it. Yeah, thanks to you I got this psychic vibe thing going on. So now, not only can I talk to the dead, but I can also pick up on your emotions and see you when you're not around. And I thought I'd only be picking up your house and my salary. Talk about added perks."

I groaned inwardly. She finally felt the bond, but I could see she was a slow one. At this speed we'd still be sniffing at each other in two years. Sniffing was good, came with the territory of dating, but not if it destined me to regular blood stained shirts and more jokes from the others.

"I could give you a hint or two." I laughed at how sleazy I sounded. Kieran was obviously rubbing off on me.

"Next time you write a classified ad for a position, you should consult me," Amber said.

I cocked a brow. "Why?"

"Because the last one was completely misleading." She sat up in a lotus position. I tried hard not to peer at her naked legs, toned in all the right places. "It should read like this: single vampire, stronger than any human on Earth, 500+ years old but still drop dead gorgeous with blue eyes and dark hair, seeks summer temp to clean his house, put up with boss's annoying and beyond cheesy brother, risk life by living in a creepy mansion, and help obtain an ancient book."

I opened my mouth to protest when she lifted a hand to stop me, then continued, "Must be quiet during the day while he sleeps and be willing to understand that his best friend is a blonde bombshell. Added perks: the gift of talking to a dead person, mind-blowing kisses, faster-than-a-speeding-bullet rides in the woods, meet nice demon friends from hell, and last but not least, a psychic connection to the boss."

Amber took a deep breath and tapped a finger against her pink lips. "Must be willing to communicate with a creepy child queen, not panic easily and keep her cool when a legion of Shadow people are after her. Endure vampire attacks, face Medusa, survive venomous snake bites, be willing to give up her espresso when turned into a vampire per boss's request, and—"

"Stop it," I said, laughing.

"Just trying to keep it real." She elbowed me in the ribs. "Forget the ad. I don't know what you're hiding, but I'll figure it out myself. Or I'll just ask Cass. She'll read your mind like nobody's business."

"Don't you dare!" I rolled her on her back, minding her sore thigh.

"Why not? I want to know everything."

I laughed. "Like hell you do."

"Oh, is that where Cass is? Let's go call her. Now get off me." Poking a finger in my chest, she pretended to push me away, but her attempt was a feeble one.

What was I doing? I should walk away, let her wiggle a bit, play hard to get like my brother suggested. But I couldn't.

"It's like we're destined to be together," I whispered in her ear, my fingers brushing her cheek. Somewhere inside my brain, I could hear my brother's voice—faint but there, and bloody annoying at that. *What the heck?*

It was too late. I lowered my mouth on her neck where her pulse felt the strongest, my teeth grazing her skin. Amber held her breath, but didn't push me away.

My hunger grew stronger, clouding my mind, consuming my body. I couldn't think straight, just let myself fall into the dark needs I had ignored for five hundred years. For a moment I hesitated, my lips lingering over her skin, then opened my mouth. My fangs touched her skin. The sudden knock on the door jolted me out of the moment. I sat up, startled.

"Go away, Kieran," I yelled.

"Don't stop," Amber whispered, sitting up on her elbow, so cute with her disheveled hair and innocent gaze.

"You've no idea what you're requesting." I pressed my eyes shut, mad at myself for what I'd just been about to do. How could I let myself lose control like that?

The room seemed to spin as one pang of hunger after another washed over me. Setting my jaw, I pulled Amber to my chest. Her blood's call tortured me, but I deserved it. I deserved any torture I'd get for being so careless.

"I know guys do the casual relationship thing all the time, and I want you to know that I'm okay with it if you are," Amber said.

"What do you mean by 'casual'?" I pushed her away as my temper flared.

Amber shrugged and pulled the covers over her body. Her face was hard, any traces of love gone. Somewhere at the back of my mind I heard Kieran's voice say, I told you so. *Damn him. Damn her. Damn that bloody bond.* Not only was I stuck with a mortal; I was stuck with a mortal *commitment phobe*, and I was growing sick of it. Fate was probably watching right now, laughing her head off at my expense.

Without looking at Amber, I jumped out of bed, shrugged into a clean shirt and left the room, slamming the door behind me.

Chapter 25

I propped up on my elbow and watched Aidan stomp out of the room like a bomb had just gone off. Okay, I didn't make the most romantic statement in the world, but after the experience with Cameron who could blame me for thinking all guys were morons? There I was, basically offering him dating with no strings attached and he acted like I just deceived him and robbed him of his most precious possession. Our knee-weakening kiss still lingered on my mind. Trust me to put my foot in my big mouth and get the nicest guy I'd ever met to make a run for the hills.

Wrapping the bedspread around me to keep off the Scottish chill, I jumped out of the bed and went in search of my clothes. My pair of jeans was torn to pieces. The shirt I'd worn the night before didn't look much better. I shimmied into what was left of them and headed for the privacy of my room. Closing the door behind me, I switched on the lights. My heart thudded in my chest as I kneeled on the floor to peer under the bed and beneath the sheets. The scary snakes were gone. Taking a deep breath, I relaxed a little.

What happened to Layla? I couldn't remember anything between the sudden, piercing pain in my thigh and then waking up in Aidan's arms. *Aidan's arms*—it sounded so right, the place I should be rather than in my pretty yet empty room, all alone with a sore thigh and no one to comfort me.

I rummaged through my bedside table until I found a pack of aspirin and swallowed another pill with the stale glass of water I'd carried upstairs the night before, then peeled off my shredded clothes to take a quick shower. The water cooled my feverish skin. With a shaking finger, I brushed over the bruise on my thigh, just above the knee, where the snake had sunk its teeth. I trembled, a sudden wave of dread washing over me. The memory of Aidan sucking out the venom was faint, but enough to remember I hadn't put up a fight. I'd found it too easy to trust him with my life.

After rubbing my body with a dry towel, I gave my teeth a quick brush and slipped into my flannel PJs, then snuggled under the covers, musing.

Should I go after him and clarify that I wasn't actually keen on anything casual? I sighed and switched off the lights. Cameron had always been the one to run and I the one to do the chasing, trying to woo him and rectify whatever I'd done wrong. In the end, he'd ended up cheating on me anyway. Whatever I'd seen in him was now gone, but I'd learned my lesson. No guy would ever make me trip over myself to please him. I figured, Aidan was a big boy. His ego could deal with a bit of rejection. And if not—I didn't want to go there. He simply had to be different and like me the way I was now that I'd fallen in love with him.

***

Living with vampires was messing up my routine big time, slowly turning me into a creature of the night, shunning daylight. I slept through most of the day, only waking twice to eat and call my parents to tell them I was all right. By late afternoon, I found myself refreshed enough to take a hot shower and go around the house, waiting for the big event. Tonight we'd retrieve the book—whatever that might involve—but that wasn't what worried me. How would Aidan react to seeing me after the previous night? Was he still mad?

The wind howled outside, rattling the shutters. I grabbed a soft drink from the kitchen and made myself comfortable on the sofa in the living room with several cushions propped up behind my back. Soon it'd be time to leave everything behind. After just a few days, I realized I felt at home and couldn't imagine myself living somewhere else. I could almost pretend the mansion was mine, forgetting that a few days ago I was a mere employee. Albeit, not a very good one, but I'd tried my best—sort of. Working for a vampire hadn't been an easy task, what with all the strange things happening and Aidan probably able to smell the dust I'd overlooked on occasion. Even Dallas hadn't failed to get Aidan's hints.

307

But I hoped Aidan would consider all those things in my reference, because with my employment history I'd be lucky to land any crappy position. For a moment, I regretted quitting my job—my heated head was causing more harm than good these days—but asking him to take me back was out of the question. He'd ridiculed my cleaning skills in front of the others. He was probably searching for a replacement already.

A car stopped in the driveway, gravel crunching under its tires. I pulled the curtains aside, but the visitors had already moved out of my line of vision. A second later, the entrance door opened and I heard Cass's chatter, assuring someone they were welcome. I sighed and plopped down on the sofa. So much for seeing Aidan before we commenced our mission.

Cass peered in and switched on the lights, looking around the room. "Gee, Amber, we need to evacuate, like, right now. There's a hurricane amidst us." She chuckled. "I thought my place was bad."

I glanced from Clare's stacks of magazines gathering dust in the corners to the half-empty glasses I hadn't bothered to pick up after Dallas's visit. For a moment, I felt guilty. Then again, I realized my bad conscience wasn't warranted. Although I basically still lived here, free of charge, I wasn't Aidan's employee anymore.

I peered around me. It didn't even look *that* bad—just a few things thrown here and there, which helped give the house a homely touch. Really, where was the charm in stacking away anything that might give away someone actually lived here? I shrugged and looked back at Cass, only then noticing Devon and Angel standing in the doorway, hesitant whether to enter. With a flick of my hand, I motioned them to come in and grabbed Angel in a tight hug.

"I'm sorry I left you behind," I whispered in her ear so Devon wouldn't hear. Cass raised an eyebrow, but didn't comment.

Angel blushed and sat down on the sofa with a shy smile. "I'm just glad you're okay." Why wouldn't I be? And then it dawned on me. The girl believed what that eerie child queen spoon-fed her and didn't question the Shadows' actions. Angel continued, "They asked me to come along so you wouldn't feel all alone among these people."

No doubt, by 'people' she meant the vampires. I cringed inwardly, biting my tongue so I wouldn't make a snarky remark. Unlike the Shadows, the vampires hadn't threatened and kidnapped me. I could see a friendship developing between Angel and me, but not when her only purpose of being around me was to earn my trust in case the Shadows could get rid of the vampires to use me for their own wants. I shrugged. Well, straying from Aidan's pack wasn't going to happen.

Devon's smile looked fake. His unnaturally black eyes betrayed reproach, as though he held a grudge that I escaped. I stuffed my hands in the pockets of my jeans and averted my gaze, lest he talk to me.

Cass inched closer and whispered, "Someone's irritated tonight. What bit your butt?" Her green eyes creased with laughter as she leaned forward, peering closer. "On second thought, the answer's right there on your neck."

Raising my hand to my throat, I blushed, the heat spreading across my skin at lightning speed. "I was attacked last night."

Cass winked. "You should've called me. I could've taught you a thing or two about dealing with that kind of assault." The familiar pang of jealousy took hold of me. No way would I let Cass anywhere near Aidan. Cass rolled her eyes. "Get a grip, mate. I was just joking. Besides, your guy isn't my type. Now, your brother's just—" she tapped a finger against her lips "—yum."

I scowled. The thought of my brother being seduced by Lucifer's daughter made me nauseous. "He's not available." Before Cass could read more of my thoughts, I jumped up and headed out the door with a false smile, calling over my shoulder, "Drinks, anyone?"

From the corner of my eye I saw Cass mutter to herself something like, "I told you to shut up for a while, didn't I? Now she thinks I'm a tart."

Good grief! The girl was weird, talking to herself and all. I shook my head and headed down the corridor to the kitchen, hoping there were enough glasses left in the cabinet. If need be, I could just serve Diet Coke cans and straws, claiming the glasses were all shattered in a recent earthquake.

Among several plates and Tupperware, I found glasses piled high in the sink, but decided against washing up. For one, I'd have to dry up and polish, which is even worse than cooking because it entails some sort of higher understanding of cloths and the right amount of pressure I didn't possess just yet. And second, last time I'd tried I ended up in an emergency room with a huge piece of glass imbedded in my finger. Dallas didn't mind driving me to the hospital, but I doubted a pack of vampires would be quite so forthcoming.

Watching from the window, I could make out the last rays of light on the horizon. Darkness had almost descended over the forest, the heavy clouds bearing the promise of another rainy night. I sighed and grabbed three cans of Diet Coke, wondering when my vampire friends would finally make their grand entrance when Angel peered in, a timid smile playing on her lips. "May I help?"

"If you're up for washing dishes." I pointed at the dirty glasses. "Nah, I'll just get us some Diet Coke."

"You shouldn't have left—" Angel said, grabbing my hand.

I hesitated. "But I thought everyone was thirsty."

"Not that. But you're funny. I've missed you."

"Deidre asked you to accompany Devon and play the friendship card to change my mind." I regretted saying the words the moment I opened my mouth. It wasn't Angel's fault Deidre knew how to manipulate people.

Angel grimaced and dropped my hand. "Let's just say things haven't been the same without you."

"Do you remember the pendant Deidre gave me?" I didn't wait for her answer. "It was infused with some sort of dark magic that influenced my mind. You can't blame me for not trusting you when you're one of them."

She shook her head, eyes wide with honesty. "I would never—"

For an instant, I almost believed her earnest gaze. Then I held up a finger, interrupting her. "Listen, I'm sorry, but I had to do what was right for me." I gave her hand a squeeze and turned to the door, hoping she'd follow.

"Now's not the time to argue. Can we talk later after we grab the book?"

Angel nodded. We returned to the living room in silence, meeting Devon's questioning gaze. When Angel shrugged, he scowled and turned away. Well, I wasn't going to feel guilty for spoiling their plans. Not when their plans involved playing with my life.

My palms turned damp as I placed the cans on the coffee table. My heart started to race in my chest. I sensed him a moment before the door was swung open and Aidan walked in with Clare and Kieran following a few steps behind.

Aidan made a derisive noise as his gaze skimmed Devon and then moved to me, gaze narrowed, nostrils flaring. He was still mad, ego bumped and all, but cute as a button in his white shirt and jeans with that disheveled mop on his head. Unable to suppress a giggle, I pictured running my hand through his hair, planting a soft kiss on his lips and—

Cass puffed somewhere to my right. "Just get a room and give me a break, will you?" I sat down, embarrassed. Aidan shot me an amused glance, and I groaned inwardly. Why couldn't Cass just keep her mouth shut?

"How did you get past the gates?" Kieran asked, suspiciously.

"That would be my doing. You see, your magic stands no chance against this little number." Cass retrieved her high-tech phone and waved it in front of Kieran's face.

"Daddy come up with a new invention?" Kieran said.

Cass raised her chin defiantly. "As a matter of fact, I did. Why? Are you jealous?"

"I see Amber has offered you refreshments," Aidan said, pointing at the unopened cans. His gaze move from the cans to the dirty glass on the sideboard and then back to me, the corners of his mouth twitching.

I glared at him. "I quit. Remember?" Surely, he could lift his manicured fingers and clean his own house?

"I've been meaning to talk to you, Aidan," Clare said. "Let's hire a new housekeeper next week."

"Yes, let's do that," Kieran said. "And this time, bro, don't date the help."

Aidan raised his brows meaningfully. "You both know I've bigger things going on in my mind than discussing the future help. Like the book."

"Or Amber." Cass smirked.

My heartbeat sped up. What did Cass hear in his thoughts? Was he thinking about me the way I was thinking about him?

"After the stunt you pulled on us, I don't care for small talk with Shadows, so let's get going," Kieran said.

Cass jumped up from the sofa. "Goody."

"We should discuss the plan one more time because we can't afford to screw up," Devon said, glancing at Kieran.

"You know what's screwed up?" Kieran said. "Those big black eyes of yours. Must be some major inbreeding problem among Shadows."

Clare grabbed his arm to silence him. "Let's go over the plan one last time, just to make everyone happy."

"There's no need," Aidan said. "We've discussed it a million times. Everyone should know their part."

Devon pointed at me. "Including Amber?"

"Let's go," Aidan said. I could hear an edge in his tone.

"So you're keeping her in the dark?" Devon shot me a disbelieving look. "What do you see in this guy?" Ignoring his remark, I stood, signaling Aidan I was ready to leave when they were. As long as we got the book, I didn't want the details because, after Aidan saved my life last night, I trusted he knew what he was doing.

"But your life is on the line," Angel said.

Same old, same old. "Isn't yours too? You're just as mortal as I am. I've been filled in on the dangers. Now, can we get on with this? My family's waiting."

"Dad might be calling any time," Cass said, nodding. "I don't want my new position as ambassador to clash with my hell duties."

"What is it that you assist Daddy with?" Kieran asked, barely able to suppress his laughter. "You help the big guy create more swarms of rats and locusts, destroy a poor farmer's crops, send out a plague or two, offer contracts to steal people's souls, perhaps start a few wars?"

Two flames blazed in Cass's eyes. "Drop dead, jerk."

"Been there, done that, hot stuff. But I came back to life." Kieran chuckled. "And when I say hot, I'm talking about temperature, not looks."

Cass's cheeks turned bright red, her hands clenching and unclenching in her lap. Geez, did she have a temper. If she couldn't even handle Kieran, she wasn't going anywhere near Dallas. "I'd rather be hot than an ice cube," she said. "Better yet, why don't you pop over and I'll show you what my new phone can do."

Kieran raised his hands in mock defense. "Did you have to invent a phone to do the work for you because you have no supernatural abilities?"

314

"I told you I get them when I turn eighteen," Cass snapped.

"Let's just go." Aidan held the door open, muttering under his breath, "Am I the only sane one here?"

I hurried after him, eager to catch a moment alone, but the others followed too close behind to the cars parked outside. Aidan retrieved the keys from his pocket and threw the bundle to Kieran who caught it in mid-air. I realized getting him alone in the car was out of the question. Sighing, I jumped on the cold backseat as Kieran started the engine. Peeking out the tinted glass, I watched Aidan pull Devon aside, talking heatedly. I craned my neck to listen, but Kieran switched on the radio as if to stop me from eavesdropping.

I punched Kieran's shoulder. "What is it you don't want me to know?"

"Ouch." Kieran rubbed his shoulder, grinning.

"Don't quit your day job. You're the worst actor ever." I rolled my eyes and threw Aidan another glance. Hundreds of questions raced through my mind. Where were we going? Why wasn't Clare riding with us? What'd happen and why did we need the Shadows? I took a deep breath and pushed my thoughts to the back of my mind, but the more I tried, the more popped up. Eventually, Aidan squeezed onto the front seat and Kieran sped off, tailing Cass's SUV.

He *did* drive like a maniac, too close, foot on the gas pedal like he couldn't wait to get to his destination fast enough. My hands clutched the leather tight, holding on for dear life. His reflexes might be supernatural, but I didn't trust them one bit.

From my seat, I watched the brothers exchanging meaningful glances a few times. Okay, if they weren't going to talk, neither would I. Who needed conversation anyway? Leaning back, I closed my eyes and let my mind drift to my post-Aidan time. He had ignored me as though nothing happened between us the night before, so there was no doubt he saw no future. While his silence drove me ballistic and made me insecure, it also put things into perspective. I had a knack for commitment phobes. *No, scratch that.* The women's magazines I read were right. Guys just didn't want relationships anymore. Mum would tell me to suck it up and keep searching, but Mum had been married for the past thirty years and to the same man—a phenomenon that probably died down with the perm.

Half an hour later, Kieran pushed the brake briskly, and I lurched forward between the front seats, knocking my head in the process. Two pairs of eyes turned to regard me, like I was some sort of freak. Dallas would've cracked up with laughter. I could certainly deal with someone laughing in my face. But Aidan and Kieran just gawked, no doubt ready to guffaw behind my back.

I straightened and raised my chin a notch, avoiding their gazes, my face burning. As I opened the car door and stepped out, my foot caught in a loose branch and I toppled forward. Talk about keeping it graceful for the guy I loved. Aidan wrapped his arm around my waist, catching my fall. I murmured a thank-you and yanked my hand out of his grip. He didn't respond, but his palm lingered on the small of my back a little too long, as he gazed down on me in the darkness.

316

"We'll be walking the rest of the way." Devon's voice startled me, breaking my magical moment, and I jumped a step back.

"Are you okay to walk?" Aidan whispered.

The cold wind blew my hair in my face, chilling me to the bone. I tested my leg. My thigh felt sore, my toes were already frozen in my leather boots, but I gathered I'd rather be in pain than let him carry me and risk standing out like a sore thumb among the rich, athletic kids, so I nodded. Frowning, Aidan turned away.

"Do you have a flashlight?" Cass asked.

Kieran snorted. "You can't see in the dark? What sort of immortal are you?"

"Why would I want to see in the night? That's the time when normal people sleep." Cass flicked out her phone and started punching. A moment later, a legion of fireflies appeared over our head, flickering like a dying flashlight. Their light barely penetrated the thick bushes, but at least it cast a dim glow on our path, warning me of impending danger in the form of stones, loose branches, and what else not.

"A bunch of insects? Seriously, that's all you could come up with?" Kieran said.

Aidan frowned. "Come on, guys. Shut it for a change. Amber has a task to finish. Your banter's not exactly helping ease her nerves."

I threw him a grateful look. The longer we stood here, the more I felt like going home. No idea how these people could just stand here in the middle of nowhere, dressed in clothes befitting a Californian barbecue evening, and continue chatting while I froze my butt off in my summer coat, denims and boots.

317

Cass appeared beside Aidan and pointed at the winding path stretching through the trees. "Wait, we're going up there?" When he nodded, she groaned. "You've got to be kidding. Had I known my job duties involved climbing Mount Everest, I'd have reconsidered my career choices."

"This is hardly Mount Everest," Kieran said.

Cass glared at him, her eyes burning bright in the semi-darkness. "What, you've been there too, moron? You don't strike me as the outdoorsy type. More like getting your Boy Scouts medal from watching the Discovery channel."

"And you strike me as a girl I'd want to throw into the nearest volcano," Kieran said. "You know, it'd be like giving you a lift back home, down into the depths of hell."

"Here we go again." Aidan slung his arm over Cass's shoulders, pushing her forward. "You said you were in a hurry. Let's get this over with, shall we? Preferably without you two killing each other."

Cass snorted, but started walking behind Devon who led the way. Smiling, Clare gave Angel a nudge. "Don't worry. They fight like this all the time. I think it's courting."

"Clare!" Cass yelled, outraged. "I wouldn't date this guy if my life depended on it."

Kieran started to speak when Aidan tugged on his sleeve. "Not another word."

We walked in silence for a while, passing yet more trees. I didn't dare look up the path in case it seemed to stretch on forever, crushing my spirits. The fireflies hovered over our heads, illuminating our way. I reached up to touch them, then decided against it because I didn't trust demonic animals.

"The question is when will the demon attack the vampire with a fire bolt and when will the vampire bite the demon?" Devon said, resuming the conversation. "It's only a matter of time until someone's seriously hurt. Hanging around with them is a lethal combination, Amber. For the life of me, I can't figure out why you're still alive."

"As you can see, she's perfectly fine and happy," Aidan said. It was nice to see him stick up for me. Wrapping my coat tighter around me, I peered at the dense woods surrounding us. The path didn't seem to be the one we'd taken only a few nights ago; for one, it was narrower and obstructed by bushes and low-hanging branches. Then again, I'd been focusing on my feet, minding the loose stones and fallen twigs, and definitely not paying much attention to the scenery.

"Want me to carry you?" Kieran whispered in my ear, his hot breath brushing my skin.

He sounded so much like Aidan that, for a moment, I stopped breathing, my brain completely fooled, until Aidan called out, "She'll walk."

Who the heck did he think he was, telling me what to do? I considered taking Kieran up on the offer, just to piss Aidan off, but then I let it pass. He was right, better get the book without any more delays and drama.

"Another time," Kieran whispered.

"Bro, I swear next time Cass tries her abilities on you, I'll be the first one to help her," Aidan hissed, annoyed.

Was he jealous? I beamed at the realization that he didn't want to see me with someone else. In spite of his cold demeanor, he cared about me. I quickened my pace and, in a bold and brainless moment, placed an affectionate hand on his lower back, remembering an article on how guys were like children who wanted to be loved and cuddled. I felt stupid, but if it helped him open up more, I could cough up a few subtle displays of affection. A moment later my boot connected with a stone and I bumped into him, cussing under my breath.

The air smelled of damp wood and earth. Twigs snapped under our feet as we moved forward at a fast speed. My legs were starting to ache; my breath came in labored heaps. I was on the verge of asking whether we were there yet, when Kieran turned to Angel, signaling trouble ahead. "The leader of the pack—" Kieran pointed at Aidan "—won't let me anywhere near Amber because he's the alpha, territorial and all. So I extend the offer to you."

"Over my dead body," Devon said.

Kieran laughed. "Two alpha males. Is there room for a third?"

"My feet are killing me," Angel whined. "If I weren't so darn scared of vampires I'd take you up on your offer."

"Better not," Clare said. "He's bad news."

In spite of the cold, my jeans stuck to my damp skin and my thighs were on fire. The path continued to incline. Although Aidan freed the way for me, the biting wind made it hard to avoid the whipping branches. With no one speaking, my panting echoed in my ears. The more I focused to silence my breathing, the more it turned into a whistling sound trapped somewhere in my chest. Annoyed, I wondered whether Aidan could hear me with his supernatural powers. Probably. If he asked, I'd just pretend to be suffering from asthma.

Somehow, I managed to reach what looked like our destination with no more embarrassing tripping over my feet. A bird cried as it circled on the horizon, lowering over our heads, then rising into the depth of the night. For some undefined reason, it sent chills down my spine.

"That's not a normal bird, is it?" I whispered to Aidan. He shook his head and gave my hand a reassuring squeeze. I spun slowly as I gazed into the pitch black at yet more trees to each side. Why had we stopped in the middle of nowhere? Maybe the immortals needed a break, too? The ground—damp and cold, but still inviting—beckoned to me. Surely no one would mind me sitting down for a while until the others figured out what they were doing here.

A light flashed to my right, flooding the clearing in glaring brightness. I shielded my eyes, ready to complain, when I noticed the tall barbwire fence inches away. A few steps and I'd have run right into it. Devon fidgeted with what looked like a control panel until I heard a crack and a gate opened.

"Hurry up! We only have five seconds," Devon said. "Then the mechanism's blocked for a few hours."

"You're kidding." Yet more walking. With a sigh, I lifted my sluggish legs and trudged forward before the gate shut.

"Follow me," Devon said.

Cass looked down at her oversized jeans covered in mud and snorted. "I'm going to send you the cleaning bill, mate."

"If you burn that—" Kieran pointed at her clothes, grinning "—I'll buy you something that isn't made out of sackcloth."

Fashion was Cass's pride and joy. He'd definitely crossed the line with that one. I watched in awe as Cass's face turned bright red. But instead of the unnatural glint in her eyes, she just smiled and said, "At least I don't need to wear tight pants to distract from a lack of brains."

"Come on," Aidan muttered as he grabbed my hand and pulled me after him. "If they don't kill each other soon, I will."

The bickering continued behind me, but I tuned out. Aidan was still holding my hand, his thumb drawing circles on my skin as we crossed an open field, passing several floodlights, and reached an incline. Aidan stopped and muttered under his breath, "Holy cow."

"What?" I followed his line of vision up the hill where the light didn't reach, but all I saw were strange shapes towering against the canvass of the night.

He intertwined his fingers with mine and hurried forward, dragging me after him, forgetting my short legs couldn't take the same long strides. I quickened my pace so he wouldn't think me completely out of shape. And then I reached the top, seeing what he'd known was there all along, and my stomach twisted into nervous knots.

Chapter 26 - Aidan

The cemetery of the dead—I couldn't believe I was finally standing in front of it. Rebecca had tried to locate it to perform the ritual, but even after stepping on Shadow territory and searching around for hours, killing several Shadows along the way, she hadn't been able to find it. She'd claimed the woods were some sort of labyrinth in which passages changed with the moon. I never doubted her words because Rebecca would never admit failure willingly. Our journey so far had seemed straightforward, but I had no doubt Devon had some trick up his sleeve that would ensure we'd never find the way back should we decide to return later.

Row after row of tall statues and gravestones stretched in the distance as far as my heightened vampire sight let me see. Soft moonlight shone down on us. A large cloud of mist gathered around our feet, hovering inches above the ground. The wind howled, scattering the leaves.

"Now, that's a nice touch," Cass said. "Gives spooky a whole new meaning. Who brought the fog machine?"

"Huh?" Kieran said.

"Not talking to you, mate. You're always in a fog."

"I don't think there's anything creepier than this place," Angel whispered.

Devon nudged her and pointed at Kieran and me. "Just look behind you."

The Shadow irritated the hell out of me, but without him, we'd never get in. So I swallowed down my anger, for the time being. The war between our races was far from over, but a fight would have to wait.

"Show some respect," Amber said. "If you're going to crack on my guy, I'll turn around and leave. Got it?"

Devon set his jaw, but kept quiet. Defying my better judgment, I wrapped my arm around Amber's waist and drew her close. The rhythm of her heart echoed in my ears, racing like she'd just run with the bulls through the streets in Pamplona. I shot her a sideway glance and smiled reassuringly, as if that'd make a cemetery a less grotesque place to visit in the middle of the night. If the legends were true, we would never even catch a glimpse of the actual horrors the Shadows kept from the Lore court.

"Stay with Kieran while I check things out," I whispered.

Kieran wrapped his arms around Amber and Clare. "You go, bro. I'll keep the womenfolk safe from the clutches of Shadow Man."

"What about me?" Cass said, piqued.

Kieran laughed. "I'd invite you over but you know the saying, four's a crowd."

324

"Hey, idiot, the saying is three's a crowd." Cass pulled Amber and Clare away. "You stay with me. Not only is he mentally challenged, all he has is a couple of scary fangs and absolutely no idea what kind of fire is in this furnace."

"I'll defuse you real quick," Kieran said.

She took a menacing step forward. "You could never put out this flame."

"Did anybody ever tell you that you suck at public relations? Since you're an ambassador, you're supposed to like me. A lot. You know that, right? But maybe you're an ambass-a-*snore* because you're sleeping on the job. I'm going to personally talk to Layla about your inability to do your job."

Cass snorted. "Yeah, if you live to tell the tale."

"She likes me," Kieran chanted.

"She loves Aidan and look what happened when he visited to complain," Cass said. "I've had enough of you. I'm never coming back to your house. Clare will have to meet me somewhere else from now on."

I opened my mouth to speak when Kieran cut me off. "Funny, every time I turn around you're parked on my sofa. You're definitely crossing the line to Stalker Ville."

Cass gasped. "You think I'm stalking you?" The fireflies flickered over our heads, a shrill, indefinable sound, like that of thousands of wasps, filled the air. I peered up, waiting for the fireflies to turn into a dragon or something. If Kieran kept winding her up, it was only a matter of time until Cass snapped.

"*Think?* I know it. You like me. You want me," Kieran said. I threw him a warning look, but he just shrugged, grinning.

"Like a bullet in my head," Cass said. Clare chuckled somewhere in the shadows.

"Enough, you two." I turned my attention to Devon. "I'm going in."

Devon shook his head. "Not without me."

My lips twitched. "Don't trust me to take a quick look?" I was his enemy. Of course he wouldn't trust me.

Devon snorted. "About as far as I can throw you."

"You know I wouldn't get far without your help. I just want to make sure you have no tricks up your sleeve."

"Fine then. We'll all go together because I don't trust your insane brother around my Angel," Devon said.

Kieran turned and looked at her. "So that's your name. I knew there was a reason you had that beautiful hair and gorgeous eyes." He kissed her hand. "Somebody call heaven because an angel just fell from the sky."

"That's beyond lame." Cass groaned. "Every guy uses that line. Find something original, will you?"

"When you get a shrink," Kieran said.

I leaned into Amber to whisper in her ear. "So, you're waiting here?"

"What?" She peeled her eyes off the bronze statue—the hideous shape of a woman and bear caught in an embrace—and turned to face me. "Oh, no. No way. I'm not staying here." She lowered her voice. "What's this supposed to be?"

"Part shamanism, part—" I shrugged "—Voodoo? Who knows?"

"Magic," Devon said, matter-of-factly. "We don't practice Voodoo. A long time ago, the souls of sacred animals entered the bodies of our ancestors to grant them

326

eternal life. As payment, our people sent their shadows to the otherworld to watch over the animals' cubs."

It was the longest explanation I'd ever received about this holy ground I'd been investigating for years. According to the rumours circulating the Lore court, a Shadow could die by finding his statue in the cemetery of the dead and piercing a dagger through the animal's heart. I waited for Devon to reveal more, but he turned away, heading down the narrow path to a low entrance in the hill.

"Are you sure you want to do this?" I asked Amber. "This is your last chance to back out."

She puffed. "No way. We're in this together, Aidan. I want you to have a life without the need for blood. Besides, even if I changed my mind I wouldn't let you go in there by yourself to tell them I'm chickening out. They'd kill you on the spot."

Shadows had tried to kill me for centuries, and didn't succeed. I took a deep breath to suppress my sudden joy. Amber's fear lingered on her like she wore it as a perfume. For the first time she seemed to worry about me. In the heat of last night's words, I figured the bond wasn't working after all and all she wanted was her old life back. Rage had driven me insane, made me curse Fate for giving me a mortal. But I could sense something about Amber's attitude had changed. Her gaze was softer and in the past few hours she'd raised her hand several times as if to touch me. And now her need to protect me had flared up. I was finally starting to see progress. Hopefully, it wasn't too late for us.

Somewhere behind me, Kieran's said, "How much does Daddy pay you to screw over other souls?"

I shook my head and pulled Amber along. I had no idea why Kieran kept winding Cass up. The girl was beyond normal, but it couldn't just be mutual dislike that drove my brother to be mean. As far as I knew, Cass had done nothing to earn our ridicule. I made a mental note to talk to Kieran about it once my problems with Amber were solved.

The heavy mahogany door stood wide open. As I walked through, I felt the invisible barrier across the threshold vibrate, holding me back for a second, and then give in. *Magic.* Without Devon opening the path, I doubted I'd have been able to pass through. It was a similar magic to the one protecting my house against immortal intruders. That Cass got in without my explicit invitation showed me she was something else, or stronger than anything the paranormal world could conjure up.

The space reeked of Shadows, dressed in black robes, watching from the countless dark corners. A huge altar, surrounded by countless white candles, was set up in the middle of the dimly lit, cave-like room.

"Look at that," Cass said. "Now that's how you woo a girl." She winked at me. "Are you taking notes?"

"Candles are overrated," Kieran said. "Just like romance."

"You just haven't found the right girl," Clare said. "She'll come along."

"And then she'll make a run for the hills." Cass laughed at her own joke.

I squeezed Amber's hand. The Shadows' glare brushed over us, their distaste for what I was palpable in the humid air. Slowly, I turned my head to my right, ready to face another abomination Rebecca created a long time ago: sitting on a high throne was Deidre, Queen of the Shadows, an ancient soul living in the pain-ridden body of a dying girl, trapped forever between life and death. The Shadows wanted the book badly so they could search for a ritual to free Deidre from her need to feed on the life force of her own people. Deidre was one of the reasons why I had found it so easy to kill Rebecca when she attacked Blake. I had enough of her love for torture.

"You—" Deidre pointed a finger at Clare, Cass and Kieran "—move over there to the wall." Kieran and Clare did as instructed, but Cass stood her ground.

My jaw set as I met Deidre's black gaze. I bowed to hide my horrified expression. A glimpse at that dying body was enough to send shivers down my spine. Deidre wouldn't harm Amber because she wanted the book more than I did. But I could be wrong. After underestimating Layla, I wouldn't trust anyone but myself. I waited for Deidre to speak, but instead it was Cass who took charge of the situation.

"I'm the new Lore ambassador, here to save the mortal from supernatural harm. Don't you dare play a trick on me, Dee Dee. I'm much stronger than the whole bunch of you together." Her eyes glinted red as she glanced at Deidre, then walked to the altar and picked up a burning candle. It melted under her fingers, wax dripping onto the stony floor. With an exaggerated sigh, she placed what was left of it back and peered from one face to the other. "Just a word of advice, guys, living in a cemetery's beyond macabre. You should look into proper housing."

Cass obviously enjoyed drama a bit too much, but as long as it helped get Amber out of here alive, I'd do anything to assist her. I tightened my grip around my mate's waist. Her heart quickened as her body—plump in all the right places—leaned into me. From the corner of my eye, I watched Deidre rise from her seat and walk to the altar, motioning Amber to step forward. I let go of her waist, but followed right behind.

"And you should look into proper manners because your demon hands have left a scent on that candle you've touched. Every single one of them has been blessed by our priests," Deidre said.

"Hey, I'm half fallen angel and half Seraph. There's a difference, meaning I'm actually holy." Cass crossed her arms over her chest, grinning.

"Pitch the candle you've defiled," Deidre said.

"I'll look for a trashcan then." Cass shrugged, but didn't budge.

"Angel, dispose of this candle immediately. And then leave." Deidre waited until Angel scurried out, then grabbed Amber's hand, addressing her. "I see you're back. You truly want to retrieve the book for us?" Amber shot me an insecure look and nodded.

"Good." Deidre pointed at the high cavernous walls where the soft light of the candles didn't reach the shadows. "This hall's special. Once the—" she hesitated and scowled as if she had to force herself to speak out the word "—vampire leads you to the threshold of death, where your physical and astral body meet, this place will help you enter the otherworld. You, then, shall be brought by hell's demons to where the book supposedly is. When your deed's done, our incantations will help you return to the physical plane. You understand you could die in the process?"

I noticed Amber flinch and put a reassuring hand on the small on her back as rage rose inside me. She wouldn't die. I'd rather break the Lore rules and turn her into what I was than have Fate take her away from me.

"I do," Amber said. I smiled proudly at how brave she sounded.

"Whoa, let's not get dramatic here. No one's dying," Cass said. "Now, without further ado, let's get this party cracking. You had enough time for chatting when you kidnapped her. Besides, I'm not paid by the hour." She turned to me, frowning. "Aidan, how am I actually being paid?"

"There's something else," Amber said. "I want something in return. You can have the book, but you have to perform Aidan's spell. Promise me."

Deidre tilted her head. "Very well. I give you my word."

Amber beamed up at me, then took a deep breath. Grabbing her hand, I helped her onto the altar, kneeling next do her. Somewhere behind us countless voices, obscured by the darkness, started to chant. Amber looked small and fragile among the countless candles that barely flickered. She shuddered, wide-eyed with fear. I remembered I still didn't have her agreement.

"What the heck am I doing here?" she whispered. "I thought you guys were going to show me how to go into a trance and talk to Rebecca to ask where the book was. And that the trance might kill me."

I shook my head. "It's a little more complicated than that."

"So you keep saying." Her voice quivered.

I grabbed her hand. "Listen, babe, try to remain as calm and still as you can."

"Am I being sacrificed in some freaky ceremony?" She laughed nervously.

How could she even think that? "No, of course not. I'll just have to drink a bit of—" I hesitated, reconsidering my words "—I promise I won't let anything happen to you. I'll get my life sorted out so we can be together. Once this is over, I won't ever have to feed again."

"I never promised you a life together because I want my old life back," Amber said.

I grimaced. "We'll talk about that later. There's one more matter to discuss."

"You haven't told her?" Cass shouted. "You're the worst boyfriend ever!"

Damn the demon. I tried to keep my composure and ignore Cass's ecstatic gaze, sucking in every chaos vibe she could get hold of. "I'll have to bite you now to slow down your heart rate until you almost die so you can cross over."

"What sort of crappy plan is that? You should've told me," Amber hissed.

"You can still back out."

She rolled her eyes. "No. I'll do it, but only because I don't go back on my word. But you better not suck me dry. Got it?"

I shook my head. "The others won't let that happen."

"Let's get this over and done with." She punched my arm, then lay on her back, her eyes bulging in their sockets, heart pumping with fear. "When I get back you're so going to get a piece of my mind!"

"I deserve it." I inched closer and whispered in her ear, "If things go wrong, please let me turn you into what I am."

She regarded me for a second, her eyes as deep as dark pools with the bright flames of the candles reflecting in them, and then she shook her head. *No.* Taking a sharp breath, I opened my mouth to speak, beg her if need be, but she turned away.

"Please, just trust me," I whispered. The chanting around us grew louder. Deidre raised her arm and signaled me to begin. The time had come. I placed a soft kiss on Amber's neck and ran my tongue over the spot where her blood pumped the hardest, then waited. She shuddered under my touch, her heart hammering in her chest. Intertwining my fingers with hers, I dared take a deep breath and let her scent invade my nostrils. She smelled of lavender and honey, of warm summer nights and rainy skies, of the home I always wanted to build and treasure.

The hunger inside me stirred, growing in intensity until I could barely restrain my vampire nature. My fangs connected with her skin, piercing the fragile barrier, and her blood, sweeter than any nectar, flooded my mouth, robbing me of my last ounce of control.

"Don't kill her." My brother's voice echoed from somewhere behind me, but I could scarcely make out the words. It wasn't right to drink from my mate and enjoy it so much, but Amber was different—in a way she was mine like no other had ever been before. I couldn't slow down.

Amber groaned and stirred beneath me. Her soft hand moved to the nape of my neck. To hold me in place? To push me away? I had no idea because her hand just lingered there. I could feel her heart racing, pumping harder to make up for the loss of blood. The color was slowly draining from her cheeks as she grew weaker. It wasn't enough; she hadn't reached the threshold yet. And then her pulse slowed down to a mere whisper, barely audible in my ears, and her hand let go.

"That's enough." Deidre put her child-like hand on my arm to stop me. I turned on her, snarling like a crazed animal trapped in a cage. For a moment, my human side switched off and I almost pounced, ready to shred to pieces whoever lingered between me and my prey. Strong hands grabbed my shoulders and pulled me away, holding me down until understanding kicked in and my human side returned.

Cass glared at me. "That love bite was more than just a nibble. You took it a step too far, mate. And you think *I'm* nuts?"

"What's wrong with you? You could've killed her," Kieran hissed in my ear. Was he talking about Deidre or Amber? *Amber.* With a gasp, I turned to face my mate, lying on the altar, pale as the dead. I struggled against my brother's iron grip, listening for Amber's pulse, but I couldn't hear it.

"Get him out of here until he calms down," Deidre said, annoyed.

"Yeah, you heard Queenie, kick his butt to the curb," Cass said.

I shook my head. I didn't want to leave. Not before someone assured me my mate was all right. I took a deep breath to steady myself and clear my mind. "I'm good." I took another look at Amber's motionless shape, so small and helpless between the candles. For her sake, I'd be strong. But just standing here and not doing anything felt wrong.

"You sure?" Kieran asked, skeptically.

I nodded.

"Let's hurry then. We don't have much time." Devon kneeled at Amber's head and placed his palms on her temples. The incantations commenced again, barely more than a soft murmur compared to Devon's booming voice. "Amber, can you hear me?" She didn't respond, but the pinkie on her left hand twitched.

"Can she hear us?" I asked. She simply had to, otherwise—

"Be quiet," Devon whispered. "Let her focus."

Deidre stepped in the middle of the circle and raised her arms. "Tonight, this gifted soul shall enter the realm of the otherworld, and we are here to guide her."

The chorus of voices rose near the wall. "Dark Lords, let us serve this congregation through our queen."

Deidre bowed her head, her voice echoing from the walls. "Amber, listen to the voice that is no servant of the power, but power itself. I pledge that I shall act as a bridge between you and the souls that will assist you on your journey in this dim hour so long as your pledge remains finding the book."

The strong wind outside shook the door in its hinges; the candles started to flicker, but didn't go out. Somewhere in the distance, glass shattered, and birds cawed. The Shadows' murmurs filled the air, sending shivers down my spine.

"Amber, can you feel the power that is present to guide you?" Devon asked. I watched my mate's eyes move beneath closed lids. A heavy weight settled somewhere in

335

the pit of my stomach as Devon whispered, "Her journey's about to begin."

Chapter 27

As the pressure lifted off my feverish neck, I descended deep into the lower fractions of my consciousness, surrounded by darkness though my eyes were open, staring at a point in the distance.

Something hit my head hard, and I stumbled forward, almost tumbling to the ground. I scanned the area. There was no one around. Who had hit me then? Where had the others disappeared? Why had Aidan abandoned me, leaving me here to fend for myself?

The cold air reeked of dirt and blood. Taking one slow step at a time, I moved around, blind in the darkness. After a while, I could feel a nameless presence pacing with me, breathing cold air in my face. I shivered, but not from the cold. A sudden drop in temperature usually means one thing—ghosts. I figured, now I'd have my encounter with Elvis. Behind me, low murmurs erupted. Invisible hands tugged at my arms and shoulders as though they wanted me to listen. I stopped mid-stride and focused on the soft voices to discern what they had to say.

"Amber, can you feel the power that is present to guide you?" Silence. Then, "Her journey's about to begin."

Someone was speaking to me, but who? My bones felt heavy, my muscles ached. I lay down on the naked ground and propped my palms under my head, closing my eyes to rest a little.

***

When I woke up, my body no longer ached, but darkness still lingered. My limbs felt frozen and numb under the thick layers of clothes. I was supposed to do something, but I couldn't recall my purpose. Was I dying? Deidre had said I might. Aidan had warned me also. Was this freezing sensation what death felt like? Where was the light and people you loved supposedly greeting you? I could see no people or tunnel; in fact, it was so dark I couldn't even see my hand in front of my eyes.

Stumbling forward, I swore I'd figure out a way to haunt Aidan for this. I snorted, annoyed. Did the otherworld have a ghost school where I could take Ghost Tricks 101? I'd sign up in a heartbeat. Not a chance Aidan would ever sleep again. I'd wear a white flowing robe, wave my arms, clank some chains and moan with all my might. Maybe I'd sing nonstop in his ear, like Whoopi Goldberg did in *Ghost*. Now, that'd drive him nuts. Since he never heard me sing he was in for a real treat because I was basically tone deaf and couldn't hit a note if my life depended on it.

My feet lifting off the ground, I started to float into the open space. Surprised, I peered up at the countless stars glittering on a black canvas, and wondered where they came from. I felt the entire universe stretched out in front of me. Yeah, I was certainly a ghost, flying and all. Aidan's doors would definitely not keep *me* out. Letting go, I could no longer feel my body. My mind fell into perpetuity, drifting into the greatest sense of freedom and tranquility I'd ever felt.

Wings flapped around me as dark, formless shapes gathered, murmuring words of wisdom in my ears. I knew they had assembled to help me, to guide me to the right place. The book. Aidan wanted it. And then I remembered the purpose of my visit.

The winged beings barely touched my skin as they lifted me up and carried me forward in their strong arms. Their smell—burnt tires and sulfur—made my stomach clench, but I didn't mind as long as they led me where I was supposed to go.

We flew past woods and mountains, valleys and rivers. A setting sun appeared on the horizon. I lifted my gaze to the large, deadly claws wrapped around my arms and legs, holding me in place. I realized the formless shapes looked like tall, muscly humans, their skin black as coal, with white wings and eyes dark as bottomless pits. Letting out a screech, they pointed down and lowered me to the ground near a hole surrounded by stones.

I stood and wiped a hand over my dusty jeans. "Is the book here?"

The tallest of the creatures hovered over me, wings flapping as it nodded and let out a guttural sound. He was so beautiful with perfect features, and yet so eerily inhuman, like a dark angel. I could barely peel my eyes off him when the scent of burnt tires on a hot summer day wafted past again, stronger than before. If they were angels, then surely not from heaven.

Holding my breath, I leaned over the edge and peered inside, my mind starting to work slowly. How was I supposed to get down there?

I shot the creature a glance over my shoulder as I asked, "Do you have a rope, an energy bar or something?" No answer. I cleared my throat. "Well then, can one of you be an angel and give a girl a lift?"

The creature let out a sound that resembled a chuckle and shoved me forward, then rose into the sky, white wings flapping gracefully, and disappeared with the others. I realized I was supposed to climb when I could barely walk without tripping over my own feet. If I fell and broke my leg, no one would ever know. Whoever came up with this particular plan to retrieve the book, sucked big time. Maybe I'd haunt them, too.

Murmurs echoed in the distance. A cold shudder ran down my spine. "Hello? Is there someone?" I spun, holding my breath as I listened for more sounds.

"Amber! I know you can hear me."

Was that Devon? It didn't sound like a voice inside my head, more like someone shouting through a loudspeaker at a football game. I peeked behind the nearby bushes. No one there, but where else could he be hiding? Maybe the voice was carrying over from inside the pit? I dared a peek

340

into the pitch-black when his voice jolted me, making me flinch.

"Look around you and tell us where you are."

I scanned the area. The thick forest stretched into the distance. Apart from trees and bushes, and yet more trees, there was nothing nearby. "Oh shoot, my GPS can't get a service down here. I'm going to really have to change providers. But let me get my map out and match it to the giant, neon, flashing road sign I'm standing under." I paused for effect. "How the heck would I know where I am, Devon? All I can tell you is I'm outside."

"You must see something."

Yeah, a future appointment with a good psychologist and a prescription for anti-depressants. Dallas had a point something was wrong with my mind. The signs were there: hearing strange voices, seeing unearthly beings, talking to myself. I sighed and opened my mouth to speak, hysteria almost choking my throat. "There's a pit."

I heard a gasp, then Aidan said, "That's it. Well done, babe. You'll have to go in now."

Snorting, I peered over the edge. "And how am I supposed to do that? Last time I checked I couldn't fly."

"Can you climb in? Or jump?" Aidan asked.

I'd feared that one coming. "Of course I can, because I'm Spiderman."

"Remember nothing can hurt you because you're not in the physical world anymore. We're standing over your body at the altar. Your soul is doing all the work right now," he said. He didn't sound convinced.

I snorted. "I'm dead already. How reassuring. Are you sure nothing can hurt me?"

341

"Positive," Devon said. Why the hesitation in his voice then?

My pulse racing, I draped a leg over the brink and dangled it as I peered in. Wherever the bottom was, it seemed to be a long way down.

"You said nothing could hurt me? So, right now I'm just a spirit?" I mumbled. "Well, in that case I'd just float my way down."

"Amber, no!" Aidan said.

"Ah, what the heck!" Taking a deep breath, I closed my eyes and jumped.

I felt myself free fall in slow motion, spinning in circles and plummeting deeper, the cold air seeping into my skin. Opening my eyes, I saw a vision of Aidan smiling inches from me.

"We'll get the book and have a life together. I promise," Aidan said.

His face morphed into Kieran's who held a camera. "Can I take a picture so I can show Santa what I want for Christmas?"

Angel appeared, her long swirling black hair made her look like a dark angel as she smiled. "If I marry Kieran we'll be sisters-in-law, and I'll never be lonely again."

"No, you're my BFF," Clare's image said.

Devon cleared his voice in the distance. "Concentrate, Amber. You're almost there."

I hit the floor with a loud thud, the impact knocking the air out of my lung. A sharp pain rippled through my shoulder. Didn't Devon say nothing could hurt me?

"Are you in?" Aidan asked.

I wiped my dirty hands on my new coat, annoyed. "I can still feel my legs, thanks for asking. My back's not even hurt that badly. Only as though I was just hit by a train."

"Good, now what do you see?" Devon's voice again.

Did they pay any attention to me? For a moment I considered ignoring them, just so I could sulk a bit, but I figured the sooner I got out of here, the faster I could haunt them. As I scrambled up, hand holding onto the wall, I saw a neon cord and pulled it. A rusty light bulb flickered on the other side of the wall. I noticed I was standing in a long, narrow room with the only entrance above my head.

The place was one dirty mess with a naked mattress covering the far side and cobwebs hanging from the low ceiling. "I'm in a room with no windows. There's a cooker in one corner and a pad on the left side."

"Describe the room. What does it smell like? Is there anything else besides the cooker?" Devon's voice was dripping with anticipation.

"It's dusty." That was an understatement. "Since I have no job maybe they should hire me as a housekeeper."

Aidan snorted. "Seriously, Amber, would it really help?"

"One more housekeeping joke from you and I'm outta here. Got it?" I walked around, taking in every detail.

"Sorry, babe. Listen, the book's there. You need to find it," Aidan said.

With trembling fingers, I picked up a dirty towel from the bare ground and tossed it across the bed when I noticed the animal fur. "Oh, God, that's just disgusting. I see skin shredded to pieces, like a beast sharpened its claws on it." My heartbeat accelerated. Whatever this place was, I wanted out. Now.

"Keep searching," Devon said.

I puffed and turned away to scan the floor. "Easy for you to say. You're not looking at dead stuff." There was nothing else. No cupboards, no trapdoors. "I don't think it's here."

"Look harder. The book's probably hidden."

"I'm not blind," I muttered under my breath as I skimmed the walls. How big was it anyway? What did it look like? The Shadows hadn't even bothered to give me any description or, even better, show me a picture. If I pretended to search hard enough they'd eventually realize it wasn't here.

I paced the room several times, swirling up the thick dust. "There's nothing else, just empty walls and filth everywhere. If I don't get a shower soon I swear I'll—"

"Search the floor," Devon said.

"Dive right in. Oh, why not? I've always wanted to die from asthma." I cowered on the ground and moved my hands about through years of dust and what else not. "Nothing."

"Have you checked under the bed yet?" Aidan asked.

My heart skipped a beat. "You've got to be kidding. What if there's a monster lurking under there?"

"Babe, what're you, five?" Aidan said.

"Yeah, right. I shouldn't believe in monsters, but then again I shouldn't believe in vampires either." The shirt on my back was soaked with sweat; my pulse started to sound like a drum in my ears. Stretching out my arms, I grabbed hold of the mattress and pulled it up. It was stuck to the floor, like someone nailed it to the spot, and much heavier than I expected. With a grunt, I took a step forward, bending my elbows to lift it. The light barely reached beneath it. As I turned away, ready to drop it, I saw a bundle pushed to the far side.

"Nothing? Maybe there's some sort of vault or corridor?" Devon said.

"Please don't let it be anything dead and foul-smelling." My stomach churned as I pushed the mattress aside. After several attempts of pulling and shoving, my arms ached. I wiped the sweat off my brows and tried again. The material ripped. I kicked at it until it slid away, revealing what lay beneath.

"Amber, can you hear me?" Devon asked. I heard him, but didn't reply. No point in raising their hopes, then crushing them if I didn't find what they wanted.

It was a bundle made from skin and fur that smelled as though the animal hadn't died long ago. Poking my foot into it, I pulled the cover aside and let out a shriek.

"Got it." Silence. Did they even hear me?

"Really?" Aidan said, eventually.

The book was thick and bound in fading leather with letters and symbols embossed on the cover. I inched closer and held my breath as I dropped to the floor to touch it. The pages were old and yellowed, worn out at the corners where fingers had chafed the paper. I couldn't stop staring at it, the smell of dust and magic making me dizzy.

"It's right here. I'm holding it in my hands." I felt proud of myself. There I was, inconspicuous Amber, finding what a bunch of immortals hadn't been able to get. It had been so easy, but who cares? I had it, and now I'd get back home.

Eventually, I shut the book and lifted it in my arms. It was heavier than I expected, but not impossible to carry. If I could pull Dallas's monster of a suitcase up a hill, I'd be able to transport an oversized book.

Aidan sounded pleased too. "You rock, babe. Now get back here."

Right. Now came the hard part. Where was the way out? I stumbled forward, standing right under the opening in the ceiling, and looked up. Whoever hid the book either had a rope with them, or could climb up walls like Spiderman.

"Guys, I've no idea how to get out." I tried to infuse cheeriness into my tone when pictures of me, trapped in this place, flashed through my mind. I wasn't going to end up a skeleton, nails scratching at the bare walls as I tried to climb my way out to no avail.

"There's got to be some sort of tunnel," Devon said. "Keep searching."

Scowling, I scanned the floor for the umpteenth time. "What do you think I'm doing? Picking flowers?"

No trapdoor, no hidden opening, nothing. I always hated playing hide and seek. Dallas's fetish for hiding my stuff and then watching me cuss my way through searching for it while he guffawed like an idiot, always turned me into a raging lunatic. I sank down next to the mattress and pressed my back against the wall, taking one deep breath after another. I'd literally skimmed every inch of this awful place. Where else could I look?

"Have you found it?" Devon asked. "You need to hurry. The book's very important."

346

Not to mention my wellbeing. I rolled my eyes. "Of course. I'm standing in front of the exit. Just taking a few pictures, you know, to remind me of my time in the otherworld."

Maybe I could summon some deceased souls and send them after Devon & co. right now, because apart from seeing a few dead people and what happened to them, the prize had brought me nothing but hassles.

"If you could just hurry up with the pictures then, we'd really appreciate it," Devon said. Not only was he annoying as hell, he was also dense. Leaning against the bed, I felt my hand sink right in. I turned to examine the wide cut at the foot of the mattress, inconspicuous in the dim light. The material seemed stretched over a long string as wide as two fingers. I pulled it out and stared at the metal hooks running every few inches. Were they supposed to fit in somewhere?

"Hey, anyone know anything about rock climbing? With hooks and stuff?"

Silence, then Aidan said, "Oh, God. Is there any other way you could get out of there?"

"I'll just grow myself a pair of wings." I bit my tongue hard, holding back another remark. No need to take it out on him just because he had a point. He had yet to see my acrobatic side—the one I'd put to use for the first time in my life. "I get it. You're clueless, too." I nodded to myself. "Doesn't matter, I'll figure it out myself."

Swinging the rope over my shoulder so the hooks dangled and clattered, I brushed my hands over the walls until I found the tiny indentations in the stone that were too small to see with the naked eye. Under my fingers, I felt the metal rings inside the indentations, smooth to the touch. I tied the rope around my waist, securing it with a knot, then wrapped it a few times around the book to keep it secured against my back, and glanced up.

"Now what?" I examined a hook as I considered my options. Obviously they were meant to clasp around the ring, but how was I going to climb up there to attach those? "Darn it."

"Are you okay? Anything happened?" Aidan's voice boomed, jolting me out of my thoughts. I could only hope he wasn't going to interrupt my concentration while I dangled from a rope in mid-air.

"Just peaches, thanks. Now if you could just keep quiet for a minute. Thanks," I said.

After a last look at the rope tied around my waist, I squeezed the hook into the first indentation and wriggled it about until it connected with the ring. Standing on my toes, I attached the next one half a foot higher, grabbed hold of it and tried to pull myself up. Groaning from the effort, I realized it wasn't going to work unless I grew myself a pair of bodybuilder biceps.

"What happened to the good ole' stairs?" I whispered.

With a sigh I heaved myself up for another try, pushing the tip of my boot into the first indentation for more leverage as I climbed up. I reached the second hook and stretched my arm as far as I could to grasp the third dent above my head, blindly fidgeting with the catch until it connected with the ring. From where I hung, I figured there were at least ten or fifteen of those. After only two, my body was already shaking from too much effort.

Setting my jaw, I took a deep breath and forced my tired thighs into motion, pushing against the wall to take the strain off my shoulders. I wasn't going to quit—not least because I had no clue how to get down again, and dangling in mid-air wasn't an option. By the time I fitted the last hook and lifted myself through the opening in the ceiling, my back was slick with sweat and my heart hammered in my chest, probably publicizing an imminent heart attack. I crawled a few feet so I wouldn't fall back in and stretched out on the grass to wait for my trembling limbs to stop shaking.

The moon stood high on the horizon. It was just a round circle, but it gave enough dim light to see as far as the woods in the distance. Pushing up on my elbows, I scanned the semi-darkness around me. So I had found and retrieved the book, but where were the black, winged guys to take me back? They either figured I'd take longer and were still on coffee break, or I was supposed to find my way home.

"Hey, can anyone hear me?" I cringed at myself for talking into thin air.

"Did you get out?" Aidan sounded nervous, doubtful.

"Yep, but there's a problem," I said. "My taxi's not here."

"Huh?"

Did I have to spell out everything? "I've no idea how to get home. I know I should've left a trail of bread crumbs or something, but you didn't pack me breakfast."

"Cass's demon guardians aren't there?" Devon asked. "That's bad."

He didn't say. I rolled to the side and went about stretching my arm muscles. "So, since you're the fabulous event organizer, how am I supposed to get home now? Do

I get a replacement car, or do you expect this tourist to walk all the way back home?"

"Don't worry, we'll get you out," Devon said.

"You'd better hurry if you want the book, otherwise I can't guarantee I won't forget to bring it with me." I knew it was petty to sulk, but you'd think after I did all the hard work for them, the Shadows could at least ensure my departure went according to plan.

Maybe the creatures lingered close by, passing the time until they were called. Lifting my aching body off the ground, I started in the direction of the nearby bushes, figuring I wouldn't venture too far in case they turned up. The scent of pines hung heavy in the air. Were there pine trees in Scotland? I had no idea, but we had flown over water, hills and woods, and the air was too dry here, and the sun had only been setting when I arrived. I figured, this place had to be somewhere in the United States, a place with a few hours time difference and where conifers grow.

The moonlight reflected in something shiny behind the bushes. I bent down to have a closer look when my sleeve caught in the thicket, a sharp twig grazing the skin on the back of my hand. I yelped at the sudden pain and pulled away, tearing a hole in my favorite coat. Then I realized this was my spiritual coat. My real coat was on my real body guarded by Aidan, Cass and Kieran. I let out a sigh of relief, stifling the uneasy feeling inside the pit of my stomach.

"Are you all right?" Aidan asked.

"I'm fine," I said through gritted teeth. Nature really wasn't my friend.

The scratch stung as though hundreds of needles pierced my skin. Something hot and sticky trickled down my fingers. I gazed in awe at the thin, almost black rivulet dripping to the ground. Blood. Great. Now I'd have to get stiches when I got home. While others brought photos and key rings from their trips, my souvenir would be a freaking scar.

I wiped my right sleeve over the wound and kneeled down, pushing the other hand through the thicket to reach for the shiny object, ignoring the voice inside my head that kept asking whether I really wanted to squeeze my hand, leg or any other part of my body in there. Hell, yeah. I had to know what the shiny thing was. The scar wouldn't be for nothing. My fingers connected with something smooth and cold, the size of my palm. Digging my nails into the ground, I scraped at the sharp borders until the object came loose, then I pulled.

The ground shook beneath my feet. I jumped back, my left sleeve catching in the same branch as before. The earth trembled again, this time harder. An earthquake below the bushes in the same moment I retrieved some sort of palm-sized mirror. What were the odds? Carefully, I squeezed my injured hand under the thicket to free my sleeve when I realized the twig that had grazed me wasn't a twig at all but an oversized, protruding nail.

A loud hiss erupted a moment before a hand appeared from beneath the ground, digging its way out of the soil, and grabbed hold of my injured arm, pulling it down into the earth. Something dug into my skin; the pain ran up my arm, almost blinding me. I opened my mouth and let out a startled scream as I yanked my hand away from the

351

iron grip, but the thing kept sucking and slurping, gurgling sounds echoing in the eerie silence of the night.

My heart hammered in my chest as I yelled, "Please, someone help me!" I felt my strength wane. My vision blurred. I was paralyzed with fear. Voices carried over from the distance, but I couldn't discern their words. At some point, one of the black winged creatures appeared beside me and fire brushed my clothes, burning my skin. I tried to breath, but the pain made me choke on my gasps.

And then I fainted.

Chapter 28 - Aidan

Something had happened, or why else wouldn't Amber answer our calls? I paced the room up and down, my wrath competing with the need to roar and punch the walls. It wasn't like me at all to lose control, but never before had I been in a situation where I felt so helpless. For the umpteenth time I wished I'd stopped her in the woods, forcing her to give me the gemstones even though using force was against the rules. Better a few broken rules and dealing with Layla's fury than hearing my mortal mate's cry for help and not being able to help. Kieran squeezed my shoulder and murmured something that sounded like "She'll be okay." They were just empty words.

Barely two hours had passed since I drank Amber's blood, but her taste still lingered on my tongue, beckoning to me. Being separated from her pained me. Literally. My body craved her scent, her touch. I knew I was going bonkers, but I didn't care because the rage inside me made me feel more alive than hope ever would.

"Amber, can you hear me?" Devon kept repeating the words over and over again. How much more of an idiot could he be? Obviously, if Amber heard him she'd respond.

"Get her out of there. Now!" I bellowed. "Or I swear you won't live to see another day." It was a threat I intended to carry out. Kill the damn Shadows one by one. If it weren't for their book, Amber would still be with me, safe in my arms. I realized I could live like before, trapped by my need for blood and darkness, but I couldn't live without my mate.

"Send out the demons, your dad's army or whatever." I heard Kieran whisper. "I can't guarantee he won't turn against everybody if Amber doesn't wake up soon."

"What do you think I've been doing for the last half hour, moron?" Cass yelled.

They all sounded worried, though probably more about the book than about Amber. I had to do something—anything—before I snapped. "I'm going after her." Peeling the collar of my shirt from where it stuck to my neck, I turned my head to the side and motioned Kieran to step closer. "Your turn, bro."

Cass rolled her eyes. "Don't be daft. You know you need the prize to astral travel. Even if you left your body without killing it, you'd be hovering over this room, either dying or stuck forever as a poltergeist."

"She's right," Kieran said. "Besides, I doubt I could drink enough of your blood before your vampire instincts kicked in, turning you into a raging psycho. Not that you're far away from being one right now."

My vampire nature would respond if I lost too much blood, forcing me to survive by attacking anyone nearby, but did I have any other choice? "Just do it. I can control it." I gazed up at Kieran's hard face, his expression betraying I wasn't going to sway him any time soon. I turned and shot Clare an imploring look. Until now she'd been silent, waiting and watching near a wall. "What about you, Clare? Will you do it?" She was my last chance. "Please," I added.

Clare hesitated, eyes darting between Kieran and me, then shook her head. "I'm sorry. There's no way you can travel without the prize. Whatever happened to Amber, she would want me to keep you here."

They had turned against me. Letting out a roar, I jumped to my feet and kicked at the burning candles, hot wax spilling onto the dirty ground. Fate had played a prank on me, sending a mortal mate and then taking her away once I fell for her. It wasn't fair.

"The demon guardians are nearby," Cass said. "I can hear them searching for her. They'll reach her in a heartbeat." She gasped as she pointed at Amber's body.

"What? What do you hear?" I turned and kneeled beside my unmoving mate, fingers digging into her fragile shoulders. She was turning a pale shade of blue right before my eyes; her skin felt cold as ice under my touch. "Cass, what's the matter? What's happening to her?"

Time seemed to stand still. Eventually Cass replied, eyes wide with something I couldn't quite place. "It's got its teeth sunk into her. Charge the creature, then. Do something, you idiots." She was talking to her demons, regarding me as she said, "I have one hundred of Dad's best men flying over this thing and twenty more jumping on it, clawing at its skin and poking its eyes. Looks like your ex isn't going down without a fight."

What was she saying? "My ex?"

"Rebecca," Cass hissed, closing her eyes. "Get the fire demons, Octavius. Turn that thing into burnt toast." She paused. "I know they're dangerous, but we don't have a choice. Release them. Do it. Now."

"Cass, is Amber safe?" Kieran asked.

She jerked her head back. "Whoa, slow down on the flames, man. You're going to singe your eyebrows. We need just enough to roast marshmallows, not set a raging forest fire."

"The forest is on fire? Are you insane? You're going to kill Amber," I roared.

"Don't you know Smokey the Bear's trademark slogan? No? Well, let me tell you. Smokey says, only you can prevent forest fires." Cass smiled bitterly. "They got Amber out."

"Is she burned?" I asked.

"Yes, and bitten. Sucked dry."

"But she's alive?" As long as Amber was breathing I could still turn things around. I glared at Cass, ready to shake the answer out of her, when I noticed her parted lips and flushed cheeks. Drama. Chaos. Havoc. Demons feed on them, and judging from the ecstasy on Cass's face there was plenty of it around.

"They're bringing Amber back," she said.

The Shadows started their incantations again. Deidre stirred for the first time since Amber's departure, smoothing a hand over her long hair, the sudden movement startling me.

I felt the pull, the bond warning me like a ringing bell that something was happening. Amber sat up with a gasp, her heartbeat speeding up, then slowing down again. Her eyes turned in their sockets before she fell back into my open arms. My gaze moved over the book tied to her middle and her torn sleeve, lingering over the caked blood on her savaged arm. Whatever bit her drew a lot of blood. As long as her heart still beat she'd live, but she needed an infusion now.

"She's back." Devon inched closer and stared hungrily at the book.

I snarled in his direction in case he made the mistake to reach for it, but I knew the Shadow wouldn't dare with Cass around. It didn't surprise me to find the Shadows cared nothing for Amber. They probably would've let her die once she retrieved the book because to them, she'd been just a means to get what they wanted. But did they have to be so blunt about it?

Scooping Amber up in my arms, I pressed her against my body and headed for the door.

"The book's ours," Devon said, reaching for the dagger tied around his waist.

Kieran stepped between us, a cocky smile playing on his lips as he untied it from Amber's waist. "You'll get it when you fulfill your part of the bargain and perform the ritual."

Devon pulled out the dagger. Cass pressed a hand against his chest, nostrils flaring as usual. "Whoa, mate, get a grip, will you? We had a deal and I'll make sure you abide by the rules."

"The ritual shall be performed now, otherwise the deal's off," Deidre said.

"No." I shook my head. "I'm taking Amber home. It's my responsibility to make sure she recovers without harm."

"She won't recover," Deidre whispered.

She was just trying to get what they wanted and for that she'd spin one lie after another. I lowered my gaze, ignoring the need to fling Deidre across the room.

"Shut up," Kieran said. "We'll get her to a hospital and she'll be okay."

Deidre shrugged. "You can hope all you want, but the girl will die. The ritual shall be performed now or never. Your call."

Kieran pulled me aside and whispered, "I think she means it. If you don't do it now, you may never get another chance. After all Amber went through, she wouldn't want you to bail out."

I hesitated. Of course Kieran was right. Amber would want me to finish what we'd started. Besides, if the ritual worked I'd never have to worry again about not being able to protect her during daylight.

"You both stay here and I'll teleport her home," Clare said. She was the least reckless of us all, faster than Kieran, but also weaker. Was she a better choice than my brother? Clare placed a hand on my shoulder. "I don't need what we came for. Your mates are still alive, mine isn't."

Kieran planted a kiss on her cheek, but his gaze betrayed hesitation. I had no doubt my brother would return to the mansion if I asked him to. It wouldn't be fair to rob him of this chance. Kieran had fought to find this book just as hard. He'd earned his right to reap the reward. "All right, Clare. We'll be as fast as we can." I pushed a strand of hair out of Amber's face before Clare scooped her out of my arms and disappeared into the night.

"That was touching," Cass said. "Better than any soap opera. I wish someone brought popcorn." Her eyes blinked brightly. She spun, oblivious to the Shadows' glares. "So, Dee Dee, where's the real party at?"

Deidre motioned us to follow her to the cemetery. We passed the tall bronze statues until we reached a small, open chapel in the far left corner. Inside, a circle of white candles cast moving shadows against the hip-high, white fence.

Cass nodded, seemingly impressed. "Quite cozy. I'd get some of this for my backyard, or a Halloween party."

"The book," Devon said, snatching it out of Kieran's hand.

"Lay down over there." Deidre pointed to the middle of a circle, then started chanting, swaying back and forth as Shadows gathered around her. Devon flicked the book open and held it in front of her, and she began reading in a melodious, childlike voice, the foreign words flowing from her tongue like she'd done nothing else for the past month.

I figured the sooner I got this over and done with, the faster I could return home to Amber. Following Kieran's lead, I lay on the cold floor, shivering but not from the cold. Something was happening; I could smell the tension in the air. Kieran shot me a questioning look, then closed his eyes, waiting just like me. A sense of anticipation washed over me, my skin tingled. Deidre's voice grew fainter as though coming through a tunnel.

How much time passed? I had no idea, but I could feel myself relaxing, letting go. Wasn't that what Deidre was telling me in that strange language? Someone grabbed my shoulder and gave it a yank.

"Hey, did you just pass out?" Cass said.

I pried my eyes open and stared at her. She still looked the same—all red, frizzy hair and gleaming green eyes. Kieran stirred next to me, pale as a ghost, but otherwise nothing seemed different. I sat up and rubbed my forehead. "Did it work?"

Deidre shrugged. "I performed the ceremony for three reasons. One, to demonstrate my gratitude for helping us find the book. Two, out of respect for your friend who will pass away tonight. And three, out of honor because I always keep my word. If the ritual doesn't work, it's not my fault."

"What, no refund policy? That sucks." Cass grabbed my arm and pulled me up. "Come on, mate. My work shift starts in four hours and I need my beauty sleep."

"Dad's being a little stingy lately, huh?" Kieran asked with a grin. "What is it that you do again? Get the rich and famous to sign the dotted line before they jump into their death? Rob a few graves?"

I nudged him in the ribs. "Let's go." I could feel the left side of my head throbbing at the prospect of yet another confrontation between my brother and Cass.

"I work in customer services and I'm quite proud of it." Cass raised her chin, defiantly. I shot her an imploring look. She paid me no attention as she continued, "Now, what do you do, moron? That is, apart from sponging off your brother's money."

Kieran snorted. "I'm not sponging; I'm learning the craft of being a bounty hunter. There's a difference."

"You mean Aidan's been taking you to job orientation days for vampires for the last 500+ years?" Cass laughed. "What are you, fourteen, or just a slow learner?"

Devon insisted we follow him the way we came. I tuned out, sprinting down the path because I couldn't get away fast enough. Amber was waiting for me. Had the ritual worked? It better had, otherwise I'd be back, and it wouldn't be a visit to afternoon tea and scones. I barely noticed when we reached the car and Devon disappeared again.

"Amber's a fighter, mate. If anyone can pull through this it's her. I'll stop by after my shift to check on her." Cass patted my shoulder. From the corner of my eye I noticed something underneath her oversized shirt, tucked in beneath her armpit.

"You're going to keep that?" The corners of my lips twitching, I pointed at the ancient book she'd just stolen from the Shadows.

She smiled. "Let's just say I'm the most trustworthy one out of this bunch."

"Thank you," I said, meaning it.

With a wave of her hand, she jumped into her car and sped off.

"You think that too?" I asked my brother.

"What? That she's trustworthy?" Kieran shrugged and opened the car door. "I'd rather see that book in hell than in my enemies' hands."

"Leave the car here. We'll get it later," I said.

Kieran raised his brows. "You're good to teleport already? What about the wounds?"

I shrugged and pictured the mansion. A second later, I materialized in the driveway, my gaze hazy, the cuts inflicted by the succubi tearing open again.

It had started to rain, thick droplets drumming against the cobblestones. Kieran appeared beside me, heading for the door when I grabbed his arm, holding him back.

"What's wrong?" Kieran asked.

"I don't know." Something was off. I could feel it in the air, smell it. *My mate winding on a bed, shivering, calling my name.* The vision broke. "You stay here while I go in and check."

"What? No way."

"I said—" I rubbed a hand over my face. I had no time for an argument. Kieran was old enough to know what he was doing. If he wanted to go in, he'd do it anyway. I walked past mumbling, "Whatever."

All lights were switched off as I entered through the front door, minding the creaking floorboards.

"I'll check upstairs," Kieran whispered. I nodded and headed for the living room, then yanked the door open. My breath caught somewhere in my throat as I took in the picture before my eyes.

Clare bound to a chair with the same chains I had used to tie the others to the tree during that fateful night of the race. And then Amber, lying motionless on the sofa, pale in the darkness, her pulse barely stronger than the fluttering wings of a butterfly. With a cry I dashed for her when something pierced my chest, missing my heart by less than an inch. I tumbled forward, hitting the floor with a thud, dizziness washing over me. I tried to stand, but my legs gave way under me, my gaze searching for Amber.

Blake appeared in my line of vision, blood dripping from the spear in his hand as he held it over my throat, rattling the chains. Amber was dying; her heartbeat was slowly fading. My chest felt as though on fire, blood oozing too fast. I had to gain time because once the chains were attached I had no way of freeing myself. I peered toward the door, hoping my brother wouldn't fall into the same trap. "How did you get hold of these?" I asked.

"You forget I used to live here," Blake said. "I know what you hide in that basement." Damn, I should've thought about finding another hiding place for the chains, but I hadn't figured I'd see Blake again so soon.

"Why're you doing this? I let you live in the woods." I tried to sit up. My vision muddled. After centuries of drinking frozen blood, what I had taken from Amber had made me temporarily weaker because my body wasn't used to it. I needed more blood, and time to heal.

Clare shook at her chains, a yelp escaping her gagged mouth. Where the heck was Kieran.

"You won't die. I missed your heart on purpose," Blake said.

"Then why all of this? You realize I will never forgive you." I could barely feel my physical pain. My chest constricted, rage surging within my veins, making me roar. Amber wasn't breathing. Fate was telling me to hurry up, or I'd lose her forever. Gathering my strength, I stumbled to my knees, only to tumble forward seconds later. My body was losing blood while at the same time it craved more to resuscitate what it had lost in power over the last centuries.

Blake shrugged. "Ever since Amber entered your life, she's been nothing but a nuisance. She solved the riddle and stole the jewels that were meant to ensure the prize was ours. No mortal's ever stolen from me. So, you see, I'm doing you a favor here." In one fluent motion, he grabbed my hands to tie them at the back when the door flew open. From the corner of my eye, I watched Kieran fling Blake to the ground. A coffee table broke into pieces under their weight. Kieran's fist connected with Blake's eye. Another punch sent Blake against the wall. Blake stood and wiped a hand over his mouth. Snarls and grunts echoed through the room as they circled each other, battling it out.

Turning away, I crawled to my mate. Amber had to be saved, even if it meant turning her. I placed my hand on her chest and tried to stand, but my legs shook beneath me. There was no heartbeat. Pain rippled through me, threatening to tear me to pieces.

Amber couldn't die. She wouldn't die, or I'd die with her.

Someone burst through the door, a pitchfork in hand. A second later, Blake cried out and the window shattered as he jumped into the night.

"We all know what you are, you vile creature of darkness. Now don't you ever come back to haunt this blessed house and the children living here," Harry said, swinging his pitchfork with Greta behind him.

"Please, help her." My voice was barely more than a whisper, choked by the guilt I felt. I should've returned home with her instead of sending Clare.

Kieran motioned the gardener and his wife out, then appeared beside me and lifted Amber in his arms. Taking a deep breath, he lowered his mouth to her neck. He'd never turned anyone. Could he do it? Would he know how?

"Trust me," Kieran whispered, voice coarse and heavy with—hunger?

"No. Don't kill her." I dropped to the floor, tiredness washing over me as I felt my mate's life waning. And now my brother was signing his own death sentence by going against Lore rules.

Clare struggled against her chains, the rattling sound grazing my mind like nails on a chalkboard. Darkness descended around me, but I could see my mate in the distance, smiling, signaling me to hurry up. Amber was leaving this world, and so was I.

Chapter 29

The room felt warm and cozy; the guy sleeping next to me smelled of sandalwood and incense. I stirred, but kept my eyes closed, relishing his scent. I'd recognize him among thousands, but luckily I'd never have to because I'd never let him go again. Pushing up on my elbow, I planted a soft kiss on his cheek when he woke up, a lazy grin playing on his lips. He regarded me, sleepily.

"Rise and shine. I thought you'd never wake up." I returned the smile, a rush of love washing over me. "A girl has needs, you know."

Aidan groaned and rubbed a hand over his face, then ran it through his already disheveled hair. I swallowed hard, unable to peel my gaze off him. How did he always manage to look so enticing?

"What time is it?" he asked.

I threw a glance at the clock on the bedside table. "Almost nine."

Light seeped through a hole in the blackout curtains, bathing the wooden floor in brightness. So we were on the second story, and these were the curtains I had watched from the garden so many times. Someone had forgotten to pull them. Why wasn't Aidan burning?

Jumping up, I reached the curtains in less than a second, marveling at my speed. My whole body felt alive, eager to move and do stuff. Like walking and climbing. Whoa, Clare and her fitness obsession were definitely rubbing off on me. Aidan came behind me and wrapped his strong arm around my waist, pulling me close. With one flick of his wrist, he opened the curtains.

The sun stood high on the grey, Scottish horizon. I turned to face him, noticing the bandage around his chest and the choked emotions at seeing the sun for the first time in several hundred years. Awe. Surprise. Happiness. And then I remembered the book and the winged beings. After retrieving it, I brought it back from the otherworld. But what happened afterwards was a big black hole in my memory. "The ritual?"

Tracing a finger along my collarbone, he nodded and planted a kiss on my lips. "I love you. We'll always be together."

"I love you too." I stood on my toes and pulled him closer. "I thought you'd never say it."

"Then you're not mad? We had no choice."

I frowned. "Huh?

"You can't remember?" Aidan asked. He seemed nervous, fidgeting like a five-year-old.

"Just say it, Aidan, or I swear to God—" Jabbing a finger in his chest, I sent him stumbling backwards. I frowned, hesitating. Something wasn't right.

I couldn't have—

I couldn't be—

"No." I shook my head as I grasped the meaning of what just happened. But why wasn't I a raging psycho, kicking the furniture in search for a few mortals and a drop of blood?

Aidan raised his hands in mock defense. "It was Kieran, not me. I couldn't stop him because I was almost dying. I pledged, but he wouldn't listen." I didn't believe a word he said. He continued, "But look at the bright side. It happened after the ritual, so you can still get your nails done without sucking the town dry."

What would Mum and Dad and Dallas think? Now I wasn't just bringing home Dracula's relatives, I was basically one of them. How could I explain why I wasn't tucking into the Christmas dinner? Mum would be so upset.

"I'll kick his butt." I stomped out the door with Aidan on my tracks.

"I'll help you," Aidan said, laughing. "Blake almost killed me because my dear brother had to take care of his hair first before jumping to my rescue."

THE END

368